Hidden Scars

A.M. Myers

The characters and events in this book are fictitious. Names, characters, places and plots are a product of the author's imagination. Any similarity to real persons, living or dead, is coincidental and not intended by the author.

Cover Design by Renee Ericson
Editing by Lea Burn
Proofreading by Julie Deaton

Copyright © 2015 by A.M. Myers

First Edition

Prologue

This can't be me.

This blank, empty girl reflected in the mirror isn't who I am, and yet, even when I think back to a time before *him*, I can't remember *that* girl. Realistically, I know who she was, but I don't feel her anymore; I don't connect with her. She is a stranger, though, somehow, I miss her. I miss her like a best friend that I lost touch with, the ache so sharp that it sometimes steals my breath.

I want her back.

I stare at my face. Smoky green eyes that used to shine with so much love and laughter look duller now. The light has left them. Everything about my demeanor screams that I am wounded, damaged. I've built walls around my heart so high that no one will ever be able to scale them. I am alone, but after everything that I've been through, everything he's done to me, I think that might be for the best. There are still days, though, when all I can think about is going back and changing things. If I could do things differently, I would. If only I knew then what I know now.

Shaking my head, I attempt to clear away the painful memories that threaten to drown me as tears fill my eyes. With my hands braced on the edges of my bathroom sink, I take a deep breath. Trying to mentally will away the physical evidence of my pain. You would think after crying for four months straight that my eyes would be barren as a desert but that doesn't seem to be the case. I just can't do this. I don't want to cry anymore. I want to be strong.

Besides, I don't have time to lose it right now, not that it ever happens at a convenient time. Moe is expecting me for my shift at the bar in a few hours and as much as I would love to hide under the covers for the next year, I know that if I call in sick, both of my brothers will be up my ass. Just as I'm convincing myself to get into the shower and get ready for my day, my phone starts ringing on the nightstand in my bedroom. I recognize the special ringtone I set up for *him*. A single tear runs down my face as my heart starts beating faster and my entire body locks up.

Goddamn it!

Is it too much to ask that he just leave me alone? That's all I want. I want him to leave me the hell alone and let me try to heal. Can I just get through one day without a phone call from him? The daily reminder from him usually sets back any progress I feel like I'm making. When I left him four months ago, he vowed that he wouldn't give up on me. I didn't take him seriously at the time but he's proving me wrong. Every single day, he calls. And every single day, I ignore the ringing phone. It's time to get a new number. Maybe that will finally stop him.

He can't possibly think that I'm going to forgive him. That after everything he's done, I would ever give him another chance. That will never happen. I shudder as a darker memory threatens to bog me down again.

Suddenly, I'm angry. So angry that I'm shaking. This has to stop. Today. I'm taking back my life and stopping this torment. I look back in the mirror and watch in fascination as determination hardens my features. I glance at my watch again before rushing into the bedroom and grabbing my phone. I shoot off a quick text to Moe to let him know that I'm going to be a little late then I jump in the shower.

After I'm done, I dress quickly and throw my long brown hair into a ponytail before racing to my car. On the drive over, the anger builds again but I'm still a little nervous about what I'm on my way to do. Who knows if it will even work? But it feels like the only option I have left. I'm so tired of being the victim. No more. Finally, I pull up in front of the Port Allen Police station. I draw in a ragged breath as I survey the brick building.

I know I need to do this and it feels right. This is how I'm going to get my life back. After a quick pep talk, I climb out of my car and make my way across the street. When I step inside, a young officer standing behind a tall desk flashes me a kind smile.

"Can I help you, ma'am?"

I nod. "Yes. I need to file a report."

Chapter One

"Are you sure about this, darlin'?" Moe asks, his golden brown eyes filled with concern. I give him a reassuring smile and nod my head.

"Yeah, I'm sure, Moe."

He narrows his eyes, watching me closely for any sign of hesitance but he won't find any. I am absolutely sure about my decision. After a moment, he sighs and runs a callused hand over his short, dark hair.

"All right, I guess I can't really stop you." A mischievous grin crosses my face and I shake my head. I've known Moe my entire life. He's been like family, having known my mom since grade school. Moe's always held the part of the cool uncle, playing with my brothers and me and never being able to tell any of us "no." Daddy has always said that we have him wrapped around our fingers.

"Maybe you shouldn't go alone, though," he adds, squaring his shoulders and straightening to his full height. When he does this, I feel dwarfed by the sheer size of him. Most people find him intimidating but I can still picture him with a pink feather boa around his neck as he pretended to sip from a plastic teacup my grandma had given me for my fourth birthday.

"Moe, how many times do I have to tell you guys that I'm fine?" He purses his lips and just watches me for a moment. Finally, he sighs.

"Is he still calling you?"

"For, like the hundredth time, no. He stopped calling as soon as I filed that report with Detective Nelson. I haven't heard from him in nearly a year."

He rubs his hand along his jaw and I know he's worried about me going into the city alone. Baton Rouge is only about five miles away from Port Allen, but to him, it might as well be a hundred. All of the men in my life have been worried about me, constantly calling to check in or dropping by my apartment to "hang out." What they are really doing is babysitting me. Honestly, though, I can't blame them. They don't know what really happened to me so all they have is whatever they've dreamt up in their imaginations.

"Just remember to keep your phone on you." I fight the urge to roll my eyes.

"I'm not some fragile little girl. I can take care of myself." His eyes grow dark and I know, for certain, that I don't want to know what he's remembering. I've worked really hard to move past all of that. "I'll keep it with me. I promise." My words seem to ease his concern some and he nods. After a few more seconds, he sighs again and slips a piece of paper into my hand.

"The address is on there. I let him know that you were coming." I unfold the piece of paper and see an address there and a name — Phoenix West, Moe's nephew. I tuck the paper into my pocket and throw my arms around Moe's neck, pulling him into a hug. He grunts as he wraps his arms around my waist.

"Thank you."

He nods. "Just be careful, okay?"

"I will. I promise."

"Love you, darlin'," he says, releasing me.

"Love you, too, Moe."

*   *   *   *

Twenty minutes later, I'm pulling up to a black stucco building in the heart of Baton Rouge. I take a deep breath and stare at the front door. It's not that I'm scared to do this. In fact, I don't think I've ever been so excited. It's been a year and I'm stronger than ever. I want — no, I need this, and more than that, I deserve it. I take a look at the sign hanging over the building and smile. After climbing out of the car, I make my way to the front door of the shop with sure, even steps.

When I pull open the door, a bell jingles over my head and a voice from the back says, "Just a second."

I scan the small lobby, taking in the blood red walls and black leather furniture. The entire wall to my left is filled with framed flash art, everything from skulls to flowers. The other three walls hold various paintings, some of which I recognize as the work of local artists. A small pang tightens my chest as my fingers itch to be able to paint again. I turn away, knowing that focusing on them will only leave me sad. I look around the rest of the space, approaching the small counter with just a cash register and a notebook sitting on top.

"Can I help you?" The voice, much closer this time, startles me and I jump. I turn to my right just in time to see the sexiest man I've ever laid eyes on chuckling at me. Oh my God...*this* is Moe's nephew? "Sorry, sweetheart, didn't mean to scare you." His piercing blue gaze focuses on me, and the amused curiosity dancing there sends my heart racing in my chest.

"Uh...sorry. I wasn't really paying attention."

He nods, an easy grin pulling one side of his mouth up. "Not a problem. What can I do for you?"

My mind immediately goes to the gutter, thinking of several things he could *do* for me. *Jesus, Emma. Get a freakin' grip.*

"Um, I'm Emma. Moe said he called you?" Recognition dawns in his eyes and he stiffens, squaring his large shoulders. I'm amazed by the similarities between him and Moe. Both men have the same large build except Phoenix obviously spends time in the gym, his muscles nicely defined.

"Yeah, he did. What is it that you were looking to get?"

I pull the design I drew last night out of my back pocket and set it down on the counter. He grabs it, studying the intricate crown I designed along with the phrase "*love is not enough*" scrawled underneath.

"This design is amazing." His gaze flicks up to mine. "Who did it?"

"I did." At my answer, his eyes widen in shock for a moment before that damn curiosity is back. He looks down at the paper in his hand again before focusing back on me.

"You sure?" My eyes drop to the paper and I recite the words in my head before nodding. This is something I am absolutely sure about. It was a hard lesson to learn and I want the reminder permanently inked on my body. He nods in agreement. "All right. Follow me back."

He turns and walks over to the doorway leading to the back of the shop. I can't pull my eyes away from him when he pushes the curtain to the side, the ripple of his muscles evident even through the material of his t-shirt. My gaze drops to his arm, where he is covered in tattoos. Some black and gray, others full of color, and I find myself wanting to trace each one. I really should not be thinking things like this.

It's been a year since I left *him* and I haven't even thought about dating until this very moment. I guess that's not entirely true. I have thought about dating as a far off concept. Something I *might* do, someday in the future. Now, though, I find myself wondering what it would be like to go out on a date with this man. After all I've been through, I know I should probably just swear off men altogether, but I've always liked to think that I'm a fairly reasonable person. I can't feasibly conclude that all men are bad. In fact, I know several that prove that statement wrong. The problem is, I don't know whom to trust anymore. After everything I've been through, I can't tell the hero from the villain. So, as much as I might want that special, intimate connection with someone, I remain frozen in fear.

"Have a seat," Phoenix says, pointing to the black leather table off to my left. I sit down as he moves things around, getting them ready and setting them up exactly as he likes. He pulls a rolling chair toward him with his foot and sits down before rolling closer to me. "Where do you want this?" He waves the design in the air and I hold out my arm, flipping it over and pointing to the inside of my wrist. He lays the paper on the delicate skin, checking that my design will fit, and smiles when he realizes that I already measured it before drawing the design.

"You're makin' my job easy."

I shrug. "I do what I can." He flashes me that laid back grin and I swear my heart stops for a moment. He turns away, grabbing a piece of contact paper and laying it over my design. His brow furrows as he focuses on what he's doing, dragging the pencil along precisely to recreate my drawing. I pull my eyes away to look around the space and I see several framed drawings on the wall.

"Are those yours?"

His head pops up and he looks where I'm pointing. "Yeah. They're mine."

"They're really great."

A shy smile slowly stretches across his face. I find it really endearing. "Thanks."

I nod and he turns back to the tattoo. Seeing his obvious love of his art makes me miss my own more than ever. Every day, I stare at the blank canvas sitting in my guest bedroom and wish that I could somehow get past this block that I've developed.

"All right, hold out your wrist for me." He turns to me, and holds the contact paper over my skin, moving back and forth and trying to find the perfect spot. He finally presses the design against my wrist. When his finger brushes over my skin, I feel a sizzle, like water in a hot pan. I barely hold in my gasp and my gaze flies up to his face. He is still focused on my tattoo and I would think that I imagined it if it wasn't for the slight twitch of his lips, letting me know that he felt it, too.

He remains quiet as he pulls the paper away from my skin, leaving the design behind. "What do you think?"

I examine the crown on my wrist and my heart swells with pride. Yeah, I definitely earned this.

"Perfect," I say and when I look up at him, his eyes are locked on me. He nods slowly, his eyes saying so much more than he is. I think I could get lost in those blue depths forever. We just stare at one another, caught up in some kind of intimate connection that makes my heart pound so hard that I can hear it in my ears. My lips part and his gaze immediately drops to my mouth. He licks his full lips and I feel like I'm going to combust. A moment later, he seems to come to his senses and shakes his head.

"Uh, go ahead and lay your arm on this table." His voice sounds like he swallowed a handful of gravel and it makes me flush with warmth. He motions to the small table to my left and I place my arm on it, with the design facing up. He finishes up his prep then grabs the tattoo gun off the tray next to him and a buzzing sound fills my ears. "Ready?"

I nod and whisper, "Yeah."

He uses one hand to hold my wrist steady and even through the rubber of the gloves I can feel sparks shooting up my arm. I'm so distracted by his touch and the heat it ignites in my body that I don't notice when he starts moving the needle over my skin. Surprised by the sting, I gasp and he stops, his gaze snapping up to mine, concern lining his face.

"You okay?"

"Yeah. Sorry. I was just surprised." His sweet, reassuring smile puts me completely at ease and I nod for him to continue.

"Is this your first?" he asks as he starts tattooing again.

"Huh?"

"The tattoo. Is it your first?"

"Gee, how could you tell?" He laughs at my comment and I'm finding that I love the sound of it.

"Don't worry. I won't tell anyone." He winks and my heart skips a beat. As much as my brain knows that liking him is a very bad idea, the message doesn't seem to be reaching my heart. I'd be lying if I said that I didn't want to find my person, the one who was made specifically for me. I've always been a hopeless romantic but the past couple years left me wondering if the idea of soul mates was just a notion I naively believed in before I met *him* and knew how much a person could truly hurt another.

Needing a distraction from the dark memories trying to surface, I turn toward Phoenix and watch him as he works on my tattoo. He reminds me so much of Moe, with the exception of his blue eyes. He has the same dark hair, although he wears his longer and messy. It looks like he's constantly running his fingers through it. His strong, square jaw is lined with dark stubble, but he has Moe's same easy smile that has always comforted me. I study him for a long time, trying to figure out what it is about him that has me so out of sorts.

"Can I ask you something?" We've been sitting in silence as he works on my tattoo but at my question, he glances up at me.

"Sure."

"How is it that I've known Moe my entire life and we've never met?"

He looks back down at my wrist and shrugs. "We're not that close."

"Why?"

When he looks up at me this time, he seems slightly annoyed but still answers.

"Moe and my dad had some kind of falling out before I was even born, so he was never around much when I was little. By the time they kind of made up, I was a teenager and didn't really know who he was." My heart aches for Moe because I know how much he's missed his family all these years, but I'm not sure it's really my place to say anything.

"Do you ever go see him now?"

"He comes into the city sometimes and we grab dinner or hang out."

"But you don't go see him?"

He shakes his head. "No."

I just nod and remain quiet. I won't pretend that I know what went on in their family but I feel for both of them. Moe, who has spent years wishing he was close to his family again, and Nix, who missed out on an amazing uncle.

Several minutes pass before he speaks again. "Can I ask you something?"

"I guess that's fair."

"What does this tattoo mean?"

My body tenses at his question. "It means exactly what it says."

The corner of his mouth tips up in a smirk. "Okay, but will you tell me the story behind it?"

"No." My answer is immediate. His smile may be charming but it's not *that* charming. I don't talk about this — with anyone. My brothers have been hounding me for almost a year to find out what happened to me and if I haven't told them, why would I tell a stranger? Except, I feel like I could tell him — if I wanted to, that is.

"You know, tattoo artists are like bartenders. People like to tell them their problems. I'm like a discount therapist."

"Well, it's good that I'm a bartender then. I know how to keep my mouth shut." He chuckles and shakes his head. I'm surprised to find myself smiling so easily with him. Not that I've spent the last twelve months with a frown permanently fixed on my face, but smiling has never felt as natural as it does right now.

"Can't blame a guy for tryin'."

"I guess not," I reply. His blue eyes lock onto me and he winks as that easy smile curves his full lips. It sends butterflies fluttering through my belly and I look away to hide the blush creeping up my cheeks. I really don't know what to make of all this. Of him.

"Well, you're all done." The buzzing stops and he sets the gun down before pulling his gloves off. He grabs a bottle of liquid off the table and squirts some onto a paper towel before rubbing it over my fresh ink. When he's finished cleaning it, he covers it with a bandage and then grabs a roll of plastic wrap, rolling it around my wrist to protect the tattoo.

"All right, leave that on for, at least, a couple hours and make sure you keep the tattoo clean. Remember to put lotion on it a couple times a day, and whatever you do, do not pick at it when it starts peeling."

"Okay." He stands and I hop off the table and grab my wallet. "How much do I owe you?"

He shakes his head and holds up his hands. "On the house."

"What?"

"Moe covered it." I grit my teeth. This was supposed to be about me. I wanted to do this all on my own. It was important to me.

Sensing my frustration, Phoenix lays his hand on my arm. Tingles race up and down my flesh from his touch, and I can't seem to form a single thought. "If you really want, you can pay me and we'll say that what Moe gave me is an extremely good tip. Or you could just give me your number and we'll call it even."

The question surprises me. So much so, that I'm left gaping at him as I try to collect my thoughts. He's so forward and I have to wonder how often he uses his job to pick up women. God, he's a player. I shake my head. "How much do I owe you?"

"It'll be one hundred." He doesn't look deterred as I hand over the cash. He lays it on the table before leading me back to the lobby. "Will you let Moe know that I'll come by the bar this weekend?"

I turn to him. "I thought you didn't come by the bar."

He shrugs. "Maybe I have a reason to now."

My eyes widen at his forwardness and I quickly stumble through a good-bye, rushing out of the shop before I say something as foolish as how I would really like to see him again.

Because saying that would be *monumentally* stupid.

*   *   *   *

"All right, let me see it." Moe rushes up as soon as I walk into the bar for my shift. I snort when I see my dad and both of my brothers following closely behind him. When they reach me, they all give me an expectant look. Shaking my head, I hold out my arm and show them my wrist, still covered by the plastic wrap. Each man takes a turn inspecting my ink before looking
up at me, concern in his eyes. I hate it.

"Did you draw it, Em?" Trey asks, and I grin, nodding my head.

"Yeah. I did it last night."

He smiles, his chocolate eyes shining with pride. Trey isn't my brother by blood but he might as well be. He and Tucker became best friends in kindergarten and he spent a ton of time at our house. His dad ran off when he was a baby and his mom was always high. When he was fourteen, his mom died and he was supposed to go into foster care. At that point, he was already like family to us so my parents adopted him without a second thought.

He and Tucker have always been there for me. From telling the neighborhood bully to stay away from me to warning all of my exes to treat me right, they've had my back. That's how I know that not knowing about the things I've been through lately is killing them. They want so badly to help, to find a way to fix this, but I won't let them in.

"Well, I'm still not thrilled about you having a tattoo but it is beautiful, baby girl," Daddy says, and I beam at him.

"Thanks, Daddy." He gives me a warm smile and wraps his arm around my shoulders, kissing the top of my head. "Oh, Moe, Phoenix wanted me to tell you that he'll be by the bar this weekend."
Moe's eyes widen in shock for a moment before a slow smile creeps across his face. He shakes his head. "Did he now?"

I can tell from the laughter in his voice that he is suspicious of something going on between Phoenix and me. I can't even tell him he's wrong because I'm not sure what I'm feeling right now and that scares me. I could be in big trouble here.

Chapter Two
Then…

Thump! Thump! Thump!

Slamming my foot on the brake, I pull my piece of shit Toyota Corolla over on the side of the gravel road and pound the steering wheel in frustration. I already know what I'm going to see when I get out of this car and that I can't afford it. Sighing, I fling the door open and step out, the dense Louisiana heat threatening to strangle me immediately.

Goddamn, it's hot out here.

I walk around to the front of the car and bend down to inspect my flat tire. I can see the nail sticking out of the almost non-existent tread even from here. A groan slips out of my mouth, and I stand before giving the useless rubber a good kick. I could just change it, but my only spare is currently taking the place of my back passenger tire.

Stomping back around to the side of the car, I reach in through the open window and grab my phone, only to discover that I don't have service out here.

Well…shit.

I know I'm going to be late for work no matter what, so my options are to either sit here and hope some Good Samaritan stops by or hoof it. The sun is already starting its descent, setting behind the line of trees to the left of the road, and that helps make my decision.

Hoof it, it is.

I can't be more than four miles from the edge of town, and the bar, so I should be able to get a signal in about another mile or so. Then again, it's getting dark and the swamp is just past those trees. I can't say I'm real eager to become a gator's dinner. I take a deep breath and grab my purse out of the car.

"Buck up, sister," I mutter to myself.

As I start walking, I think about how the hell I'm going to pay for two new tires. Truthfully, all my tires need to be replaced, but I know there is no way I'll be able to afford that. I'm going to have to dip into my savings just to replace the two and there won't be much left. Disappointment envelops me. I had just started saving up to put a down payment on a new car but now I'll have to start over. Even though I didn't have much, it's still disheartening.

I could just call Daddy and have him get me new tires or buy me a new car like he has offered before but my stubborn side won't allow it. My dad has owned a garage on the other side of town my whole life, and he's been trying to get me to let him buy me a new car for the last year. I just can't bring myself to say yes. I like taking care of myself. It's why I work so hard, both at the bar and with my art. I glance at my phone again, checking to see if I have a signal yet.

No luck.

I've got to be getting close at this point. I just have to keep walking…and not get eaten by an alligator.

Yeah, that sounds like a good plan.

Trudging along the gravel road, my heels keep catching on the little rocks, making me stumble, and I curse myself for wearing heels to work. Yeah, I get better tips when I'm all dolled up but they aren't exactly ideal right now. The tall grass to my right rustles, startling me, and I barely hold back my scream.

"Please don't eat me," I whisper repeatedly, clutching my phone to my chest.

I wipe a bead of sweat from my forehead and another trails down my cheek and drips onto my chest, practically bare in a tank top. God, it's so hot outside. I'm suddenly wishing that I had brought a water bottle. My throat is so dry that I swear it's closing up. I probably look like a hot mess right now. Between all the sweating and the dirt I keep kicking up, Moe is going to think I was attacked.

Just as I'm checking my phone again for a signal, headlights shine on the road to my left. I breathe a sigh of relief before a troubling thought enters my mind. What if it's a serial killer or something? That's about exactly how my luck is running tonight.

What's worse, getting hacked into pieces by some psychotic redneck with a machete or getting my leg chewed off by a gator?

I think I might prefer the gator…

I'm contemplating making a run for it when red and blue lights illuminate the area around me. I spin around to find that my savior is none other than one of Port Allen's finest.

Oh, thank God!

The blinding light cuts off and he climbs out of the car, shutting the door behind him, and my breath falters. Is he a mirage? I couldn't possibly be that dehydrated yet. Could I? Oh, who gives a damn? Even if he is a figment of my imagination, it's a damn fine view. His long legs eat up the space between us. His

21

stride is one of a man full of confidence, and I can't stop my eyes from traveling up and down his long frame, thoroughly enjoying the view.

"You all right, ma'am?" he asks, his voice smooth with a hint of a southern drawl.

"Not really. My car got a flat." I point to the road behind him. His stunning hazel eyes flick in that direction before turning back to me.

"That maroon Toyota about a half mile back?"

"That's the one. It's okay, you can call it a piece of shit," I joke and he laughs freely.

"Well, I didn't want to be rude, but yeah." I shrug my shoulders because I know it's true. "Well, I can't help you with the car but would you like a ride?"

"Do I have to sit in the back?" I flirt and he shocks the hell out of me when he reciprocates.

"Only if you're bad." His eyes flash with humor and heat. My body thrums with excitement.

"Oh, Officer Wheeler," I say, looking at his name badge, "I'm always bad."

He smirks. "You can call me Ryan."

I smile up at him. "Okay, Ryan."

He jogs around to the passenger side of the car and opens the door for me. I thank him before sliding onto the soft leather seat. As he walks around to the driver's side, I realize that I can't remember the last time a guy opened a door for me. After he climbs in, he grabs a bottle of water out of the cup holder and offers it to me.

"Water?"

I forget everything else except my intense thirst as I grab the bottle out of his hand.

"Thank you!" I exclaim and proceed to chug the entire thing. When I'm done, he chuckles and I look down at the bottle, blushing. "Sorry."

"No big deal," he assures me. "Where am I headed?"

"Uh...Moe's. Do you know it?"

He grins. "Sure do. It's one of my favorite bars. Do you work there?"

"Yeah, I've been there for about six months."

"I don't think I've ever seen you. I'm in there with my friends almost every weekend."

"Maybe you just missed me."

He smiles and shakes his head. His eyes rake over my body and I suddenly have a hard time breathing. When he looks back at me, lust is so clear on his face that I would have to be blind to miss it.

"Naw, I wouldn't have missed you." I blush, looking down at my hands and he chuckles. "I never did get your name, by the way."

Didn't I tell him my name? Thinking back over our conversation, I realize that I didn't.

"Oh, sorry. I'm Emma."

"Emma...?"

"Harrington. Emma Harrington."

"Well, it is very nice to meet you, Emma Harrington."

"It's very nice to meet you too, Ryan."

My phone starts buzzing frantically in my hand, going crazy with missed texts. I smile when I read the messages from Moe.

Moe: Where r u?

Moe: R u ok?

Moe: EMMA!

Moe: U better answer me, girl.
B4 I call the cops.

I giggle as I read the last one, amused at the situation. With a big grin on my face, I quickly text him back, letting him know that I'm okay and on my way.

"Your boyfriend worried?"

I shoot a sly grin over at him. "Why, Officer Wheeler, is that your way of asking if I have a boyfriend?"

A slight blush stains his cheeks. "Guilty," he admits with a chuckle and my smile grows.

"I don't have a boyfriend." As soon as the words leave my mouth, his eyes light up like a kid on Christmas morning.

Oh boy…

"Would you be opposed to a date with a police officer?"

I shrug. "Depends on the police officer."

He laughs and shakes his head. "You're not gonna make this easy on me, huh?"

"Never," I tease, laughing.

We make small talk the rest of the way; well, mostly I complain about dipping into my car fund and he listens. He stops the car and I realize that we're already at the bar. He turns in his seat to face me.

"All right, let me try this again. Would you like to go out on a date with me, Emma Harrington?"

"*Hmm*," I hum, pretending to think about it and almost burst out laughing when his eyes widen.

"Come on! Give me a break!" he pleads and a wide smile stretches across my face.

"Okay, Ryan Wheeler. I would very much like to go out on a date with you."

His victorious grin is totally worth it. We exchange numbers before I climb out of the car. Resting my arm on the open door, I lean down to talk to him.

"Thanks so much for the ride. You're a lifesaver."

"Kind of in the job description," he says, pointing to the badge on his chest. I laugh.

"Saving damsels in distress?" He grins and nods his head. His smile is mesmerizing and I forget to breathe for a minute.

"Do you need a ride home after work?"

"That's really sweet of you but I'm sure I can find my way home." I can't imagine that he wants to wake up at three in the morning to drag his ass to a bar and give me ride home.

"Are you sure?"

"Yeah."

"All right, but you call me if you can't find a ride. Promise?" His tone and his eyes tell me he's completely serious. Who is this guy? I've known him ten minutes and already he's better than all my ex boyfriends.

Combined.

"Yeah, okay."

He grins, almost knocking me off my feet yet again. How the hell am I supposed to function around him if he keeps smiling at me like that?

"Goodbye, Ryan."

"See you soon, Emma," he calls out, and I shut the door before making my way into the bar.

*   *   *   *

After Moe closes up the bar at two, Bree and I clean in comfortable silence while he goes into the office to close out the registers and count out the deposit for the night. When he comes back out to help us finish up, I remember that I need a ride home.

"Hey, Moe, can I get a ride?"

"Already plannin' on it, darlin'." I smile my thanks at him. "Say, you gonna be at the market in the mornin'?"

"Yeah, I'll be there tomorrow only."

The Artist's Market is in downtown Baton Rouge and I sell my paintings there every weekend. Art is my true passion. Even though I love working here, I would be lost without my art. Baton Rouge has a revolving door of tourists and I do pretty well selling my work on the weekends. I don't think I'll ever be rich and famous, but I'm okay with that.

"How is that going, by the way?"

I'm the only artistic one in my family and no one really understands that part of me, but they always make the effort to ask about it and I appreciate that.

"Pretty good, actually. I sold four pieces last weekend. Made four hundred bucks."

He lets out a whistle and smiles proudly at me. "That's our girl!"

I beam, soaking up his praise. Pride courses through me. Even if they don't understand, I know they are proud.

"Thanks, Moe."

"What time do you have to get there in the morning?" Bree asks.

"I've gotta wake up at seven thirty." At the reminder, I peek at my phone to see the time.

Three fifteen.

Ugh, I need some sleep.

"I don't know how you do it, girl. I would be running on fumes."

"Eh...coffee helps." We both start giggling. I don't ever see it as a bad thing. Sure, I'm tired sometimes, but I'm making a life for myself and I love what I'm doing. How many people can say that?

"All right, ladies, let's get out of here," Moe calls, grabbing his keys from under the bar. He follows behind us as we step out of the bar and then turns around to lock up. I freeze when I find my car sitting there.

What the hell?

Moe bumps into me from behind and I almost fall flat on my face before he catches me.

"Sorry, darlin', I didn't see — hey, what is your car doing here?"

I shake my head. "I have no idea." I make my way over to the car and there's a single rose and a piece of paper trapped underneath the blade of my windshield wiper. Grabbing both items, I hold the rose up to my nose before opening the paper, gasping when I see what's written inside.

Emma,
I couldn't stand the thought of you
being stranded again so I replaced the tires for
you. I know you're probably freaking out about
it
but please, humor me. I'll talk to you soon.
Ryan

Holy shit…like holy effing shit.

I circle the car and see four shiny new tires. He replaced them all. When I reach the front again, Moe snatches the note out of my hand. He lets out a low whistle when he finishes reading it.

"This the cop?" I nod. He chuckles. "Boy's got it bad."

"How am I going to pay him back?" I ask, more thinking aloud than actually asking anyone.

"Pretty sure he's not wantin' cash, darlin'."

"Moe!" I gape at him. Bree's jaw hits the dirt before we both burst into giggles. He has the decency to look down and blush.

"Aw, hell, that's not what I meant."

I nudge him with my shoulder and wink. "Sure ya didn't, Moe." When he returns my smile, I see that mischievous twinkle in his eye and I know that is exactly what he meant.

"As much as I would love to sit around and discuss what the officer wants from me, I've got to go home and get some sleep," I say, yawning loudly.

Moe wraps his arms around me. "See you tomorrow, baby girl."

"See you later, Bree," I call to her when Moe releases me.

"Bye, Em."

I slink over to my car, exhaustion weighing me down. God, my car looks ridiculous right now. The maroon paint is faded by the sun and peeling in places. There is a huge crack running down my windshield, and four brand spankin' new tires. They look so out of place. Shaking my head, I climb in and roll down the window before peeling out of the parking lot, letting the wind whip through my hair as I dream about collapsing into my bed the second I get home.

Chapter Three
Now

     Three days. That's how long it's been since I last saw Phoenix, the man who has taken over my thoughts and dreams. It annoys me that I can't seem to stop thinking about him. We only spent a couple hours together but there was definitely something there. But, what? What is it about this man that I've heard stories about my whole life but never laid eyes on until now that gets to me? It feels almost like he calls to me on a deeper level. Maybe it's just because I've known Moe so long and Moe always talks about him. The more I think about it that has to be it. Right?

     Except the moment that I close my eyes, he's staring back at me and my heart kicks into gear, pounding against my ribs at a furious pace. I am at war. My head, the always-practical part of me, is screaming to just forget about him, saying that I can't afford to take a chance on him. My heart, though, my heart is telling me that I shouldn't ignore this. That this is different, special. But can I trust myself?

     I've just been going around in circles for three days and never getting anywhere. One minute, I decide that I should go for it, but it doesn't take long for the fear to take hold and remind me why I need to be careful. Shaking my head, I sigh as I wander down the sidewalk in downtown Baton Rouge. It's Saturday. Before *him*, I would spend the day at the market, selling my art and mingling with other artists in the area. I loved it. It fed my soul, but now that I'm not able to paint, I don't know what to do with myself. I'm lost. So, I wander. Nothing helps the ache deep in my chest though.

I wish that I could tell you that there was one defining moment that stole my art from me but that's not the case. Even now, when I think back, I can't tell you exactly when I lost it. The one thing I do know for certain is that it's gone. I've started so many paintings in the past year, only to give up halfway through when that little voice in my head started second guessing every single brushstroke. In my frustration, I would chuck the canvas in the trash and mope for a few days.

"Holy shit! I think it might be my lucky day!"

I recognize the deep, masculine voice instantly because it's been playing on a loop in my head for the last seventy-two hours.

"Phoenix." My voice is breathless, rich with nervousness and an intense feeling of relief that confuses me even more. His blue eyes sparkle with a genuine happiness that floors me. Could he really be this sincere? The side of his mouth tips up in a smile that has me fighting back one of my own.

"How are you, Emma?"

"I'm good. How are you?" I reply, finding my voice again.

"My day is certainly looking up. What are you doing in town?"

My gaze rakes over his body, perplexed by his honest interest in me. The sleeves of his plain black t-shirt are so tight around his biceps that it looks like it might rip at any moment. The thought has me feeling all sorts of things that I definitely should *not* be feeling.

"Just wasting time, I guess." He tilts his head to the side as he studies me.

"Why do I get the feeling that there is more to the story?" I just shrug. I'm not talking about this with him. Finally, he nods. "Do you want to grab some lunch with me?"

I'm stunned by the question and immediately try to come up with an excuse. Although, I'm not sure why. "I…uh…I have to get going soon."

"Why?" He takes a step toward me.

"Um…I have to work."

"At the bar? What time?"

Shit. Shit, shit, shit. The bar doesn't even open until four, and I'm sure he knows that. Even if it took us a couple hours to eat, I would still get back to Port Allen with plenty of time to get ready.

"Uh…"

"Come on, Emma. Please? I promise I'm a nice guy. Just have lunch with me. I can hear your stomach growling from here."

My traitorous stomach chooses that exact moment to grumble loudly and he flashes me a victorious smirk. When I see those dazzling eyes sparkling back at me, I know I'm going to fold like a cheap suit.

"Okay."

His grin turns into a full on, mega-watt smile, and the corner of my mouth curves up. He gestures to the sidewalk behind me.

"There is a great little burger place down that way."

My stomach rumbles again and I nod, earning a laugh from him.

"That sounds great." We begin walking in silence and I can't stop my gaze from flicking over to him. His hands are down by his sides and when I look at him, the hand closest to me twitches. Now, my mind is spinning, wondering what it would be like to feel my hand in his. My heart races at the thought of him intertwining our fingers and pulling me closer to him. After that, I can't help but wonder what his lips would feel like pressed against mine. Would they be soft? Commanding? Would that sizzle I felt when we touched several days ago explode and consume us both?

"Here we are." His voice cuts through my vivid daydream and I startle. "Did I scare you?"

"Sorry. I was just lost in thought."

"I can tell. Care to share?"

My cheeks flush and I shake my head. "No."

His lips mash together as he holds in a laugh. God, does he know what I was thinking? He opens the door and stands back, holding it for me. "Ladies, first."

"Wow. A gentleman," I say as I walk into the restaurant. I slowly make my way through the dining room and to the front counter, all the while feeling Nix behind me. We step up to the counter and he moves to my side, keeping his arm wrapped securely around my waist. My body tenses slightly and I tell myself to just relax. When I peek in his direction, he's watching me, brows furrowed and curiosity in his eyes. He releases my waist but doesn't move away so every time he shifts his weight, he brushes up against me.

When the cashier steps up to help us, we both order burgers, fries, and milkshakes. Nix pays, despite my objections, and leads me to a table in the back. We sit down and chat about silly little things, like the weather and sports. It's so easy to laugh with him and before long, my belly aches from all his antics. Then, he turns serious on me.

"I want you to know something." They call out his name and he glances toward the counter before looking back to me.

"What?" I whisper.

"I'm not here playing games. I'm not just looking for some quick hook up. I'm here because I like you, really like you. Please don't think I'm *that* guy."

He stands without another word and walks over to get our food. I watch him the entire way, my heart aching. God, how I wish my issues were something as simple as that. He has no idea that my pain cuts so much deeper. But his words do something else for me, something I didn't expect. They let me know that he really is a good guy. And I wonder if maybe I can actually trust him. I'm still thinking about it as he sits back down and hands me my burger.

"So, tell me," he prompts, popping a French fry into his mouth, "what should I know about you?"

My brow quirks up. "What do you want to know?"

"Anything. Everything." His answer is so immediate and sure that it has me thinking my earlier feelings of trustworthiness are right.

I smile. "Be more specific."

He laughs and nods his head, grabbing some more fries. "Okay. You have two brothers, right?"

"Yeah."

"What's that like?"

My brow furrows. "You don't have any brothers or sisters?"

He shakes his head. "Nope. It's just me."

"Well, let's see, my brothers have always been pretty protective of me. They are bossy and think they know everything, but they have always had my back and protected me from anyone that tried to hurt me. Trey is the more laid back one of the two and he likes to joke around. Tucker is short-tempered and like I said, bossy, but he has a good heart." The more I talk to him, the easier it gets, like we've known each other for years. "What about you? Tell me all about you."

"Be more specific."

I giggle as he repeats my words back to me, actually enjoying the light flirting going on between us.

"Okay, how did you get started tattooing?" A look of complete bliss crosses his face and I know that he really loves what he does.

"Well, I've always loved art. There's nothing like it, ya know?"

My smile slips as I nod and his brow furrows. "What's wrong?"

I quickly shake my head. "Nothing." He watches me and I know that he doesn't believe me but he doesn't push either, and I really appreciate that.

"So, when I was eighteen, I met my friend Jason and he was an apprentice at a tattoo shop. I used to go there and hang out sometimes and one of the artists saw me drawing one day. He told me that I had a lot of talent and asked if I wanted to learn how to tattoo. I started apprenticing with him later that week." He shrugs. "The rest is history."

I nod my head. "That sounds cool."

"Yeah. Or lucky." He pauses for a moment before looking back up at me. "Tell me something else. What do you do for fun?"

"Well, I actually like working at the bar. Meeting all those people, you know? And I love movies. I probably have over two hundred at home."

"No shit?" I shake my head. "That's cool. I like movies."

I lower my head and focus on my food. After a moment, I meet his eyes again.

"What about you? What do you do for fun?"

He shrugs. "Go to the gym, hang out with my friends. The usual stuff." I nod and there is a bit of an awkward silence between us but he speaks up again. "So, what's your favorite movie?"

I throw my hand over my chest and gasp in mock horror. "I could never choose. I love all my babies." He roars with laughter and I find myself giggling too.

"You're cute," he says. My immediate reaction is to blush and look down at my hands. He nudges my leg with his under the table, drawing my eyes back to his smiling face. It's so perfect that I feel like my insides are melting. "Don't do that. I mean it, you're cute."

"Thank you." My voice is weak but I know that he heard me.

"So, I'm gonna say something that might freak you out a little, but I want you to know that I'm being sincere and despite the fact that we just met, I care about you."

"Okay," I say, nervous about whatever is going to come out of his mouth next.

"I want you to know that you can talk to me. About anything." He leaves the statement hanging there between us and for just a moment, I think about telling him my secrets.

The thought causes panic to rise up inside me though so I shut it down. The more I analyze what he just said, the more I begin to freak out. What does he know? Why would he say that to me unless he knew something? Oh God, what did Moe tell him? The panic consumes me and I stand up quickly, my chair scraping along the floor. His concerned gaze locks on me and I grab my bag off the back of the chair, needing to get out of here.

"I have to go." As I try to brush past him, he stands and grabs my arm gently, stopping me.

"Emma, I'm not going to push you but I'm not going away either. I haven't been able to stop thinking about you since you walked into my tattoo shop three days ago. Never in my life have I felt a connection like the one I do with you. And I think you feel it too."

My eyes flick back and forth between his face and his hand on my arm as my mind spins. Finally, my gaze settles on his face and he gives me a little nod of encouragement.

"Bye, Phoenix."

He winks and releases my arm. "See you later, Emma."

*　　*　　*　　*

"Emma? You okay, girl?"

37

I wince at Moe's question as I wipe down the table in the bar after closing. I had really been hoping that no one would notice how distracted I've been all night. I should know better than to think that I had been hiding it well or that these guys wouldn't say anything if they did notice. Ever since my lunch with Nix earlier, I haven't stopped thinking about him. His words run in a loop through my head, one minute exciting me and the next scaring the shit out of me. I'm terrified of opening up to him, of letting him into my damaged, fragile heart. I'm not stupid enough to toy with the idea that whatever is between us could be casual. Nix doesn't seem like that kind of guy and I'm definitely not that kind of girl. I just don't know if I'm ready.

"Yeah, I'm good, Moe. Just tired." I'm crossing my fingers, hoping and praying that he'll buy that excuse but I know the chances are slim. He surprises me, though.

"Well, why don't you go home and get some rest? Trey and I can finish up here."

Trey's head snaps up. He smiles at me and nods. I decide to take his advice. I really am exhausted. Not that I think I'll actually get any sleep, I'll probably spend all night thinking about Nix and these feelings he's stirring up in me.

"Okay. Thanks, Moe."

"I'll walk you out," Trey says, propping the broom up against one of the tables.

"Thanks." Making my way behind the bar, I set the rag down and untie my apron before grabbing my bag from underneath the bar. I quickly say good-bye to Moe, giving him a hug, and make my way toward the door. Trey meets me halfway through the room and drapes his arm around my shoulders.

"How are you really doing, baby girl?"

"Trey, I'm fine. I swear." I wrap my arm around his waist and give it a squeeze to reassure him. He smiles at me but I still see the doubt in his eyes. We reach the door and Trey opens it for me. I quickly duck through and he follows behind. As soon as I step outside, the sound of chirping crickets and frogs greets me. We walk side by side, making our way to my car in the back of the gravel lot.

"What the fuck?!" Trey growls, startling me, and my head snaps up.

I scan the area around us but I don't see anything out of the ordinary. I look back to my brother and find him focused on my car, his jaw clenching. Turning, I look toward my car and I finally see it. All four tires have been slashed. It feels like a rock dropped into the pit of my stomach when I see the note trapped under the windshield wiper.

Tentatively, I walk forward and grab the note. All the air is sucked out of me as I read the words written there.

Did you forget who you belong to?

I'm gasping for breath as Trey grabs the note from my hand.

"Motherfucker!" He paces back and forth, kicking dirt up around him as he does. Finally, he turns to me with wild eyes. "I cannot believe this asshole. Tuck and I are going to take care of him, once and for all."

"You know you can't, Trey."

He runs his hands through his blonde hair and lets out a roar. I flinch automatically but thankfully, he doesn't see. That would only add fuel to his fire right now.

"Why would he do this?"

"I don't know." God, why is he doing this to me now? Just when I was considering moving on with my life, he rears his ugly head again.

Chapter Four
Then…

It's two o'clock in the afternoon and I am literally running on fumes. When I got home last night and tried to sleep, I couldn't get thoughts of Ryan and what he had done for me out of my head. I ended up sleeping only a couple hours. Now, my morning coffee has worn off and I'm fighting to keep my eyes open. Overall though, today has been very successful. There is something going on at the college and I've had a lot of people coming by my booth. I sold three pieces and had two other people ask about custom pieces. I love doing custom pieces.

It's not about the money, either. Sure, I make more money on a custom painting but what I really love is that the customer liked my work so much that they wanted something by me. Let's be honest, any artist can paint a lily, but when a client loves your style so much that they want your lily, it's an amazing feeling.

My phone buzzes on the table with an incoming call and I smile at the name on the screen. "Officer Wheeler, what can I do for you?"

His deep chuckle greets me. "Well, Miss Harrington, you could go on a date with me tonight, as previously discussed." His tone is serious and all business. It makes me giggle. "Man, I love your laugh."

A blush creeps up my cheeks as I bite down on my lip.

"I'm really sorry but I can't make it tonight. I'm working at the bar." For the first time, probably ever, I'm bummed that I have to work. I think I could really like Ryan.

"That's all right. When are you free?"

"Monday is my only night off."

He mumbles something and then is quiet for a moment. I think the call may have dropped, but when I pull the phone away from my ear and check the screen, it's still connected.

"Okay, I'll just switch shifts with someone," he finally says and my mouth drops open in shock. He's getting out of work for me?

"Where did you come from, Ryan Wheeler?"

He chuckles. "What do you mean?"

"I mean, no guy has ever gotten out of work for me or paid to put new tires on my car. You're almost too good to be true."

He laughs again. "I don't know about all of that but I like you. If I have to switch a shift to be able to see you, I will. And as for the tires, I'm glad I could do that for you."

"You gotta let me pay you back."

He scoffs through the phone. "Not a chance."

"Ryan—" I start but he cuts me off.

"No, Emma. Just let me do this. I liked doing it for you and now you still have your money for a new car, which will be safer for you. If you think about it, this is really for me. It's a totally selfish move. I'm really a jerk," he jokes and I laugh. "There's that beautiful laugh."

"Oh, Ryan," I sigh, at a complete loss for words.

"So, seven on Monday night? I'll pick you up?"

"Yeah, that works for me." I rattle off my address for him.

"All right, well I've got to get back to work. I'll see you soon."

"Bye, Ryan."

"Bye, Emma."

After hanging up, I sigh as I lean back in my chair. My heart is beating like crazy, attempting to burst out of my chest. I knew that I had dated some real assholes in my past, but it's never been more apparent than at this very moment.

*   *   *   *

Sunday morning, I'm driving to my parents' house for brunch with thoughts of Ryan filling my mind. He's full of surprises. Like stopping by the bar last night just to see me and we've been texting every night. And he kissed me, right there in front of everyone. The only sour note was Trey getting pissed about it. It took me a full hour to convince him to give Ryan a chance. I swear, my brothers take the overprotective thing to a whole new level.

My phone starts rattling around in the cup holder and I glance down, Ryan's name lighting up the screen. Grabbing it, I quickly hit the green phone icon and press it to my ear. "Hey."

"Hey, gorgeous, what are you up to?" His voice is deep and gravelly.

"Did you just wake up?"

"Yeah, why?"

I shake my head, smiling so wide that I just might crack my face.

"And the first thing you did was call me?"

"Yeah."

"You are somethin' else, Ryan Wheeler."

"Why do you say that?"

"Just never met anyone like you."

"I hope that's a good thing."

"Oh, it is."

"So, what are you up to?" he asks.

"I'm just going over to my parents' house for brunch."

"Are you driving and talking to me right now?"

"Yeah, why?"

He groans. "Seriously? Did you just ignore the fact that I'm a cop?" I giggle. "Mmmm, that sweet laugh makes it a little better though."

"I'm sorry. Do you want me to go? I could hang up right now," I tease.

"No, don't do that."

I grin. "Okay, I won't."

"What are you doing today, besides brunch?"

"Just working tonight."

"Babe, I can't wait for our date tomorrow. Can I tell you a secret?"

My heart flutters when he calls me babe, a smile playing on my lips. "Absolutely."

"I don't think I've been this excited to take a girl out…ever."

All the air whooshes out of my lungs and my eyes grow wide. I haven't even been out on a date with this man and he is sweeping me off my feet.

"I don't know what to say. You've rendered me speechless," I tell him and he chuckles.

"Well, that wasn't my intention."

I'm unable to wipe the damn grin off my face. I pull up in front of my parents' house and sigh because I know I'm going to have to hang up.

"Hey, so I just got to my parents' house and I gotta go."

"Oh, okay. Well, I'll let you go then. I'll see you tomorrow, Emma."

"See you tomorrow, Ryan." I hang up the phone and just sit in my car for a minute. I'm grinning like a lunatic and my heart feels so light. Like I'm floating. Ryan is so damn charming and it's crazy but I feel like he's already working his way into my heart.

Someone bangs on the window, making me jump as a yelp flies out of my mouth. My brother Tucker stands there, grinning at me like an evil villain.

"What's got you so happy, baby girl?" he asks as soon as I climb out of the car.

"Nothing." The last thing I need is Tucker on my case about Ryan.

"Is it about that guy that made out with you in Moe's?" I glare at him. How does he — oh, of course. Trey.

"No," I grumble and he laughs.

"Liar." We walk into Mama and Daddy's house, the smell of bacon and eggs greeting us instantly. My stomach growls.

"Who's a liar?" Daddy asks, coming toward us.

45

"Hi, Daddy."

He smiles down at me as he wraps his arms around me, his signature motor oil scent enveloping me. His long salt and pepper hair is pulled back into a ponytail today, and his goatee looks like it needs a good trim.

"Hey, baby girl." His blue eyes sparkle at me.

"Emma's a liar," Tucker says, cutting into our exchange. I shoot him my best glare but he just grins at me. Jerk!

"Is this about that boy Trey was just telling us about?" Daddy asks and I gape at him. Trey promised to give Ryan a fair chance but it won't happen if he told everyone else about him. I feel totally ganged up on right now.

"I don't know why you guys take pleasure in my unhappiness." I know I'm pouting like a child but this is ridiculous. Daddy laughs, throwing an arm over my shoulder.

"Come on, now, darlin'. It ain't like that."

"Yes, it is absolutely like that. Every time I like a guy, you have to send in the goon squad and scare him off!"

"Did she just call us the goon squad?" Trey asks as soon as we step into the kitchen.

"Yep, she sure did," Tucker answers him.

"I think I like it." They both start laughing. Ugh. I'll never understand how two grown men turn into mischievous ten-year-olds as soon as they are in each other's presence. I roll my eyes at their antics and make my way toward Mama. She is standing over the stove, cooking bacon, with her long brown hair falling over her shoulder. She looks up at me, her green eyes, identical to mine, oozing warmth.

"Hey, sweetheart." She sets the fork in her hand down to wrap me up in a hug.

"Hey, Mama."

"Are they ganging up on you again?" I adore my mom, she is always so kind and sweet, but she is also who I got all my *sass* from. She's slim and always smells like vanilla and sugar from the bakery.

"Yeah."

"Poor girl." She pats my cheek and winks at me. "All right, everyone, food's ready!" she hollers, her voice booming above everything else in the room.

The boys all race over to the table, practically falling into their chairs, and I shake my head and laugh at them. I grab a plate of pastries and a big jug of orange juice and carry them over to the table. Before I can even set the plate down, Trey and Tucker are grabbing for the pastries.

"Boys! Manners!" Mama snaps, and both boys sit straight up in their chairs and pull their hands back. I grin evilly at them, childishly pleased that they got in trouble. Mama motions for me to sit and we all dig in, laughing and joking the entire time.

*   *   *   *

"Oh God," I whisper as I inspect myself in the mirror again. My dark brown hair is in waves down my back and my smoky green eyes are shimmering with excitement. I stuck with my basic look tonight, eyeliner and mascara with just a hint of blush. I'm wearing my favorite white skinny jeans and a black sparkly tank top, finished off with my black peep-toe pumps. I swipe on a light layer of lip gloss and nod my head.

All right, I'm ready.

I didn't think I would be this nervous for our date, but the anticipation has been building for days and now I feel like I'm going to burst. I am already so invested. Ryan has been so sweet and perfect. I can't help but already feel something for him. He's unlike any other guy I've ever met.

A knock at the door interrupts my thoughts and I take a deep breath to calm my frantic nerves. I grab my bag off the table and swing the door open. Ryan's smile slides off his face as his eyes travel down my body. I do my own perusal and grin as I take in the insanely handsome man in front of me.

He's wearing jeans that hang off his hips just right and I'd bet money that his ass looks fantastic. His white button up shirt, the top two buttons un-done, shows off just a hint of the muscles I know are lurking underneath. On top of that, he's wearing a dark gray blazer that somehow makes his hazel eyes pop.

When our eyes meet, he grins at me and I can feel it all the way down to my toes.

"Hey, gorgeous."

I return his smile. "Hey, yourself."

In an instant, he's flush against me with his arms around my waist.

"So, I realized something kind of troubling."

I cock my head to the side as I look at him. "Oh yeah? What's that?"

"Well, the other night I wasn't very gentlemanly. Kissing you right there in the bar, in front of everyone." To my shock, he actually looks a little ashamed.

"It's okay. I liked it."

His eyes flash with desire and he drops his gaze to my lips. My tongue darts out involuntarily and slides along my bottom lip. He groans and his arms tighten around my waist before he looks up and blows out a breath.

"We should get to dinner."

I look at him in confusion. He is really taking this gentleman thing seriously, isn't he?

"Ryan, it's okay," I reassure him but he shakes his head.

"No, I really like you and you are smokin' hot, but I'm going to do this right. I want more than sex with you."

Oh...I don't even know what to say to that.

"Okay." He smiles and grabs my hand, lacing his fingers with mine after I lock up my apartment. When we reach his car, he opens my door for me and I blush at all the attention. This is all so crazy but like the most amazingly wonderful crazy I've ever experienced.

Ryan makes his way around to the driver's side and slides in, starting up the car before taking off.

"So, I hope you like barbecue."

I snort. "What self-respecting southerner doesn't like barbecue?" I ask and he laughs.

"Good. I know this great little place."

"Sounds perfect." He grins over at me. "Did you work today?"

"Yeah, I switched my shift with another guy so I could work this morning."

"I can't believe you got off work to go out with me."

"Hey, I wasn't gonna miss my one day to take you out! So, why do you only work nights at the bar?"

"It doesn't even open until four and I'm usually working on my art during the day."

"Your art?"

"Yeah, it's my passion. I usually paint all during the week and then I sell my stuff at the market on the weekends."

"Oh, that's cool. I can't wait to see your work."

"I can't wait to show you," I reply with a shy smile.

"Do you do pretty well with that?"

"Most of the time. I've been getting more popular lately and so more people are asking for custom pieces, which is really cool."

"Custom pieces?"

"Yeah, people love my style but they are looking for something specific or they want an original just for themselves."

"How much do you make on something like that?" He looks over at me with genuine interest in his eyes and I want to squeal in excitement. Sure, my family is proud of me but they never really ask a lot of questions.

"Depends on the size. Anywhere from a hundred dollars to a thousand. Most of the time, people spend around three hundred."

"And how long does it take you to finish a piece?"

"Again, it depends on the piece. Sometimes, I get stuck and other times, I feel inspired and stay up all night working." He nods and when I look up, I realize that we have parked next to the restaurant. "Oh, geez, sorry for rambling."

"Don't apologize. I love hearing about all this. One sec," he says as he jumps out of the car and hurries over to my side. He opens the door for me and holds out his hand. I place my hand in his and get out of the car. After shutting the door, he wraps his arm around my waist and leads me into the restaurant.

I love the quaint little space as soon as we step through the door. There aren't many tables, maybe twenty tops, but they are all full of people laughing and enjoying the food. My stomach growls as I smell the delicious aromas swirling around us and Ryan chuckles. He presses his warm lips against my cheek and I can't fight the smile on my face. Country music is playing over the sound system and servers are bustling by us constantly. It feels so homey and comforting.

"I love it here," I say to Ryan and he grins.

"Wait 'til you try the food."

*　　*　　*　　*

Ryan was right. The food is phenomenal. I ate so much that my belly aches. I groan and lean back in my chair, looking up to find Ryan grinning at me.

"Full?"

"God, I ate so much!" I moan and he laughs.

"You ready to get out of here?"

"Absolutely." He stands and throws money on the table for the bill before grabbing my hand. He leads me out of the restaurant and just when I think we are going to go back to the car, he turns to me.

"Do you want to take a walk? There's a park over by the river."

"I'd love to." We set off along the empty sidewalk, hand in hand. "So, tell me about being a cop?" I ask and he glances over at me.

"What about it?"

"Why did you decide to become a police officer?"

He looks off into the distance for a moment, thinking. "I'm not sure that I ever really decided. My dad was a cop and it was just...expected of me, I guess."

"Do you like it?"

"Yeah, it's all right. Some days I hate it but it's not so bad most of the time."

"You said your dad was a cop. Is he retired now?" I ask and something dark crosses his face.

"Uh, no. He died a couple years ago."

"Oh my gosh, I'm so sorry." My heart hurts for him. I don't know what I would do without either one of my parents. It must be so hard for him to not have his dad around anymore.

"It's okay."

"What about your mom? What does she do?"

"Well, when dad was alive, she stayed home with us kids but when he died she had to find something to do so she opened a flower shop. My older brother, Zane, helps her run it."

"Do you have any other siblings?"

He snorts and nods his head. "Yeah, I've got two little brothers too, Caleb and Jake. They are a pain in the ass."

"Your poor mother."

"We were definitely a handful," he agrees. "What about you? Do you have any brothers or sisters?"

"Yeah, you actually met one of them at Moe's."

"The guy behind the bar the night I came in?"

"Yeah, that's Trey. My parents adopted him when his mom died."

"Wow, that's really cool."

"Yeah, I guess. It just seemed kind of obvious. He already spent most of his time at our house and we considered him family so they just made it official."

"I can see where you get it from now."

I shoot him a puzzled look. "Get what?"

"You're just so...bright. I can't think of any other way to describe it. You just light up a room with your spirit. Your parents sound like amazing people, you must have got it from them."

I look down at my feet, unsure of how to respond. We reach the park and walk over to the railing by the water. Placing my hands on the top bar, I lean forward, resting my weight against it. Ryan comes up behind me, trapping me between his arms as we gaze out at the water. The lights from the city reflect off the smooth water and I breathe deeply, just enjoying the serene moment.

"So, tell me something else about you, Emma," Ryan whispers in my ear, and I lean back into him.

"What do you want to know?"

"Whatever you want to tell me."

"Can I ask you a question first?"

"Of course."

"Do you have like a book or something at home that tells you how to sweep a girl off her feet in a week?"

He chuckles in my ear and tightens his arms around me.

"Maybe. Is it working?"

"Yeah," I sigh, "it is."

"Okay, now answer my question."

I close my eyes as I try to think of something interesting to tell him.

"I don't know." I'm drawing a blank. This may be due to the fact that his lips are hovering over the skin on my neck, making it difficult to breathe, let alone think.

"All right, favorite flower?"

"Any kind of lily."

"Favorite food?"

"Sweet."

He moves his hands off the rail and wraps his arms around my waist.

"Oh ya? My girl's got a sweet tooth, huh?"

I desperately want to say something about the 'my girl' comment but chicken out. "Yeah, what about you?"

"My favorite food?" he asks and I nod. "Hot wings."

I laugh, shaking my head. "Oh my God, that is such a guy answer."

He shrugs his shoulders. "What can I say, I'm all man, baby."

Oh…my…God.

A tidal wave of lust rushes through my body and I shiver.

His arms tighten around me. "You cold?"

"No," I squeak out and he growls.

"I'm really trying to be a good guy here."

"You're doing a good job."

He doesn't say anything else; we just stare out at the water and watch as boats pass by. I'm perfectly content to just stand here in his arms. Jazz music plays from somewhere nearby and Ryan pulls away from me. When I spin to face him, he holds his hand out to me.

"Dance with me?" he asks, a playful grin on his face. My face mirrors his as I nod my head.

"Absolutely."

He sweeps me up in his arms, swaying our bodies to the music. His eyes sparkle in the moonlight as we stare at each other as we move, tingles shooting through me.

"I really like you, Emma Harrington," he whispers and I feel a blush creeping up my cheeks.

"I really like you, too, Ryan Wheeler."

His gaze drops down to my lips and my body instinctively moves closer, hungry for the feel of his lips on mine. Heat flashes through his eyes just before he leans down and captures my lips. The kiss is slow and sensual. He nips gently at my bottom lip and I gasp. He takes advantage of the opportunity and slips his tongue between my parted lips to stroke and caress my own.

Good God…

I'm about to go off like a firework. I lean into him further, pressing my body up against his, earning me a growl from deep in his chest. His hand slides into my hair and he angles my head as he kisses me deeper. My hands grip the lapels of his blazer, pulling him into me. My hips grind into his and he pulls away with a groan, panting. He presses his forehead to mine as he tries to get his breathing under control.

"God, you're killin' me," he groans and I fight back a giggle.

"I'm sorry."

He leans back and smirks at me. "No, you're not. Come on, let's go back to the car." He reaches for my hand, lacing his fingers through mine, and we head to the car.

"All right, Officer Wheeler, your turn. Tell me something about you?"

"Well, I'm classically handsome, obviously—"

I giggle and bump him with my shoulder. "Be serious!"

"Okay, let's see, I like football."

"Duh."

"How am I ever suppose to do this if you keep interrupting me?" he asks, teasing.

"Sorry, I'll stop." I pretend to lock my lips and throw away the key.

"You're so cute." I wrinkle up my nose at him and shake my head. He laughs loudly. "Yeah, you are." I pull my hand out of his and give him a little shove. He turns to me with wide eyes and a maniacal smile on his face. He scoops me up in his arms and twirls me around, drawing a yelp of surprise out of me.

"Put me down!" I squeal and he sets me back on my feet, laughing.

"All right, back to me. I like football," he says, giving me a pointed stare to keep my mouth shut. "And I like playing pool with my friends, I'm an excellent gardener, thanks to my mom, and I can cook like, two things, well."

"What two things can you cook?"

"Pancakes and steaks."

A laugh bursts out of my mouth. "Diet of champions."

"You know it." I look up to see that we are back at the restaurant and Ryan jogs forward to open the car door for me. After he slides into the driver's seat, he takes me home where he drops me off at my front door with a searing kiss goodnight that leaves me breathless.

*   *   *   *

"Emma Nicole Harrington! You've been ignoring us!" Addilyn shouts at me as I'm working at the bar the next night. She and Daisy come strutting toward the bar, determination on their faces.

Shit...

"I haven't been ignoring you," I say. "I was just texting you yesterday."

"And when was the last time we saw you?"

"Well... uh..."

"Exactly!" Daisy yells and I shake my head. Sliding out from behind the bar, I make my way over to my two best friends and give them each a hug.

"Sorry."

"We will forgive you…if you come out with us tonight."

I frown and look back at the bar. "I can't. I'm working."

Daisy opens her mouth to say something but someone else calls my name.

"Emma Harrington?" I turn around and find a young girl with red hair and blue eyes staring back at me.

"Yeah, that's me."

"Wait right here, please," she says before scurrying out of the bar.

"What the hell was that?" Addilyn asks.

"I have no idea." A second later, the bar door opens, casting sunlight onto the wooden floor. In her hands is a large bouquet of lilies and a huge grin spreads across my face.

"Oh my God," Daisy and Addilyn say at the same time.

"These are for you," the girl says, handing me the vase and an envelope.

"Thank you." I set them down on the bar and she quickly leaves.

"Those from the cop, baby girl?" Trey calls from the other end of the bar.

"I don't know, let me read the note!" I pull a blank card out of the envelope and smile when I see the familiar handwriting.

Emma,
The next chapter in my handbook says to
buy the girl flowers so…here you go.
I had an amazing time last night and

I can't wait to see you again. Have a good night, beautiful.
Ryan

I giggle as I'm reading his words and when I look up, three pairs of eyes are staring at me.

"What?" I ask, looking around at Addy, Daisy, and Trey.

"Let me see it," Addy demands and I hand it over to her.

"From the cop?" Trey asks.

"Yeah." I'm unable to wipe the stupid grin off my face.

"What handbook?" Addy asks when she finishes reading.

"I made a joke last night that he must have a handbook at home that tells him how to sweep a girl off her feet."

A grin slowly curls her lips. "Oh, he's good."

"Yeah."

"I don't like this," Trey growls. Snapping out of my happy thoughts, I roll my eyes and turn to glare at him.

"Why, Trey? Why is it a bad thing that he likes me?"

"He's just too smooth."

I shake my head and ignore him.

"Oh, back to why we originally came here," Daisy cuts in. "We're taking you out tonight."

"Guys, I really can't. Moe needs me here."

"Moe!" Addy hollers and Moe's head snaps up. "Can we take her?" She points to me and pouts. She's so ridiculous.

"Absolutely. Girl needs a night off."

I growl at Moe, he knows I need all the money I can get while I'm saving up for my car.

"I need the money," I say, to no one in particular.

"I'll pay you for the hours you were gonna work tonight," Moe offers. My eyes narrow on him.

"No, you will not!"

"All right, fine but get out of here before I change my mind."

Ugh. I guess I have no choice. I grab my flowers off the bar and turn back to the girls.

"Well, let's go, I guess."

Chapter Five
Now

"Guys, this is ridiculous. You don't need to be here."

Tucker and Trey both shake their heads without saying a word. I sigh and turn away from them. The morning after I found my tires slashed, they showed up at my door and said that they wanted someone with me at all times. I know they are worried but it's insane. I don't need a bodyguard.

"Hey, Emma."

Looking up from the bar, I come face-to-face with a set of blue eyes that set my body ablaze. "Phoenix."

He shoots me a crooked grin and I forget to breathe for a moment. His smile gets me every time.

"My friends call me Nix."

"We're friends?" I ask, sarcastically.

"Oh, come on, now, sweetheart. We could be." My body tingles with excitement and desire before my brain reminds me that I need to proceed with extreme caution.

"Don't call me 'sweetheart'."

At my words, his smile grows, stretching across his entire face. He places his hands flat on the bar and shifts his weight so he is leaning closer to me.

"Would you prefer 'baby'?" he asks, the word almost a purr rolling off his tongue. My breath falters and I grip the rag in my hands tighter.

Hell yes...

NO!

"Do you need something, Nix?" I need to get him away from me before I spontaneously combust.

"Aww, see we're friends now." He smirks and winks at me. Cocky Bastard.

Damn it! I didn't mean to do that. He makes it hard for me to think. "No, I'm just lazy."

He laughs. "Playin' hard to get, huh?" The instant the words are out of his mouth, all the blood drains out of my face and his demeanor changes. He stands back up and the playful expression is gone. He looks concerned.

"Don't ever say that to me." My voice is strained with barely concealed panic.

"Shit. I'm sorry, Emma," he apologizes and I believe him, surprising even myself.

"It's okay." I inhale deeply, willing the poisonous words out of my head.

"No, I can tell it's not. I'm really sorry. I didn't mean anything by it."

I nod, acknowledging his words. Logically, I know this. I know that they are just words but the memory they conjure up is so horrid that I'm practically shaking.

This.

This is why I'll never be able to have a relationship again.

I'm ruined.

"Emma." That voice. The voice sends a wave of dread washing over me.

He steps up next to Nix and the sight of them together is so wrong that I want to rush over there and pry them apart. In that moment, I know Nix is different. Surely, my gut reaction wouldn't be like this if he wasn't, right? I look back between the two men and I just can't take it anymore. It's too much. I've reached my limit of things I can handle in a day.

"Ryan, you need to leave." I wish my voice was stronger right now. I wish that he couldn't hear the fear his presence brings. I glance over to see Nix watching the exchange and I want to die right on the spot.

First, I embarrass myself by freaking out about those silly words and now Ryan shows up. Is Nix going to think I'm insane? The more important question is, why do I care so much?

"Baby, come talk to me." It's clear from his voice that he's not asking but I won't give in. I shake my head, emphatically. I will not go anywhere with him. "Emma," he growls. It takes every ounce of self-restraint I have to fight my body's reaction to obey him.

I know the consequences if I don't.

No, that's not true. He doesn't control me anymore.

"I think you need to go, dude," Nix says, standing toe-to-toe with Ryan.

"Fuck off, asshole."

"She said leave." Nix puffs out his chest to make himself even bigger. Not that he needs it. He's already taller and wider than Ryan. Ryan's eyes shoot to me and he glares.

"You little slut. You're fucking him?"

I snap. A rage that I didn't even know was in me comes barreling out and I completely lose it. "Fuck off, Ryan. Even if I was fucking him, it's none of your Goddamn business. You need to leave!"

Our yelling catches the attention of both Moe and Trey, who come marching over.

"What are you doing here, asshole?" Moe growls.

"I came to talk to my girl," Ryan snaps right back, not backing down.

"She's not your girl anymore. That's what happens when you beat the shit out of her!" Trey yells and I turn to him with wide eyes. I can't believe he just said that in front of the entire bar. I'm completely mortified. A deep blush crawls up my cheeks and my gaze drops to the floor.

It's completely silent around us. You could hear a pin drop. From the back corner, three of our regular customers jump up and come over toward us.

"He hit you, darlin'?" One of the men, an older, grizzly looking man, puts his hand on my shoulder. I know that not one of the men standing here right now is going to let this go. It's all about minimizing the damage now.

"Please, just get him out of here," I plead with them.

"Let's go, you piece of shit." Another begins pushing Ryan toward the door. Moe and Trey follow while Nix stays back with me.

"You're mine, Emma!" Ryan yells, right before he gets pushed outside. I feel Nix's eyes on me but I can't bring myself to look at him as the embarrassment seeps through me.

"Hey," Nix says softly and his voice coaxes me into action.

Ever so slowly, I raise my head until I'm looking into his addicting blue gaze. He raises his hand to my face and gently brushes his thumb over my cheek. I'm shocked when I find myself leaning into his touch.

Holy shit, what is he doing to me?

"I'm beginning to understand, Emma," he says. A warm smile on his lips as he stares down at me.

"My friends call me, Em," I whisper.

He grins. "You got it, baby."

*　　　*　　　*　　　*

The constant ringing of my phone wakes me up from the first nightmare-free sleep I've had since I found that note on my car. Rolling over, I grab it and resist the urge to chuck it at the wall. Instead, I press the green phone icon and press it to my ear.

"What?" The words come out in a growl from just being woken up and my irritation. A hearty laugh greets me.

"Oh, man, you sound so cute in the morning." Heat courses through my veins and at the same time, chills run down my spine. How the hell does he do that? I ignore the butterflies in my belly and try to remember to breathe.

"How did you get my number, Nix?"

"Your brother gave it to me." His answer surprises me. I would have never expected my brothers to ever give my phone number to a guy.

"Which one?"

"Does it matter?"

"Yes. I need to know which one to kill."

Still laughing, he says, "Aww, baby, you don't mean that."

I sigh because he's right. Not only would I never do anything to my brothers but also I actually do like talking to him. The second I heard his voice, my heart skipped a beat and I was fighting back a smile.

"Why are you calling me, Nix?"

"Well, apparently, I have Emma duty today." My brow furrows. Emma duty? What the hell is — no! Oh God, no.

"Please tell me that my brothers didn't add you to their ridiculous bodyguard detail."

"I would, but I'm not a liar, sweetheart."

Shit.

Fuck.

Goddamn it. How am I supposed to spend all day with him and resist these feelings I have? I bury my head in the pillow and groan, earning another chuckle from Nix.

"This is so stupid!"

"I disagree. After the things he said in the parking lot last night, I think you having some protection is a fantastic idea." I swallow hard as my mind works through all the things Ryan could have possibly said to Nix and my brothers.

"What did he say?"

"You don't need to hear that, baby." Fury boils inside at the thought of another man trying to control me.

"First of all, Nix, stop calling me *baby*," I growl. "Second, don't you dare do that to me! I won't let anyone take away my choices ever again. You need to tell me." He sighs into the phone and the sound has me picturing him running his hands through his thick hair in frustration.

"All right. Come open the door and I'll tell you everything." His comment makes me come to a screeching stop.

"What?"

"I'm at your front door. Come let me in."

Suddenly, there is a knock at my front door and I look down at my body, covered only by a thin tank top and a pair of panties.

"Uh…just give me a second." I hang up on him without another word and jump out of bed. I quickly find a pair of shorts on the floor and pull them up my legs. Racing into the bathroom, I pile my long brown hair in a bun on top of my head and wash my face.

Finally, I make my way into the living room and fling open the door. Nix's head shoots up in surprise, his brow furrowed. My eyes travel down his body, taking in the tight, black t-shirt that stretches over his bulky muscles perfectly, and his dark wash jeans that hang off his hips in a way that has me biting down on my lip. When I meet his eyes again, he's smiling at me.

"Hey, baby."

"Nix," I warn. He holds his hand up in front of him.

"Okay, I'll stop. I promise."

I'm not sure that I believe him but I stand back to let him into my apartment. When he passes by me, his hand brushes mine and I wonder if it was intentional or not. He walks over to the love seat and plops down, making himself at home. I join him, sitting down on the couch across from him.

"Let's hear it."

"What? No, 'Hey, Nix, how are you doing?' first?" His eyes sparkle with mischief and I'm wavering between wanting to kiss him and wanting to throttle him. I make a big show of rolling my eyes and sighing.

"Hey, Nix, how are you doing?"

He gives a victorious smile. "Oh, I'm so much better now that I'm here with you."

I giggle in spite of my annoyance and roll my eyes at him again.

"Oh my God. Can you be serious for just two seconds and tell me what he said?" I'm still giggling but he slowly stops laughing and nods his head.

"All right. I'll get serious for a second. He said a lot of shit to your brothers before I got out there and I have no idea what it was but they were pissed. If you want to know about that, you'll have to ask them."

I nod. "Okay."

"When I got there he started screaming at me that you were his. He said that I might get to have you for a little bit, but that you would be his again soon. That he would get you back, no matter what it took."

I shudder and lean back into the couch, my mind spinning. *No matter what it took.* Those words shouldn't be so ominous but coming from Ryan, they are, especially since I would never go back willingly.

"Can I ask you something?"

My gaze snaps up to Nix. "Yeah."

"Did you really love that asshole?"

I sigh and bite my nail. "It's complicated."

"How so?" He tilts his head, his brow furrowed as he tries to understand how I could possibly love a man like Ryan Wheeler.

"It was like he was two different people. I loved the man that I thought he was and I hate who he really is but I can't separate the two."

He looks past me, out the window and appears to be lost in thought for a moment before he locks eyes with me again.

"Do you still love him?"

"Oh God, no."

"Good," he says, flashing me a satisfied smile.

"Oh yeah? Why's that?"

"I like you, Emma. I think I've made that pretty obvious. I would hate to lose my chance with you, especially to a guy like that."

"Yeah, all right, Casanova."

"I'm serious."

My eyes dart to his and I see nothing but honesty staring back at me. It's unnerving. "You don't even know me, Nix."

He smiles. "That's just semantics, sweetheart."

I stare at him as he leans back, all the while smiling at me.

"What do you mean?"

"It means that I know enough about you to know that you are a good person and that I want you in my life. It means that I feel a crazy connection between us, this spark, and I can't think of a single thing you could tell me that would make me not want you."

All I can do is watch him. I'm still not sure what to make of him. I think that had I met him only a few years ago, I would have been swept off my feet by his words but now, as much as the girl in me is swooning all over the place, I find myself questioning his motives. Does he really like me? Or is he just using his charm to suck me in? Like *he* did.

"You're awfully confident," I finally say and he just nods.

"I am."

Needing to change the subject, I plaster a smile on my face.

"So, since you're stuck with me all day, what are we going to do?"

He returns my grin and scans my apartment, stopping on a painting on the wall. It's one of mine and I freeze.

"Wow. That's incredible. Who's the artist?"

"I am." My voice is small, laced with pain. His head whips back in my direction.

"You paint?" His eyes are shining with excitement and I really wish I could tell him that I do. Instead of, I did.

"Not anymore."

His gaze softens and he looks at me like he's really trying to understand. "How come you don't paint anymore?" His genuine blue eyes nearly gut me. God, he barely knows me and he seems to actually care about me.

"I just don't."

He cocks his head to the side, never once taking his eyes off me.

"You've got to give me more than that."

My nervousness makes me snap at him. "I don't have to give you anything!" As soon as the words are out, I regret them. It's not his fault and I know it. He's just trying to get to know me and it's been a while since someone has tried to get through my armor. "I'm sorry," I whisper.

He smiles. "Sweetheart, you don't have a thing to be sorry for." I stare at him in shock for a moment. Everything he says and does throws me off balance. "Hey, how about you show me this legendary movie collection?"

I nod, surprised and more than a little pleased that he remembered. "Okay. It's over there. Go ahead and pick one out."

I grab my phone as Nix makes his way over to the bookshelves along the wall to look through the movies, and text my brother.

Me: Since when did you start giving my number to strangers?

Tucker: Nix?

I roll my eyes. Yes, Nix. Who else has he been giving my number to?

Me: Duh

**Tucker: He's not a stranger, he's Moe's nephew.
Besides, he's a good guy.**

I look up from my phone at Nix still searching through all my movies. I believe that he's a good guy but it still makes me nervous.

Me: How do you know that?

**Tucker: We talked. Trust me, baby girl.
Give the guy a chance.**

I'm shocked. If my seriously overprotective brother approves of Nix then maybe this isn't such a bad thing.

Chapter Six
Then…

We walk back into Moe's an hour later, all of us looking like sex on legs. When we got to my apartment, Daisy confessed that she kissed Tucker and that she likes him but she has no idea how he feels about her so I devised a little plan. I know for a fact that as soon as Trey sees what I'm wearing, he will call Tucker. And I also know for a fact that my brother will come running down here to *protect* me. When he does get here, he's gonna get a load of Daisy, looking smokin' hot, dancing with her friend Joel. Joel happens to be gay but Tucker doesn't need to know that.

Sure enough, like clockwork, as soon as Trey sees me, his eyes bug out of his head and he pulls out his phone, typing furiously.

"Trey Andrew Davis! Don't you dare!" I yell, playing my part to a T. He shrugs and looks over at me.

"Already done, sis."

I growl at him and he just shrugs again. I can't say that I blame him. My dress is risqué…to say the least. It's a purple V-neck dress with lace cutouts all the way down the side. I can't even wear panties with it. If Tucker isn't too preoccupied with Daisy, he's going to have a coronary.

"Put this on," Trey barks at me from behind, holding out a zip-up hoodie.

"No way, Trey."

"I swear to God, Em. Put the sweater on. Every asshole in here is staring at the side of your boob!"

"That's kind of the point, dear brother."

"I'll call Dad," he threatens and I gape at him. We both know Daddy would haul my ass out of here and not think twice about it.

"Jerk!" I snatch the sweater out of his grasp and pull it on. I expect to hear a retort out of him but when I look over, he's gawking at Addilyn. She decided to wear my favorite little black dress and it looks amazing on her. Her fire engine red hair is pin straight, falling to the top of her shoulders, and her bright blue eyes are rimmed with thick liner and false lashes.

Well…isn't that interesting.

How have I never noticed that these people in my life have a thing for each other? I'm feeling a little blind right now.

"Emma!" Tucker calls from behind me. Holy crap! He got here really quickly. When I turn around, his eyes are locked on Daisy.

Bingo!

Jealousy flashes through his eyes as he watches Joel put his hands all over her. He is clenching and unclenching his fists, looking ready to burst. Daisy catches my eye and I motion her over to us. She grabs Joel's hand and I swear my brother is going to explode.

"Hey, Trey. Hey, Tucker," she says, completely out of breath.

"Keep the sweater on, Emma," Tucker growls before turning and stomping out the door.

"What am I missing here?" Trey asks. The three of us dissolve into giggles with Trey watching us warily.

*   *   *   *

We decide to leave Moe's and go find a club downtown when our plan fails. I ditch the hoodie as soon as we are in the car, ready to let loose and have a little fun. After finding a place we all agree on, we make our way to the bar and order drinks then find a table in the back and sit down.

"So, your plan didn't work," Daisy grumbles.

"Actually, I think it did."

"I agree. Did you see his face?" Addy asks and I giggle.

"Oh, yeah. He was about to have a stroke. It's obvious that he has feelings for you, now he just needs to pull his head out of his ass."

"Yeah, we'll see," she complains.

"I was super interested in the fact that Trey couldn't take his eyes off you, Addy." Her eyes widen and a blush creeps up her cheeks.

"What do you mean?"

"Oh my God, when did y'all stop telling me shit?!"

"There really isn't anything to tell. We just flirt but nothing has happened."

"Well, let's make something happen then."

"No way. If it's supposed to happen then it will."

"Oh, all right." I huff out a breath at her stubbornness and pout — just a little.

"So, tell us some more about Ryan. Where did he take you on your date?" Daisy asks.

I launch into the whole story about how we met and where he took me on our first date, sparing no details. When I get done, both girls are gaping at me.

"Wow, he sounds perfect," Addy says.

"Yeah, he's somethin' else." Even I can hear the giddiness in my voice and both girls smile at me.

"We're glad you're happy," Daisy says. Just as I'm about to respond, my phone rings. I pull it out and grin. Ryan's name illuminates the screen. I tell the girls I'll be right back and run outside to answer the call.

"Hello?" I say into the phone, completely out of breath.

"Hey, baby. Where are you?"

"Uh...I'm out with my friends."

"I thought you were working tonight."

"Well, I was but my girls showed up at the bar and practically kidnapped me."

"Oh ok," he sighs, sounding sad.

"What's wrong?"

"Well, I really wanted to see you tonight so I'm here at the bar."

"I'm sorry," I coo.

"It's okay."

"Can I make it up to you?" I lean back against the brick wall outside the club and look up at the stars, thinking about our date the night before.

"How were you planning on doing that?" he asks, his tone playful and a little naughty.

"Breakfast in the morning?"

"Sure. That sounds good…hey, hang on a sec." Someone starts talking in the background before Ryan gets back on the phone.

"Uh… I'm supposed to ask you if you're still wearing the sweater?" he says, confusion clear in his voice.

"No, I'm…wait, is my brother still there?" I hear Ryan talking to someone and then muffled voices in the background. What the hell is going on?

"Yeah and he said that you're wearing practically nothing." There is a hint of a growl in his voice and I'm not sure if I love it or hate it.

"Oh my God, they are so overprotective. My dress is fine."

"I'm coming to get you," he announces and before I can respond, he hangs up. I gape at the now-black screen of my phone. Seriously? The last thing I need in my life is another guy that thinks he needs to protect me. Ugh. Whatever. I'm going to go back in to my friends and have some fun. Besides, he doesn't even know where I am.

I stomp back into the club and over to our table before throwing myself in the chair with a huff.

"What's up, girl?" Addy asks.

"My stupid brother was still at the bar and Ryan came by to see me."

"Uh-oh. Did they beat him up?" Daisy asks. I want to smile that they know my brothers so well but I hold back.

"Uh, no. Apparently they are best friends now and ganging up on me about my dress choice. Ryan said he's coming to get me." They both look at me with wide eyes. "Oh, whatever. He doesn't even know where I am. Let's go dance."

They share a look before agreeing and we make our way out onto the floor. I start dancing in an attempt to forget about my crazy brothers and overprotective boyfriend.

Wait…did I just call him my boyfriend?

Nope, not gonna think about it. Just dance.

I throw my hands over my head and swivel my hips as I get lost in the music. Addy and Daisy mimic my pose, losing their inhibitions and start dancing. We really get into it, huge grins on our faces as we sway around each other. Daisy wiggles her hips suggestively and we all start giggling when suddenly, hands are on my waist. I turn to tell the guy to get lost when I come face-to-face with Ryan's heated gaze.

I stare up at him with wide eyes and my mouth in a perfect *O*. His gaze travels down my body and his eyes flash with desire when he sees my bare skin through the lace.

"We're leaving," he growls in my ear and the only thing I can do is nod my head.

I wave good-bye to Addilyn and Daisy as Ryan leads me out of the building, my stomach churning with a mixture of excitement and apprehension.

*   *   *   *

The second I close the door to my apartment, Ryan is pinning me up against it with his body. He rolls his hips into me, his rock hard erection poking my belly. I moan and press into him.

"I'm trying so hard to be a good guy here," he groans.

"Don't."

It has the opposite effect on him and he pushes away from me, running a hand through his hair.

"Can I borrow your shower?"

"Uh…yeah."

He nods and takes off for my bathroom. What the hell just happened? I know he wants me, I could feel it, but he turned away. I think he's taking this good guy thing just a little too far. I sigh and mentally will the throbbing between my legs to go away.

Making my way into the kitchen, I chug an entire bottle of water, trying to get my body under control. It seems to work, at least a little bit. I go into my bedroom and strip out of my dress and throw on a tank top and shorts. Falling back on the bed, I close my eyes and breathe in deeply.

The door to the bathroom opens and Ryan walks into the room in just his jeans. My mouth goes dry all of the sudden, as beads of water run down his defined chest and six-pack. I barely hold in a moan.

"I want to talk to you."

"Then put on a shirt," I groan.

He smirks but doesn't listen. He sits down on the edge of the bed and turns to look at me.

"Do you want to see other people?" he blurts out and my eyebrow shoots up.

"What?"

"Cause I don't. I don't want to see anybody else and I don't want you to either."

"Uh, okay," I mutter, not sure what the hell is going on here.

"I know I've kind of been hot and cold but you've got to know that you are gorgeous and I'm insanely attracted to you." Okay, this is getting better.

"Okay."

"But I don't want you think that I'm only after sex. I want to be exclusive. I want to introduce you to people as my girlfriend."

"Oh…" I breathe out.

"Do you want to…be my girlfriend, I mean?"

A slow smile spreads across my face as I nod my head. "Yeah."

His answering smile is dazzling. He lies next to me on the bed and presses his lips to mine in a tender kiss. My entire body goes lax, like I could just melt into him. His hand darts out and pulls my body to his until there isn't an inch of space between us. His tongue nudges my lips, urging them open, and I comply immediately. When I reach for the button of his jeans, he grabs my hand and pulls away from me.

"We're not doing that tonight," he says, sternly.

"What the hell?! Why not?"

"I didn't ask you to be my girlfriend so I could get laid," he explains and I pout. "Don't worry." He starts kissing all over my face and I try to hold back my smile. "We will soon. Just not tonight." He plants one more kiss on my swollen lips and I moan.

"You're trying to turn me into a crazy person, aren't you?"

He laughs. "No, I'm not trying to turn you into a crazy person. Why don't you show me some of your art?"

"Okay." I may not be getting laid tonight but I have to admit that I'm excited to show him some of my pieces. I grab his hand and lead him into my spare bedroom where my easel is set up. I let go of his hand and prop some of my finished paintings up against the wall. When I stand back up, he comes up behind me and wraps his arm around my waist.

"These are really good, babe," he says and I smile as I lean back into him.

"Thanks."

"Are you doing any custom ones right now?"

"Yeah, that one is." I point to the landscape that is perched on my easel.

"Where is that?"

"Hawaii," I answer as I study the beach scene I've been working on. "It's where my client got married and she wanted a painting done of it to give her husband for their anniversary."

"Wow, that's really cool." We are silent for a moment before he releases me and backs up.

"What's up?"

"Nothing. You want to go lie down? It's kind of late...or early, depending on how you look at it."

"Yeah, that sounds good."

He scoops me up in his arms and carries me off to the bedroom. When we get there, he lays me down on the bed and turns off the light before crawling in next to me.

"Come here." He lies on his back and positions my head on his chest, hitching my leg up and over one of his. When he has me how he wants me, he sighs and I smile into his skin. "Go to sleep, baby."

Chapter Seven
Now

It's been two weeks since Nix had his first shift on "bodyguard detail" and he has become a constant in my life. One or both of my brothers are with me during the day but every night Nix shows up at my door and stays over. We didn't talk about it, it just kind of happened — like that's the way it was supposed to be all along.

I thought for sure that my brothers would object to Nix spending so much time with me but they haven't said a word. It seems that they like Nix. I hate to admit that I'm starting to really like Nix, too. My walls are slowly crumbling and I feel more at ease with him every day. He's smart, funny and sweet — not to mention, hot as hell.

The sexual tension in my apartment is so thick that I have trouble even forming thoughts. It doesn't help that Nix walks around without a shirt on, showing off his large shoulders, bulging pecs, and ripped abs. The first time I caught sight of the V leading into his faded jeans, I almost spit coffee all over the kitchen table.

"You know, I could help you out with that, sweetheart," Nix comments as I make my way out of the bedroom. He's standing by the counter in just a pair of jeans holding a coffee cup in his hand, smirking.

"What?" I barely get the word out, too distracted by his shirtless body.

Jesus...look at his abs!

My mouth waters as I think about running my tongue down them to the band of his boxer briefs poking out over his jeans. I bite down on my lip and my eyes skim over the growing bulge in his pants. I wonder what he would sound like moaning my name.

"I said, I could help you with that," he repeats, adjusting himself, and I quickly avert my eyes. From the look on his face, I know I've been caught.

"Help me with what?"

"I heard you, baby." He delivers that statement with a wink. I tilt my head and scowl in confusion for a moment.

He heard me?

When I finally grasp the meaning of his words, my eyes shoot wide in surprise, and a blush creeps up my cheeks. My belly flips as I think about him doing what I just finished doing in my room to relieve the ache between my thighs that's been constant since he started staying here.

Oh God...he *heard* me.

He smirks and leans back against the counter, raising his coffee cup to his mouth, and I follow its path. He takes a sip and licks his lips, and I gulp.

Sweet mother Mary...

"What do you say, baby?" he purrs and my brain completely stops working for a moment. I can't get thoughts of him out of my mind. Him kissing me, licking me, fucking me. I think I'm going to go crazy.

This is a bad idea, I repeat to myself, over and over again. Maybe if I say it enough times, my body will start to believe it because right now it doesn't give a shit that getting involved with Nix would be a terrible idea.

"In your dreams, big boy."

He laughs. "Oh sweetheart, the things in my dreams would make you blush a whole lot more than that." My cheeks burn in embarrassment and I look down, doing anything to avoid his eyes.

I need some air.

If I stay in this apartment any longer, I might just let him do all the things he's dreamed about, and I can't do that. I hate this feeling, like I'm stalled in the middle of the highway. I don't know what to do, I don't know where to go, so I just sit there, doing nothing.

"I...uh...I have errands to run," I stutter, grabbing my bag and heading for the door.

"All right, just give me a second and I'll come with you."

With my hand on the doorknob, I pause and blow out a breath. "I haven't heard from Ryan since that night. I think you guys can lay off the protection detail."

"Em, I think you and I both know that he's not going away. We just want to keep an eye on you." He's standing so close behind me, the heat from his body radiating off him and straight into me. I fight my body's desire to just melt into him and let him wrap me up in his big strong arms. "That's not the only reason I want to come with you though."

"Why do you want to come?" He places his hand over mine on the doorknob and slowly turns me around to face him.

"Come on, baby. We both know what's happening here. I really like you and I want to spend time with you."

I get lost in the ocean that is his eyes and more than anything, I wish I could lean forward just a little bit and press my lips to his. Something still holds me back though.

"I can't."

He smiles slightly, raising his hand, and cradles my face. Without a thought, I lean into his touch.

"I know you're not ready yet, but I'll be right here until the day you are. You're worth the wait."

Shaking my head, I say, "I'm really not. I'm ruined."

He scowls, stroking my cheek with his thumb while he searches my eyes. "You are fierce, funny, sweet, smart, sexy as hell, and so many other things, but you are not ruined." My breath catches in my throat as I gaze up at him, tears filling my eyes. One spills over and trails down my cheek. He wipes it away and kisses my forehead. "Let me get dressed and we'll go, okay?"

All I can do is nod. He smiles again and drops another kiss to my forehead before pulling away, grabbing his bag off the floor, and disappearing into the bathroom. His words bounce around in my head and the way he said them — it makes me *feel* them. His confidence in me makes me feel strong but a sliver of uncertainty still lingers.

I know I have feelings for him. It was unavoidable. With our connection and us spending so much time together, it was inevitable. I just can't take that next step and act on it. Somehow, I know that he would never hurt me like Ryan did, but I don't know if

I have the confidence to put myself out there. How long will he really wait around for me?

* * * * * *

"You gonna tell me what's going on between you and Nix?" Trey asks a couple hours later at work.

"There's nothing going on."

He shoots me an *oh please* look and shakes his head. "Come on, tell the truth."

"That is the truth, Trey. There is absolutely nothing going on between us. I…just can't, okay?"

Trey looks over at me and understanding dawns on his face. "Okay, baby girl. I hear ya."

"Don't you think it's about time ya'll stop with the bodyguard bullshit?"

Trey scowls and shakes his head. "No." He doesn't say anything else and I roll my eyes at the stubbornness of all the men in my life.

"We haven't heard anything from him since he showed up here. I think I'm fine," I point out.

"No," he snaps, sternly. "Listen to me, Em. The fact that we haven't heard from him makes me even more worried than if he was calling you every day like he did at first. We have no idea what he's thinking right now."

"God, you guys are so damn stubborn," I growl, rolling my eyes again.

"Don't downplay this, Emma. I remember what you looked like the last time he got ahold of you." I blank out for a moment at the memory that his words bring up and shudder.

"Shit. Are you all right, Em?" Trey touches my arm gently and I blink. His eyes shine with regret and concern. I hate that people feel like they need to walk on eggshells around me. I've been doing better.

"Yeah. I'm okay."

"I didn't mean to bring up all that bad shit. We're all just really worried."

"I know, Trey. I'm really okay."

He smiles and gives me a wink before heading back to the other end of the bar. It surprises me that I actually mean those words. Sure, I had the memory but the usual panic and despair I feel isn't there. Maybe Nix is right, maybe I am getting stronger.

"Hey, baby." Speak of the devil...

"Nix, don't call me that."

He gives me a cocky grin that makes my heart skip a beat...or two. "You know you secretly love it, Emmy." Well, shit. I can't even deny it. I do love it when he calls me that but I really shouldn't.

"Do you need something, Nix?" I ask, feigning annoyance.

"Only you, sweetheart."

I roll my eyes and laugh. "You just think you're so smooth, don't you?"

"Oh, I know I am. And you know what else?"

I shouldn't. I really, really shouldn't, but I do. "What?"

"You love it. You can't resist me forever, baby."

I snort but I know his words ring true. "We'll see about that, big boy."

His grin grows.
"Yes. Yes, we will."

*   *   *   *

"Hey, Emma, wake up." Nix's voice drags me out of my dream and when I open my eyes, he's hovering above me. My cheek feels wet and when I press my hand to it, I realize that I'm crying. I sit up in my bed and quickly wipe the tears off my face. I was dreaming about the good Ryan, the Ryan I fell in love with.

"Are you okay?" His eyes are soft as he searches my face, trying to decide if I really am okay.

"Yeah, I'll be all right." I look around and then it hits me...he's in my bedroom. "Uh, Nix, why are you in my room?"

He smirks, wiggling his eyebrows at me, and I can't stop the small smile that forms on my face.

"Naw, nothing like that, sweetheart. I heard you cryin'."

"Oh." I don't have anything to say to that. Should I tell him why I was crying? He sits beside me on the bed, our hips touching, and wraps his arms around me. My body is tense at first but after a moment, I feel myself relaxing into him. He lets out a sigh, like all is right in his world.

"Do you want to talk about it?"

I shake my head into his chest. "No."

"Okay," he whispers. He runs his hand over my hair and his lips press down on my head.

Closing my eyes, I soak up the comfort his embrace provides. When I open them again, I look at the tattoos decorating his arm. There is a small black gator and I trace over it with my finger.

"What's this one for?"

He glances down and his lips stretch into a smile against my skin.

"Would you believe me if I said that I got it for Louisiana?"

I snort and shake my head. "No."

He chuckles. "My dad is the president of the Bayou Devils. That's their patch."

The Bayou Devils is a local motorcycle club. In fact, they are kind of notorious in the area for causing a lot of trouble but I have also heard that they do good work. There was a rumor that they would help battered women escape their abuser but I didn't know how true that was.

"Why an alligator?"

"'Cause they're bayou devils. Have you ever seen a baby alligator? They look like little demons."

I start laughing at his description, realizing how accurate it is.

"Are you a member?" I can't ever remember seeing a motorcycle when I've been around Nix so I'm not sure.

"Naw. That wasn't for me."

"And your dad was okay with that?"

His body tenses underneath me. "No. He wasn't."

I pull back to look up at him and I can see the storm building in his blue eyes. "What happened?"

His gaze flicks down to me, and he studies me for a moment. "You really want to know?"

"Of course." I find myself wanting to know everything about him. He sighs and runs a hand through his hair.

"I already told you that I met my friend Jason when I was eighteen, but that was kind of the end of the story. My dad had been pressuring me to join the Devils for a while and I couldn't decide what to do. It wasn't really my thing but Dad always went on and on about legacy, and it being my responsibility to take over the club someday. When I met Jason, I really fell in love with tattooing and I told my dad I wasn't going to prospect." His arms tighten around me and I snuggle into him. After a moment, he takes a deep breath. "He cut me out of his life after that. Didn't speak to me for a couple years."

"What changed?"

"He got shot."

I gasp and pull back to look at him again with wide eyes. A soft smile graces his lips just before he presses them to my forehead.

"I guess after that, he decided that life was too short to hold onto his anger. We still aren't as close as we were when I was a kid but we're better now."

"I get it, you know. You have to do what you love."

This time, he pulls back with an expectant look on his face.

"You gonna tell me why you don't paint anymore?"

I bite my lip, unsure of how to open this dam. It's almost like I physically can't force the words out of my mouth.

"I…I just can't."

"Physically?" he asks and his body tenses again. Lord knows what he's imagining right now.

"No. Mentally. I've got a block and I don't know if I'll ever be able to get past it."

His lips press to the side of my forehead and I close my eyes, my body tingling with…excitement. "'Cause of him?"

"Yes. Because of him."

He squeezes me to him and kisses me again.

"You ever get a tattoo for a girl?" I ask to distract him and he laughs. He's holding me so close that it jostles me.

"No. Never felt strongly enough about a girl to permanently mark my body for her."

"Oh, come on. Not even in high school?"

He grins, shaking his head. "You really want to do this?"

"Do what?"

"Talk about all our exes?"

My eyebrows shoot up in surprise. "All? Jesus, how long is it gonna take to get through *all* yours?" That earns another laugh and he pulls me into him.

"Smart ass."

My cheeks ache from the smile on my face but I don't even care. I haven't felt this carefree in so long and it's really nice.

"All right. Let's hear it. How many?"

"Five."

"Girlfriends? Or women you've had sex with?" He has the decency to blush and I have a feeling I won't like his answer.

"Girlfriends. Including you."

"I'm not your girlfriend."

He shrugs. "I'm a patient man."

I scoff and shake my head at him. "You're a cocky man." He just shrugs again, not arguing with my assessment.

"How many for you, Emma?"

"Boyfriends?"

His eyebrow shoots up and his jaw ticks. I have trouble holding in my laugh as I see him thinking about the implications of my statement.

"That would be what we're talking about."

"Four."

"Including me?"

I shake my head, pressing my lips together to hide my smile. He pretends to look wounded and presses his hand over his heart.

"That hurts."

Shaking my head, I laugh at him. "You're impossible."

"Yeah, but you like it." And damn it, he's absolutely right.

Chapter Eight
Then…

"Is that the last of it, baby?" Ryan asks.

"No, there is one more bag in the front seat."

He hustles out the door to grab the last of my stuff to move into our new house. When I think over the last few months, all I can do is smile. Ryan is amazing and we've been enjoying getting to know each other. I agreed to move in with him last week when he started talking about us getting married. I knew there was no way in hell I was ready for that but I also knew he wanted our relationship to progress somehow so this seemed like the next logical step.

The fact that my brothers still don't like him is really hard. I've given up arguing with them and I can only hope that in time they will come around. They aren't exactly ignoring me but things have definitely seemed strained between us. At least Ryan is always there for me. Every time I've come home crying because things are so weird with them, he holds me and tells me it will be okay. If they ever do come around, I'm not sure if we will be able to work things out. I love my brothers dearly and I want them in my life, but Ryan gets so angry over every tear I cry because of them.

I'm grateful that Addilyn and Daisy like Ryan and still want to hang out with me. It would break my heart to lose them, too. Hell, it's already breaking my heart that my brothers are so mad at me. I plop the box down next to the others and let my gaze wander around our new home.

After agreeing to move in together, Ryan decided that neither of our apartments would be big enough so we went looking for a new place. We were lucky enough to find this little house. It isn't much but it's perfect for us. It has two bedrooms and two bathrooms, but the best part is the studio apartment outside that I'm using for my art.

"Uh, babe…what's this?" Ryan asks, holding up a teddy bear I've had since I was little.

"It's my teddy bear."

"It's disgusting."

I feel a little disgruntled by his comment. That bear is special. I can still remember the day I spent at the fair with Daddy where he won that for me. I mean sure, he doesn't look brand new but I've had him forever. I'm not gonna throw him away.

"Leave my bear alone." I snatch it out of his hands.

"God, you are such an idiot. Does he have a name, too?" he teases. I know he's just joking around but I find myself getting irritated with his total disregard for my feelings.

"Don't call me an idiot."

"Why? Did it hurt your feelings?" he taunts.

"Yeah, it did."

He laughs and wraps his arm around me. "You're too sensitive. It was just a joke, baby."

I feel thoroughly chastised. Am I too sensitive? I don't know… maybe I did go a little overboard there but it still hurts that he called me an idiot. What is that saying they teach all little kids? *Sticks and stones may*

break my bones but words will never hurt me? I just
need to buck up.

"So, what do you want to do for dinner?"

"The girls wanted to go out tonight for Addy's
birthday."

"Seriously, you're going to ditch me?"

"How about we do something special tomorrow
night?" I say, in an attempt to compromise.

"Yeah, sure." He walks away from me.

"Ryan," I call to him but he ignores me and lies
down on the bed in our room. "Ryan."

"What?"

"Please don't be mad at me."

"It's fine. Go get ready."

I huff in annoyance and march into the
bathroom to take my shower. Fine. If he's gonna be an
ass then I'll just go have fun with my girls.

*   *   *   *

When I arrive home a couple hours later, Ryan
is sitting on the couch, watching baseball with a beer in
his hand. He refused to speak to me before I left and he
doesn't even look up when I come into the room. I
glance around nervously for a minute before I sit down
on the couch next to him. He still doesn't acknowledge
me. Biting my lip, I try to think of what I should do or
say here. I reach out to touch him and he jerks away,
tossing the remote back on the couch and standing up.
He sets his beer down on the coffee table and starts off
toward the bedroom.

"I'm goin' to bed," he tosses over his shoulder as he's walking away from me.

"Ryan," I call to him, but he ignores me. "Ryan!" When he still doesn't answer me, I turn off the television and go back to the bedroom. He's lying on the bed on his side, facing away from the door, when I enter.

"Ryan, please talk to me." My pleas are met with silence and the ache in my chest grows. "Baby, please."

More silence.

I quickly retreat to the living room when I feel the tears welling up behind my eyes. As the first one spills down my cheek, I throw my body onto the couch. It hurts so much to have him ignore me. I don't feel like I did anything wrong. He knew I was going out tonight and it was a special occasion. Why is he acting like this?

I lie there with tears silently running down my cheeks, racking my brain for any way to make this better. I go back and forth between being angry that he is acting this way to just wanting him to talk to me and being willing to do anything to achieve that.

Finally giving up, I make my way back into the bedroom and slip out of the clothes I went out in. I decide to take another shower so I go into the bathroom and pin my hair up before sliding under the warm spray. As the water runs over my skin, I replay the entire night. I still don't understand why he is being so unreasonable. He goes out with his friends all the time. Why is it not okay for me?

More than anything, I would love to have him wrap his arms around me right now and hold me. He always makes me feel better. Fresh tears spring to my eyes as I think about Ryan lying in the other room, angry with me. I vow to myself that I will do whatever it takes tomorrow to get him to forgive me.

Whatever it takes.

*   *   *   *

The next morning, I wake up to the smell of bacon and coffee. The sheets next to me are cold, letting me know that Ryan has been up for a while. I take a deep breath to prepare myself for whatever I'm going to face in there.

"Breathe, Emma," I whisper to myself. It's gonna be fine. I'll just go in there and say I'm sorry for hurting him. He'll understand.

Yep…that's what I'm gonna do.

With renewed hope and strength, I fling the covers off my legs and make my way into the kitchen. When I round the corner, I find him standing at the stove cooking bacon in just a pair of sweats.

"Hey," I call, testing the waters to see if he's still mad. He looks over at me but doesn't say anything. That's a good sign, right? "Can we talk?"

He shrugs. "Sure."

Okay, here goes. "I'm sorry."

He turns to me and narrows his eyes as he takes a sip of coffee.

"What are you sorry for?"

"For ditching you and going out with my friends."

He scoffs and turns back to the stove. Shit…was that the wrong answer?

"That's not why I'm mad."

"Why are you mad, Ryan?"

"You were such an inconsiderate brat!" he explodes, spinning back around to face me. "We spent all day moving in together and then you just took off and didn't even take me into consideration."

"I'm sorry. I didn't think it would be a big deal." I still don't understand. He goes out with his friends all the time. He ditches me for them a lot and I never complain.

"Well, it is a big deal. My feelings matter."

"Babe, of course they matter. That's not what I was saying."

"Yeah, whatever."

"Ryan, I am so sorry. I didn't realize how much it bothered you."

His eyes soften slightly and I take a chance, sliding my arms around his waist. His arm drapes over my shoulder and he pulls me into his body.

"Will you at least talk to me before you make plans next time?"

"Yes, I will."

"Okay, I forgive you then," he says and kisses the top of my head. I hug him tighter, so relieved that there isn't any more tension between us. "I love you."

"I love you, too." And just like that, the last bit of stress leaves my body.

*   *   *   *

"Hey, I'm gonna go out with the guys for a while," Ryan says after walking into the bedroom, where I'm trying to choose an outfit for dinner.

"I thought we were going to dinner."

"We'll do it another night." He shrugs and I openly gawk at him.

"You're going to ditch me after the fit you threw yesterday about me going out with my friends?! And we didn't even have plans yesterday!"

He rolls his eyes at me. "Stop being so dramatic. It's no big deal."

"It is a big deal! We made plans!" I'm so angry right now that I'm shaking. I can't believe he is doing this to me. Especially after last night.

"Why are you being so mean to me?"

WHAT?!

I'm being mean to him?

"Are you serious?"

"Yeah. I'm just going out with my friends. We'll have dinner tomorrow or something."

"No. You don't get to do this to me."

He rolls his eyes again and grabs his keys off the dresser. "All right well, I'm leaving. Try to put the bitch away before I get back."

My jaw hits the floor as I stare at him. I can't believe he just called me a bitch. He turns to walk out the door but looks back at the last second.

"You may be a spoiled brat but I love you. You're hurting me so much right now by doing this." With that, he leaves the bedroom.

When I hear the front door open and close, a rage filled scream flies out of my mouth as I throw my hairbrush at the wall. I drop to the floor in anger and disbelief. I know I'm right here. He bailed on me. And yet, there is a small sliver of doubt. Am I really a brat? Was I overreacting?

Before I get bogged down with insecurities, I jump up and call Addilyn and Daisy to come keep me company. They agree to stop over and I quickly hop in the shower to wash off the make-up I just put on. When I get out, I throw my hair up into a messy bun and slip on some sweats and a tank top.

Just as I'm looking through the fridge for some wine, the doorbell rings. I jog into the living room and throw open the front door. Addilyn and Daisy stand there, with smiles on their faces and each with a bottle of wine in hand.

"Oh! You two are angels!" I exclaim, ushering them inside. "I don't know where my wine glasses are yet."

"Whatever. We'll just drink out of the bottle," Addy says, plopping down on the couch.

"Okay." Daisy opens both bottles. "Thanks for coming over, guys." I take a big gulp of my wine.

"Sure, sweetie," Daisy coos and I smile at her.

"Are you going to tell us what happened?" Addilyn asks. I sigh and nod my head.

"So, yesterday when I went out with you guys, he got all mad at me and said that I ditched him. I mean, we didn't even have plans last night but I apologized for hurting his feelings and we were fine today. We made plans to go out to dinner together and as I'm getting ready, he comes into the room and says his friends want him to go out and he's leaving."

"Oh, fuck no," Addy growls. I grimace and nod before continuing my story.

"Anyway, so I started freaking out and he called me a bitch," Both girls gasp, "and said I was being dramatic and that I'm a spoiled brat...I don't know. Do you guys think I'm a brat?"

"Absolutely not!" Addy yells. "You listen to me, you are an amazing person. You've always been there when I needed you. Don't you dare believe that asshole."

Her words help me feel a little better about the situation but it still hurts to think that Ryan thinks that about me. There is still a little doubt there. Maybe they are wrong...besides, they weren't there. Maybe I really was being an unreasonable bitch.

"Yeah." Even I can hear the disbelief in my voice but neither girl says a word about it.

"Come on, turn on some music and let's dance," Addy commands, jumping up. I laugh and shake my head before grabbing my laptop and turning on some music. Daisy tucks her phone into her purse and gets up to dance with us.

It doesn't take long for the music to seep into me and make me forget my troubles. I laugh and dance around my living room with my two best friends. After a while, we all crash on the couch in a sweaty heap.

"Let's watch a movie," Daisy suggests and Addy and I agree. As Addy is digging through boxes looking for the movies, my phone starts ringing.

"Hello," I answer.

"Did you tell your fuckin' brother that I called you a bitch?" Ryan growls from the other end of the phone.

"Uh…no."

"Did you tell anyone?"

"Um…"

"Goddamn it, Emma!" he explodes. "Why can't you keep our relationship between us? Why do you have to bring everyone else into it?"

"What's the big deal, Ryan? I didn't say anything that wasn't true."

"Like I believe that! You are such a fucking drama queen! I'll deal with you when I get home." He hangs up the phone before I can answer. I pull it away from my ear and stare at it in shock.

"What's wrong?" Addy asks. My eyes shoot up to my two best friends and I glare at them.

"Did one of you text my brothers about what I told you tonight?"

"I'm sorry," Daisy squeaks.

"Why would you do that?"

"Whoa, what's going on?" Addy asks.

"That was Ryan on the phone. He's super pissed. I'm guessing my brother got involved after you talked to him."

"Emma, I'm sorry," she says.

"I think you guys should leave."

"Emma…" Addy says, trying to calm me down.

"Please, leave." My voice is hard and cold. I'm so angry that my friend went behind my back and told my brother what I told her in private. I thought I could talk to them. I thought they would keep my secrets.

"Okay, we're going. Call me tomorrow, okay?" Addy asks and I nod. She gives me a hug.

"I really am sorry, Emma."

"I don't want to hear it, Daisy. You've been my friend a lot longer than you've been hooking up with Tucker. You should have known that I wouldn't want him to know."

"Come on, Daisy," Addy urges and Daisy follows her out the front door. "I'll talk to you tomorrow, Em." She closes the door behind her and I flop down on the couch.

Now all I have to do is sit here and wait for Ryan to get home to 'deal' with me.

Chapter Nine
Now

"I need to show you something," I say to Nix as he lounges on the couch. He smiles at me and my heart does that crazy flip-flop thing in my chest. I can't believe I'm even considering this. There won't be any more hiding after he sees what I'm about to show him but I'd be lying if I said I wasn't concerned. It's been weeks since Ryan showed up at the bar but I can feel the threat hanging over me, like a dark cloud.

"Sure, babe. What's up?" I sit down next to him and hold the photos of my bruised body against my belly so he can't see them yet. "I've been thinking about what you said about Ryan possibly waiting for an opportunity to get at me and I need to give you something, just in case."

"Jesus, Em. Just in case what?" His eyes are full of fear and a protectiveness that I'm used to seeing from my brothers. The emotion throws me off a little. I knew there was something between us but I didn't understand the depth of his feelings until right now. "Just in case he gets me or—"

"Or what, Emma?" he growls. His body goes impossibly tense and he gives me an expectant look.

"Or worse."

"Fuck! I don't want to talk about this, sweetheart."

"I need you to have these, Nix. It's important."

He glances down at the photos in my hand and takes a deep breath. When he blows it out, his eyes flick up to mine and the look he gives me knocks the wind out of me. No one has ever looked at me like that.

Total devotion.

"Yeah, all right. Let's see 'em," he finally agrees, his deep voice gruff with fear.

I hand him the photos and as soon as he looks down at the first one, his body goes rigid and he sucks in a breath. He flips through them quickly, growing more agitated with each new image of my battered body.

"Jesus fucking Christ." He tosses them onto the couch next to him, as though they disgust him. He tips his head back and rubs his large hands over his face. Intense shame rises up inside me. I wouldn't be surprised if he was repulsed by me now.

"I'm sorry."

"No!" he explodes and my body reacts instantly, before my mind can process what just happened. I recoil from him and regret transforms his handsome face.

"Shit, I'm sorry, baby." He scoots forward and wraps his arms around me. My muscles are tense at first but after only a second, I'm relaxing into him and breathing in his masculine scent. I fight back a groan and pull away from him slightly. He releases me and cups my face in his hand, looking deeply into my eyes, searching for something. "You never have anything to be sorry for. Especially this. It's just hard to look at, okay? I'm so sorry I scared you."

"It's okay. I wasn't really scared of you. I just reacted."

He sighs and runs a hand through his hair, looking back over his shoulder at the photos still lying on the couch. I'm reminded in this moment, how much is between us. "What do you want me to do with those?"

"Listen, I think you are all crazy for pulling a Kevin Costner on me but if you need them for any reason, I want you to have them."

"Kevin Costner?" he asks, a smile teasing his lips.

"Yeah, you know, *The Bodyguard.*" He shakes his head like he still doesn't know what the hell I'm talking about. "A movie. With Whitney Houston."

"Babe, I've got no freakin' idea what you're talkin' about." He laughs and I join him.

"Man, you ruin all my good movie references. You can't be my lobster." As the words leave my mouth, a strange sensation washes over me as I realize that Nix very well *could* be my lobster. I've never felt anything like I do with him and he heals me a little bit more every day that he's here.

A totally confused look crosses his face and he says, "Lobster? Em, what the fuck are you talkin' about?"

I laugh loudly and shake my head. It brings me back to a time when Addy, Daisy, and I would spend all day watching *FRIENDS* reruns, quoting all the best lines. "Nope, not tellin' you that one."

"Stubborn ass woman," he teases with a huge grin on his face and pulls me back into his arms. The sudden move surprises me and the next thing I know, Nix and I are nose to nose, centimeters away from each other. My breath quickens as I look into his alluring blue eyes and see so many things looking back at me.

God, how much longer can I fight this?

Do I even want to anymore?

Nix's eyes flick down to focus on my lips and his tongue darts out, trailing along his bottom lip. My mouth tingles and my breath comes out in short, sharp pants. Part of me is screaming for him to take me, smash his lips against mine, and kiss me with all the promise I see lurking in his eyes. The other part of me is still hesitant. But, why? Why am I still running from him? I truly believe that he is a really good guy so what is still holding me back?

"I can't, Nix," I breathe. He nods and meets my eyes again.

"Soon, baby," he promises and I know his words ring true. I don't have much fight left in me.

*   *   *   *

"What ya thinkin' about, baby girl?" Moe asks, drawing my attention to him. I shake my head, clearing away the memory that was just haunting me.

"Nothing."

"You and Nix are getting pretty close, yeah?"

I shrug my shoulders. "I guess."

"Naw, that boy is crazy about you," he assures me.

"I don't know about that, Moe."

"Mark my words, darlin'."

I shoot him an incredulous look and nod my head. "All right."

"Say, you wouldn't know anything about his sudden change of opinion where I'm concerned, would ya?"

"Nope, sure don't."

"Uh-huh, sure," he teases, shooting me a wink. "Thanks, girl."

I grin at him. "Anytime, Moe."

"Hey, Moe, can I steal this girl for the night?" Nix calls from behind me.

I feel lightheaded and I have to mash my lips together to keep from grinning like a loon. Moe notices and that knowing smirk on his face irritates me. I whirl around to face Nix and he smiles down at me. His blue eyes sparkle, and I'm completely swept up in him. The rest of the world fades to a blur around us as I get lost in his eyes. How does he do this to me?

"Sure thing," Moe yells back, snapping me out of my daze and I sigh. Why are these people always meddling in my life?

"What are you doing?" I ask Nix.

He grins and shakes his head. "It's a surprise. Come on."

I remove my apron and throw it under the bar. "You should know that I really hate surprises."

"You'll like this one." He grabs my hand, intertwining our fingers and I follow him out to his truck. He opens the passenger door for me and holds out his hand. "Madam."

"Who says chivalry is dead?" I tease as I climb into the truck. He closes the door and leans in the open window.

"Truth be told, I'm just trying to get in your pants."

"Phoenix!"

He laughs and I can't help but join him.

"Uh-oh. She used my full name, I'm in trouble," he teases, winking at me before making his way around to the driver's side.

We drive in silence for a little ways before I look over at him. "So, I heard a secret today."

His gaze flicks over to me quickly before focusing on the road again. "Oh yeah? What was it?"

"That you're crazy about me."

He smiles. "Was that a secret? Damn, I've got to step up my game."

I shake my head, trying to clear my thoughts. "I can't think straight around you, Nix."

"Maybe it's time to stop thinking, baby."

*   *   *   *

As I'm walking up the stairs to my apartment with Nix's hand securely in mine, I smile. What Nix did for me tonight is nothing short of amazing. He gave something back to me tonight. It may seem silly that something as simple as taking me to a football game made a small piece of me click back into place but that's what it did.

I love football.

Growing up with guys all around me, I didn't have much of a choice. Before meeting Ryan, I was an avid fan. I would get dressed up on game day, go to the stadium, and scream at my T.V. when I couldn't be there. Ryan would tease me relentlessly for liking football so much. Each week, my voice got quieter and quieter until I wasn't saying anything at all then I just stopped watching. He took the fun out of it for me and made me self-conscious about supporting my team. The longer we were together, the louder that little voice in my head got — telling me that I looked stupid.

"Give me your keys," Nix commands.

I comply immediately, pulling them out of my pocket and handing them to him. As he's unlocking the door, my eyes sweep over his body and I'm flooded with lust. Everything about him just does it for me, even the way the muscles in his arms flex as I watch him work.

Biting my lip, I imagine what it would feel like to have those arms wrapped around me, his brightly tattooed skin contrasting against my pale flesh. Fighting back a shiver, I sigh and open my eyes to find him staring at me with the front door wide open. Fire blazes in those blue depths as he meets my gaze before his eyes slowly trail down my body.

My breath hitches when his eyes meet mine again and he takes a step toward me. He's so close, close enough to touch, and I'm frozen, needing him to make the first move. He does just that and takes another step, pulling me into his arms at the same time. I lay my hands on his strong chest, his heart pounding furiously against my palm. I look down at it in wonder. I've never believed his words as much as I do right now. He really does feel the same way for me.

He reaches up with one hand and runs his fingers down my cheek as his eyes search mine, looking for something. Hesitance, maybe? He won't find any. The usual fear isn't there anymore. I'm nervous but I know that I want his mouth on mine more than I've ever wanted anything in my life.

"Can I kiss you, Emma?" he asks, his voice soft, wrapping me up like a warm blanket, and I relax into his arms completely.

"Yes."

Victory and satisfaction flash in his eyes a second before he's pressing his lips to mine. Every thought leaves my mind, every ounce of fear I felt, completely unfounded.

This feels so right. Nix kissing me, his lips moving against mine, with mine, is the most perfect thing I have ever felt. Like two magnets finally coming together. It's where I belong. Before this moment, I thought all those little kisses he planted on my forehead were hot but I was so, so wrong.

This.

This is hot. His arms tighten around my waist and he lifts me up, never taking his lips off mine. My hands slide into his hair and I nip at his bottom lip as I gain a little bit of confidence. His answering groan gives me another self-esteem boost and I slip my tongue past his parted lips, his arms tightening around me in response. His hand slides into my hair, cradling the back of my head, and I want to weep at just how amazingly right this feels. Why did I ever resist him? He pulls away, panting, his cheeks flushed, and I can feel his erection poking my lower belly.

"Let me clear up any confusion," he says. His raspy, desire fueled voice sending another shiver through me. "I'm crazy about you, baby."

"Yeah, okay." *I'm crazy about you too*, I think, but the words get lodged in my throat.

*　　　*　　　*　　　*

"Nix, where are you taking me?"

He grins back at me as he pulls me along behind him.

"All will be revealed soon." I snort and shake my head. He sounds like a fortune cookie and I tell him so. He laughs. "Just be patient, baby."

Warmth flushes through me at his term of endearment. I'm surprised by how easily we fell into this new aspect of our relationship. It's been four days since the football game but sometimes, it feels like it's been this way between us all along. Maybe it had been and I'd just been blind to it.

"Nix, seriously, where are we?"

He stops and turns to me with a grin on his face. "You are the least patient person I've ever met in my life."

I shrug because I know it's true. "So?"

"So, nothing," he says and leans in, pressing his lips to mine in a quick kiss. Well, it was supposed to be a quick kiss but we get carried away and I wrap my arms around his neck, pulling his body into mine. He nips at my bottom lip and pulls away. "You're trouble. Come on, it's only a little bit farther."

He starts walking again, tugging me along behind him, and I strain my eyes trying to see through the darkness. Finally, I give up. I have no idea where we are. I stumble forward when my foot catches on something, and I hear Nix curse as he spins to catch me. I land in his arms and he stands me back up.

"Wait here," he instructs and then he's gone.

There is a splash and my head whips in the direction of the noise. Are we near water? In the next second, soft light is flooding the area, and I let out a little gasp. Nix comes back over to me and wraps his arms around my waist from behind. "What do you think?"

I trail my eyes over everything, from the strings of lights strung up in the trees to the small stereo set up on the side of the large dock. I spin in his arms to face him. "You did all this?" He nods. "For me?" This time he smiles and nods.

"All for you, baby."

I shake my head, in a daze. "I don't know what to say."

He slides his hand into my hair and tilts my head back to look up at him. The look in his eyes takes my breath away. He smiles briefly before leaning down and sealing his lips over mine. I let out a sigh and my lips part. He takes full advantage, slipping his tongue into my mouth. A groan sounds from deep in his chest and he pulls me closer to him.

"Nix," I pant, yanking my mouth away from his but he just holds me closer and begins kissing down my neck. Goose bumps race across my flesh and moisture pools between my thighs. I let out a moan when his teeth sink into my skin. "Nix," I say again, firmer this time. As much as I would love to continue this, we are on the edge of a swamp. He slowly pulls away and when he meets my eye, I'm ready to say screw it and go right back to what we were doing.

"Sorry." He brushes his thumb over my cheek and leans in to give me one more quick kiss. "I got a little carried away."

"I'm not complaining. I just think maybe we shouldn't do it here."

He grins and I melt. "Yeah. I'd feel really bad if you got eaten by a gator."

I scoff and slap his arm, playfully. "What makes you think I'd get eaten?"

He gives me a look that screams *duh*. "All I gotta do is run faster than you, sweetheart."

I sputter out a laugh and cover my heart with my hand.

"My knight in shining armor." My tone is rich with sarcasm and he shakes his head, muttering something about me being a smart ass.

"Come sit," he commands, holding out his hand to me. With a smile on my face, I lay my hand in his and let him lead me to the edge of the dock. He sits first and then helps me to sit down next to him. He presses a button on the stereo and it comes to life, playing "My Eyes" by Blake Shelton. He wraps one arm around me and I lay my head on his shoulder, content to just sit here and enjoy his company.

"You doin' all right, baby?" he asks after a few minutes. I pull back to look at him.

"Yeah. Why wouldn't I be?"

"I just don't want you to be worried about all this shit with your ex."

I spend a couple moments thinking it over before shaking my head.

"I'm really okay. I'm a little stressed but not too bad. I wish I could just move on, though."

He tucks me into him and I lay my head on his chest again.

"We will figure this out, Em. Your brothers and I will find a way to end this." I stiffen as I think about how much my brothers or Nix still don't know.

"What have they told you?" I ask, my voice barely audible among the chorus of frogs around us.

"They told me everything they know. That Ryan was an asshole to you a lot of the time but you never said anything and that they saw you with bruises more than once. Is there something else you want to tell me?"

"No."

"Emma, baby, I know there is more."

I jerk away from him and in his surprise, he lets me go. I jump up and start walking back the way we came. It doesn't take long for him to catch me. He wraps his big arms around me and scoops me up into the air.

"Don't run from me, Em."

"I'm not talking about this, Nix." I'm practically screaming and he slides me down his body before turning me to face him.

"I just want to help you."

"I can't talk about it." My voice cracks and I feel tears burning my eyes. He lets out a rough breath and pulls me into him.

"Okay, baby. Okay." He presses me closer still until my face is buried in his chest and I feel secure again. "Come sit back down with me, Em." I nod and he picks me up again and carries me back over to the dock. He sits down a few inches from the edge and lets me curl up in his lap. His hand rubs over my side and leg, soothing me.

"Why don't you tell me about you?" I ask.

"What do you want to know, sweetheart?"

"Anything." His lips brush the side of my head and then his breath is drifting across my ear. I shiver.

"Be more specific."

I grin, thinking about the lunch we had not so long ago. "You never talk about your mom. What's the deal with that?"

He shrugs his shoulders. "Don't really know. She was a club whore and she ran off when I was a baby."

I hold back my wince at the term club whore. "So you never knew her?"

"Nope." Hearing that makes me feel for him but he doesn't seem bothered by it. I guess if you never know your mom then you never really know what you're missing.

"Were you and your dad close when you were little?"

He chuckles. "Oh yeah. I followed him everywhere. I would sit in the garage with him while he worked on his bike. He bought me these bottles of root beer that looked just like beer bottles and I thought it was the coolest thing ever. We would hang out and I would have my bottle of root beer. It made me feel like a grown up."

I giggle and cuddle into him more. "That's adorable."

"I guess."

"What else did you guys do?"

"All sorts of stuff. He took me fishing a lot and taught me how to shoot a gun." The ache is clear in his voice the more he talks about his dad.

"Do you miss him?"

His arms tighten around me and he lays his forehead on top of my head. "Yeah, sometimes I really do but I'm not willing to change who I am to please him either."

"That's gotta be hard."

He scoffs and pulls back so he can see my face. "You of all people shouldn't be saying my life is hard."

"Why not? My situation doesn't diminish everything you've gone through. Besides, I have people that I can lean on but you've said that you and your dad aren't all that close anymore."

"I have people. I've got you, don't I?"

I smile. "Yeah, you do."

Chapter Ten
Then…

I must have fallen asleep at some point because the next thing I know, Ryan is stumbling in the front door. I sit up on the couch in silence and wait for him to make the first move.

"Oh, you're still up," he snarls.

"Yeah."

"Are you done being a fucking bitch?"

Every time I hear that word come out of his mouth, directed at me, it's like a bee sting to my heart. Just a small prick at first that almost makes me wince, but it leaves a mark and throbs and aches long after the initial pain.

"I don't want to fight anymore, Ryan." And it's the truth. I let go of my anger hours ago and now I just want to curl up in his arms. I hate when he's mad at me. My whole world feels off kilter.

"Yeah, well…I'm still pissed."

"About what?"

"You! You go and tell your brother that I'm this asshole. It's no wonder he doesn't like me. I never even stood a chance with you playing the victim to him all the damn time!"

"Ryan, I never talk to my brothers about us."

"Then how did he know?"

"I told Addy and Daisy," I admit, quietly.

"Why? Why can't you keep our relationship between the two of us? I don't like you telling them stuff about us. They're going to try to break us up!" He sounds crazy right now. I mean, I know he's drunk but he actually sounds out of his mind.

"Baby, they wouldn't do that."

"Really?! And what did they do the second you told them? They went and told your brother!" He drops to his knees in front of the couch and grabs my face in his hands. "I love you. Don't let them come between us. It's you and me, babe. No one else."

"Okay, baby. I won't, I promise."

He leans in and kisses me, the smell of whiskey wafting off him.

"I love you," he says.

"I love you, too, Ryan."

"Come on, let's go to bed."

I stand and he puts his arm around me as we walk down the hall to our bedroom. I feel better, relieved that he's no longer mad at me.

*　　　*　　　*　　　*

Two Months Later…

"Baby, you home?" Ryan calls out, his voice drifting through the open door of my studio.

"Back here."

A few seconds later, he comes strolling into the door and wraps me up in his arms. "I missed you today," he whispers in my ear. I lean my body back into him and feel a calm wash through me from his touch.

"I missed you too, baby. How was work?" He lays feather-light kisses along my neck and a shiver runs down my spine.

"Terrible," he growls. "Put your paints away. I made plans for dinner for us."

I scowl in irritation. "Ryan, I really have to finish this. You should have asked me before you made plans."

He releases me and takes a step back. "What's the big deal? Just finish it tomorrow."

I set my paints down and turn to him, my irritation growing with every word he says. "It's a custom piece and she needs it tomorrow."

He chuckles and shakes his head. "Babe, she doesn't need it. She wants it. You can finish it tomorrow and give it to her the day after."

"Uh…no. I told her it would be done on time. I need to finish it tonight."

He chuckles again and I start to get really upset. It feels condescending almost, the way he's talking about my work.

"What is the big deal? It's just a painting." An air of superiority radiates off him.

"It's not *just* a painting. It's important to me and it would be unprofessional to be late."

"Unprofessional?" He bursts out laughing, and my irritation immediately morphs into intense anger.

"I'm not going out tonight," I state, my voice strong and unwavering. I turn back toward the easel and grab the paintbrush.

"Baby," he coos, coming up behind me and wrapping his arms around my waist again. "Why are you doing this to me? I just want to spend a little time with you." When he uses his charm, I don't stand a chance. I sigh and close my eyes, my resolve weakening.

"Yeah, okay. What are the plans?"

"Just go get ready. It's a surprise."

Sighing again, I nod and put the paints away before making my way into the house to shower and get ready for a night out.

*　　　*　　　*　　　*

We pull up in front of Moe's and I turn in my seat to look at Ryan.

"What are we doing here?"

"The guys wanted to meet up to play pool."

My jaw drops as I stare at him. "Are you serious?"

"What?"

"I thought you wanted to spend time with me?"

"Babe, that's what we're doing," he answers, pointing toward the bar. He can't possibly be serious. Before I can say anything, he gets out of the car and opens my door. I climb out, anger pouring off me though he seems oblivious. When we walk inside, I see Trey and Bree behind the bar. They both wave at me, which I return as Ryan steers me over to the pool tables.

"Hey, guys," he calls and shakes hands with his friends. I've only met them twice before and I don't remember their names. I don't particularly like them and I get the impression that they aren't all that impressed with me.

Whatever.

I honestly don't care. I plop down in a chair while Ryan and his friends walk over to the pool tables.

"Babe, can you go grab us beers?"

I grind my teeth together while standing up. "Yeah." I turn and start making my way over to the bar.

"Hey, baby girl, what's going on?" Trey asks when I reach him.

"Nothing."

"Come on, now. You know I'm not going to believe that."

"I don't want to talk about it, Trey." Especially not after the last time I talked to someone about my relationship with Ryan. That's the last thing I need tonight, him getting mad because I talked about him to one of my brothers.

"All right, sis." He nods in agreement.

"Holy shit! Emma Harrington?" a voice says from behind me. I turn to find a guy who looks vaguely familiar.

"Uh…yeah."

"I haven't seen you in ages! It's me, Drew Lynch."

Realization dawns and I gasp. "Oh my gosh! Hey. How are you?" I ask, jumping off the bar stool to give him a hug. He wraps me up in a tight embrace.

"I'm good. How have you been?"

I pull away and offer him a warm smile. It's been years since I've seen Drew but we used to be really good friends in high school. We were both into art and had a lot of classes together.

"I've been good, Drew. You wanna have a beer and catch up?"

122

"Emma!" Ryan snaps from behind me. I spin around and take in his narrowed eyes and angry glare. "Come here." I find myself instantly obeying.

"Yeah?"

"What the fuck do you think you're doing?" he growls under his breath so only I can hear him in the noisy bar.

"I was just talking to an old friend from high school."

"It looks like a whole lot more than talking. What are you doing flirting with another guy?"

"Ryan, I wasn't flirting with him."

"Don't lie to me. Are you trying to embarrass me? You're mad that I wanted to come out tonight so you act like a whore in front of my friends?" He takes a step closer to me but I don't take my eyes off his face.

"I wasn't flirting with him, I swear."

He grabs my face in his hands. "Don't lie to me."

"Hey, get your hands off her!" Trey shouts from behind me, attracting the attention of the people around us.

Ryan releases me instantly and backs away. "Go home," he commands and I nod. I really don't want to be here anymore. I feel everyone's eyes on me and the embarrassment is building. I really shouldn't have been hugging another guy. That was stupid of me.

"Trey, could you give me a ride home?" I ask when he comes out from behind the bar and approaches me.

"Sure, sis. Just let me tell Moe." Trey jogs back to the office and Drew walks up to me.

"Are you okay, Emma?" He looks so concerned and I feel bad for getting him involved in this.

"Yeah. I'm sorry, Drew. I have to go."

Drew looks like he wants to say something else but Trey comes back out with his keys in his hand.

"Let's go, baby girl." He wraps his arm around my shoulders and leads me out of the bar. "You're staying with me tonight."

"No, Trey. I just want to go home." I don't know how long I can stand to be in a car with him. I feel so embarrassed that I flirted with another guy and made Ryan mad.

"I'm not letting you be alone with that guy," he growls and shakes his head.

"It will be okay. When he gets home, I'll apologize and it will be okay."

Trey looks at me with wide eyes as he opens the car door for me. "You don't have anything to apologize for."

I grab the door and close it after climbing inside. He makes his way around the front of the car and gets in.

"I shouldn't have been flirting."

"Emma, you can't be serious. You didn't do anything wrong. Ryan is an asshole."

The need to defend the man I love is overwhelming. I'm not happy with Ryan's behavior tonight but I made a promise to him that I wouldn't talk about our relationship to other people and that means something to me. Even though he was acting crazy jealous, I know that he loves me.

"No, you're wrong. Ryan loves me and I shouldn't have been flirting." I can feel his eyes boring into the side of my head and I turn to look at him. His face is a mask of confusion.

"Emma—"

"Please take me home, Trey."

He puts the car in drive and starts off toward my house without another word.

*   *   *   *

Ryan stumbles through the door just after midnight and stops when he sees me sitting on the couch, reading a book.

"What are you still doing up?" he asks, throwing his keys on the entry table.

"I wanted to talk to you." I keep my voice calm, doing my best to say this just right.

"About what?"

"About you acting like a crazy jealous asshole."

His brow furrows in anger and he storms over to me, yanking me up off the couch. "You were flirting with that guy!"

I shake my head. "No, I wasn't. He was a friend from high school."

"I saw you hug him!"

"So, I'm not allowed to hug people now?"

"No," he snaps back at me.

"Ryan, that is ridiculous."

He shakes his head back and forth, tightening his grip on my upper arms. "No, it's not!"

I manage to wiggle out of his grasp and back away from him. When he comes toward me and reaches for me, I flinch. He recoils, looking at me in horror.

"You're afraid of me?"

"You put your hands on me tonight."

His face softens and he slowly extends his hand out toward me, silently asking permission with his eyes. I don't pull away and he cups my face in his hand.

"Forgive me, sweetheart. I love you so much and I got so jealous when I saw him hug you. I can't lose you. I need you."

I sigh, relaxing into his touch, and cave. "It's okay. Just please don't do it again."

He nods and leans down to kiss me. When he pulls away, he drags me closer and wraps his arms around me.

"Please don't ever leave me, baby. I need you."

*　　　*　　　*　　　*

It's my birthday today and I seriously love my birthday. Maybe it's because I'm the only girl in my family and the guys always liked to spoil me on my special day. Or maybe I just love my birthday because it's my birthday. Either way, it doesn't really matter. My dad and my brothers usually go all out for it and they definitely didn't disappoint this year.

When I walk into Moe's around five, the room is crammed with all my family and friends. There are purple and white streamers strung all across the place. There is a live band playing country music over in the corner, and I can smell barbecue as soon as I walk in the door.

"Happy Birthday, baby girl," Tucker hollers, scooping me up in his arms and twirling me around. I laugh and squeal as he spins me through the air. He sets me back on my feet, planting a kiss on my cheek and smiling at me.

"Thanks, Tucker." I beam at him.

"Happy Birthday, lil' sis," Trey calls, wrapping me up in a hug and kissing me on the cheek.

"Thanks, big brother."

He studies me for a moment before pulling me in again to whisper in my ear. "Can I talk to you?"

I nod and he leads me to the back room. He locks the door before turning to me. "Are you okay?"

It's been a couple days since the incident in the bar and I haven't seen Trey since. I know he's been worried because he's been calling me non-stop.

"Trey, I'm fine. Honestly."

"I'm worried about you. I don't like what I saw the other night." His worry is evident on his face. He has dark circles under his eyes like he hasn't been sleeping well.

"Are you okay?"

"Yeah, I'm just worried about you."

"Trey, you don't need to be worried. All couples fight. Ryan and I are good now," I assure him but he doesn't look convinced. Not even one little bit.

"Emma, that asshole put his hands on you."

"He didn't mean it and he apologized. It's really okay."

He shifts his eyes away from me and runs his hand through his hair. "I should just tell Dad and Tucker," he says, almost to himself.

"NO! Trey, please don't."

The frustration builds on his face as he thinks about my request. "Why? Why shouldn't I, Em?"

"Because I love him, Trey, and if you tell them, it will only make things harder on me. I don't want to lose any of you, but if you make a big deal out of this I'm afraid that that is going to be what happens."

He never takes his eyes off me and I can practically see the wheels turning in his head. He sighs and looks up at the ceiling.

"Okay, baby girl. I won't say anything, for now, but you have to come to me if you're in trouble, okay?"

I nod. "Promise."

He opens his arms and I launch my body into them. He hugs me and sighs again. "I don't like this."

"I know," I whisper.

*   *   *   *

Around ten, I decide to head home. I'm exhausted and the longer I wait around here to see if Ryan will show, the more frustrated I get. As I'm walking out of the bar, Ryan pulls up. I cross my arms in front of my chest and wait for him to get out of the car. When he does, he smiles and makes his way over to me.

"Hey baby," he coos and I arch a brow at him. "What?"

"Where have you been?"

He watches me for a moment before answering. "I had to work a little late and then the guys wanted to grab a beer."

I scoff and push around him, heading toward my car. I'm so angry that I'm not even sure I could form words right now. He just ignored my birthday and went out with his friends?

What. The. Fuck?

"Emma! What is your problem?" He catches up to me and grabs my arm, spinning me around.

"Are you fucking kidding me?" I scream, drawing the attention of a few of my guests by the door.

"What's the big deal?" He looks truly stupefied. Surely, he can't be this dumb.

"It's my birthday."

"I know."

At this point, I don't even know what to say or do.

He knows?

"And you just decided 'fuck her, who gives a shit about her birthday'?"

"I'm here. I went out with the guys for a bit, but I'm here now to celebrate your birthday." He makes it sound so rational. I'm anything but rational right now.

"I'm going home, asshole. The party is over."

He glances toward the bar before turning back to me. "It doesn't look like it's over."

"Yeah, well, getting stood up by your boyfriend tends to dampen the party mood." He moves in closer and I back away from him, not wanting him to touch me. He advances on me quickly and wraps me up before I can get away. "Let me go!" I growl, the menace clear in my voice.

"Calm down. You're overreacting. I didn't realize it was such a big deal, okay?"

He didn't realize?

"Ryan, it's my birthday. How could you possibly think it would be anything but a big deal?" I ask, completely baffled.

"Birthdays aren't a big deal in my family."

I gape at him before snapping my mouth shut, feeling exhausted. "Let me go. I'm going home."

The disappointment is crashing down and I would like to be in the comfort of my own bed when it hits. No matter what he says, it hurts that he didn't care about my birthday.

"Okay, I'll follow you."

I shake my head and pry myself out of his arms. "No. Find somewhere else to sleep tonight."

His jaw drops in shock and if I wasn't so upset, I might laugh. I can imagine that he never expected me to kick him out.

"You can't be serious."

"Do I look like I'm joking?" I shout as I fling open the door to my car and climb in. I start up the engine and roll the window down.

"Baby," he pleads.

"Goodbye, Ryan," I say, before driving off into the night.

*   *   *   *

I wake to incessant ringing of my phone, the sound invading my dream. Rolling over and grabbing my phone, I groan at Ryan's name on the screen. I debate on answering it when it stops ringing. I sigh and close my eyes, attempting to fall back asleep when I hear the front door unlock and open. I groan again and pull the pillow over my head.

Ryan's footsteps shuffle into the room and a second later, the bed dips as he sits on it. "Baby?" he asks, his hand running lightly over my back. I ignore him and his touch becomes firmer. "Emma."

I groan and roll over to face him. "What?" I growl but stop when I see the bouquet of flowers in his hand. My mouth pops open and I sit up in the bed.

"Happy Birthday, baby. I love you." He hands me the flowers. I watch him cautiously as I bring the bouquet to my nose.

"Thank you."

"I got you this, too." He hands me a velvet jewelry box and my eyes shoot up to his. He smiles and nods, encouraging me to open it. When I flip open the lid, a gasp leaves my lips. Nestled inside is a pendant necklace with a jagged line, like the one on a heart monitor, and a dangling heart with diamonds embedded in it.

I meet his eyes and he smiles again. He grabs my hand and kisses it. "I love you and I need you. I would die without you. I'm so sorry about last night, baby. Forgive me?"

For a split second, I feel like he's manipulating me but I shake it off. He wouldn't do that to me. He loves me.

I nod my head. "I forgive you."

131

He slides his hand along my face and into my hair, pulling me forward and pressing his lips to mine. I melt into him, his touch righting my world like it always does.

"I love you," he whispers against my lips.

"I love you, too."

Chapter Eleven
Now

I crack open my eyes and bright morning sunlight has me immediately shutting them again. I take a deep breath and just relax into Nix as he holds me in his sleep. After a moment, I open my eyes again and turn my head to look at him. He lets out a snore and I smile as my gaze travels over his handsome face. When he's sleeping, he looks so peaceful but I miss that sexy smirk of his that I am beginning to love. I reach out and brush the hair off his forehead.

His eyes blink open in surprise, and it takes him a moment to fully wake up but when he does, he smiles at me.

"Sorry," I whisper, feeling bad for waking him.

"Mmm, don't be." He turns toward me, threading his other arm around my waist and nuzzling into my neck. A sigh slips out of my parted lips as soon as he grazes his mouth over the column of my neck.

"Nix," I breathe.

"Mmm," he hums again. "I don't know if I can keep my hands off you after last night." The scruff on his jaw scrapes against my skin and I gasp when I feel his kiss on the same spot a moment later.

"I can't think with you doing that to me."

"Stop thinking, baby," he growls, the sound vibrating through me, all the way to my core.

"I don't want you to keep your hands off me," I admit and he instantly pulls back to look at me. His eyes connect with mine and I see so much swimming through his blue orbs — hope, devotion, and nervousness.

Why is he nervous?

"Answer something for me," he prompts and I raise an expectant brow. "Are you my girl, Emma?"

All the air whooshes out of me as I stare up at him. *His.* Is that what I want? "What?" I ask, my voice shaky.

"'Cause that's what I want, baby. I want you to be mine."

I suck in a breath, hearing the exact same words Ryan said to me. Nix makes the connection almost immediately and shakes his head. "Not like that, baby. It's not something I ever want to take from you but it's something I would very much like for you to give me. I want the privilege of you being mine."

My heart stutters and I'm pretty sure I sigh, like a lovesick teenager.

"Yeah, I'm yours, Nix."

His answering smile is blinding. "About damn time, Sweetheart."

I shoot him a look and he gives me that grin that makes my heart flip-flop in my chest.

"Shit, they'll probably take my balls for saying this so I'm only gonna say it once: I adore you, Emma."

I scrunch up my mouth at the uncertainty running through me and look away from him. He grabs my chin, bringing my gaze back to him. "I. Adore. You."

"That was twice."

His lips twitch as he fights back a smile and growls, "Smart ass." He leans down and presses his lips to mine and any insecurity, any doubt I had, disappears from just his kiss alone. When he touches me, I know that he truly does mean everything he says. I can feel it in every kiss, every caress.

He pulls away and just stares down at me, his eyes soaking up every detail of my face for a moment before he lays down next to me and pulls me into his arms. I run my fingers along the lines of one of his tattoos, a mass of flames with a skull in the middle.

"Will you tell me some more about him?" he asks a moment later. His question is so unexpected and out of place in this blissful moment between us that I immediately tense up in his arms.

"Why would you want to ruin a great moment with all that crap?" I snap, thoughts of Ryan already swimming through my mind.

"I don't want to mess this up so I've got to know what he did to you so I won't unknowingly do something to hurt you."

"Nix, if I get upset by something like that it's not on you. These are my issues, you shouldn't have to worry about them."

He cradles my face in his hand and guides my eyes up to his, his blue eyes looking so sincere. "Talk to me, Em. Open up to me. I want to be your lobster."

I gasp and my mouth pops open in surprise. I stare at him with wide eyes and he just smiles back at me.

"How?"

"I looked it up online. You're going to have to explain that story though."

"Uh…Daisy, Addilyn, and I were obsessed with *FRIENDS* in high school and we've just always used it.

We wanted an epic love like Ross and Rachel. I don't think you really get it, though. It seems hasty for someone I just started seeing like four minutes ago," I tease and he smirks at me.

"Baby, you've been mine since the moment I laid eyes on you. I was just waitin' for you."

"You are too smooth, Phoenix West. You say all the right things."

"You know what I think it is?" he asks and I get lost in his eyes for a moment. God, they are so blue, so intense, and I feel like when he looks at me, he sees me. Sees the real me, not all the stuff I've been faking for everyone else for too long. "Baby?"

"Huh? What?" I ask, snapping out of my daze. He smiles and shakes his head before leaning down and taking my lips again. I sigh as soon as we connect, and he pulls me into his body as his tongue slips into my mouth. I thread my fingers through his hair as our tongues dance together, caressing and stroking. With a groan, he pulls away, breathing heavily.

"What was I saying?" he asks, looking drunk. Drunk on me.

"Um…something about why you are so smooth." I don't sound much more coherent than he does.

"Oh, right. I think it's you — us. I've never felt anything like this, Emma. It's like I've known you my entire life or loved you in a previous one. I don't know. I can't find a good way to explain it but we're just connected. Don't you feel it, baby?"

"Yeah, I feel it."

"See? We were inevitable."

"Inevitable," I say, testing the word out for myself.

"Like two magnets." I'm shocked when he somehow says what I've been thinking all along. "When they are far enough apart, they will stay apart but as soon as you move one closer to the other, they have no choice but to crash together. As soon as you walked into my tattoo shop, this was the outcome. We couldn't fight the pull of *us*."

"Oh, Nix."

He leans down to kiss my cheek. When he pulls away, he settles back into the bed and pulls me close. I hook my leg over his and lay my head on his broad chest.

"Will you tell me about him?"

"No, I won't. Please don't ever think that I compare you to him because I don't. You are so much more than he ever was, even on his best day."

He looks down at me and for a moment, I think he's going to push me but I should know better. Nix never pushes me, never makes me go further than I want to go.

"Okay." He wraps his arms around me and just holds me close. It doesn't take long for me to fall back to sleep, safe in his arms.

*   *   *   *

"Not gonna lie, baby girl, I've missed that smile," Moe says as I'm working my shift at the bar. I look over at the burly man and my brow furrows.

"What are you talkin' about?"

He grins widely and shakes his head. "I think my nephew is bringing you back out of your shell."

I scoff and roll my eyes. I've been pretty tight-lipped about what is going on between Nix and me, not wanting my family to get involved before I know how I'm feeling. But it's been a week since Nix's impromptu swamp date and things have been flowing so…smoothly.

"I think you're losing your mind in your old age, Uncle Moe."

Moe roars with laughter and slaps his hand down on the bar. It takes him a moment to regain his composure and when he does, he still has a huge smile on his face.

"That right there. That's the girl we've been missing."

I blush and look down, shaking my head at my crazy uncle.

"You been sampling the merchandise tonight, Moe?" I ask and he chuckles again.

"That's all right, girl. You just keep playing it off. I'm smarter than I look." With that, he turns and goes back to the office to do paperwork. I get back to serving customers with Moe's words on my mind. I know he's right. The more time I spend with Nix, the more I feel like my old self. Sometimes, I would wonder if I would ever get that girl back.

"Emma Harrington?" a young girl asks on the other end of the bar. I glance in her direction and my heart drops as I recognize the girl who always delivered my flowers from Ryan.

"Yeah." I raise my hand as I make my way over to her. She smiles and hands me a small bouquet of roses. My stomach rolls as I watch her walk away. A hand settles on my lower back, making me jump. When I turn, I find Trey behind me with concerned eyes.

"Find the card, Em."

I nod and start digging through the small arrangement until I find the little envelope. Sucking in a breath, I open it and pull out the card.

Emma,
I miss you, baby. That yellow dress always was
my favorite. See you soon.

I gasp and the card falls from my hand, fluttering to the floor. Trey bends down and picks it up while I try to breathe. It's proving difficult though. I know when Trey reads it because he curses and his arm tightens around me.

"When did you wear a yellow dress, Emma?"

"Today."

"Goddamn it. Come with me. I'm taking you home." He guides me to the back of the bar where we tell Moe what's going on. He sends a sympathetic look in my direction and I do my best to muster up a smile but even I know that it's weak. Trey drives me back to the apartment, calling Nix and Tucker, who meet us there. While I go to bed, the boys spend all night in the living room, trying to come up with a plan.

*   *   *   *

"Emma. I told you that I would get you back."
His voice makes my skin crawl and I look around
frantically for him but I can't see him. "Did you really
think that you would ever be free?" I have to run. It's
the only way I'll get away...but, which way? There are
trees all around me. I'm lost. One wrong move and I
could be dead. I spin to check the other direction but it
doesn't look any better.

"Trying to escape, baby? You'll never be free."

"No!" I scream. The only response is his
sinister chuckle.

"Did you really think your brothers or that guy
would be able to save you? You're mine, Emma.
Forever."

"NO!"

"Emma. Wake up, baby," Nix says, breaking
through my dream as he shakes my body a little. I peel
open my eyes and see bright blue globes staring back at
me. He offers me a soft smile and wipes a tear off my
face. "Bad dream, again, sweetheart?" he asks, brushing
away more tears. I just nod and cuddle into his huge
body.

"You wanna talk about it?" I bite my lip as I
pull away and stare up at him. The look he gives me in
return makes me feel safe in spite of the story I am
about to tell.

"Mmm, I guess," I whisper as I shrug my
shoulders. He waits patiently for me and after a few
moments, I begin telling him about my dream.

140

When I finish, he mutters, "Jesus Christ," with rage burning in his eyes. "I want to kill him for hurting you. I don't know what else to say."

"There are no words." Shrugging my shoulders, I roll onto my back and look up at the ceiling. "Do you know how easy it is to break a person?" I ask him and I can feel his muscles grow tense next to me.

"No." His voice is raspy with barely concealed rage.

"It's easier than you think. When you love someone, they have the power to destroy you. It's insidious and you never see it coming. All it takes is some careful maneuvering to make a person think that they are losing their mind."

"Baby, I don't want to talk about this," he growls, his body still tense underneath me.

"No one does. That's why people get away with it. Some people don't even know what emotional abuse is, or it's not taken seriously because the victim doesn't have bruises as proof. I mean, look what Ryan did to me. He didn't scream at me all the time. Those times still stung but they were easier to dismiss than when he came to me in a loving manner and planted something evil in my head."

"Enough, Emma!" he yells, startling me and shoving me out of his arms. He sits up and scoots to the edge of the bed, dropping his head in his hands. Once the immediate fear dissipates, I realize that I pushed him too far. I was so lost in what I was saying that I didn't listen when he said he didn't want to talk about it.

I sit up and scoot across the bed until I am behind him. I wrap my arms around him, kissing his back and giving him a good squeeze. "I'm sorry," I whisper. He blows out a breath and shakes his head, still in his hands.

"Baby, please don't apologize. I just need a minute." If I didn't realize it before now, this moment proves that Nix is nothing like Ryan. Not once has he blamed me for anything and he is so considerate of what might cause me to freak out.

"This time I owe you an apology. You told me that you didn't want to talk about it and I should have listened to you."

He's suddenly moving, spinning around, and grabbing me before pulling me into his lap and positioning my legs so that I'm straddling him.

"I owe you an apology, too. I'm sorry for freaking out. It's just...I...I care about you so much and it guts me to think about the things he did to you. In my entire life, I've never felt as much rage as I do when I think about him putting his hands on you."

"I know," I tell him, laying my hand on his cheek. "I can see it in your eyes."

"Oh yeah? What else do you see in my eyes?" he asks, raising his brow at me.

"Lots of things."

"Like what?"

"Well, I can see how much you care about me and I see that I can trust you. I know that you'll protect me and I can see how much you want me." I wiggle in his lap and rub my core over his hardening cock. His eyelids droop and he groans, locking his hands on my hips and grinding up into me.

"You can read me like a book, baby."

"Mmm," I hum, my body instantly swamped with desire. His eyes open and meet mine, blue depths blazing with need for me. "You're right. That's how I know the filthy thoughts you're thinking right now." I wiggle my hips again and my nipples pebble, poking through the thin fabric of my tank top.

"God, Em, you're such a tease."

"It's not teasing when you can have it." I have his full attention, instantly.

"Really? Are you sure?"

"Yes, I'm sure." I know that I want nothing more at this moment than to be with him.

"I really don't mind waiting until you're ready, Em. I can wait."

"Oh for Christ's sake," I growl. "Shut up and kiss me, Nix." I grab his face in my hands and smash my lips against his before he can reply. He squeezes my hips and he groans, the sound racing through me, straight to my throbbing sex.

One arm slides around my back, pulling me in even closer, and his other hand fists into my hair, manipulating my head to deepen the kiss. His tongue glides between my parted lips and dances with mine, flooding my body with white-hot need. I thought that this would be hard after everything I've been through. I thought that Nix would have to take control and guide me through this first time but my body reacts to him instinctively. We mold and fit together perfectly. He moves and my body follows with no direction from him.

Like magnets.

I grind down on him, needing the friction before I go crazy. He rips his lips away from mine, panting as he looks over my body. I reach down for the hem of my tank top, a sugary sweet smile on my face as I rip the thin white material over my head. My breasts bounce free and he cups one in his large hand.

"Emma," he groans, stroking his thumb over my nipple. I moan and arch my back, pressing my breast further into his hand and he leans down, taking it into his mouth. He swirls his tongue around the sensitive nub and my hips buck against him.

"Nix." I'm begging. My skin is aching to feel his rough hands on me, holding me. I want to feel him everywhere, all at the same time, and never stop. "Please," I add and his answering growl only serves to make my desire for him skyrocket. He stands, holding me in his large arms and turns toward the bed, laying me down ever so gently, and stretches out over me.

He leans down and kisses me again. This time slower and softer than the last, his lips moving with mine. In sync. In this moment, I feel it stronger than I ever have before — this *thing* between us, whatever it is. It pulls me to him.

His hand scrapes against my belly before it disappears into the waistband of my panties and his finger brushes over my clit. I cry out and arch off the bed, meeting his hand, my body eager for more.

"God, you're so fuckin' wet, Em," he growls, ripping my panties down my legs.

"You make me wet." I'm feeling very bold all of the sudden. He groans again just before pressing his lips against my lower belly. He bites the same spot and I jump, but oddly enough, even that turns me on. "Please, Nix. I need you." I'm begging again, practically reduced to a shaking mess on the bed.

I glance up just in time to see him lick his lips and his fingers find my clit again.

"*Yessss,*" I hiss and he sucks in a breath. He slowly slides one finger inside me and I clench around him.

"Fucking Christ, Emma," he groans, pumping his finger in and out of my wet, aching core. His lips brush against my skin again, trailing kisses up my body as he continues sliding his finger into me. "You ready, baby?" His concern only makes me fall for him harder.

"God, yes."

He pulls his finger out of me, standing up and quickly taking his boxer briefs off. My gaze zooms in on his body, following the line of his abs, to the V leading to his impressive cock, jutting out proudly from his body. I lick my lips and he groans as he takes it in his hand, stroking himself slowly a few times.

My breath stutters and I can't take my eyes off him. When I meet his eyes, I melt beneath the fire in his gaze. Pulling my bottom lip between my teeth, I lie back and spread my legs open so he can see me. I slowly start sliding my hand down my belly toward the apex of my thighs. His eyes lock on my hand immediately, and he stops stroking his shaft. When my fingers skate over my clit, I sigh and he starts pumping himself again.

"Emma," he groans. After a moment, he stops and grabs a condom.

"Are you clean?" I ask.

"Huh?"

"Are you clean, Nix?"

"Yeah."

"Then no condom. I want to feel you."

He tosses the condom onto the nightstand without another word and joins me on the bed. He lines himself up with my entrance and looks back up at my face, locking eyes with me as he slowly slides into me. My eyes flutter closed and a satisfied moan leaves my lips as he fills me to the hilt.

"Jesus," he breathes, through clenched teeth. "You're so tight, baby."

I open my eyes and all I see are bright blue oceans staring back at me. It intensifies the sensation of him gliding into me again and again, as we connect on another level. The depth of my feelings for this man in such a short amount of time knocks the wind out of me. And a part of me is terrified. I push the thoughts out of my mind, determined to focus on the amazingly pleasurable things he's doing to my body right now.

"Harder," I plead and he complies, pulling out and shoving back into me with a little more force. He swivels his hips and I gasp before he pulls out and rocks back into my core. God, he's a master. It has never felt this good before. I'm already teetering on the edge of the cliff, just needing a little more to push me over.

"Baby, I need you to get there," he says and the strain in his voice is my undoing. I shatter around him, calling out his name as I grip his wide shoulders. He groans and really lets loose. Pounding into me relentlessly as he chases his own orgasm.

His muscles tense just before he stills and groans, "Fuucckk!" His head drops to my shoulder and he releases a breath. Holding his weight off me, he kisses up my neck until he finds my lips and then shoves his tongue into my mouth. He draws another moan out of me as my hands fist in his hair and I kiss him back with just as much enthusiasm.

When he pulls away and stares down at me, his chest is heaving as he tries to catch his breath. "God, that was—"

"Incredible?" I say and he smiles. "The best I've ever had."

His eyes widen and he shakes his head. "Em, I...you are amazing," he says and I get the distinct feeling that he's holding something back. I search his eyes and the emotion I find there scares me so I let him keep it to himself. But in this moment, I trust him to protect not only my body but my heart, too.

Chapter Twelve
Then...

Ryan is being super suspicious today. In the two weeks since my birthday, he has been nothing short of amazing. He's been sweet and attentive, surprising me with flowers several times and taking me out to romantic dinners twice.

But today, he's being fidgety and, well, weird. It's throwing me off balance.

He sent me away, saying that he has some surprise planned for me that he needed to get ready. So, I called Addilyn and Daisy. We started out the day by grabbing lunch. Then, we went to get our nails done, and followed that up with some shopping. We were on our way over to Addy's when Ryan texted me around eight and said I could come back home.

I walk in the door and am greeted by total silence.

"Ryan?" I call out, making my way through the living room to the kitchen.

"Out here." His voice drifts in through the screen door. There is a faint glow filtering in and I cock my head to the side in confusion.

What is that?

Laying my purse and shopping bags down on the counter, I walk toward the door. When I get closer, I gasp. Candles cover almost every inch of the back yard. I step down onto the first step and find rose petals leading to an open patch of grass in the yard. Ryan stands there with his hands behind his back and a smile on his face. I can't help the grin that spreads across my own face as I take him in.

"What is all of this?"

He grins and holds his hand out to me. I follow the petals through the path outlined by candles until I reach him.

"Hey baby," he says and I giggle.

"What are you doing?"

He winks and drops down to one knee, earning a loud gasp from me as my hand shoots up to cover my mouth.

"Emma, I love you so much and I can't live one second of my life without you. I need you. Will you marry me?" He pulls a small box out from behind his back and opens it. Another gasp escapes as I take in the solitaire diamond ring.

Good God.

It's absolutely stunning. It's a simple ring with a plain band and a large diamond in the center. I absolutely love it.

"Yes," I whisper with a nod and he shoots up, wrapping his arms around me and planting a kiss on my lips.

"I love you." He slides the ring on my left hand.

"I love you too." I stare at my hand, mesmerized by the ring on my finger. In that moment, there is small sliver of something that makes me pause.

Doubt?

Fear?

I don't know what it is but I push it aside. I'm sure that every bride feels a little nervous at one point or another right?

Bride…

Oh my God, I'm going to be a bride.

Ryan leans down, capturing my lips in another kiss that makes me forget everything except the feel of his mouth on mine.

*   *   *   *

"What the fuck is that?" Trey seethes when he catches a glimpse of my ring.

"What does it look like, Trey?"

He grabs my hand and pulls me into the back room, leaving Bree on her own behind the bar.

He shuts the door and whirls around to face me. "You can't marry him, Em."

"Why not?"

He paces back and forth, running his hands through his hair.

"You deserve so much better. I thought that this would fizzle out by now. I never expected you to marry the guy," he rants, more to himself than me.

"Trey, please, I'm happy. Please be happy for me."

"I'm calling Tucker," he states, pulling out his phone and dialing.

"Please don't do this." He ignores my plea.

Twenty minutes later, my brother comes marching into the bar, picks me up, and carries me outside. Trey trails behind us, looking grim. When we get behind the bar, Tucker sets me back on my feet and I slap his chest.

"What are you doing, Tucker?"

He ignores me and reaches for my hand. "Let me see it." He inspects the ring for a minute before looking back up at me. "You can't marry him."

"Guys, please don't do this. I'm happy."

Both of them stand firm as they look at me. "He's not a good guy, Em," Trey says and Tucker's head whips around to him.

"What are you talking about?"

I look at Trey and silently plead with him not to say anything. He releases a breath and shakes his head.

"He put his hands on her."

Tears roll down my face as the man who's been like a brother to me my whole life betrays my trust.

"He hit you?"

"No, he just grabbed my face when we were arguing."

"You are not marrying him." The command in his voice leaves no room for argument but I won't give in.

"I love him and you can't stop me."

A look of total desperation crosses my brother's face as he frantically tries to come up with something. I wish that he could just be happy for me.

"If you marry him, I'm not going to be around to see it."

The tears start pouring down my face.

"You won't come to my wedding?"

He shakes his head, his mouth in a thin line. "I won't be a part of your life at all. It's him or us."

151

A sob rips through me and Tucker's face softens for just a moment before he finds his resolve again. Trey looks like he's going to be sick.

"Please don't do this."

Neither one says anything. I remain silent also, making my decision. I can't believe my brothers would do this to me. It hurts more than I could ever describe.

"You choose him then?" Tucker asks.

I nod and whisper, "Yes."

Tucker grunts and Trey releases a stuttered breath. When I look at him, there is so much pain and sadness swimming in his eyes. Tucker turns and grabs Trey's arm, pushing him along with him. Just when I think that's it, Tucker turns back to me.

"Bye, baby girl," he says and I sob harder.

As they walk away, I can hear Trey arguing with him but they don't turn back to me again. I fall to my knees, the gravel tearing up my skin, and cry. Fat tears spill out of my eyes as I lean my back against the building and sob for the loss of my brothers.

I'm in shock over what just happened. It feels surreal, like I dreamed it or something, but the pain in my heart lets me know that it really happened. I always thought my brothers were the two men who would never abandon me. I guess I was wrong.

"Emma? Baby, what's wrong?" Ryan yells after coming around the side of the building to find me crying in the dirt. He kneels down next to me and runs his hands over my face.

"M-m-my brothers," I say but can't get any more out before another sob racks my body.

"What about your brothers, sweetheart?" He looks more and more concerned with every passing moment.

"They m-made me ch-choose. Them or you."

Shock registers on his face and he wraps me up in his arms.

"Who did you choose?"

"You."

"Oh, baby. I love you," he replies, squeezing me tighter. "What can I do for you?"

"Just take me home, Ryan." He nods, scoops me up in his arms, and carries me to the car.

*   *   *   *

Answering the door, I almost pass out from shock when I see who is standing on my front porch.

"Can we talk?" Tucker asks.

In the two weeks since our huge fight, neither he nor Trey has spoken a word to me. They even went as far as to avoid Sunday brunch with mom and dad. To say that I've been miserable without my brothers would be an understatement but I won't give in to their demands.

"What is it that you want to talk about?"

Tucker sighs. "Baby girl, can we please just come in and talk?"

I bite my lip, watching them for a moment longer, and then nod. They shuffle past me into the house and sit down on the couch. I take a seat in the recliner and face them.

"What do you want?" My voice comes out harsher than I intended but there is still so much hurt from their actions. I know I need to steel myself against what they might say to me. If they came here to badger me further, it might break me.

"We came to apologize," Tucker states and I flick my eyes to him and gawk.

"What?"

"We were wrong. We shouldn't have given you an ultimatum," Trey says.

"I still don't agree with you marrying him, and I pray that we're wrong about him, but if we're not then you're going to need us and we'll be here for you," Tucker adds.

"I always need you."

"Em, we're really sorry. Dad straightened our asses out," Trey explains.

Oh, now it makes sense.

"Is that the only reason you're here?" Even as I ask the question, I hope that I'm wrong.

"No, Dad just made some valid points that I hadn't considered before but we really missed you," Tucker clarifies.

"I really missed you guys, too." I jump up to hug him.

"There's one more thing though," Tucker says. I look over at him, waiting for him to continue. "I love you but if you choose to marry him, I'm still not coming to your wedding."

"Tucker," I gasp, feeling heartbroken all over again.

"I'm sorry, sis. But I can't stand there and act like I like the guy."

"No one is asking you to! You're my brothers, you're supposed to be there for me!"

Trey stands and wraps an arm around my shoulder. "I'll be there, baby girl." I give him an appreciative smile and loop my arm around his waist. I watch as Tucker's face cracks, the toll this is taking on him evident.

"Tucker, you don't have to worry about me. Ryan loves me."

He shakes his head and runs a hand over his almost-bald head.

"There is something off about that guy, Emma. I don't trust him." A throat clearing behind me catches my attention and I turn to find Ryan standing there, a thunderous expression on his face.

"Emma," he growls and I know I'm in trouble. I turn back to my brothers and try to plaster a smile on my face.

"I'll see you guys at brunch tomorrow, okay?"

They look at each other, seemingly having a silent conversation. Trey and Tucker were always like that. They have always just known what the other was thinking.

"Em, I don't think we should leave," Trey whispers in my ear so Ryan can't hear.

"I'm fine. I promise. I'll see you tomorrow, okay?"

Both boys still look unconvinced but they nod, each giving me a kiss on the cheek before heading to the door.

"We'll see you tomorrow, baby girl," Tucker says, staring right at Ryan.

"Okay. Love you, guys."

"Love you too, sis," they respond in unison and walk out the front door.

I take a deep breath, preparing myself for whatever is coming next before turning around to face Ryan. He glares at me, so much anger in his eyes that I'm actually scared for a moment.

"What the hell were they doing here?" His voice is a low growl that sounds more menacing than anything I've ever heard. I'm just not sure if he's mad at my brothers or me.

"They came to apologize."

His jaw ticks as he stares at me and I wait with bated breath for his reaction.

"And you forgave them, just like that?"

"Yes." Of course I forgave them. They are my brothers and I love them. Plus, I could tell they were genuinely sorry for what they did.

"You can't do that."

"Why not?"

"Look what they did to you!" he explodes. "I was there! I carried you home because you were too weak to walk on your own after bawling your eyes out!"

"Ryan, they're sorry."

"God, you're so stupid! You don't even see it. I'm trying to protect you! I love you!"

Did he really just call me stupid? And he doesn't need to protect me from my brothers. I know, beyond a shadow of a doubt, that my brothers love me. As his words sink in, I feel the anger build.

"Don't you dare call me stupid!"

He laughs. The sound of it grates on my nerves.

"That's all you heard? You're so fuckin' dramatic! Of course that's all you heard. You just love to create drama wherever you can. Now that you've made up with your brothers, you have to fight with me? Did you ever notice that we were great when you were fighting with them? You just have to have drama in your life. You crave it!"

"That's not true!"

"Yes! It is!" he screams. "Cause that's what drama queens like you do!"

"Don't call me a drama queen!"

"Why not? It's true. Why the fuck do I even put up with this anymore? I don't need this in my life. No one else would put up with all your shit!" He paces back and forth through the kitchen and then throws his hands in the air. "Fuck it! I'm out of here!" He storms through the kitchen and kicks open the back door.

I watch him go, anger surging through my body and putting me on edge. The more I think about everything he just said, the angrier I get. I've always thought of myself as a pretty levelheaded person, but every time he calls me a brat or dramatic, I want to scream. I didn't start this fight. All I did was forgive my brothers.

Why is that such a crime in his eyes?

At times like this, I wonder if I really should marry him. This can't be normal, right? Then as soon as that thought crosses my mind, the guilt takes over. I love Ryan, even despite all of this, and I made a commitment to him. I know he loves me too and he's told me so many times that he needs me. What would he do if I ever left?

Even considering leaving makes my chest ache so badly that it's difficult to breathe, and just like that, my mind is made up. I want this. I want a life with Ryan. We'll work through the rest and figure it out. I love him and that is the most important thing.

*   *   *   *

Around midnight, Ryan shuffles into the bedroom and sits on my side of the bed. I've been lying here for hours trying to sleep, but worrying over where he was and what he was doing.

"Baby, you awake?" He runs a hand down my back, the alcohol flowing through his system making him slur his words.

"What do you want, Ryan?"

"Oh, come on, baby. Don't be like that."

I roll over to face him and look him right in his bloodshot eyes.

Jesus…

How much did he drink?

"Don't do what, Ryan?"

He scowls and runs his fingers across my jaw. My automatic response is to relax into his touch but I resist. I need to get my point across.

"Don't be mad. I didn't mean anything by it. I've just been stressed with work."

"I don't like it when you talk to me like that."

He chuckles. I'm getting angry all over again so I take a deep breath, trying to control it.

"I wasn't serious, babe. You're too sensitive."

"Leave me alone," I growl, hating when he says that to me. Like my feelings don't matter, at all.

"Aww, you don't mean that, baby." He slides into bed and wraps his arm around me. I press my palms against his chest, trying to shove him away.

"Stop, Ryan."

"Shhh, sweetheart. I know what you need," he whispers before plastering sloppy kisses along my neck. His hand dips under my shirt and I struggle to get away from him.

"Ryan, I'm serious. Cut it out." Frustration bubbles up in me, along with a small sliver of fear that I don't quite understand.

"You can't resist me." He taunts, ripping my shirt over my head and leaving me in only a pair of panties.

"Ryan! Stop!" I push against his firm chest and squirm, trying to free myself.

"You know you want it, Emma."

The next thing I know, his pants and boxers are on the floor and he's pulling my panties down my legs.

"I said no!"

"Baby, stop fighting me," he coos in my ear after he throws the red material to the floor. I struggle against him and he pins my hands above my head with a grin on his face. "Wanna play hard to get, huh?"

When he slides into me, the fight leaves my body entirely. I stare up at the shadows on the ceiling made by passing cars with one thought running through my mind:

What the hell is happening right now?

*　　*　　*　　*

My eyes open and the sun has yet to rise, so I just lie here, staring at the ceiling. Something feels off...wrong. But I can't, for the life of me, figure out what it is.

Ryan lets out a snore beside me and I glance over at him, remembering last night. He pressured me to have sex but that's not anything new. He is usually pushing me for sex. Why does it feel different?

He opens his eyes slowly and blinks before smiling at me. "Hey, baby doll." His voice is still heavy with sleep.

"Hey."

"What's wrong?" He quirks an eyebrow, suddenly more awake and alert.

"Nothing." If I can't even figure it out, how am I going to tell him?

"Last night was amazing." He drapes his arm over my belly and pulls me closer. I fake a smile and he kisses my cheek. "Go back to sleep, babe."

I shove what happened and my insecurities to the back of my mind, trying to forget about it. I smile and close my eyes, snuggling closer to him, and fall back to sleep almost immediately.

Chapter Thirteen
Now

"Wake up, baby," Nix whispers in my ear, running his fingers down my bare spine as I lie on my stomach. I groan and try to roll away from him but he just hooks his arm around my waist and pulls me into his body. "Nu-uh, beautiful. Time to wake up."

"No." My voice is more of a growl and it makes him laugh.

"Yes. Come on, let me see those gorgeous green eyes of yours." His words do the trick. I peek my eyes open and meet his sparkling blue gaze.

"Why?"

He runs his knuckles down my cheek, his eyes flicking down to my lips before meeting my stare again. He leans down and gently kisses me. I sigh. My body feels boneless as I lean into him and kiss him back. He pulls away far too quickly and I pout, earning another laugh from him.

"Later, sweetheart. It's your birthday and I have a surprise for you."

I startle in his arms and my eyes shoot up to his handsome face. "You…you did something for my birthday?"

He frowns at me in confusion. "Of course I did, baby. Your brothers warned me all about your birthday." There's humor in his tone but I'm so surprised that I just stare at him with wide eyes. When I don't return his smile, his frown returns and he searches my face. "What am I missing here, Em?"

I sigh and look up at him, feeling stupid already for the story I am about to tell. "These past couple years, my birthdays have not been...good. I didn't even celebrate last year and the one before that, Ryan ruined."

"Why?" I find myself launching into the story without a second thought, feeling safe enough to tell him.

"Of course, he showed up at the house the next morning with a diamond necklace and flowers. He was always doing that. Showing up after a fight with flowers or something." The memories of how much Ryan manipulated me are ramping up my irritation.

"Remind me to never buy you flowers."

I snap out of my thoughts to look up at him. "Flowers are good, for the right reason."

"And what's the wrong reason?"

"Hey, sorry I just beat the shit out of you. Here are some flowers, please don't leave me," I say, imitating a guy's voice. Nix laughs, the sound bringing a small smile to my face.

"I'm sorry, it's really not funny. It's just the way you said it."

I nod. "I know."

"Well, let's clear something up, Emma. Today is the day that you came into the world and that is definitely something that we are celebrating."

"Phoenix West, how did I ever find you? I didn't even dare hope that someone like you would come into my life and you're so much more than I ever even dreamed of."

He smiles but doesn't say anything, just stares down at me. In these small moments, I believe in fate. How could I not? After everything I've been through, I thought no man would want me and then here comes the most amazing, patient man I've ever met. What else would bring me someone who could not only deal with the darkness and pain lurking within me but also be strong enough to pull me out of it?

Fate, destiny, chance, whatever you want to call it, it brought me Nix.

"Come on, let's get out of bed. Your surprise is in the kitchen." He swats me on the ass and I yelp.

"I don't want to get out of bed." I cuddle into my pillow more. "I'm the birthday girl, shouldn't I get what I want?"

"Shit!" he teases. "Your brothers didn't tell me you were this bad on your birthday." I know he's joking but it makes me frown for a moment. "Hey, don't read into that. I didn't mean anything by it."

I release a breath and nod at him. "Okay."

"Now, would you be more agreeable if I carry you?"

The thought of being carried in his arms makes me smile and my heart beat faster. "Yes. Yes, I would."

He jumps out of bed like he's on fire and I laugh as he bows down in front of me. "At your service, madam."

He scoops me up in his arms. I squeal in surprise but quickly settle into his embrace. I feel completely secure, his strong arms supporting me with ease. I lay my head on his shoulder and bury my nose in his neck, inhaling his manly scent and sighing.

"Keep doing that, baby, and we're going back to bed."

A mischievous smile forms on my face. "Why turn around when you could just fuck me on the counter?" I'm doing my best to sound innocent right now. His steps falter and his eyes widen before he returns my grin.

"Oh, baby, I might do just that." A shiver races down my spine. "But, first…" We step into the kitchen and I look down at the dining table to see it set for breakfast with pancakes, sausage, eggs, and orange juice. "Happy Birthday, Emma," he whispers and my heart pounds in my chest.

I love him.

The thought flits through my mind, taking me by surprise and causing a new sense of fear to build within me. God…I do love him. I know I do. And loving him exposes me to a whole new level of hurt. I'm too broken. Too damaged. I can't handle it. I can't live with the fear that comes with my new revelation.

Jesus, I need to breathe.

"Em, what's wrong?" Nix asks, noticing my obvious distress.

"Please, put me down." My voice is shaky and uncertain. As soon as my feet touch the tile floor of my kitchen, I begin pacing back and forth, my mind racing, and I run a hand through my hair.

"Baby, please talk to me." The strain in his words is clear and it hurts me more than I expected. In my panic, all I want is to have him wrap his arms around me and tell me everything will be all right. The fact that he has this power over me doesn't help my current state of mind.

I need him to leave. I just need to think.

"I need you to leave," I finally say. Collapsing in one of the chairs at the dining room table, I put my face in my hands and will away the tears that threaten to fall.

"Absolutely not. Talk to me, Emma." He crouches down in front of me. He pries my hands away from my face and tries to force me to look at him but I don't budge. I know what he'll see in my eyes. And I can't allow that.

"I just need you to leave, Nix."

"No, I'm not leaving you. Not ever," he proclaims, adamant. His new declaration brings on a whole new wave of fear. Not ever? As in forever? As in marriage? My body freezes on the last word, thinking back to the only comparison I have — Ryan.

"I just need some time, some space," I choke out and he balls his fists up. I have a moment of panic before I remember that Nix is nothing like Ryan. He's just frustrated, I reason. I know he doesn't like it but I also know that he'll do it, for me.

"Goddamn it!" he growls. "Okay, I'll give you some time but you need to call someone to be here with you."

"I'll call the girls."

He watches me for a moment before nodding. He stands and starts walking to the door, me trudging along behind him. When he reaches it, he stops and turns to me.

"I'll be back, Emma. I'll give you the space you need right now but I'm not going to give you up."

I nod as he opens the door and steps into the hallway. I feel torn right now. I wanted him to leave, needed the space, but now, watching him walk away is ripping me apart. He braces his hands on the doorjamb, the two of us just staring at one another.

"I love you, Emma," he says, his voice so low and sincere that my heart stalls and races at the same time.

How in the fuck does he do that?

I knew he felt this way. I saw it in his eyes when we made love for the first time, but hearing him say the words makes them real and scares the shit out of me. My muscles lock up and my eyes widen as I stare at him.

I know as soon as he gets it. Understanding dawns on his face before his eyes soften and he gives me a small smile. I panic, slamming the door in his face and collapsing against it as a sob rips out of my mouth.

Nix is still there, I know he is. I can feel him through the wood of the door. My magnet, pulling me back to him.

"I'm leaving right now *because* I love you so much, Em. I know this scares you but I will fight for you. I'll be back," he says softly and then, he's gone. I feel his absence throughout my entire body, it aches to rush after him. Aches like I'm missing a limb or a vital organ. Like I'm missing…*my heart.*

*　　*　　*　　*

"Emma, what happened?" Addilyn asks as soon as she steps through the open apartment door twenty minutes later.

Sighing, I shake my head. Fresh tears well up in my eyes and I dash them away

"He told me that he loves me," I admit, my voice wavering.

"Why is that a bad thing?" She steps up to me and rubs her hands down my arms while she waits for my answer.

"I'm scared."

Her face softens. She hugs me and I start crying again, already missing Nix more than I ever thought I would.

"Do you love him, Em?"

I tense up and pull away. Shaking my head, I step back and wipe away my tears. "I can't."

"That's not what I asked you. Do you love him? Because let me tell you something, that man is head over heels in love with you, Emmy."

I look up in shock. "How do you know that?"

"Sweetie, anyone with two eyes and half a brain can see it. It's plain as day on his face. Plus, he called me because he was so worried about you."

"He did?"

"Yes, he did. He loves you, Emma."

So many emotions are swirling through me that I can't sort them out, can't deal with even a single one of them.

"What's going on in your head, Em?" she asks. I sit down on the couch and she sits next to me, waiting for me to start explaining.

"There's so much."

"I know but let's break it down, okay?" God, she makes it sound so simple. Maybe it is.

"I'm scared," I admit. She nods slowly, thoughtfully.

"What are you scared of?"

"What if he hurts me?"

She balks. "Seriously? Emma, Nix is absolutely nothing like Ryan."

"How do I know? How do you know? Ryan fooled people for so long," I point out and she just shakes her head.

"No, we were never really sure about Ryan but you seemed happy so we let it be. Nix is an amazing man and it's so obvious that he worships the ground you walk on."

"What if we break up? I just can't handle all this, Ad."

"Honey, that's a risk that everyone takes when they start a new relationship but no one would find their lobster if they didn't give it a shot. And for what it's worth, I don't think Nix is ever going to let you go." Her words bring a smile to my face as I remember a comment Nix made.

"What's that smile for?"

"I made a joke to Nix that he couldn't be my lobster because he didn't get a movie reference I made. He didn't know what I was talking about but he looked it up online. He said he wanted to be my lobster."

She gawks at me for a moment before her lips quirk up into a huge smile. "He said he wants to be your lobster?" I nod and her grin grows. "See, that man is nothing like Ryan. How many times did we talk about that in front of him and he never once even asked about it?"

"A lot," I admit.

"Nix went out of his way to find that reference because he loves you."

"Addy, the only other man who has even said, 'I love you' to me like that is Ryan. The words are bad for me."

She shakes her head, still smiling. "Em, the words aren't bad. Ryan was. Let Nix love you, the right way."

"I guess."

"Just talk to him, Emmy."

"I'll think about it," I promise her.

*   *   *   *

I'm fucking miserable. More miserable than when I left Ryan and I was this broken shell of a girl, more miserable than all the days I spent terrified that some misstep on my part would cause another blow-up and leave me bruised again. Why am I doing this to myself? What's the point? Am I really going to let my fear take Nix away from me?

I want to call him. Pick up that phone and dial his number. I want to hear his deep voice in my ear, sending chills down my spine. I want to hear him call me "baby" and revel in the high that it gives me. He swooped into my life at the worst time possible. He took the shattered pieces that were left of me and he put them back together, put me back together, but it's not enough.

I want more.

I need more. What the hell is wrong with me? The fear doesn't stop me from *knowing* what I want, it just stops me from having it. I know he's waiting to hear from me because he's been by the apartment four times in the past two days.

Just pick up the damn phone, Emma.

My gaze drops to the coffee table where my phone sits, silent and like a sign from the gods, it starts ringing, Nix's face popping up on the screen. I suck in a breath as I stare at the handsome photo of him that I snapped at the LSU game. He's grinning at me, his entire face lit up with so much happiness that I can't help but smile every time I look at it.

"Answer the phone, Emma," I whisper, my scolding voice the only sound in my empty apartment besides the ringing phone. Just as I'm reaching to answer it, I hear him saying those words again.

I love you, Emma.

Fuck! Why the hell does that scare me so much? Why is it different now that he said those words to me? Ryan is the only other man that has ever said that to me in that context and look what he did to me — could it really be that simple?

Even though I know that Ryan didn't mean them, those words meant something to me because I did love him and now they have awful memories associated with them. All the times that Ryan would show up after a terrible fight. All the times that he would use those words to control me, bend me to his will.

The screen of my phone fades to black as it stops ringing and I blow out a breath in annoyance and throw my head back, looking up at the ceiling. Jesus, I'm more messed up than I thought. I should just let him go now, set him free. There's no way he's going to want to deal with all my crazy. Maybe it's just better to break things off before they get too serious.

God, I miss him so much though. The ache in my chest just won't go away and every time I hear a noise outside my door, my heart skips a beat, hoping that it will be Nix. Not that it matters much if I can't work up the courage to answer the fucking thing.

I'm such a coward. I told myself that I would stop letting Ryan control me and look at me now — pushing away the most amazing, patient man that I've ever met because I'm scared. I'm so disappointed in myself. I know what I want… Why is it so hard to just go after it?

Just do it, Emma.

Just grab the phone off the table and dial his freakin' number. I just need to do it. I quickly sit up and snatch the phone off the coffee table, twirling it in my hands as I try whatever I can think of to work up the courage. I'm probably just making a bigger deal out of this than it needs to be.

Just. Call. Him.

I unlock my phone and my finger hovers over the *Contacts* icon as I second-guess my decision.

I can do this, I tell myself.

I click on the phone book and breathe a sigh of relief for making it one step closer to actually talking to him. I scroll down until I find his name and open his contact information. When I see his photo again, I get lost in it, just like I did when I snapped the shot. He looks at me with such love and devotion, even through a camera lens. God, this was before we were even together and he looks like he already loves me.

Shit…

I can't do this. He's so amazing. He should have a woman who isn't broken, who can give him the love he deserves in return. At least, that's what I tell myself as I toss the phone onto the couch beside me and groan.

*   *   *   *

"Emma," Nix says, his deep, raspy voice sending chills up my spine.

I look up from the bar and meet his dazzling blue gaze, my heart skipping a beat at the look he's giving me. Dragging my eyes down his body, I take in the wrinkled t-shirt and jeans that he's wearing. He has dark circles under his eyes and he looks miserable.

Just like me.

It's been a week since I kicked him out of my apartment and despite Addy's advice, him constantly coming by the apartment, and the number of times I've picked up the phone just to hear his voice, I haven't actually spoken to him. I didn't really know what to say. I'm still scared. Terrified, in fact, that this will all end in heartbreak for me.

I watch as he slides behind the bar and steps into my space. He cups my face in his hand, rubbing his thumb over my cheek. The feeling of his hands on me is divine. One touch from him and all my fears seem to fade away. They are still there. Just less loud now.

"I'm thrilled to see that you still look at me like this," he murmurs, staring into my eyes.

"And how is that?"

His body visibly relaxes as soon as he hears my voice. Like all is right in his world again. "Your eyes tell all your secrets, baby. You can't hide from me."

"I know." Feeling unsure, I drop my gaze to my shoes. He guides my eyes back up to his.

"Can we talk, Em?"

All I can do is nod. Honestly, I would do anything he wanted, especially if it prolonged our time together in this moment. I've missed him so much, more than I ever thought possible and I'm not ready to let him go. I need this. I need him.

"Come with me," I say, grabbing his hand from my face and pulling him to the storage room. Once we reach it, I close the door and turn to him.

"Baby, I miss you so much. I told you I was going to fight for you if I have to. I wasn't lying. Whatever you want, I'll do it."

"I miss you too." I keep my eyes trained on my sneakers as I talk to him, still incredibly insecure.

"Look at me, Emma."

I take a deep breath and raise my head. The look in his eyes blows me away. There is so much love shining back at me. If he hadn't already said the words to me, I wouldn't be able to deny it or push it away. It's so blindingly clear.

"Can you give this thing a chance, sweetheart?"

I bite down on my bottom lip again. "I'm scared."

Relief washes over his face. He nods and takes a step toward me, holding my face again.

"Do you know what scares me, Em?" I shake my head. It's hard for me to picture anything scaring Nix. I know it's ridiculous but he just seems so strong, in every way. "It scares me to think about you not giving this thing a chance. It scares me that I may miss out on the love of my life to the bastard that came before me. Because let's be clear here, baby, he did this to you. Sometimes I wish I would have met you before you met him. I would give anything to take away all this pain that weighs you down, and I would carry it for you if I could."

"Nix," I breathe.

"I love you, Em. I know that scares you and I know that word is warped for you after everything you've been through, but let me change that. Let me show you my love, baby. Let me take away your pain. Let me be the one to protect you."

"Nix…" I'm unable to get anything else out. A single tear falls from my eye and trails down my cheek. Nix leans down and kisses it away.

"Let me love you, baby. Please?"

"I love you" is running on a continual loop through my head but I can't make it come out. I'm still too scared to tell him. Like somehow I'll become infinitely more vulnerable as soon as the words pass my lips. I didn't think it was possible but I think that I love Nix more than I ever loved Ryan. It's different with him. It feels so right…

He is my lobster.

"Emma, please say something," he pleads. The stress is so clear on his face and I feel bad for getting lost in my own thoughts and forgetting to answer him. "I'll do whatever you want, baby. Whatever you need."

"Okay."

"Fuckin' hell, woman." All the tension leaves his body at once. He swoops down and claims my lips in a fiery kiss that leaves me panting. His arms wrap around my waist and he pulls me up in his arms, my feet dangling over the ground.

"Well, it's about damn time!" Moe yells and I jerk away from Nix's kiss. My cheeks are burning as I look over at the door and see Mama, Trey, Addy, Tucker, Daisy, and Moe standing there. Cheers and applause ring out around us. Smiling, I shake my head before burying it in Nix's chest.

Once I'm over my embarrassment, I look back up at Nix. He smiles and winks at me.

Shooting a fake glare at the door, I say, "What? Ya'll couldn't get Daddy here, too?" Nix's body shakes as he laughs and everyone at the door joins in.

"Naw, he was busy," Tucker remarks, walking up to us and prying me out of Nix's arms. Nix growls, making me laugh again. "You'll get her back in a second. Happy for you, baby girl," he whispers in my ear.

I pull back and gape at him. "Wait. You're okay with this?"

He shrugs. "Yeah. I told you, Nix is a good guy."

"Holy shit, ya'll feel that draft? Hell just froze over."

Trey barks out a laugh as the rest of them join in. Nix comes up behind me and loops his arms around my waist. He kisses my neck.

"Hey, Moe, can I steal her?"

"I don't see why not."

His lips brush over my ear, sending shivers racing through me and he whispers, "Let's get out of here, gorgeous."

Chapter Fourteen
Then…

Ryan: Where R U?

I sigh and quickly type back that I'm at the mall with the girls. It drives me crazy that he constantly checks up on me like this. Shaking my head, I shove my phone back into my pocket.

"What's up?" Addy asks, looking concerned.

"Nothing. Just Ryan checking up on me." As soon as the words leave my mouth, I wonder if I should have said anything. I know Ryan doesn't want me talking about him to people but I didn't say anything bad, did I?

"Em, I wanted to talk to you about something," Daisy says from my other side.

"What?" Things are still kind of awkward between Daisy and me. We haven't talked about what happened when she told my brother about Ryan and me. It seems like we both are avoiding it.

"I need to apologize for talking to your brother. You were right, I am your friend first, and I shouldn't have said anything."

Well, I guess we're not avoiding it anymore.

"It's fine, Daisy. I honestly got over it a long time ago."

She lets out a huge breath and wraps me up in a hug, stopping right in the middle of the mall.

"I'm so glad! I missed you!" she exclaims and I giggle.

"I missed you, too."

She releases me and we start walking again. "So, how are things going with Ryan?" Addy asks and I shrug.

"Good."

"That's all I get?"

I briefly consider telling her more but if Ryan ever found out, I know that he would be pissed. How is he ever going to find out though?

"I don't know. All couples fight, ya know?" I finally say, deciding that it's safe to talk to them.

"What are you fighting about?" Daisy asks.

I scoff and shake my head. What don't we fight about? "Everything…anything."

"Like what?" Addy probes.

"Oh, he just hates when I talk to you guys about us and he calls me a drama queen."

"You are not a drama queen. Out of the three of us, you are the least dramatic, by far," Addy points out and I laugh.

"Yeah, I know."

"Is that all?" Daisy asks.

"Um…no, he makes fun of me a lot but when I tell him I don't like it, he says I'm too sensitive and I need to lighten up."

"Tell him to knock that shit off. That's rude," Addy rants and I smile.

"Yeah, I'll do that," I joke and nudge Addilyn. "Let's go eat. I'm starving." They both agree and we head off to find some food.

*   *   *   *

"What the fuck is this, Emma?" Ryan growls, holding my phone up to my face when he marches into the bedroom. On the screen is a text from Addy telling me to confront Ryan about treating me better and not back down.

Shit.

Wait a minute…why is he looking through my phone?

"Why were you snooping through my phone?" I ignore his question completely.

"I wasn't." He shifts his eyes from mine for a fraction of a second. In that instant, I know he's lying. "It went off and I checked it. Don't ignore my question! Are you talking about us to your friends?"

"You're lying! Why were you looking through my phone?" Both of us are now ignoring the other's question. I have a sickening feeling that this is going to be a doozy of a fight. I'm filled with anger that he's been spying on me.

"Answer my question!" He gets right up in my face, screaming.

"Answer my question!" I scream back at him.

He takes a step back from me and chucks my phone at the wall. It falls to the ground in three separate pieces, the back and the battery falling off from the contact.

"Why do you do this to me? You know it bothers me!" He stands and begins pacing the room, like a caged tiger. I watch him carefully, taking in every minute movement he makes.

"I should be able to talk to my friends."

"No! We always end up fighting when you do. They are poisoning you against me. Why do you let them do this to us? Look what they do to us!"

I watch him, unsure of what to say to his comments.

"Ryan, it's not like that. They just listen to me and let me work through my thoughts."

He drops to his knees in front of the bed and grabs my face in his hands. "Baby, I love you. Please don't let them come between us. If you have a problem, talk to me. Don't let your friends and family take away what we have." He looks so distraught that my immediate reaction is to say whatever it takes to ease his fears.

"Okay, baby. I'm sorry. I love you," I whisper. Relief floods his face and he pulls me into his arms.

"I can't lose you, baby. I need you." He pulls me down and presses his lips to mine. I kiss him back, several different emotions warring inside me. Relief that we are no longer fighting and that I could ease his distress. Anger that he went through my phone and confusion about what is going on. Something doesn't feel right…I just wish I could figure out what it is.

*   *   *   *

"Hey, Em! Come here!" Ryan calls as I'm laying in bed reading. I grumble and throw the covers off my legs before making my way to the kitchen, where I find Ryan standing by an open dishwasher.

"What's up?"

"Did you load the dishwasher?"

I resist the urge to roll my eyes. "No, the gnomes did it," I reply, sarcastically and he growls.

"Stop being a brat."

I sigh and nod my head. "Yes, Ryan, I loaded the dishwasher."

"You did it wrong. The dishes are never going to get clean this way."

Oh my God, seriously?

"Ryan, this is they way I've been loading the dishwasher my whole life and it's always been okay." It feels a little surreal that we are actually arguing about how to load the dishwasher right now. It might be the most ridiculous conversation I've ever had with anyone.

"Well, you've gotten lucky then, because it's wrong."

"You know what, Ryan? I'll load the dishwasher my way and if you ever actually do the dishes, you can do it your way." I mean, seriously. He doesn't even help out around here and now he's going to criticize the way I do things?

"Baby, I'm just trying to help you," he says, softly.

"If you want to help me, you could clean up after yourself once in a while."

"Are you serious? I work all day. The least you could do is have the house clean and dinner ready for me when I get here." I blink, unable to believe he just said that me. What is this? 1950?

"I work, too." I'm seething.

He chuckles and shakes his head. "Yeah, in a bar."

I feel very small. I've always loved working in the bar but he's making me ashamed of it. Should I be doing something else? I push away my doubts and cling to my anger at his almost pre-historic idea of gender roles.

"Fuck you," I bark before turning and marching back into the bedroom. I throw my body onto the bed and he comes stomping in a second later.

"What the hell is wrong with you?"

I shoot up to a sitting position and glare at him.

"You! I like working in the bar and your job is not better than mine!"

He throws his head back and laughs loudly. "Uh, babe, I save lives."

"You write parking tickets."

His laughter dies quickly. "You have no respect for me at all."

"That's not true!" Of course, I respect him. I didn't mean what I said, I know his job is important but he got me so mad that it just came out.

"Yes, it is and maybe if you did a better job around here, I would respect you but you're not even trying. If you really loved me, you would want to do those things to take care of me."

I've reached my limit and I know I need to get out of here and get some air. I stand up from the bed and brush past him out into the living room without uttering a word. Just as I'm slipping my shoes on and grabbing my keys off the table, he comes barreling out of the bedroom.

"Where the hell do you think you're going?"

181

"I'm leaving."

"The fuck you are."

I'm reaching for the doorknob when he grabs my arm and spins me around. He pins me against the door and glares down at me.

"Let me go, Ryan," I say, calmly, trying to diffuse the situation.

"Never."

"Let me go."

"Not a chance."

I begin to feel trapped. All I want is to get on the other side of that door. I just want to be able to think for a minute. I push against his chest and he grabs my wrist, pinning it above my head. He squeezes so hard that pain shoots down my arm and I yelp. His face softens as he looks down at me but he doesn't let me go.

"Do you see what you make me do?" His eyes flick up to my hand. "If you would just listen to me, none of this would happen. All I want to do is help you be better but you're just so damn stubborn and dramatic." His voice is soft, caring almost, and for the first time in my life, I question my own sanity. Did I do this? Is there something wrong with me?

"I love you so much and all you do is fight me. Why? Why are you always fighting me?" he asks, voice almost pleading.

"I'm sorry," I answer in a complete daze. The pressure around my wrist disappears and he wraps his arms around me, capturing my mouth in a kiss.

"I forgive you." When he pulls away, I look up at him. A storm of emotion brewing inside me. What the hell is wrong with me? Something doesn't feel right but I can't put my finger on it.

What is going on?

*   *   *   *

Bright sunlight streams in through the French doors of the hotel room, drawing me out of a deep, relaxed sleep. I smile at Ryan sleeping soundly next to me. Looking out the window at the ocean, my smile grows. Yesterday, Ryan whisked me off to the airport, telling me he had a huge surprise for me. I couldn't believe it when we boarded a plane for the Bahamas. I know he needed this though.

He's been working so hard to make detective and it's made him so stressed. That stress has been making us fight even more lately. This trip will be really good for both of us. I just know it. I roll over and snuggle into Ryan. He grunts and wraps his other arm around me, pulling me close. I lie there, somewhere between awake and asleep, reveling in the sensation of being surrounded by the man I love.

"Morning." His gruff voice startles me and my eyes snap up to his face. He leans close and plants a kiss on my neck, right under my ear. I sigh loudly as a shiver races through my body and his lips stretch into a grin against my skin.

"Good morning."

He pulls away, half of his large body still covering mine, and looks down at me. He brushes the hair out of my face then runs his thumb down my cheek. His gaze drifts down to my lips and he licks his own. My breathing becomes labored as I imagine what he's thinking. His gaze flicks back up to mine, his eyes like molten pools of golden desire. He leans down, his eyes never leaving mine, until our lips meet and my eyes flutter closed as my lips part and his tongue glides along mine in a slow caress that sets my body on fire.

He groans, the sound swallowed by my kiss, and I hitch a leg up over his hip. He grinds into me and I break away from his lips, gasping, as I feel his rock hard erection against my core. His lips trail over my cheek, down to my neck where he nips and licks his way to my collarbone. My body bows off the bed, grinding into him, earning me another deep groan.

His hand slides over my hips and he hooks his thumbs into the waistband of my panties, slowly pulling them down my legs. He quickly shoves his boxers off and once he's naked, I reach out, brushing my fingers over the smooth head of his cock. He groans. In an instant, his lips are back on mine as he positions himself at my entrance and thrusts into me. I wasn't quite ready for him so there is a bite of pain and my body tenses. He slowly pulls out and thrusts back in. I throw my head back and gasp at the delicious full feeling as my body expands to fit him. He thrusts again, getting deeper this time and I can't stop the loud moan that leaves my mouth.

"Ryan," I gasp and he thrusts harder, rendering me mute. The only noises I can make are incoherent gasps and moans of pleasure as he continues to power into me. My fingernails dig into the skin on his back and he groans loudly in response. His thumb finds my clit and he rubs small circles over the sensitive nub as he thrusts harder.

"Get there, babe," he says through clenched teeth and I know he can't hold on much longer. He leans down, flicking my nipple with his tongue and I explode without warning. I pulse around him as he lets out a long groan and I feel him empty into me. He releases a breath and lays his head in the crook of my neck, careful not to put his full weight on me as he tries to get his breathing under control.

I relax into the bed as I wait for him to move and kiss along his neck. He finally lets out another long breath and rolls off me, pulling me into his side and kissing the top of my head. We lie there, cuddling while his hand trails patterns over the skin on my hips and back.

"I'm glad we did this," he says, just as I was falling asleep and I open my eyes again.

"Me too. Speaking of...how did you afford this?"

"I have a bunch of money that my mom gave me when my dad died that I've been saving, and I thought, why the hell not? We definitely needed some time away. I've been so stressed."

"I know you have, baby. I hope it gets better soon."

"Yeah, me too." He chuckles. "'Cause when it does, I'll be a detective." I smile as I think about how proud of him I am. He really is working so hard. I have to try to make things easier on him. "Hey, I wanted to talk to you about something." He sounds a little nervous and I perk up, very interested in whatever he's going to say.

"What's up?"

He takes a deep breath. "I want you to stop working. I want to take care of you."

I bite my lip. We just said no more fighting but I know I'm not going to give in on this.

"Can I think about it?" I ask, feeling extremely guilty for lying to him.

"Of course, babe. Take all the time you need."

I smile in response. Maybe things really are going to get better.

*   *   *   *

I can tell Ryan is stressed with work again. I do everything I can to make things easier on him. I keep the house clean and make dinner for him every night, doing everything possible to reduce any stress at home.

After checking the food in the oven, I glance up at the clock and see that Ryan should be home any minute. I get a beer out of the fridge for him and set it down on the table when I hear the front door open.

"Hey, babe," he calls just as I walk into the living room.

"How was work?"

He frowns before shrugging his shoulders. "Fine, I guess."

"'Kay, well I've got dinner ready."

He nods and kicks off his shoes before following me into the kitchen. Grabbing the food out of the oven, I fix us both a plate and go back to the table.

We eat quietly for a while and when the silence becomes uncomfortable, I say something, anything to break it up.

"I've got to work in a couple hours and you'll probably be asleep by the time I get home."

A scowl mars his handsome face. "Have you thought about quitting like I asked?"

I wince at his question. I knew this topic would come up again and I had been hoping to put if off for as long as possible.

"I have."

"And?"

I take a deep breath, trying to prepare myself for his reaction. I know he's not going to be happy but I need to work.

Here it goes…

"I'm not quitting."

The next thing I know, his plate is shattering against the wall, quickly followed by his fist smashing into the kitchen table. I gasp and look up in shock. I knew he wouldn't be happy about my answer but I never expected anything like this.

"WHAT THE FUCK?" I flinch. "I don't ask that much of you, Emma! I ask for one fuckin' thing and you can't even do that for me? If you really loved me, you would do what I fuckin' ask!"

It takes me a minute but eventually, I find my backbone and stand up, ready to defend myself.

"Don't you dare! I have done everything around here to make your life easier! I like working at the bar! I'm not quitting!"

He watches me, his jaw twitching and for the first time ever, I'm genuinely scared of what he may do.

187

"You don't do anything! You sit around the house all Goddamn day long, doing absolutely fucking nothing or you stay out in that studio, painting and neglecting me. You're so lazy! Such a selfish, lazy bitch. Nobody else would put up with you."

I feel the fury coursing through my body. How dare he say I don't do anything? This house is always clean. I always have dinner ready. He always has clean clothes…what more does he want? Maybe I should just stop and then we'll see what his reaction is. The more I stand here with the words he just spewed at me running through my head, the angrier I get and I know I need to walk away right now. Huffing in annoyance, I take off down the hallway to the bedroom so I can get ready for work.

"DON'T WALK AWAY FROM ME!" he screams and his footsteps echo down the hallway as he rushes after me. Before I can react, he grabs my arm and spins me around, slamming me into the wall. Tears well in my eyes and I look up at him but his hazel gaze shows no sign of the man I know and love. I'm not even sure he realizes that he hurt me.

"Let me go," I say through a veil of tears.

"Oh, don't cry. This is your fault. If you would just do the one thing I asked you then this wouldn't have happened!"

I squirm, trying to worm my way out of his grip but he just holds me tighter. "Let me go," I repeat, a little stronger this time and he releases my arm.

"You know what, screw it. The last thing I need to deal with is you being a bitch. I should just let you keep that job. You're so stupid, it's probably the only thing you can do," he spits at me before stalking back into the living room and throwing himself onto the couch.

When I hear the T.V. turn on, I escape to the bedroom and lock the door. The tears stream down my face as sobs rack my body. I fall to the floor and cry harder, replaying the last five minutes in my mind over and over again.

What happened? I don't understand where I went wrong. He just blew up for no reason, and why did he say such hateful things to me? I've been trying so hard to make him happy. Maybe he doesn't want to be with me anymore. That thought causes a new kind of pain to surge through my chest.

My phone chimes in my back pocket and I pull it out to find a text from Bree reminding me that I took her shift tonight. I shake my head in an effort to steel my heart and lock my emotions down deep inside. I can deal with this later. Right now, I need to get ready for work and I can't start bawling in the bar in front of everyone. Time to suck it up.

Chapter Fifteen
Now

I'm stirring creamer into my coffee when Nix steps up behind me. His arms lock around my waist and he pulls me into him, my back to his front. He doesn't say anything for a moment, just holds me, and I have to admit that I love it. It's been about a week since we made up and just like the transition from friendship to relationship, things have been flawless. It's all just so natural with him. So easy. It feels like this is how it should have always been for us.

"I missed you in bed, baby." His warm breath washes over my neck and I lean back into him as a shiver racks my body.

"Oh yeah?"

"Mmhmm." He runs the tip of his nose along the column of my neck and I release a breathy moan. I set the cup of coffee down on the counter and lean back into him further. His large, rough hands slip under the material of my tank top.

"Nix."

"Love hearing you say my name, baby." He nips at my earlobe as his fingers connect with my nipple. My body arches, hips crashing back into him while my chest presses further into his hand. He withdraws his hand and I make a small sound of protest. He chuckles and grabs the bottom of my tank top, yanking it over my head. My breasts bounce free and he groans right in my ear. "Lovin' this view, gorgeous."

"You're good for my ego."

I feel his smile as he presses his lips to my neck in a quick kiss. In the next second, his tongue darts out, swirling over my flesh. Goose bumps pop up over my arms and my head drops back to his shoulder.

"You want to hear what I have planned for you this morning?" His voice holds so much filthy promise that I'm panting and rubbing my ass against his growing cock.

"God, yes."

"First, I'm going to peel all of these annoying clothes off of your gorgeous body." His hand glides along the skin of my belly. So close and yet, so far away from where I want him. "Then, I'm going to kiss you from here." He points to a spot right below my ear. He drags his finger over my shoulder to my breast, down my belly, and finally stops just above my aching core. "To here."

"Oh God."

He kisses the spot where his finger just was on my neck and the muscles in my lower belly clench. I'm grinding my ass into him shamelessly, his breath heavy on my neck. I don't know how he's still so in control.

"Then, I'll slide my fingers into this sweet pussy and get you ready for me."

At this point, no intelligible words are coming out of my mouth, just moans and sighs of pleasure. He hooks his thumbs into my shorts and slides them down my legs, along with my panties. I step out of them quickly. He stands and presses into my back again. His hard cock nudges against my ass and I moan, thinking about it between my thighs.

"When I have you dripping wet, I will bend you over this counter, and slam my hard cock into you."

"Nix." His name is a plea as I stand here, panting and losing my mind over his words.

"Is that what you want, baby?" From the teasing tone in his voice, I know that he's enjoying this, immensely. I'm too far gone to care though.

"Yes. Please."

"Right here? On the counter?"

I moan. "God, yes." His answering groan spurs me on and I grind my ass harder against him. "Please, baby. Fuck me."

"Jesus, Emma," he growls. "Put your hands on the counter." I immediately obey. When my hands are flat on the surface in front of me, Nix pulls away. This time, my groan is one of frustration. I turn to look at him but he stops me. "Stay still."

I face forward again, my chest heaving as my body buzzes with anticipation. One large hand lands on my hip and the other reaches between my legs. As soon as he makes contact with my throbbing clit, I moan loudly. His lips land on my shoulder as his deft fingers swirl over the little bundle of nerves. Small gasps of pleasure leave my mouth and my hips buck against his hand.

"God, you make me crazy, sweetheart," Nix groans. I can't take any more of the teasing. Reaching between my legs, I shove his hand away.

"Nu-uh, baby." His hands lock onto my hips and he spins me quickly so that I'm facing him. My gaze meets his and the desire there has my skin prickling with need.

"Please." My one word plea falls on deaf ears as he slowly, seductively presses his lips to the spot just behind my ear. My head drops back and I release a heavy breath. He slowly kisses down the same line he drew on my body just moments ago. Each time his lips press against my skin, I mewl, my desperation growing exponentially.

"Baby," I croak out when his tongue swirls around my nipple. His lips stretch into a grin against my flesh and I groan in frustration. I'm honestly shocked that I don't have juices running down the insides of my thighs at this point. I need him now.

He crouches down in front of me as he starts kissing down my belly, and the closer he gets to my pulsing core, the harder it is to breathe. His thumb circles my clit as he nips at my hipbone, and I buck against him. His large hands caress my skin as he moves them up and brushes them over my stomach. He kisses just below my belly button and all the air rushes out of me. I glide my finger through his hair. He nuzzles into my belly and I sigh, feeling more content than I can ever remember.

"I'm going to worship you like you deserve, baby. The way you should have always been adored." With that, any restraint I had snaps and I can't hold back any longer.

"Nix. I need you. Now." Without a word, he stands, spins me around, and pulls my hips back toward him. When he has me where he wants me, I plant my feet. He lines himself up at my entrance, teasing me with the head of his magnificent cock before plunging into me. I cry out. He pulls out and thrusts in again, making me moan. Warmth coats my back as he leans over and braces his hands on the counter next to mine. He keeps up a steady pace, kissing and sucking the skin behind my ear, making me climb faster than I ever have before.

Everything about him gets me off. From the way he thrusts into me to the noises he's making, to the occasional kiss he plants along my spine. All of it just works for me.

"Emma," he groans in my ear, his pace increasing.

"Oh, God," I moan as I feel the pressure building in my belly. "More," I demand and he groans again. He rears back and drives into me even harder than before. My hand slips on the counter from sweating. He reaches around and his finger swirls over my clit. My knees buckle. He catches me, holding me up with one hand while the other continues its assault on the sensitive bundle of nerves.

"Baby, you gotta get there," he says through clenched teeth, pumping his hips faster. He moves slightly, changing the angle, and hits the perfect spot.

"Yes!" I cry out. One hand grabs my breast as the other stays around my belly, pulling me into him as he powers into me. My orgasm hits me. Stars explode behind my eyes and I call out his name as I clench and pulse around him. He thrusts into me one more time before stilling and letting out a low groan.

After a moment, he collapses on me, trembling. His breath feathers over my back and I soak it up, loving every single second. Warm lips meet my skin as he kisses up to my neck.

"I love you, Emma," he whispers.

I love you too, I think but the words don't come out.

*   *   *   *

"You wanna do something, baby? Watch a movie, maybe?" Nix asks as I'm sitting on the couch reading.

"Sure. What did you have in mind?"

He pulls a DVD case for *The Bodyguard* out from behind his back and I burst into giggles.

"I figured I needed to know your movie reference."

"Nix, it's gonna take a whole lot longer than one day for you to learn all the movie references I have in my head."

"Hey, I'm game," he answers, shrugging his shoulders. Just as I'm opening my mouth to say something else, there is a knock at the door. His brows furrow. "You expecting someone, baby?"

I shake my head. "Nope."

He approaches the door cautiously, like at any moment, someone is going to break it down and come charging in. I scoff and roll my eyes. He shoots me a look of warning. When he reaches the door, he checks through the peephole before turning back to me with confusion on his face.

"There's no one there."

"Well, open it. Maybe it was the UPS guy."

"Did you order something?"

"Uh…no."

"Then why would it be—"

"Oh, this is ridiculous," I say, interrupting him and jumping off the couch. I stalk past him and rip open the door. All I see is empty hallway. When I step out to get a better look, I kick something small on the ground. Dread fills me as soon as I see the small velvet box.

Please, dear God, don't let that be what I think it is.

Slowly, I crouch down, pick up the box, and open it. My breath lodges in my throat and the world spins as I look at the diamond heartbeat necklace I never wanted to see again. This necklace used to be something I cherished, something that reminded me of Ryan and his love for me. Now, it just makes me sick. And angry. The manipulation is clear to me now. The way he showed up with his charm, pretty words and even prettier presents, and I fell for it, every single time. And he never said sorry. Not even once.

"Em, what is that?" Nix asks, softly, sensing my unease. Closing the door, I hand the box to him.

"It's one of his presents."

Nix looks down at the necklace and my unease only increases. Seeing him with it is just so wrong. Nix is the best thing in my life and that necklace represents the worst. They don't belong together.

I need that thing out of here.

Snatching the box out of his hand, I march into the kitchen. My eyes focused on my end goal — the trashcan. Nix catches my hand just as I'm raising it over my head to chuck the vile jewelry.

"What are you doing?"

"I need it out of here, Nix!"

"Okay, baby." He wraps his arms around me and I bury my head in his chest. "We'll call your brothers and they can come get it but we need to keep it."

Tears well up in my eyes. "No! I need it gone forever. I need it to not exist anymore!"

"Shhh, sweetheart," he whispers, wiping my tears away. "I know, but for right now we need to keep it. When this thing is all over we can crush it or burn it or toss it into the swamp. Whatever you want."

"Do you promise?"

"Absolutely, baby."

I bite my lip and nod at him. "Okay."

"There's my girl." I smile and he pulls me back into his arms. "I love you," he adds and I just nod, still unable to say the words.

"Will you tell me the story about this necklace?" After a moment, I nod. He scoops me up and carries me over to the couch, sitting me on his lap. I sigh and unload the story about that morning. When I finish, he just nods.

"One sec," he finally says, setting me off to the side and striding into the bedroom. He comes out a moment later and sits down beside me again. "Get back over here," he commands and I scramble into his lap.

"What's up?"

"Well, speaking of birthdays, I didn't get a chance to give this to you." He pulls a velvet box out from behind his back. I gape at him, my eyes flicking between his blue gaze and the black jewelry box in his hand. We had just started dating right before my birthday and he got me a present? And not just any present but jewelry.

"You didn't have to do this."

"Naw, I wanted to, baby. I'm sorry it's late. I actually just got it a few days ago. I had to have it specially made."

Specially made?

"This is too much."

"Nothing is too much for you, baby. Open it."

Glancing down at the box in my hand, I slowly peel the lid open. Inside is a silver bracelet. A charm that connects the two pieces of the bracelet catches my eye and I gasp when I realize what it is.

Oh my God.

"It's a…" My voice fades off, unable to finish my sentence.

"Lobster," Nix finishes for me. It's more than a lobster. It's two lobsters, twisting to form an infinity symbol. The bracelet itself and its symbolism steal my breath away.

"Nix." Tears well up in my eyes as I look at him.

"Hey, what's wrong?" he asks, wiping a tear that falls down my cheek. "If you don't like it, it's okay." His voice is full of disappointment.

"These are happy tears. I love it."

A slow smile spreads across his face. "Really? You wouldn't lie right?"

"Never."

"I love you." His lips brush again mine in a sweet kiss. A sigh slips out of my mouth as he pulls away.

"I'm sorry."

"For what?"

"Not being able to say it."

"Don't be. I understand. Besides, I can see how you feel about me in those gorgeous eyes. You can't hide from me, sweetheart. Now, movie or should we call your brothers first?"

"Call the goon squad. Let's get this over with."

*   *   *   *

"So, did either of you actually see him?" Trey asks as we all gather around my dining room table.

"No, but it had to be him. I left the necklace at the house when I left."

"What's the deal with the necklace, Em?"

"What do you mean?"

"I mean, why did he give it to you?"

"It was a gift." I focus on the floor, avoiding my brothers' stares, and hoping to get out of this without having to tell them the ugly truth.

"No shit, Emma. A gift for what?" Tucker snaps, clearly losing his patience already.

"What does it fuckin' matter?" Nix barks. Both of my brothers look to Nix in shock and then back to me. Nix is usually pretty levelheaded but I can tell all this is stressing him out and he knows I don't like talking about this.

"Uh…what just happened?" Trey asks.

"She doesn't like talking about this. Why does it matter why he gave it to her?" Nix growls and I lean into him. I'm so thankful for his support through all this. Besides my brothers, no one has ever stuck up for me like this.

"I think it's important."

"*Why?* Why is it important, Trey?" I ask, getting irritated that he's not answering the question.

"Because if we know why he gave it to you the first time, maybe we can figure out what he meant by leaving it for you now."

Well, damn.

When he says it like that, it actually makes a lot of sense. I don't want to talk about this though. I don't want my brothers to know these things, just the thought has my stomach churning.

"I don't know if I can," I whisper.

Nix pulls me into his body. His lips brush over my ear as he whispers, "Close your eyes. It's just you and me here, baby." I follow his instructions. Closing my eyes, I imagine only telling my story to Nix.

"It was one of his 'I'm sorry' presents. He said that he needed me and that he couldn't live without me. That I was his heartbeat." I release a breath after I finish and open my eyes to see both of my brothers staring at me.

"How many 'sorry' presents were there, Emmy?" Tucker asks, his voice soft. Anguish fills his green eyes and my own burn as tears well up.

"It doesn't matter right now," Nix comments, rubbing his hand across my back. Soothing me.

"I wish you would tell us everything, baby girl," Trey urges and I shake my head.

"No."

"So, what does him leaving the necklace here now mean?" Tucker asks. We all look at each other as we try to work through it. It hits me all at once. The tires, the notes, and now the necklace.

He can't live without me.

He won't live without me.

"It means he isn't going to let me go," I whisper and Nix's entire body goes rigid underneath me.

"We'll he's S.O.L. cause I'm not letting him anywhere near you." He pulls me closer, loops his arms around me, and kisses my cheek. Almost like he needs me for comfort. It occurs to me that I don't know what Ryan will do if Nix tries to stop him. The thought of Nix getting hurt is too painful to even think about.

"Yeah, what he said," Tucker says and Trey nods in agreement. I'm thankful for their protection but I can't shake the feeling that it may not be enough. Who knows what Ryan has planned? I don't think I even know what he's truly capable of.

Chapter Sixteen
Then…

At work, I am quieter than usual and everyone has noticed. More than once, Moe and Trey have pulled me aside to ask what is wrong with me. When they do, I fake a smile and brush off their concerns, but as soon as they turn their backs, I'm on the verge of tears.

When Addilyn shows up around eleven, I pull her into the back to ask if I can stay the night at her house.

"Of course you can, sweetie. What's wrong?" I desperately want to tell her but after what happened earlier, I don't want to do anything else to piss Ryan off.

"Nothing's wrong," I say, my smile as fake as a stripper's boobs. "Ryan is just working tonight and I haven't seen you in forever." Her face brightens immediately.

"Oh, ok. Well, I'll call Daisy and we'll make it a girls' night."

"Yeah, that sounds really great."

"'Kay, I'll go rent some movies. Any preferences?"

"Comedy," I practically shout and wince at my reaction.

"All right. I'll go do that now. See you later, girl." And with that, she twirls around and leaves me standing in the stockroom. When the door closes, I practically collapse on a stack of boxes. Who knew that acting was so exhausting? I feel like I ran a marathon.

"Come on, Emma. Get it together," I say to myself.

I stand and brush my hands down my apron to compose myself and then I head back out to the bar before someone comes looking for me. Luckily, the place is busy and I am able to avoid any more questions for the rest of the night.

*   *   *   *

I wake up just as the sun is shining through the windows, practically blinding me. Groaning, I roll over to cuddle closer to Ryan and almost fall off the bed.

Wait…what?

No, I'm not in bed. I'm on a couch. Opening my eyes, I look around the room and it takes me a minute to realize I'm in Addy's living room. Then it all comes back to me. Tears sting my eyes as I remember Ryan's words. Checking my phone, I see that I have twenty-nine missed calls and it's only seven a.m.

Great.

Just as I'm contemplating what I should do, my phone rings in my hand. Ryan's face pops up on the screen and I just stare at his picture as it continues ringing.

"You gonna answer that?" Addy asks, startling me, and I drop the phone on the floor.

"Huh?"

"Are you going to answer your phone? And are you going to keep lying to me about why you stayed the night last night?"

I bite my lip and shoot her a guilty look. "I'm sorry."

She sighs. "Hun, I don't care that you lied. I just want to make sure you're okay."

I sit up on the couch and fold my legs under me as she sits on the other side. "Yeah. We just had a fight."

She nods like she already knew that. My phone starts ringing again and I roll my eyes before rejecting the call.

"You gonna answer that at all today?" she asks again and I shrug. "Do you know what you're going to do?"

"No," I admit. "We left things kind of badly last night."

"Well, talk to him." My phone starts ringing yet again. I shake my head and she huffs before grabbing the phone out of my hand.

"Ryan," she answers. "it's Addilyn…She's fine…I don't know if she wants to see you…No, I'm not giving you my address…Oh, shove it, asshole." She hangs up the phone and hands it back to me.

"There. Now he knows you're not in a ditch somewhere, at least." She cracks a smile. I can't help but follow her lead and a second later we're both giggling. My phone rings again, effectively shutting us both up. I just stare down at Ryan's picture on the screen while I wait for it to go to voicemail.

"You know what?" Addy says and I look up at her. "Let's go shopping." She nudges me with her shoulder and I grin despite myself.

I seriously don't know what I would do without this girl.

Addy and I spend a couple hours at the mall, window shopping, and my mood does improve. But as soon as I pull into my driveway, a rock takes up residence in the pit of my stomach. I just stare at the front door, trying to work up the courage to go in… or run away — I'm honestly not sure which. I sit for what feels like hours before I come to a decision.

I love Ryan and I just need to go in there and talk to him. I'll tell him how much he hurt me and we'll work it out.

With newfound confidence, I throw open the car door and walk up to the house. Inside, I notice that the place is spotless, the scent of soap from the washing machine hanging in the air.

"What the heck?" I whisper to myself.

A noise rings out from the kitchen, startling me and I head in that direction. Along the way, I notice that there isn't a speck of dust on anything. Did some magical cleaning fairy descend from heaven and invade my home? In the kitchen, my eyebrows shoot up in surprise at the sight of Ryan scraping food off the wall where he threw his plate last night.

"Uh…hi," I say and his head shoots up. Before I know what's happening, he jumps up and throws his arms around me.

"I didn't know if you were gonna come back," he admits as he releases a breath and his entire body relaxes.

"We need to talk."

I feel his muscles go rigid.

"Okay." He releases me and follows me into the living room. We sit on opposite ends of the couch, just staring at each other in silence.

"What happened last night wasn't okay."

He nods his head. "I know I lost my temper, baby." Is he kidding? He did a whole lot more than lose his temper.

"It was more than that. I was scared of you last night. I thought you might hurt me."

"I love you, baby, but you are so damn dramatic," he says with a soft chuckle. I can feel myself getting angry again and I close my eyes, mentally counting to ten to calm myself back down.

"You called me stupid and a bitch. You hurt my arm!"

"You're crazy. I didn't call you stupid and I didn't hurt you. I barely touched you."

I gape at him. "Are you serious right now?"

"Show me your arm," he demands.

"What?"

"If I hurt you so badly then show me your arm."

I rip off my sweater and hold my arm out to him. He studies it before looking at me with a furrowed brow.

"Baby, there isn't even a mark. See, this is what I'm talking about. You're so dramatic and you are making this into a huge deal when it wasn't. Yes, I lost my temper. I yelled and I threw a plate against the wall and I'm sorry for that, but I didn't hurt you," he explains in a soothing tone and I begin to doubt my own memory.

Did I really blow this way out of proportion?

I look down at my arm and even I have to admit that there isn't a mark there. Did he really call me a bitch? Did he say I was stupid?

"Do you think I'm stupid?"

Shock crosses his face for a second before he shakes his head.

"God! No, baby. You are so gorgeous and kind and smart. It's one of the reasons that I love you so much," he says, his eyes soft with love and compassion.

Jesus...

I think I might really be losing it. Reality blurs. Did it really happen the way I remember it or did I manufacture things in my mind? Am I really so dramatic that I dreamed up some insane story? I think I might be going crazy.

"I'm so sorry, Ryan," I choke, a sob escaping my mouth. He immediately moves forward and pulls me into his lap, hugging me tightly.

"Oh, sweetheart. It's okay. I forgive you." Tears begin to fall down my face, drenching his shirt. "Shhh, it's okay, baby. I love you. We're going to be okay."

I sob harder. I don't deserve him.

*   *   *   *

I've been off lately, since the big fight Ryan and I had. I'm so embarrassed that I blew the whole thing so out of proportion. And it has put me in a terrible mood since. Add in the fact that Ryan wanted to go out tonight and I had to work, and I'm especially surly.

Trey really is doing everything he can to try to cheer me up. Apparently he has been working on his bartending skills. He is spinning bottles, throwing them through the air and behind his back as he makes drinks tonight. He's got a crowd of adoring fans around the bar cheering for him. Moe is loving it. He says we've done more sales than ever before.

As I'm going back to the stockroom to grab more liquor, my phone rings. I dig it out of my pocket and see Daisy's picture on the screen.

"Hey, chica, what are you up to?"

"Um… Em, I think you should sit down," she says and I freeze.

"Why, Daisy? What's wrong?"

"Okay, so I was downtown and I saw Ryan outside of this strip club and I followed him inside cause I was suspicious."

"Yeah…and?" I have to admit that the strip club is bad enough. I hate the thought of Ryan watching some other girl grinding all over a pole. Suddenly feeling inadequate, I send up a silent prayer that he's not doing anything else. It already hurts so much to think about him being there.

"Um…well…there's no easy way to say this. His friends bought him a lap dance and he is making out with her," she says softly, pity heavy in her voice. I gag around the bile rising in my throat.

"Send me a picture, Daisy."

"I don't think that's a good idea, sweetie."

"Please!" Silence greets me and she takes so long to answer that I have to check my phone to make sure the call is still connected.

"All right, I'm going to hang up now. You'll get it in a second."

"Thank you."

She hangs up without another word. I clutch my phone in my hand, waiting for the photo that I know is going to shatter my heart into a million pieces.

Just as Trey walks into the room, my phone dings with a message and I ignore him as I open the picture. As soon as I see the slutty brunette straddling my fiancé's lap with her lips plastered to his, I collapse onto a stack of boxes nearby.

An unintelligible grunt of pain escapes me seconds before tears start streaming down my face, and I clutch my phone to my chest. Trey rushes over to me, kneels in front of me, and lifts my chin so my eyes meet his. His lips are moving but I can't hear what he is saying over my sobs and the ringing in my ears.

What did I do to deserve this? Why would Ryan do this to me? It's not because I had to work tonight, is it? Trey tries to pry my phone out of my hand and I jerk away from him, holding my phone tighter.

"Emma! What is going on?" he asks, his voice finally breaking through the noise in my head.

"N-n-n-nothing," I stutter and hiccup.

"Do you really think I'm going to believe that?" he demands. I need to leave here. I can't stay here any longer. I need to go home and fall apart in peace and quiet.

"W-will you t-take m-me home?" I ask and he arches a brow as if to say, "Are you nuts?"

"No! Tell me what the hell is wrong with you."

"I j-j-just want to g-go home."

He stands, throwing his hands in the air before he pulls out his phone.

"I'm calling Tucker."

"NO!"

Moe comes barreling into the back room and stops short when he sees my face.

"Darlin'," he coos and I shake my head to stop him. He frowns.

"Will y-you take me home p-please, M-m-moe?"

"Of course," he answers immediately.

"No!" Trey yells at the same time but Moe ignores him.

"Trey, watch the bar." Moe guides me out the back doors and to the parking lot. I curse when I notice my car sitting in the lot.

"Moe, I totally forgot I had my car here. I can get home."

He eyes me skeptically. "Are you sure, darlin'?"

"Yeah, I'm all right."

He watches me for a little longer before he nods. "Call me when you get there, okay?"

"I will."

"Are you going to tell me what happened?" he asks and I shake my head.

"I don't want Trey and Tucker knowing and everyone knows you can't keep a secret."

He grins. "Ya, you got me there." He wraps his arm around my shoulders and gives me a squeeze, a fresh wave of tears welling up in my eyes.

"Thanks, Moe."

"Anything for you, darlin'. You're like the daughter I never had." I smile, immensely grateful for such wonderful people in my life.

Chapter Seventeen
Then...

Hours later, I'm parked on the couch, staring blankly at the wall as I wait for Ryan to come back home. I think I've cried my body weight in tears and the pain is still as raw as it was when I first saw the photo.

That photo...

I've looked at it a hundred times, memorizing every inch of it. It's burned into my memory, his hands on her hips, her hands clutching at his chest, and her nasty cooch rubbing against his cock. And then there are the details that my imagination had no trouble filling in for me. Like her tongue in his mouth and how he was turned on by her.

I wonder if he fucked her.

I feel numb. My body, my soul...it all feels numb, empty. I love him so much but I don't even feel that right now. I feel nothing. Yet, somehow, the doubt and insecurity has crept in. Am I not pretty enough? Am I too fat? Have I been a total bitch to him? Is this my fault for not calling in sick to work tonight to go out with him? All these questions swirl through my brain, like a tornado of emotional destruction, leaving only agony in their wake.

The slamming of a car door startles me and I glance up at the clock.

Three a.m.

My mom always said nothing good ever happens after midnight. When I was a teenager, I thought she was crazy. It seemed like all the good stuff happened after midnight but I've been working at the bar long enough to know that her words ring true. Tonight just really drives the point home.

The front door opens and Ryan walks into the living room, stopping short when he sees me.

"Jesus, babe! What are you doing sitting in the dark?" He flips on the lamp beside the couch.

"Where have you been?" He looks away from me for just a split second and I know that whatever comes out of his mouth next is going to be utter bullshit.

"I was over at my brother's house. We just had a few beers and hung out."

I nod as if I buy the crap he's spewing.

"Why are you so late?" My voice is filled with fake concern. Hell, if he can lie right to my face then I can do the same.

"Oh, we just got to talking and lost track of time." Wow…he's an even better liar than I realized. "I'm gonna jump in the shower and go to bed. I'm exhausted."

I force a smile to my face and nod. As he starts heading down the hallway to the bathroom, I stand.

"Did you screw her?"

He freezes mid-stride and turns to me, slowly. I see the panic clearly on his face before he masks it. "Huh?"

I take two slow deliberate steps toward him. "Did. You. Fuck. Her?" I say, enunciating each word clearly.

"Baby, I have no idea what you're talking about."

I'll give him this, he's good. It makes me wonder what else he's been up to that I don't know about.

"I have a picture. Would you like me to remind you?" I'm feigning sweet and innocent but I feel violent. His face pales and his eyes widen as he looks at me. I can practically hear his mind racing.

"Baby...," he starts but stops and snaps his mouth shut.

"Yeah, that's what I thought." My tone is full of so much venom and hatred that he flinches at the weight of it. His eyes flick down to the bag I packed, sitting by the front door.

"Babe...I just went to a strip club. It's not that big of a deal," he says, condescending, ratcheting my anger up another level.

"I saw the picture, Ryan! You were making out with her!"

A confused look crosses his face. "What are you talking about? I got a lap dance but I didn't kiss anyone."

For a second, I believe him. He's that convincing.

Or maybe I'm that stupid...

I grab my phone out of my back pocket and pull up the photo before shoving it in his face. His brow furrows as he studies it.

"Okay, I'll admit that this looks bad but I swear I didn't kiss her. She kissed me and I was pushing her away in this photo." His voice and his body language lead me to believe he's telling the truth. Then, I remember that Daisy saw him.

"No, Daisy saw you making out with her. Don't lie to me." I'm desperately fighting my body's desire to forgive him and end the tension between us.

"Sweetie," he says, walking up to me and wrapping his arms around my waist. I try to pull away as fresh tears well up in my eyes at his touch but he tightens his grip. "Your friends don't like me. Daisy is lying to you. I don't know why she would want to hurt you like this but don't let her destroy us."

At his words, the only thing I can feel is confusion. Would Daisy really do that me?

"Wait, what about the lap dance? Do you really think I'd be okay with some slut grinding all over your lap?" I say, renewed anger in my voice.

Don't give in, I scold myself.

He sighs and looks up toward the ceiling.

"Emma, you're making a big deal out of nothing. It didn't mean anything."

"It's not nothing to me! You had some other girl all over you! Were you turned on by her?"

He chuckles and shakes his head.

"You are too sensitive. I swear, it didn't mean anything, baby. I was more there to hang out with my brothers and friends than anything else. Besides, if you hadn't ditched me tonight, I never would have ended up there," he tosses out.

Guilt floods me that I wasn't there with him. Should I have called Moe and asked for the night off?

"I'm gonna hop in the shower. Why don't you go calm down and when I come out, we can go to bed,"

215

he instructs, kissing my forehead and I feel like crying again.

What the hell is going on with me?

*   *   *   *

"Good morning, beautiful girl."

I roll over and come face-to-face with Ryan. I just watch him, not saying a word, and after a moment, he narrows his eyes at me.

"What's wrong?"

"Nothing," I say with a sigh, rolling away from him.

"Bullshit. Come on, Emma. What's going on? Are you still upset about last night?"

I nod my head. He sighs, heavily and lays his chin on my shoulder.

"Sweetie, you are really blowing this out of proportion. It didn't mean anything."

"Yeah, okay."

He wraps his arms around me, his front to my back. His erection presses against my butt and I freeze.

"I love you, baby. Can we please have fun today? You said we would spend the day together."

I feel guilty because I did promise him that yesterday when I couldn't get out of work. I take a deep breath and try to get past what happened last night. If he says it meant nothing, then it meant nothing.

"I love you, too."

He smiles against the skin on my shoulder. "There's my girl." He rolls my body toward him. He skims his thumb over my nipple and kisses my neck. "I bet I can make you feel better."

I try to get into it, I really do, but every time he touches me, that picture flashes in my head. My hands fall away from his back and he looks at me in confusion.

"I'm not in the mood." I try to roll away from him but he stops me. He climbs on top of me and spreads my legs with his knee, despite my resistance.

"Just give me a minute and I'll get you in the mood. You can't resist me." One hand goes between my legs, rubbing across the thin fabric of my panties. My hips lift into his touch without any instruction from me, and I get mad that my body is reacting to him.

"No, Ryan."

He chuckles against my neck. "Always playing hard to get, baby. I can feel how much you want me."

I scowl, angry that he is right. My body wants him but my mind is such a mess right now. He takes advantage of my confused state, moving my panties to the side and sliding into me. I gasp at the intrusion but…oh, it feels so good.

I hate myself right now, I think, as I surrender myself to him.

*   *   *   *

"Who is she, Ryan?" I ask from my perch on the couch as soon as Ryan steps into the dark house. I had naïvely hoped that the strip club incident a couple weeks ago would be a one time thing but apparently, I was wrong.

"Holy shit! Babe, you scared the hell out of me!"

"Who is she?"

"Who's who?" he asks, flipping on the light by the door. I scoff when I see the lipstick stain on his collar. He's not even trying to hide it.

Bastard.

"Addy saw you on your date." I say it coolly, like I don't give a shit. In reality, I'm burning with rage inside. How dare he cheat on me? I've done everything he wanted.

"What date?" he asks, continuing with the dumb act.

"The one in this photo." I fling the picture I printed off of my phone at him.

"Baby, she's just a friend from work."

I shake my head. "Don't fuckin' lie to me. You're caught, Ryan. Just give it up."

He gazes at me and I can see his mind racing to come up with anything to salvage this situation. Apparently, he hasn't noticed my bag by the door.

"Baby." He's got that tone. The one that lets me know that he's about to lie his ass off. He's going to spew a bunch of crap at me and hope that I'm dumb enough to believe it again. Not. Happening.

"Stop lying!"

His face changes instantly. "Don't yell at me," he warns, his voice low and menacing.

"Fuck you!" I'm so mad right now that I'm doing this even though I know I shouldn't be.

"What did you say?" He takes a threatening step toward me.

"Screw this. I'm done, Ryan. Have a nice life." I step to the side, trying to go around him to my bag. He looks over his shoulder and sees my things sitting there, waiting for me.

"'No. You're not leaving me, bitch." Hooking his arm around my waist, he lifts me off the ground. He starts walking down the hallway as I yell at him flailing in his grasp.

"Put me down, you asshole!"

"Every time we fight, you do this. You always try to leave me." I beat my hands on the arm wrapped around my waist but it doesn't do any good.

"I said, put me down!"

"Do you see that ring on your finger? That means you're mine forever. It means that you don't get to leave. You need to figure out just what being married to me means. It means that I will never let you go!" He walks into the guest bedroom and I look around in surprise.

Why did he bring me in here?

He drops me on the bed and grabs my face in his hand, squeezing hard. I'm almost certain there will be bruises there in the morning.

"We will talk in the morning when you can stop being so Goddamn dramatic." He releases me, turning and marching out of the room without another word. The door shuts behind him. Until I hear the lock click, I don't fully understand the gravity of the situation. Rushing to the door, I try the handle even though I already know what I'll find.

I'm locked inside.

He locked me in the room? Oh my God, he locked me in this room.

With panic building inside me, I rush to the window and try to open it. It doesn't budge. I'm well and truly stuck. How long will he leave me in here? What will happen if he decides to let me out? All these thoughts twist around in my head on an endless loop as I collapse to the floor, tears welling up in my eyes.

*   *   *   *

I don't know how long I've been in here. I do know that the sun has already risen so if I had to guess, I would say seven hours. Eight, maybe. I'm so thirsty and my body aches from spending the night on this bed. And I'm angry. Angrier than I can ever remember being before in my life. The knob turns suddenly, startling me, and my gaze flies to the door. Ryan walks in and in that moment, I hate him.

"You ready to talk, baby?"

I nod my head, afraid that if I open my mouth I will just start screaming at him.

"Say it, Emma. I want to hear you say that you are sorry."

My lip curls back into a snarl and I shake my head. "Go fuck yourself."

He clenches his fists and his lips form a thin line. I think he's going to leave but a second later, he's marching over to me and grabbing me by the arm. He yanks me off the small mattress and shoves me into the wall so hard that I see spots. His hand closes around my neck and my eyes fly open. When I look up at him, there is nothing staring back at me. He's completely blank.

"Why are you such an ungrateful little bitch?" His hand tightens around my neck and I wonder if I'm ever going to make it out of this room. It's getting really hard to breathe but he just stares at me as his grip tightens further. I claw at his fingers but he grabs my hand and smashes it against the wall next to my head. Pain shoots down my arm as tears pour down my cheeks.

"Do you know how much I do for you? You wouldn't have anything if it weren't for me. You're going to stay in this room until you learn to have some fucking respect."

He lets go of my hand and pulls his arm back, curling his hand into a fist. He releases my neck and I duck as his fist comes flying at my face. He barely misses me, his hand going through the drywall, and then he turns and leaves, like nothing happened. I hear the lock click again and I collapse to the floor, sobbing. I can't help but wonder how the hell I got here.

*   *   *   *

It's starting to get dark again. My stomach growls and my mouth feels like it's been stuffed with cotton balls. It's so hard to swallow. I think I'd do anything to get out of this room right now. Even apologize to Ryan, but he hasn't been back since this morning.

Then, I hear the front door open and my heart flips with excitement. I pray to every God that I can think of that he will come to let me out. A moment later, my prayers are answered when I hear the lock click and the door opens.

The look of pity on his face almost has my anger resurfacing but I push it back down. "Why do you make me do this to you, baby?" he asks. I say nothing. "Are you ready to apologize?" I nod my head. "Let's hear it."

"I'm sorry." My voice is so quiet that I'm not even sure he heard me.

"For?" I guess not.

"For accusing you and yelling at you."

He smiles, swooping down and scooping me up into his arms. He carries me into our bathroom and turns on the water. He carefully strips me and places me under the stream of water.

"Get cleaned up and I'll make you some food. See how much easier things are when you just listen to me?"

As soon as he leaves the room, I curl up into a ball and sob.

Chapter Eighteen
Now

"Jesus, Em! Wake up, baby," Nix calls to me and my eyes pop open.

I breathe a sigh of relief as I take in the familiar walls of my apartment. That dream was so real.

"Are you okay, sweetheart?" he asks, cradling my face in his hand and searching my eyes.

I nod and force a smile to my face. "Yeah, I'm okay."

He eyes me warily. "You wanna talk about it?" I just shrug my shoulders. He snuggles up to me and lies back down. I run my finger along the intricate lines of the tattoos on his arm.

"I caught Ryan cheating on me once. Well, actually Addy did."

His hold around me tightens. "Yeah, you told me before that he cheated on you."

I nod again. "When I confronted him and told him that I was leaving, he locked me up in the guest bedroom overnight. He said I needed to calm down."

"What do you mean he locked you up?" The tension in his body grows.

"He had installed a lock on the outside of the door so he could lock me in. And he did something to the window so it wouldn't open anymore. I was trapped in there until he decided to let me out."

"Jesus fucking Christ," he growls through clenched teeth. "He planned to lock you up?"

"I dunno. I have no idea what he was planning to do with that room before that night." He just nods. "The next morning, he let me out and asked if I had calmed down yet. I told him to go screw himself so he locked me back up until he came home from work."

"Holy fuck, Emma." He jumps out of bed and begins pacing next to the bed, running a hand through his hair. His body is absolutely rigid, muscles bulging from the stress.

"Do you want me to stop?"

His eyes shoot to me. They instantly soften and he crawls back into the bed. He lays his hand on my face and draws me closer, claiming my lips.

When he pulls away, he whispers, "I love you." I just nod. He kisses my forehead and lets me cuddle back into him. "Okay, keep going."

"When he came home from work, he let me out again and asked if I had calmed down. I was so hungry and thirsty that I told him I was sorry so he let me out."

"God, Emma. The things he did to you." His voice cracks. I look up at him and grab his face between my hands.

"It's okay. I'm okay."

"You are one of the sweetest people I know, Emma, and he used that against you. And somehow, you still blame yourself."

"I was stupid, Nix."

"No, you weren't."

"Fine. I was naïve, then."

"You got played, baby. It happens to the best of us."

I lean in quickly and kiss him again. "You always see the best in me, Nix."

He smiles and wraps his arms around me.

"That's 'cause there isn't a single piece of bad in you, Em."

I scoff and shake my head. He smiles against my skin as he kisses my cheek. I relax into him. We fall into a comfortable silence, just lying there in bed. After a while, my fingers begin to dance across his washboard abs, dipping lower and lower on each pass.

"Mmm, baby," he hums, closing his eyes.

I smile and drag my fingers along the waistband of his boxer briefs. His sigh encourages me and I hook my fingers in them, pulling them down his legs. Coming back up, I wrap my hand around his cock and he groans.

Slowly, I work my hand up and down his growing erection, drawing noises of pleasure out of him. When he starts thrusting up into my hand, I sit up in bed and lean over him. I run my tongue along the underside of his dick and he throws his head back into the pillow.

"Emma," he groans.

I hum as I wrap my lips around him. His fingers slide into my hair and he grips a handful, guiding himself in and out of my mouth. When I swirl my tongue around the tip, his grip tightens and he groans again. I suddenly have the urge to watch him. My eyes flick up and the sight has me moaning around him. Blue fires gaze back at me and as soon as our eyes meet, he squeezes his eyes shut, groaning loudly.

I can't take it anymore. My core is aching, begging for relief. I slide a hand between my legs and swirl my fingers around my clit. I moan again. With my free hand, I wrap my fingers around the base of his cock, stroking in rhythm with my mouth.

He looks back down at me and growls. "Jesus, Emma."

My fingers slip inside my slick entrance and I break away from him, gasping. Nix moves quickly, grabbing my arms and tossing me to the bed next to him. He hovers over me. His fingers slide between my legs. When he touches my clit, we both moan together.

"You're going to be the death of me, woman."

"Why?" I breathe, throwing my head back as two fingers enter me.

"It's so Goddamn hard to hold back with you. I wake up in the morning, aching to slide inside you. Some days, it's all I can think about. Getting back to you and ramming into this sweet pussy."

Good God.

His words cause a rush of warmth to race through me, straight to my core. "Why the hell are you holding back?" I ask. "I want all of you, baby."

His fingers are suddenly gone from my body. I cry out in protest. Before I can say anything, those magic fingers are back. He adds a third and slides back into me. He pulls them out slowly and glides back in, creating the most deliciously agonizing torture I've ever felt. I need more.

"Nix."

At the sounds of his name on my lips, he groans. "You want more, sweetheart? You want all of me?"

I nod, frantically. "God, yes." He pulls his fingers almost all the way out and stays there for a moment, tormenting me some more. Finally, he pumps his fingers back inside me and pulls out again, moving faster than ever before. I scream, my back arching as he brings me closer and closer to a blissful release. But then, he stops, his fingers gone, and I almost sob.

"You ready for me, Em?" he asks, leaning in, his perfect body hovering just above mine and providing me with a whole new kind of anguish. His dick presses against my core and I shudder.

"Yes." My voice is hoarse, rich with need. He slides into me slowly and my eyes roll back into my head as a low moan slips out of my mouth. He grunts as he buries his head in my neck and pulls out slowly before thrusting back in.

"Give me all of you, Nix," I demand.

With a groan, he starts moving, pounding into me like a jackhammer. He presses his lips to mine, his tongue gliding between my lips and strokes my mouth, swallowing my moans. One hand threads into my hair and holds my mouth against his while the other grips my ass as he relentlessly drives into me.

"Nix," I call out, pulling away from his mouth.

"Is this what you wanted, baby? All of me?"

"Yes!" I scream and he makes a sound that is a mixture between a grunt and a growl. He thrusts harder.

"Like this, Emma?"

"God, yes! Don't stop! Don't ever stop!" I cry, my mind completely blanked out. Overloaded by the pleasure coursing through my body.

"Look at me, Em."

My eyes immediately open and lock onto his. He gazes down at me through hooded eyes, fighting to hold on. The look in his eyes makes my release come racing to the surface. I yank him closer and smash his lips to mine. He groans into me. His hips start moving faster and I explode around him. Stars dance behind my eyes as I rip my mouth away and cry out.

He buries his head in my neck. Grabbing my hip in his hand, he thrusts, chasing his own release. I feel him swell just a moment before he's pulsing inside me. His low groan in my ear sends a whole new wave of shivers down my spine.

"Emma," he sighs, kissing my neck as he stills over me. "You're gonna kill me, it's too good."

I grin. "There's no such thing as too good."

He smirks back at me, face filled with so much love that my heart expands in my chest, trying to break through my rib cage. "I love you," he whispers. I nod, my usual response. He winks at me and stands. "Don't move."

I turn my head to watch his fine ass walk into the bathroom. When he returns, he has a washcloth in his hand. He kneels down on the bed and gently wipes between my legs. He tosses the washcloth onto the floor when he's finished and lies back down on the bed, pulling me into him.

Snuggling up to him, I realize that I'm actually happy. It's not an act anymore. I'm not pretending around everyone. I'm genuinely happy, but more than that, I'm healing.

And I have Nix to thank for that.

I want to tell him that I love him because I do, but I'm not ready yet. All I can do is hope that he means it when he says he'll wait for me. It would destroy me if my fears took this away. He may be the best thing that has ever happened to me.

*   *   *   *

On my way to the car to go to work, I get the sensation that someone is watching me. I can't shake it. I can feel eyes boring into my back. Am I being watched or is all this stress with Ryan getting to me? Not willing to take the risk, I quicken my steps. I sigh with relief when I reach my car.

I open the door and slip behind the wheel. Leaning my head back against the headrest, I take a couple deep breaths and scold myself for overreacting. God, with Nix and my brothers all stressed out, I'm becoming just as paranoid as them. I'm honestly surprised Nix left me alone to go into the shop earlier. I had to promise I would call him before I left and as soon as I got to work.

I blow out a breath and open my eyes. Staring up at the roof of my car, I let my mind wander a little. I can't seem to get my mind around the idea that Ryan would actually hurt me. Which is absurd because he has already hurt me. What is it with me always believing that there is some redeemable quality inside of him? He has proven over and over again that he doesn't deserve my concern or faith. Especially with Nix in the picture now.

Let me show you my love, baby.

His words from that night at the bar flow through my mind and I smile. I'm thankful that I didn't let my fear stop me from saying yes. But more than that, I'm thankful for Nix. It takes an incredible man to deal with all this. From my fear to my flashbacks, and add in the threats Ryan sporadically makes — Nix is my rock.

Eager to talk to him again, I turn to set my purse on the passenger seat so I can head to the bar and freeze. A small package wrapped in brown paper sits in the seat. Unease washes over me. How long has that been there? Did I even lock the doors when I got in the car? Shit, I need to be more careful. Nix, Tucker, and Trey would have a coronary if they knew I was being this careless.

My eyes dart up to the street, remembering the feeling of being watched as I made my way to my car. Scanning the area, I don't see anything weird or out of place. This only serves to make me more nervous. I lock all the doors, but it doesn't go away so I hit the lock button again. It still doesn't help. I feel trapped in this car.

With trembling hands, I reach over and pick up the small box. I recognize the shape as another jewelry box instantly and I can feel the tears welling up in my eyes. I've never wanted to be left alone so much in my life. I want nothing more than to move on and be happy again. Why can't he do that for me?

Slowly, I rip the paper off the box and my breath catches when my suspicions are confirmed. It's another jewelry box. Briefly, I debate on whether I should open it or not, but in the end, I decide to just get it over with. I take a deep breath and lift the lid. A gasp flies out of my mouth.

It's the engagement ring. I look down at the simple solitaire diamond ring nestled in the box. This ring used to mean so much to me but now it just makes my stomach churn. All I can see is pain and manipulation. My mind begins to wander again, wondering what would have happened if I hadn't left, if I would have gone through with the wedding. I shudder. Shutting the thought down immediately because the reality of it is too ugly to even consider, I lay my forehead against the top of the steering wheel.

When I open my eyes, I see the wrapping paper on the floor below me where I tossed it. I notice another piece of paper inside it. I scowl and lean down to grab it. I unfold it and read the note written there.

Roses are red,
Violets are blue,
You belong to me,
I'm coming for you.

A sob rips through my body and tears start streaming down my face. I think about the story I just told Nix a few days ago, about Ryan locking me in that room. The thought of that happening again makes the panic build. It claws at me, making it difficult to get air into my lungs. I need to run but I'm frozen here.

I need Nix.

Just as the thought crosses my mind, my phone starts vibrating in my pocket. I pull it out and breathe a little easier at Nix's face on the screen. I scramble to press the green icon as fast as I can.

"Nix," I choke out.

"Baby, what's wrong?" he asks, sounding panicked.

"I need you. And my brothers."

"Where are you, Em?"

I hear shuffling in the background and he curses.

"I'm at the apartment. Well, outside of it, actually."

The noise on the other end suddenly stops.

"Are you safe, baby?"

"Yes, I'm locked in my car."

"Shit! All right, I'm on my way, Emma. I'll be there as soon as I can. I love you." He hangs up. I take a deep breath and triple-check the locks. I just need to hang on for a little while longer. As soon as Nix is here, everything will be okay.

Chapter Nineteen
Now

I don't know how much time has passed since I talked to Nix but it feels like forever. Every little noise has me practically jumping out of my skin. Occasionally, I scan the street, trying to figure out where Ryan is. If there is one thing I've figured out, for sure, since hanging up the phone, is that Ryan is watching me. I know it.

A knock at the window scares the hell out of me. I jump and scream. Nix's face appears through the glass a second later and I sigh, clamping a hand over my heart.

"Unlock the door, baby," he instructs through the glass. I hit the unlock button and he yanks the door open.

Pulling me out of the car and into his arms, he says, "Are you okay?"

"What took you so long?" My voice is high and squeaky, full of the panic racing through me.

He scrunches up his eyebrows as he runs a hand over my cheek. "Hey, calm down. I sped the whole way here. It's only been ten minutes."

"He's here."

His eyes widen and he starts looking all around us. "Where?"

"I don't know but I know he's here."

His eyes land back on me and his gaze softens. He leans in and plants a kiss on my forehead. Closing my eyes, I soak up the feeling.

"Let's go inside the apartment and we'll figure this all out, okay?" I bite my lip, looking at the neighborhood surrounding us. "Em, don't worry. I've got you."

"Okay." I grab my bag, the ring and note inside, and we start making our way up to the apartment. Both of us are silent as we keep our eyes peeled on the area.

"Did you call my brothers?"

He squeezes me to him. "Yeah, they are on their way."

We reach the door and I hand my keys to Nix. It feels like an eternity as he unlocks the door. My mind begins to wander. Ryan has found a whole new way to torment me. I feel like this is worse. At least *with* him, I knew I wasn't safe. Now, I have no idea. Maybe he's not even here. Maybe I'm overreacting.

"Emma?" Nix's voice breaks through my panic attack and I meet his eyes. The door to the apartment is open and he is holding his hand out to me. "You okay, baby?"

"Yeah," I whisper and place my hand in his. He leads me into the apartment and over to the dining room table. He plops down on the chair next to me and grabs my hand again.

"All right, sweetheart, what happened?"

I shake my head, clearing away the fog of panic, and look into his crystal blue eyes. Everything about him gives me the strength I need and I take a deep breath.

"I was going out to my car and I just felt like someone was watching me, ya know?" He nods. "So I got in the car and this was waiting for me." I pull the ring box out of my bag and set it on the table.

"What is it?" he asks, his voice rough with contained emotion.

"My engagement ring."

The growl that comes from deep in his throat sends a shiver down my spine. "Was there anything else?"

"Yeah, this note," I answer, setting it down. He picks it up and reads it. When he's done, he slams the paper down and grinds his teeth.

"What kind of sick fuckin' game is he playing?" I hate seeing him so upset. The only thing I know to do is go to him. So I do. I climb into his lap and straddle him. As soon as his hands are on my hips, he exhales a breath. "Baby," he sighs, his deep voice breaking halfway through. I know this all has to be so hard on him. It's way more than he ever signed up for.

I cradle his face in my hands and force his eyes to mine. "I'm so sorry, Nix."

His hands tighten on my hips and he shakes his head. "No, don't do that. I would walk through fire for you, Emma. I'm only worried about you here."

Emotion chokes off my voice and makes tears well up in my eyes as I look into his eyes and find nothing but honesty. He means every word he says to me.

"I…" I start to say, *I love you,* but the words get stuck in my throat. I know he can see it in my eyes. He knows what I was trying to say to him. But I still feel awful that I can't force the words out. I feel them —

feel every single ounce of them, but for some reason I can't say them.

I'm already vulnerable.

He's my weakness and he has the ability to destroy me. If Ryan ever knew the depth of my feelings for him, I fear that Nix would be in more danger than I am. I guess, in that sense, I'm lucky. Ryan is so egotistical that it will probably never occur to him that Nix is the love of my life.

Nix's eyes soften and I do the only thing I can to show him how I feel. I pull him to me and press my lips to his. As soon as we connect, we sigh in unison. His kiss is firm, taking control, and I let him. His lips move with mine and he slips his tongue into my mouth, groaning. His hand slides into my hair and gives it a little tug so my head falls back. He kisses down my face to my neck.

"Nix," I moan.

He guides my eyes back to him. "I love you, Emma."

"Me too," I whisper and he beams before claiming my mouth again.

A knock at the door drags us apart and we just stare at each other for a second. My chest heaves as I try to catch my breath. I look down to see his doing the same.

"See something you like?"

I nod.

"Emma?" Tucker calls through the door.

"Come in!" I holler back, not moving from Nix's lap. Nix leans in and presses a whisper of a kiss against my lips just as the boys walk into the room.

"Jesus, can't you two just knock it off for five minutes?" Tucker growls. Nix's lips curl into a smile as he pulls away from me.

"No," I answer, shrugging my shoulders, and Nix's whole body shakes with laughter.

"Whatever. Why are we here?" Tucker asks, still sounding irritated.

"Sit your grumpy ass down, Tuck."

His only response is to gape at me with raised brows.

"When did you get all that sass back, Emmy?" Trey asks.

A blush creeps up my cheeks and I shrug. "I dunno." I stare down at my hands in my lap.

"Shit, sis. He didn't mean anything by it."

"I know." My voice is barely audible. I hate that I got a small piece of myself back only for it to be claimed by the self-consciousness again.

"Seriously, what's going on?" Tucker repeats and my muscles tense, remembering the reason we called them over here.

"Ryan left her another *gift*," Nix snarls, possessiveness and protectiveness dominating his voice. It does so much for me. On the one hand, it makes me feel safe, cherished, loved, and on the other, it excites me. Knowing that he feels this way about me makes me want to drag him off to the bedroom.

"What is it?" Trey asks.

I snap out of my dirty thoughts and look over to the ring box and note still sitting on the table. Trey grabs the ring while Tucker snatches the note up. I watch Tucker read it, his muscles tightening with rage the further he gets. When he finishes, he slams his hand to the table with the note underneath it.

He opens and closes his mouth as he tries to come up with something, anything, to say but I know there are no words. Ryan's notes and "gifts" are getting increasingly more disturbing. This one almost seems to be taunting me with its playful, poetic nature. It takes a moment but Trey is finally able to get the note away from Tucker. His face morphs into one of pure rage that honestly surprises me. He's spent his life chasing off my asshole boyfriends and defending me but I've never seen him *this* angry.

He lays his head in his hands and his chest expands as he takes several deep breaths. After a moment, he looks up and meets my eyes. "Why is he sending you the ring, Em?"

I freeze. My body locks up to the point of being uncomfortable as I think about telling them what I think the ring means. Telling them about how he locked me in that room and the words he said to me then. Nix's mouth brushes over my ear and I relax into him slightly.

"It's okay, Em. You can tell them. I'm right here."

Taking a deep breath, I look at my brothers, both standing, too wound up to sit still at this point. "You better sit down."

"Shit, that bad?" Trey asks, looking to Nix for confirmation. Nix just nods. Tucker growls while Trey blows out a breath and runs a hand through his hair but they both do as I ask.

"All right, out with it, Emma," Tucker says.

I go rigid again. My mind is racing, trying to find the best way to tell them something like this. The little voice, his voice, in the back of my head is telling me to keep it to myself, that they'll never understand. They'll think I'm just being overly dramatic.

"Em!" Tucker barks and my head snaps up to look at him.

"Give her a Goddamn minute, dude!" Nix's voice is like valium, taking the edge off my panic and giving me courage to tell them what I know they need to hear.

"Holy shit," Trey whispers once I finish, his eyes dropping to the floor. I'm kind of surprised by their reactions. It seems stupid now but I really expected them to call me crazy or dramatic.

"Like a motherfuckin' prisoner?" Tucker asks. I nod. "How long, baby girl?" He is staring at me, his eyes burning with a fury I've never seen in either of my brothers before.

"Um…almost twenty four hours."

Trey gasps and Tucker slams his fist into the table. I jump, my body locking up in fear on instinct.

Nix's arms tighten around me and he kisses my hair before turning to my brother and growling, "Don't do that."

"Don't do what?"

"Don't get fucking violent around her."

"Holy fuck," Tucker rasps as he finally gets what Nix is saying. "Goddamn it, Emma! You are going to tell us everything!"

"Everyone chill the fuck out!" Trey barks, making everyone turn to him in shock. "This isn't about anyone but Emma so shut the fuck up and just chill out!"

"Sorry, baby girl," Tucker mutters and Nix squeezes me closer to him.

"Em, what does the ring mean? It's not making sense to me."

"When he threw me in the room, he told me that ring meant that I was his and that he would never let me go." All three of them draw in ragged breaths and I can almost see their minds racing.

"We need help," Trey pipes up. "We are in way over our heads. We've barely scratched the surface of what this guy has done to you, Em, and it's already clear that he's insane."

"Could we go to a different precinct and report this? I mean, they didn't really do a whole lot the last time you went in there," Trey asks. All three guys look back and forth between each other.

"I don't know," Tucker says.

"I could ask my dad for help," Nix says, his voice tight and I know instantly that he's not exactly fond of the idea.

"You don't have to do that, baby." I grab his face in my hands and direct his gaze to mine. He smiles up at me and lays his hand over mine.

"Walk through fire, sweetheart," he says, reminding me of his earlier declaration. "Asking my dad for help is nothing."

"You hate it. I can tell. You don't have to do this for me. We can find another answer." He slides his fingers into my hair, curling his hand behind my head, and pulls me toward him.

His lips find my cheek and then he whispers, "I will do anything I have to do to protect you, and my dad is a really good option. Stop pushing me away and let me take care of you."

His words make me frown. Was I doing that? Maybe I was or maybe I just didn't want to drag any more of his family into this mess. What if someone gets hurt because of me?

"Baby, I can hear your brain working. Just stop and please trust me." His words melt me and I nod against his face. He releases a breath and gives me a quick peck on the lips before releasing my head.

"Wait, who is your dad?" Tucker asks.

"He's the president of the Bayou Devils," Nix says, his voice tight.

"Holy shit," Trey and Tucker say at the same time.

"We've known Moe all our lives and we never knew that your dad was a Devil?" Tucker adds.

Nix just shrugs. I get where they are coming from but Moe never really talked about his family except to say that they had a falling out.

"You don't have to do this," I whisper to him, one more time. His lips smash together as he shakes his head at me.

"Stop, Em."

"This shouldn't be your problem."

Nix stands abruptly, holding me in his arms and turns to my brothers. "Give us a minute, guys." He doesn't wait for their response as he starts carting me off to the bedroom. He tosses me on the mattress and slams the door behind him. He kneels down in front of the bed and grabs my face in his hands.

"Listen to me, I don't ever push you on anything but I'm going to push you on this. I love you and I'm not going to let this asshole anywhere near you. If that means I have to go ask my dad for help, then I will. I need you to not fight me on this. Okay?"

"I don't think that—"

"Stop! No negotiation on this, Emma. I'm not him. I'm not trying to control your life. I'm just trying to keep you safe," he growls.

I grab his hand, still holding my face, and squeeze. "I know you're not him."

His gaze softens and he presses a soft kiss to my lips. He pulls away and looks at me with pleading eyes. "Don't fight me, Em. Just let me take care of you."

"Okay."

He releases a huge breath and looks down. I run my fingers through his hair and he hums in response.

"Thank you, baby," he whispers. "I love you."

"Me too." He looks up at me, smiling, and kisses me again.

*   *   *   *

Meeting Nix's dad, Blaze, was a lot different than I thought it would be. From everything I heard, I expected this hard, unforgiving biker. Instead, he actually reminded me a lot of Moe. Tough looking on the outside but a teddy bear on the inside. Unless, of course, you messed with someone he cared about, which apparently now includes me.

The nerves hit as soon as I heard him pull up on his motorcycle, the pipes roaring from a mile away. He was just as tall and broad as both Nix and Moe, making me realize that it must just run in the family. He had long dark hair and Nix's blue eyes.

We all sat down and enjoyed dinner before getting into the heavy stuff. He listened as I explained as much as I could get through before breaking down. I noticed the pride in his eyes as Nix scooped me up and finished telling his dad all that he knew. Blaze's immediate response is that he and the boys would just "take care" of Ryan. It didn't take a genius to connect the dots.

I flinched in Nix's lap and told him I didn't want anyone getting in trouble because of me. He seemed irritated but agreed. Before he left, he said that he would send guys over to watch over us. Sure enough, an hour later, two guys rode up on motorcycles and started standing guard outside my apartment.

"Should I go ask them if they want some food or something?" I feel bad that they are just going to spend all night outside on guard detail because of me. Maybe we're all blowing this out of proportion.

"Naw, babe. I just asked 'em. They're all good." I purse my lips and twist my fingers together as I look back at my front door. "Emma, what's wrong?" Nix walks up to me and pulls my hands apart so he can hold them.

"I just feel bad that they are stuck out there because of me."

"Don't. They are here to keep you safe and besides, if they were in here then I couldn't do this," he says, sealing his lips over mine. I moan and melt into him almost instantly. He pulls back and smiles. "Gotta say, I love when you do that, sweetheart."

"What?"

"When you just melt into me like that."

"I can't help it," I tell him. "You do crazy things to me."

His eyebrows quirk up and a smile stretches across his lips. "Oh yeah? Like what?"

"Like you make my heart practically beat out of my chest and my entire body tingles anytime you're near. You make me feel your love. Words don't mean much to me anymore if actions don't back them up and you somehow know that. You just know that I need to see your feelings for me instead of just hear them. But the best thing is that you make me feel safe — in every way."

His eyes are soft as he looks at me with so much love and devotion that I risk melting into him again. He places another quick kiss on my lips before pulling me into his arms and squeezing me to him. Now that he's not distracting me, my thoughts float back to Ryan and I wonder again if we're making too big of a deal out of this.

"Nix?"

"Yeah, babe."

"Do you think maybe we're overreacting to this whole Ryan thing?"

His body tenses and he pulls away to look at my face. Just as he's opening his mouth to say something, my phone rings on the kitchen counter. Now it's my turn to tense up because I recognize the ringtone. It's like a sign from God.

When I got myself a new phone, I still made sure to program Ryan's number in there with a special ringtone so I would know to never answer the call.

"Whose ringtone is that, baby?" From the tone of his voice, I know he knows the answer. He just needs me to say it. The better question is, how the hell did Ryan get my new number?

"Ryan's"

He clenches his jaw and releases me, marching over to my phone, intent on answering it.

"No! Don't!"

He stops and turns to me with wide eyes. "Why?"

"If he leaves a voicemail, it will be more evidence."

He studies me for a moment, seeming to think it over before nodding just as the ringing stops. A minute later, it beeps with the notification for the voicemail.

"You want me to play it, sweet girl?"

My face must show my fear as I try to steel myself in preparation for hearing his voice. I nod and then he scoops up my phone, messing with it for a couple seconds before Ryan's voice fills the room.

"What the fuck, Emma? You a little biker slut now? Did you forget who you belong to? He may get you for now but I'll find a way to get you back. We're meant to be together. See you soon."

Silence fills the room and I grab the back of the couch to brace myself as I gasp for air. Tears well up in my eyes. I haven't heard his voice since that night in the bar so long ago and hearing it now makes me feel weak.

Why can't he just leave me alone? That's all I want. It's not asking much. Nix crosses the room to me and scoops me up in his arms. He carries me over to the couch and sits down with me in his lap.

"Shhh, sweetheart. You're going to be okay." He rubs his hand over my back gently. "I won't let him get you. Do you trust me?"

"Of course I trust you, Nix."

"I love you so much, Emma. I'll die before I'll let him anywhere near you."

"Don't say that. I need you."

A slow smile spreads across his face. "You do, huh?"

"Yes."

He pulls me into him tighter and just holds me close to his body. "I love you, baby."

"Me too."

Chapter Twenty
Now

I wake from another nightmare with a start and sigh as I realize that I am safe, in my bed. I sink back into my pillow.

"Good morning, baby girl," Nix whispers as he rolls toward me and wraps his arm around my belly.

"Hey, handsome. How did you sleep?" Turning to him, I push my dream to the back of my mind.

"I always sleep great when I'm with you."

"Mmm, me too."

"I wanted to talk to you about something," he prompts and opens his eyes, watching me carefully. I instantly feel nervous.

"Okay…what's up?"

"What do you think about moving in with me?" My eyes pop open in surprise and I just stare at him, unable to say anything. "Shit, babe," he curses. "Just forget I said anything, okay?"

I shake my head, partially to clear my thoughts and partially to reassure him. After the initial shock, I'm not so freaked out about it but I'm not sure I'm ready to say *yes* either. "Let me think about it, okay?"

He nods. "Absolutely. You take all the time you need, baby."

I make a promise to myself in that moment that I can't move in with him until I can say the words I know he's dying to hear.

"I have a surprise for you, baby," Nix whispers in my ear. He steps up behind me so that his front is pressed firmly against my back, and I lean into him, my eyelids fluttering closed at his warmth.

"Oh yeah? What kind of surprise?"

His arms snake around my waist and he nuzzles into my neck. He plants a kiss there and says, "A secret one. Come on."

He grabs the mail out of my hand and sets it down on the counter. Putting his hands over my eyes, he begins guiding me through the apartment, whispering in my ear to help direct me. His warm breath washes over my bare shoulders and a shiver winds its way down my spine.

We finally stop and he pulls his hands away from my face as he says, "Surprise."

Blinking in surprise, I look around my spare bedroom that houses all my art supplies, which have been unpacked. "I don't understand."

"You're going to paint." He nods toward the easel with a fresh canvas on it.

Apprehension fills me. I want to paint so badly that my body is twitching to reach out and grab that brush but I don't think I could handle not being able to finish another one. "No, Nix. I can't." My voice cracks. I start stumbling back, trying to get away and save myself the heartache but his arms lock around me.

"Do you trust me, Em?" He presses up against my back and despite my reluctance, I melt into him just like I always do. He calms me.

"With my life." It's really not even a question. I trust him more than I've ever trusted anyone. He knows things I've never told anyone else.

"Fuck, baby. You can't say shit like that 'cause now all I want to do is forget about painting and make you deal with this." He rubs his hard cock up against my ass.

I release a soft moan and whisper, "With my life," fighting a smile the whole time.

"Jesus," he sputters out on a laugh. "You're such a fuckin' smart ass sometimes, you know that?"

"I could be worse. I *used* to be worse." His hands tighten on my hips.

"Right. That's why we're here. Time to get a piece of you back, Emma."

I eye the canvas in front of me, fear and intense nervousness running through my body, leaving me rigid. "I...I don't know if I can, Nix."

"Shhh, sweetheart. I'm going to help you, okay?"

"Nix..." I start but I don't know what else to say. The last time I was this anxious I was still living with Ryan. Not that I think Nix would do anything to hurt me but I'm so afraid of getting my hopes up again. I miss painting. I don't feel like myself without it.

"The problem isn't your talent, baby. It's your head and I'm going to help you get out of your own way. Just give it a try, okay?"

Putting my faith in him, I nod my head and say, "Okay."

"I've got all your colors laid out for you already." He points to a piece of cardboard with globs of paint on it. My eyebrow quirks up when I see the colors he's chosen — red, pink, purple, gray and black.

What is he up to?

"Trust me, baby." Taking a deep breath, I nod again. With his hands on my hips, he positions us in front of the easel. "Pick a color, Em." My body is still tense but I listen to him and dip my paintbrush in the red glob of paint.

"Good, sweetheart. Now, close your eyes." My brow knits in confusion and I try to turn around in his arms to look at him. His hands tighten on his hips. "Close your eyes, Emma." I suck in a breath and do as he says, curiosity starting to override my trepidation. "Just *feel*, Em. Feel me." One hand leaves my hip and slides across my lower belly.

"What are you doing?" I can't stop my eyes from opening.

"Such a stubborn woman," he mutters, almost to himself. "Close your eyes, Emma, and don't open them until I say so."

I growl in frustration but listen to his instructions. His lips meet the skin on my neck as he lays kisses down the side and pulls me back into his hips. A moan slips past my lips. He kisses back up my neck to nip at my ear and my body bows against him.

"Nix."

"That's it, baby. Don't think, just feel."

I do my best to turn my mind off and just feel him. His hand slips under the material of my tank top and my breath hitches.

"You feel me, Em?"

"Yes."

"Good, now open your eyes and paint." His words startle me and my eyes pop open. Again, I try to turn but his hands lock on my hips again. "No, baby. Don't think. Just feel and paint."

I try to listen to him but my mind is racing again and I can't help the doubts that fill me. "Nix, I can't."

"Okay. We'll start again. Close your eyes, Emma."

Now that I know his plan, I close my eyes immediately and wait for his touch. He doesn't disappoint. His hand slips under my tank top again and he moves it up to cup my breast. When his thumb brushes over my nipple, my breath stutters and a shiver races through my body.

"Nix," I moan.

"Okay, now paint, Em." He kisses just behind my ear. My eyes pop open and my mind completely blanks out as I raise my paintbrush to the canvas and begin painting. "Good, baby. Keep going," he coos in my ear, kissing down my neck again. Goose bumps break out over my body and I press my hips back into him. His touch grows firmer as he rubs his solid length into me.

Before long, my brush is flying across the piece and I realize that it's working. It's not a huge piece and it's not anything that I carefully planned out but I am painting.

Nix slides his hand from my breast down to the band of my shorts, slipping under it and finally stopping between my legs. His fingers swirl over my clit and my eyes drift shut as I drop my head back onto his shoulder and moan. The brush stops moving as I just soak up his touch.

His hand disappears from my body and I cry out in frustration. "As long as you're painting, I'll keep touching you."

"Do you have any idea how hard this is?" I'm all but stomping my foot at him. He chuckles at me.

"Paint, Emma."

The command in his voice should make me freeze up, should turn me off and bring up my past, but it doesn't. Not even close. That authoritative tone makes me feel hot. Makes me crave his touch even more than I did before. I begin painting again, needing his hands on me. As soon as the brush begins stroking over the canvas, I get my reward.

His hand slips under the band of my shorts again and he slides two fingers inside me. I moan loudly and my legs shake. I do my best to keep painting but between him sliding his fingers in and out of me and his lips kissing a trail up my neck, I'm barely getting by.

"You're so beautiful." His warm breath rushes over my ear. My teeth sink into my lip and I have to fight to keep my eyes open. "Inside and out," he continues. "I've never met a girl like you. You are kind." Lips press against the skin behind my ear and my breath stutters. "Sweet and smart." Teeth sink into my earlobe and my fingers tighten on the paintbrush. "And funny and everything I never even knew I needed."

"Nix," I moan as his words bring tears to my eyes.

"And so incredibly strong, baby. I love you so much." I moan again and he bites my earlobe a little harder. "Don't stop painting."

Growling, this time in frustration, I keep gliding my brush across the canvas and he pumps into me faster.

"Yes." I sigh, feeling the orgasm build inside me. He groans, burying his head in my neck. He rocks his hips against my ass, rubbing himself on me. He pants into my neck, short little bursts of air rushing over my sensitized skin.

"Don't stop painting."

This time I nod. His other hand dips into my shorts and starts rubbing my throbbing clit. I grind into his hands, my brushstrokes growing harsher and more dramatic with each swipe of his talented fingers.

When my release crashes over me, I throw my head back and the paintbrush slaps against the canvas before trailing off. I sigh and relax into him.

"Do you want to stop or do you want to finish it?" He nuzzles into my hair.

Opening my eyes, I gaze at the piece for a minute. I'm actually quite impressed with it. It's certainly abstract but the whole thing looks sensual. The lines and curves of each brushstroke reveal my feelings while I was painting and I can see my release building as I stare at it. It just needs a little bit more to finish it off.

"Give me like an hour, okay?"

His lips stretch into a grin against my neck. "You got it, sweetheart." He kisses along my throat up to my cheek before leaving me to finish my first painting in over a year.

*   *   *   *

"Hey, Em, it's gettin' late. Are you about done?" Nix asks, poking his head into the room. He just has on a pair of black, mesh workout shorts. My eyes trail down his stomach, taking in every single inch of his defined abs and locking onto the *V* leading into his shorts. "Emma?"

"Huh?" My gaze snaps back up to his face. He chuckles and nods his head to the canvas behind me.

"Is it done?"

I twirl back around and stare at the piece again. I added in some more color and made everything flow together.

"Yeah, I think so."

Nix comes up behind me and wraps his arms around my waist. "It's amazing, babe. Makes me want to fuck you." A shiver races through my body.

"That's just 'cause you know what you were doing while it was being painted."

"Naw. It just looks…hot. You should hang it up in your bedroom."

I laugh and relax into him. "I'll take that under advisement."

"Told you that you could do it, Em."

I turn in his arms and wrap my arms around his neck. Smiling up at him, I say, "You gave me my art back." I can't even explain half the emotions coursing through me right now. I'm so proud of myself and grateful to Nix for pushing me to do this. I feel more like the old me than I ever have. Art was a huge part of me and without it, I just wasn't the same.

Nix returns my smile and kisses my cheek. "I just got Ryan out of your head for a little while, baby."

"That might be even better!"

He laughs loudly and holds me against him tighter. "I'm glad, sweetheart." Leaning down, he presses his lips against mine, a sweet kiss that makes my heart expand with love. When he pulls away, he rests his forehead against mine and asks, "Are you ready for bed?"

"Yeah, I guess."

He gives me another quick kiss before turning to leave the room, thinking I'll follow behind him.

"Nix...I love you," I blurt out.

He freezes for a second before turning to face me. His eyes are wide but there is a smile slowly curling his lips.

"What?" He's gonna make me say it again.

"I love you."

All I get is a flash of teeth before he's marching over to me, wrapping his arms around my waist, and hoisting me up in the air. He smashes his lips to mine in a no-holds-barred kiss that steals the breath from my lungs. Everything happened so quickly that I don't even have time to think until I'm in his arms, legs dangling off the ground, his mouth bruising mine.

It takes my body less than a second to catch up and I loop my arms around his neck, kissing him back with as much intensity. My legs wrap around his waist and he groans, pushing me up against the wall. His hand threads through my hair as he grinds into me.

I break away, panting and moan, "Nix."

He growls. Setting me back on my feet, he wastes no time ripping the tank top over my head and shoving my shorts down my legs. I'm suddenly glad that I didn't put panties on earlier because I need him. Now. When I'm completely naked, he quickly pushes his own shorts and boxer briefs down his legs and kicks them off.

He picks me back up and my legs encircle his hips again. I'm slammed back against the wall with a little more force, his erection rubbing against my core. A low, seductive moan slips out of me and Nix is kissing me again. One hand gripping my hair and the other squeezing my ass, he rubs me against him.

"Baby," I plead with him. I don't know how much longer I can stand the torture. I need him inside me. He rips his mouth from mine and starts kissing down my neck. He hooks an arm under each of my legs and grabs my ass as he pins me to the wall. He lines his cock up with my entrance and plunges into me.

He's so deep in this position and my muscles flex around his hard length. The move draws a groan from him and his hips begin moving, thrusting into me at a punishing pace. It's so animalistic, so primal. Like he's claiming me, marking me as his for the rest of the world to see. Who knew saying those three little words I've been avoiding would result in some of the best sex I've ever had?

"Phoenix," I moan when his teeth sink into the skin on my neck. I run my fingers through his dark hair and give it a little tug, causing his head to drop back. Just as I'm moving in to slam my mouth back to his, he lets out a growl and drives into me harder.

"Holy fuck." It comes out as more of a growl and I love it. With both his hands occupied, I'm able to control this kiss and he takes everything I'm giving. I've never felt so wild, never needed someone this much in my life. Pressure begins to build inside me and I clench around him again. He latches onto my bottom lip with his teeth as he groans loudly.

"Shit, baby." His words are barely understandable with all the panting and grunting. He thrusts into me harder. I'm dangling right there on the edge, needing just a little more to fall off the cliff. He leans in and bites my neck again. That's all it takes. My body locks up around him as fireworks explode behind my eyes. I throw my head back and call out his name.

His grip on my ass tightens and he slams into me, panting against my neck. Only a moment later, I feel him swell and release inside me before his body goes lax and he has to slide to the floor. He doesn't pull out of me and he doesn't move me off him. He just hugs me to him as hard as he can without cutting off my air.

"Say it again, baby," he prompts, pulling away to look at my face. A satisfied smirk spreads across his face.

"I love you, Nix."

"Mmm, I love you, Emma."

*   *   *   *

"Baby, there's paint in your hair." He laughs, pointing to the top of my head as we lie on the floor of the spare bedroom wrapped up in each other's arms. We've been here for the past hour just talking and laughing about everything. My cheeks hurt from smiling so much.

"Yeah, well, you've got some on your face." I scoop a red blob of paint off his cheek with my finger.

"God, I love you." He smiles, running his knuckles gently down my cheek. My eyes flutter closed at his touch and I lean into him.

"I love you, too."

He leans in, presses his lips to mine. He kisses me slowly, chasing every single thought from my head. When his tongue pushes past my parted lips, I sigh. He pulls away and kisses my forehead before tucking me back into his arm.

"I think I'm the happiest man alive right now."

"Naw, it's just all the sex going to your head."

He laughs, shaking my entire body. I love watching him laugh like this but more than that, I love knowing that I made him laugh like this. It's a happiness unlike anything I've ever experienced.

"Come on, dirty girl, let's go take a shower."

"Okay."

He stands up next to me. Extending his hand, he pulls me up and into his arms. He doesn't say anything, just kisses my head. In the next second, I am being scooped up in his arms and I squeal. He chuckles and heads for our bathroom.

My thoughts come to a screeching halt as I realize that I just referred to it as our bathroom. His request to move in has been on my mind pretty much every day since he asked. On the one hand, I really do want to move in with him and we have practically been living together for damn near three months. On the other hand, there is still a large part of me that is really nervous at the thought of moving in with him. It's not that I think Nix would ever hurt me because I know that he wouldn't but what if it ruins our relationship.

I love him so much. What would I do if I lost him? Is it too much pressure to put on our relationship at this point on top of all the Ryan stuff? Nix sets me down in the bathroom and turns on the water as my mind keeps spinning, going back and forth between my two options.

"Em?"

My head snaps up and I meet his eyes. "Huh?"

"Water's ready." He points to the shower behind him and I want to smack myself on the head. God, I really get lost in my own little world sometimes. "You okay?" He frowns, concern marring his handsome face.

"Yeah, I'm good." I wave my hand through the air as if to brush off his worry. I step into the walk-in shower and he follows, shutting the door behind him. Arms wrap around my waist and he kisses my neck as the hot water beats down my front. It doesn't take long for me to fall back into my thoughts from earlier. It's like a tennis match in my head. I go back and forth, deciding something and then changing my mind a second later.

Nix tenses behind me. "Em, what's wrong?"

"Nothing."

He spins me so fast that I don't even have time to react. He tilts my face up to his and uses his thumb to pull my bottom lip out of my teeth.

"Talk to me, sweetheart. I can practically see steam shooting out of your ears."

"I was just thinking about your request to move in together."

His eyebrows shoot up and he looks down at me, waiting for me to continue. When I don't, he says, "And?"

"I don't want to screw this up with you." My teeth sink back into my lip as I wait for whatever he's going to say next. He scowls at me, searching my face for something.

"Baby, there is absolutely nothing you could do that would make you screw this up. I love you."

"I love you, too."

He gives me a full smile that reaches his eyes and I can't help my own grin from forming on my face.

"Why do you think you would mess this up?"

"I don't know. What if it's too soon? What if living together ruins what we have?" I can see him fighting back a chuckle and it pisses me off. He holds his hands up in front of him and I curse myself for giving away exactly what I'm thinking again.

"I'm sorry, Em, but we are already living together. Just not officially."

"Yeah, but if we get in a fight, you could go home. What are you going to do if there is nowhere else to go? What if you need a break from all this Ryan shit?"

"Sweetheart, there isn't much of a chance that I will leave you anywhere until that sick son of a bitch is behind bars or dead."

I huff in annoyance and grit my teeth. "What if you get mad at me? Where are you gonna go if you can't leave?"

"I'll go to another room and take a chill pill. Why are you picking a fight with me right now, Em?"

As soon as he says it, I realize that is exactly what I'm doing. Why? Am I trying to test him right now? What the hell is wrong with me? Tears well up in my eyes and I drop my head.

"Shit, baby. I didn't mean to make you cry." He panics and wraps me up in his strong arms.

"You didn't make me cry!" I yell at him through the tears that are now pouring down my cheeks.

"Then why are you, Emma?"

My hands ball up into fists and I smack them against his chest.

"'Cause I'm awful and I feel bad. I don't know what's wrong with me right now."

He shushes me and runs his hand over my wet hair as he holds me tightly against his body.

"Hey, it's okay. Let's just drop it for now. We don't need to make a decision right this second. I'll wait forever for you, baby." More guilt fills me and I start sobbing. "Jesus, what did I say?"

"You shouldn't have to wait around for me! You should just go find a nice normal girl who can give you everything you need."

"Emma, baby, I love you but what the fuck are you talkin' about right now? You are everything I need. I only want these things with you."

I shake my head against his chest. "You could find someone so much better."

His arms squeeze me and he snaps. "Emma! Listen to me, stop doing this. I want you, baby." He takes a deep breath and runs his fingers through my hair. His muscles relax as he does it so I just let him.

261

After a second, he sighs and kisses the top of my head. "You know what I think?"

"Huh?"

"I think maybe this stuff with that douchebag is really starting to get to you, yeah?"

"Maybe," I agree, nodding my head.

"Just relax, sweetheart. We will move in together when the time is right. Don't stress so much, okay?"

Before I can say anything, I hear Tucker and Trey calling for us from the living room. We both sigh at the same time and I start to giggle.

"I so planned on this shower going a little differently." At the disgruntled look on his face, I giggle some more. "Just a minute!" he yells to my brothers as he turns me to face the showerhead again.

"Hurry! It's important!"

Dread immediately washes over me and Nix's hands clench my shoulders. Whatever is out there waiting for us, it's not going to be good.

Chapter Twenty-One
Now

Nix and I make our way into the living room ten minutes later to find my brothers lounging on the couch watching football. When they see us, Trey turns the T.V. off and sits up. Nix settles onto the love seat and pulls me into his lap.

"All right, what's the big emergency?"

My brothers share a look of trepidation that's really starting to irritate me. I swear, every time I see them it's stressful. Tucker clears his throat and I direct my attention to him.

"So, we were just coming over to hang out, Em, but when we pulled up in front of your apartment, I saw Ryan sitting in his car. He was just staring at your window."

Nix's body instantly tenses up. "Where the fuck are the guys?"

"They're outside in the hallway but they can't see the street from where they are. Ryan's very good at not being caught."

"Jesus," Nix growls, pinching the bridge of his nose between his fingers.

My gaze drifts to the window between my living room and kitchen that faces the street. Muscles all throughout my body tense as I think about him down there, watching me. Nix wraps his arms around my waist and squeezes, trying to reassure me.

"He drove off before we could grab him and kick the shit out of him but then Trey found this on your windshield." Tucker holds a piece of paper out to me and I look at it like a snake that might bite me. Familiar feelings of fear start to work their way through my body as I remember his last note to me. One that was so dark despite the fact that it was practically a nursery rhyme.

When I don't reach out and grab it, Nix does. He slowly unfolds the paper and holds it out so both of us can read it.

Blood is Red,
Bruises are Blue,
It's time for you to pay,
I'm coming for you.

Nix makes a choking sound behind me but I'm frozen. All I can do is stare at the words scribbled on the page, my mind racing a hundred miles an minute. This doesn't make sense. These words don't seem like Ryan. Even at his worst, he was never this obvious. Then again, it makes perfect sense for Ryan.

It's time for you to pay.

He's mad. Furious that I am with Nix and that must be what's driving his actions now. At least, for the most part. He has always said that I was his, and that he would never let me go. I think that is still there but now it's just intensified by the fact that Nix and I took our relationship to the next level.

"Em?" Trey croaks and my eyes snap up to his. Both Tucker and Trey look ready to commit murder, and I'm sure Nix is sporting a similar face. I glance down and read the note twice more, trying to figure out where Ryan's head is at.

"Emma, you gotta say something, baby."

I slowly shake my head back and forth. Maybe it's stupid or crazy of me to think this, but I just feel like this escalated so quickly. I can't wrap my brain around it.

"I...he...what the hell is happening?"

Nix pulls me into him and just holds me. It does help me clear my mind and breathe a little easier. Holding me seems to calm him, too. His shoulders relax and he takes a deep breath.

"Did you guys read it?" I peek up at my brothers from Nix's hold.

"Yeah, Emmy, we read it," Tucker grits out.

One question keeps running through my mind: what the hell are we going to do? I'm scared now. Terrified. And I don't know how to keep myself and the ones I love safe.

"I think maybe we should go to the police." I'm musing to myself more than anything. I don't know what else to do here. We don't know how to handle this situation. A plan slowly begins to form in my head and I start to feel a little more confident.

"Why? They didn't do anything last time," Trey growls.

"I didn't really follow up with that. I was happy that he was finally leaving me alone."

"I don't think they'll actually help you, Em," Tucker adds and I nod.

"They probably won't but I want something on the record in case something happens to me."

Nix is tense again. "Baby, I won't let anything happen to you."

My brothers nod their heads in agreement and I sigh.

"Guys, as much as I appreciate the sentiment, something could happen to me. I know you all will do your very best to protect me but I really think it would be a good idea to have a report against Ryan, just in case."

"No, I don't like this." Nix sets me next to him on the love seat and leans forward, bracing his elbows on his knees and running his fingers through his hair.

"I agree," Tucker snaps and Trey nods. Jesus. It's impossible with these three.

"Listen to me, really listen. I think this is the best option. We know that they will probably dismiss it but they will have to investigate it. And even if they don't, I can say that I did everything I could to protect myself. We have to try everything. We need that report too. If, God forbid, something happens to me, they will have to look at Ryan first if there is a report against him."

"What makes you think they won't just ignore it again?"

"I won't let them."

"Baby, how?"

"They will have to investigate because if they don't then they are obviously covering for a cop and I'll take it as high as I need to. Right now, our evidence is mostly he said/she said. We have the pictures of me but the notes don't ever have his name on them."

"And what if you go as high up as you can and they still cover for him?"

"Then we go to the newspaper and tell them a little story about the Port Allen Police Department covering up domestic violence," I say, with a sly smile forming on my face.

"Shit! Did you two know she was so damn devious?" Nix asks my brothers, laughing.

"She hasn't been for a while," Tucker answers, with pride shining in his eyes.

"Are you sure about this, baby girl?" Tucker questions.

"Yeah, I think it's our best option."

All three of them nod, reluctantly.

"Yeah, all right," Trey finally says.

"I need all of you there tomorrow.

"We'll be there, Emmy," Tucker assures me and I take a deep breath, summoning the strength I'm going to need.

*   *   *   *

We're lying in bed after saying good-bye to my brothers, and I can't seem to turn my mind off. I'm so nervous about tomorrow and I'm wondering what happened to the other report I filed. Is it still there? What if it's not? I never considered it before but maybe I can't trust Detective Nelson.

I was incredibly stupid. I was just so happy that Ryan was finally leaving me alone that I never thought to follow up with the original report. I thought it was all over.

"Baby?"

My head turns to the side, taking in the gorgeous man next to me. He has a worried expression on his face that I hate. I wish I wasn't bringing all this ugliness into his life.

"Yeah?"

"I need you to tell me."

My body tenses and I lock eyes with him. "Tell you what?"

"Everything." His voice is barely audible, rough with the emotion he's feeling right now. "I need to hear it all."

I balk. I'm not telling him this. I don't even know if I can. "No."

He turns on his side to face me and offers an encouraging smile while he strokes my face with his big hand.

"Baby, I've got to know what I'm gonna hear tomorrow. I can't hear all that for the first time in that interrogation room."

I watch him carefully. He's got a point. It would be unfair of me to ask him to live through all that with me in front of total strangers. When I don't say anything, he scoots closer and kisses my forehead.

"Whatever you tell me won't change the way I feel about you. I just think it might be a good idea for you to tell the story before tomorrow."

Damn it, he's got a point.

"I...I..."

"Shhh, sweetheart. I know it will be hard but I'm right here and I'm not going anywhere. I love you."

I watch him, my brain working at a furious pace and finally, I nod.

"Okay."

Chapter Twenty-Two
Then…

"Baby!" Ryan yells as soon as he comes in the door Friday evening.

"In here," I call from the bedroom and he stomps down the hallway. He busts through the door with a huge smile on his face. I raise a brow at him.

"Get dressed. We're going out!" he exclaims and I scowl.

"Ryan, I have to go to work, I was just getting ready to leave," I say and the smile immediately drops off his face.

"Baby, I made detective! We have to celebrate."

"Oh my God! Ryan, I'm so proud of you," I squeal and jump into his arms. He laughs and kisses me quickly before setting me back on my feet.

"Okay, so go get changed!"

"Babe, I still have to go to work but I'll get someone to cover my shift tomorrow and we can go celebrate," I say, hoping to reason with him.

"What the hell, Emma?"

"I'm sorry. My shift starts in fifteen minutes. I can't call in now. We'll celebrate tomorrow."

He stares at me with hard eyes for what feels like forever before he turns and stalks out of the bedroom. I tilt my head back and close my eyes, taking deep breaths. After I feel mentally prepared to face him,

I go out in the living room. I find Ryan sitting on the couch staring at the T.V.

"I have to go." He just sits there in silence, not even sparing me a glance. "Please don't be mad, baby. I am so proud of you and I promise we are going to celebrate tomorrow."

Silence.

"I love you," I say and still get nothing. He sits like a statue, not moving, not looking at me and completely silent. I sigh, fighting back tears over him being so difficult about this. Finally giving up, I grab my keys off the entry table, and spare him one last glance before walking out the front door.

*   *   *   *

When I come home from work, Ryan looks like he just walked in the door himself. His jacket is still on and he's kicking off his shoes.

"Hey. Where did you go?" He sends a glare in my direction but doesn't say anything. "Ryan, please talk to me. I'm sorry that I had to work tonight." My apology is met with more silence as he throws himself onto the couch. "Goddamn it, Ryan. I'm tired of this shit."

"Yeah, well I'm tired of you never being able to do anything because you won't quit working at that damn bar."

I roll my eyes. I'm not having this fight with him again.

"Will you let me make it up to you?"

His eyes narrow in my direction. "How?"

"Let's do something fun tomorrow. Anything you want." He watches me closely for a moment.

"You'll spend the whole day with me?" I nod and finally, he nods in return. "Okay."

*   *   *   *

Ryan and I spent the whole day together, just like I promised. He borrowed a boat from one of his friends and we spent the day relaxing on the water. It was actually really nice. Now, I'm getting ready for dinner. I was glad that I was able to find someone to cover my shift tonight. I didn't want to have another fight with Ryan.

I finish getting ready and do a little spin in front of the mirror to inspect myself. The pale green maxi dress really plays up the color of my eyes and my peep-toe wedges give me a couple more inches. Running my finger under my eye, I fix a little bit of smudged liner before exiting the bathroom.

Not paying attention to where I'm going as I walk into the hallway, I slam right into Ryan. His arms immediately wrap around me, preventing me from falling to my ass.

"Oh, hey, I was just coming to find you," he says. "My brothers called and wanted to take me out to celebrate my promotion."

My eyes widen as I look up at him.

Is he serious?

"Uh…we have plans and I thought you saw your brothers last night?"

"No, I was out with my friends last night. We spent all day together. Besides, I've barely spent any time with my brothers since you and I got together. I'm always with you. Don't be so selfish."

I take a step back, looking at him in shock.

"Are you serious? You're going to ditch me?"

"It's not like that. I haven't seen my brothers in a really long time. Please don't start with the drama tonight."

"I just spent the last hour getting ready."

He rolls his eyes and sighs. "I see you're going to be an unreasonable bitch about this so I'm going to leave now," he says, leaning down to kiss the top of my head. "I love you, baby." With that, he turns and walks out the front door, leaving me gaping after him.

"What the fuck just happened?" I whisper to myself. Was I being unreasonable? I know he hasn't seen his family much lately but he hasn't been with me either. He's been working so much that he hasn't had time for anyone.

God…I am a bitch.

He deserves to go out and have fun. He has been working so hard lately. I shouldn't have picked a fight with him over this. Pulling out my phone, I send him a text to apologize.

Me: I'm sorry. I love you, have fun.

I plop down on the couch and stare at the blank screen of the T.V. What should I do tonight? Maybe Addy and Daisy would like to go out. Just as I'm getting ready to call them, my phone buzzes in my hand.

Ryan: Thanks, baby. I love you.

I smile at his reply, feeling like all is right in my world again. I decide to call my friends.

Hell, if he can have a night out so can I.

* * * *

The three of us strut into the bar. It's really busy tonight so we should be able to dance and have a good time. On Saturday and Sunday, Moe hires a DJ to draw in a bigger crowd, and I'm grateful for it tonight. I just want to let loose and have a little fun.

"Let's go get drinks," Daisy says and I nod in agreement before following her over to the bar. A loud wolf whistle erupts and I look up to see Moe grinning at me.

"Well, look what the cat dragged in," he says with a wink.

I just shake my head and laugh. I have to admit that I do feel great tonight in my black skinny jeans and blue strapless top. My four-inch electric blue heels giving me an extra pep in my step.

"Jesus! Are you trying to get Tucker and me arrested?" Trey asks when he sees me. I just send a wink his way. He fights a grin as he shakes his head. "Fuckin' little sisters are a pain in the ass." I burst out laughing. His lips stretch into a grin, unable to fight it any longer.

"Oh, Trey." He turns back to me. "Call Tucker and I'll post those pictures of you and Tucker playing superheroes when you were five all over Facebook," I threaten and his mouth drops to the floor. I fight back a smile as I think about the photos I just referenced. Tucker and Trey had just watched Batman and decided they needed to be superheroes so they put underwear on over their pants and tied fabric around their necks like capes.

"You wouldn't."

"Try me."

"Pain in my Goddamn ass," he mutters as he turns to grab me a beer. When he sets it on the bar, I give him my best innocent smile.

"Thanks, Trey." I see the corner of his lips quirk up as he turns away from me to hide his smile.

"Let's go dance!" Addy yells in my direction.

"Fuck me," I hear Trey grumble and I motion to Addy that I need a second.

"Trey." He glances up at me with an expectant look on his face.

"Yeah."

"If you like her," I say, motioning toward Addilyn, "then make a move." He turns bright red and looks back down at the bar top.

"Trey."

"What?" he grumbles.

I lean in close so only he can hear me and offer him an apologetic smile. "You know I love you, and FYI, she likes you too…so make a move." When I back up, his eyes are wide with shock.

"Are you serious?"

I nod and give him a thumbs up. Hopefully, he'll take my advice. I would love to see my friends happy.

I join Addy and Daisy on the dance floor and we really start getting into it. We are all laughing and having a good time when a hand closes over my arm. I turn to tell whomever it is to leave me alone when I come face-to-face with a very pissed off Ryan. His grip on my arm tightens and I wince from the pain shooting up my arm.

"What the fuck do you think you're doing?" he spits, right in my ear.

I try to pull away but he only grips me harder. A whimper of pain escapes me. "What are you talking about?"

"We're leaving."

What is going on? Feeling terrified of what is going to happen if we leave this crowded bar, I shake my head.

"I don't want to go."

His angry gaze feels like it's burning a hole through me and he begins pulling me to the exit. At the exact moment, Trey comes up to us, looking every bit the protective older brother that he is.

"You need to let her go," he demands, his voice like steel. I've never heard him sound like this before.

"This doesn't concern you," Ryan snaps and Trey clenches his fists. I look around and realize that almost everyone is staring at us. Embarrassment floods me. I can't believe this is happening right now. I need to get Ryan out of here. Once we get home, I can apologize and he won't be so angry.

"Trey, it's okay," I whisper, my voice shaky and unconvincing. "Baby, let's go," I say, turning to Ryan.

"Emma, no!"

I shake my head at my brother. "I'm fine, Trey." I wrap my free arm around him and give him a hug. "See you tomorrow."

As soon as I release him, I am being tugged out the door of the bar. Ryan drags me around to the passenger side of his car and practically throws me in before slamming the door. I look out the windshield to see Trey, Addy, and Daisy watching the scene unfold with a myriad of expressions on their faces. Trey stares murderously at Ryan but when he looks at me, I see fear staring back at me. Addy and Daisy both have expressions of concern, neither one taking their eyes away until the car is out of sight.

Now, I'm stuck here with a Ryan that I don't know, that scares the crap out of me.

*   *   *   *

We've been home for thirty minutes and haven't said a word. It's so quiet in here that I can hear my heart race. I haven't been able to relax as I wait for Ryan to say or do something. Finally, it becomes unbearable.

"Will you please talk to me?"

Ryan turns to me slowly. When our eyes meet, there isn't a single thing I recognize there.

"What is there to say?" he asks, voice calm. It contradicts the tension threatening to drown me and a shiver runs through my body. The hairs on my arms raise and I feel like a cornered animal.

"Ryan, I didn't do anything. I was just dancing with my friends," I try to reason with him.

"YOU DIDN'T DO ANYTHING?" He shoots up off the couch and I flinch. "YOU THINK IT'S OKAY TO GO AROUND ACTING LIKE A TOTAL SLUT? MY FRIENDS WERE THERE! THEY CALLED ME!"

"I wasn't acting like a slut!"

Wrong move. His hand flies out and connects with my cheek. I gasp as tears fill my eyes, my face stinging.

"Shut up, you bitch! I saw you, that kind of dancing belongs in a strip club!"

"Well, you would know," I mumble before I even think about it. My eyes widen as I look up at Ryan.

Shit.

His eye twitches as he glares at me.

"What did you say?" he growls and I shake my head.

"Nothing."

The next thing I know, his hand is gripping my jaw and forcing my gaze to his.

"Don't lie to me."

I struggle to free myself from his hold but he only grips me tighter.

"Let me go."

His fingers press deeper into my skin and I cry out in pain. I swat at his hand and he releases my jaw to grab both wrists, squeezing so hard that he cuts off the circulation.

"Do you see what you're making me do to you? If you would just tell me the truth and stop fighting me, this wouldn't happen!"

"Let me go!" I scream, getting right up in his face, tears running down my cheeks.

"Do you even love me? Do you care that you embarrassed me? How could you do this to me? I give you everything! All I want to do is love you and take care of you but you won't let me, and you force me to do this!"

"Let me go!"

"Fuck this! God, you are so mean to me. I don't even know why I put up with you anymore. No other man would want you!" He finally releases me and takes a step back. "I'll be in the bedroom. When you decide that you are ready to stop being a spoiled brat and apologize to me, you can come find me."

With that, he turns and marches out of the room. As soon as I hear the door close, I fall to the floor, tearless sobs filling the room. I rub my wrists, gasping for breath as I try to come up with a plan. I've never felt so trapped in my life.

What happened? Where is the man I love? Where is the man that loves me? When I get my breathing back under control, I glance up at the front door.

Yes!

That's what I'll do. I just leave for the night, give us both a chance to cool off and then we can talk about this tomorrow. I get up off the floor and notice that Ryan's keys aren't hanging in their usual spot. I glance around the room as I hop around, trying to get my shoes on, and finally see them on the floor by the kitchen.

Oh yeah…he threw them at the wall.

I make my way over to them and flinch when I pick them up and they jingle. I creep to the door as quietly as I can and turn the lock.

"Where do you think you're going?" Ryan snarls from behind me as I pull the door open.

I jump and let out a small cry of surprise. Fight or flight kicks in and I throw the screen door open, praying I make it to the car before he catches me. Even as I'm doing it, I know I'm screwed.

A scream rips out of my body when Ryan's arms wrap around my stomach and he hoists me up in the air.

"Shut up." He carts me back into the house. He doesn't release me until we're back in the bedroom. He throws me across the room and I land with a thud on the floor. I glance up at him with tears pouring down my face as he advances on me. He grabs my face again and pulls me up so we're nose to nose. "You think you get to leave me?"

"I wasn't…" I start to say but stop when his fist connects with my stomach, knocking the wind out of me.

"Don't you dare lie, you little whore. You need to apologize."

I look up at him and try to force the words out but they feel so wrong. I didn't do anything wrong. Why should I apologize to him? Slowly, I shake my head, watching the rage build in his eyes.

"No?" he asks.

I shake my head again. With his hand still firmly holding my face, he pulls my head away from the wall and slams it back into the drywall. I gasp at the pain that radiates through my skull.

"No?" he repeats.

What will he do if I refuse? Will he continue to slam my head into the wall? His fingers dig into my jaw and my mouth pops open.

"You're hurting me," I whisper, my voice scratchy and unrecognizable. He moves in closer, his breath wafting over my face.

"Don't you see? You make me do this. If you really loved me, you would do what you're told. Now, apologize."

"I'm sorry." Fear and guilt have me submitting to him.

He releases me immediately then steps back. My knees give out and I collapse to the floor. Without another word, he gets into bed and turns away from me. I gingerly stand and walk over to my side of the bed. As I pull the covers back and slide under them, I know that what he said is true. If I had just listened then none of this would have happened. Another part of me wonders when the hell I became so weak.

Chapter Twenty-Three
Then...

Ryan is already gone for work by the time I wake up the next morning and I breathe a small sigh of relief. I didn't sleep well last night and the last thing I need to deal with today is more fighting. I throw back the covers and swing my legs over so I'm sitting on the side of the bed. My body is incredibly sore and achy.

Finally working up the energy to get out of bed, I make my way to the bathroom. I flinch when I turn on the light and look in the mirror. Dark purple bruises line my jaw where Ryan grabbed me last night. When I raise my hand to inspect the marks on my face, I see marks on my wrists also. My ribs ache where he punched me and my head is pounding.

Sighing, I leave the bathroom and go back into the bedroom. I know Ryan didn't mean to hurt me. If I had just listened to him, this wouldn't have happened. I can be so stubborn sometimes. I know this. I need to do better. It's not fair to Ryan.

With a renewed resolve to do what it takes to make this relationship work, I jump in the shower and wash away the stress of yesterday. I dress and am brushing my hair, when there's a knock at the door.

I look at myself in the mirror and know that I am not going to answer that door. I'm certain it's one of my friends and if they see the bruises, they will freak.

They'll jump to conclusions before I can explain that it was an accident.

I'm so lost in thought that I don't hear the door unlock or Addy and Trey walking into my room.

"I'm going to fuckin' kill him," Trey yells, snapping me out of my thoughts.

I turn toward them and blush, embarrassment overwhelming me. Trey looks like he is about to pull his hair out as he paces back and forth and Addy looks at me with tears in her eyes.

"Sweetie," she says, reaching for my hand. She gasps when she sees the bruises decorating my wrist and Trey is immediately at her side. He makes a pained sound as he delicately runs his fingers over my wrist.

"Guys, it's okay. It was an accident."

Trey's eyes bug out of his head and he resumes his pacing as Addy gives me a look of pity.

"Em, it's okay. You don't have to cover for him anymore," she consoles.

I shake my head. "I'm not covering for him. It was an accident. He didn't mean to hurt me."

Trey explodes. "Are you serious right now?" Addy goes over to him and places her hand on his arm. They share a look and Trey nods at her.

"Sweetie, come sit down. I want to show you something," she says, patting the bed.

Giving in, I walk over and sit down. Trey moves to the other side, sitting so close our legs are touching. He wraps his arm around my shoulders and I shoot him a perplexed look, he just smiles in return.

"Okay, so I found this article and I want you to read it," Addy says as she digs around in her bag. She pulls out several pieces of paper, folded up, and hands them to me. I unfold them and scan the title: "Am I being emotionally abused?"

I look back up at her.

"Seriously, Addy? This is crazy!"

"Just please read the article, Em."

Trey gives my shoulders a squeeze. I sigh and pick the paper back up. I begin reading, feeling like this is a joke. But the further I get, the harder it is to breathe. When I finally reach the end, tears are filling my eyes.

"There is a checklist on the next page," she informs me, and I quickly flip to the next page. When I'm finally done reading, I'm gasping for breath. Trey is rubbing soothing circles on my back and Addy is saying comforting things to me.

I can check off every single box on this list.

A light bulb has been switched on inside me. I feel like a completely different person than I was even ten minutes ago and I know I can never go back. It's like there is a deep gorge running through me. On one side is the bright, spunky girl I used to be and on this side is this broken, abused woman.

Abused.

Ack! I hate the word. I can't even force myself to say it. Staring longingly at the other side of the gorge, all I want is to go back. How did this happen to me? I should have seen the signs. Why didn't I realize? How could I let him treat me like this? I'm not stupid. I should have known better. How did he fool me for so long?

"Emma, please talk to me," Addy whispers and I look up at her through my tears.

"I…I…I don't know what to say."

She bobs her head in understanding. "Pack a bag. You are coming to stay with me and the boys can come get your stuff sometime soon, okay?"

I nod, like a robot. My tears have dried up and now I just feel empty. I'm not sad. I'm not angry. I'm not anything.

"Come on, sweetie," Addy says, coaxing me to move.

"It will get better," Trey assures me.

Will it?

*   *   *   *

When we left the house, I left that article on the table with a good-bye note on top of it. A part of me feels bad about leaving him. I'm worried about how he'll react. I don't want to hurt him. I love him despite what he did to me. The fact disgusts me but it's true.

I can't seem to wrap my head around the fact that he knew what he was doing the whole time. Maybe he didn't… maybe he didn't realize what he was doing. Is that possible? I don't know what to think anymore. Everything that I know is turned completely upside down. I can't even trust my own emotions. Even they have betrayed me.

There is a commotion at the front door and Tucker comes barreling into the room. He stops short when he sees me before rushing over and crouching down in front of me. He runs his hands over my hair as tears well up in his eyes. He looks down at my lap and picks up one of my hands as he examines my wrist.

He meets my eyes again and I see a single tear slip down his cheek. I just stare blankly at him, feeling so empty and numb.

"What's wrong with her?" he asks, turning to Trey and Addy.

"I'm not sure, but I think she's in shock."

"She's been like this since we left the house," Addy chimes in.

He watches me, his eyes flicking down to my jaw. His own jaw clenches in response.

"I'm going to kill that bastard."

"I'm right there with ya, brother," Trey says.

"You can't," I respond, my voice just as empty as the rest of me feels. "He's a cop. He's going to get away with it." A slightly hysterical giggle escapes me.

"Emmy, you're scaring me," he whispers hoarsely, concern evident in his tone. I just shrug my shoulders.

"Why don't you get some sleep?" Addy asks and I nod my head. Yeah… sleep sounds like a really good idea.

*   *   *   *

When I wake up the next morning, I'm not empty anymore. I can think clearly again and it's a relief because I have to admit that I was scaring even myself last night. Staring at the shadows cast on the ceiling by the morning sun, I try to figure out how I ended up here. How did my life take such a wrong turn? How did I fall in love with a man like Ryan Wheeler?

Then, I think that maybe he really didn't realize what he was doing. I know he loves me, I've seen it in his eyes, and you would never treat someone you love like this so maybe he truly doesn't know.

No, there's no way it's possible. How would he not realize? The things he spewed at me were so awful that it has to be intentional, right? He had to know that hitting me last night was wrong. Right?

God, I feel like I'm going insane.

I can't trust my own emotions right now. I can't trust anyone. To have someone you love, that you trusted, tear you down like this elicits an emotion I can't even put into words. I feel violated. How do I ever trust anyone again?

"Em?" Addy's voice snaps me out of my thoughts and I look up at her, offering her a small smile. A startled look crosses her face. "Well, you seem better this morning."

I sit up in the bed. "Yeah, I feel a little better this morning."

"So, listen, I need to talk to you about a few things," she says, glancing nervously down at her hands.

"'Kay, what's up?"

"First, your phone has been blowing up since last night." She hands me my phone. I look down and see one hundred and eight missed calls.

"Jesus."

"Yeah," she mutters, shaking her head. "Second, I took pictures of your bruises last night, and the boys and I think you should go file a police report."

"Addy, you know that's pointless. He's one of them. They are going to cover his back."

"Okay, then let us take new pictures with like the newspaper or something to show the date. You know, just in case you need them later."

I look at her with a mix of apprehension and horror.

"What do you think is going to happen, Addilyn?"

"I don't know what he's capable of and that scares me."

"Ad, I don't think he meant to hurt me. He loves me. I know he does. Maybe if I just go talk to him."

She shoots off the bed, giving me an "are you insane" look.

"Trey! Tucker!" she yells and seconds later both boys come barreling into the room.

"What?" Tucker shouts, looking around for some hidden threat. I giggle at his ridiculous behavior. Addy's apartment is on the third floor. What is Ryan going to do, scale the wall? Trey grins and I know he's thinking the exact same thing I am.

"She wants to go talk to him. She said that she knows he loves her," Addilyn rants.

A frown instantly replaces the smile on Trey's face as Tucker stares at me like I'm crazy for a second before his expression turns pitying. I'll tell you one thing. I'm getting pretty damn tired of that pity look. He sits on the bed in front of me and grabs my hand.

"Emmy, he doesn't love you. You don't do this to someone you love."

In an instant, I feel myself getting defensive of Ryan. It pisses me off.

"You guys don't know him like I do. He didn't mean to hurt me. He
DOES love me!"

"You can't be this stupid!" Tucker yells and I immediately pull my hand away, tears stinging my eyes.

"Shit, sis. I didn't mean that."

I see my opening. "Do you love me, Tucker?"

"Yeah, of course I do, Em."

"But you just said that mean thing to me so you couldn't possibly love me because you don't do that to people you love."

"That's different, I didn't hit you!"

"Neither did Ryan."

"I can see the bruises!"

"That was my fault. I didn't listen and I tried to walk away."

"Guys, can I talk to you both in the hallway?" Addy asks and both boys walk out of the bedroom clearly frustrated with the situation. Addy shuts the door behind her and I creep closer to listen to their conversation.

"He has obviously been conditioning her for a while now," Addy says and someone growls.

"God, I want to kill this son of a bitch," Tucker seethes.

"Agreed."

"Well, she's right about one thing. You guys can't touch him. It will only land you in jail and the cops probably won't help her," Addy points out.

"So what do we do?!" Tucker yells.

"I don't know," Addy answers.

I huff out a breath in annoyance and roll my eyes before walking away from the door. I plop down on the bed and look at my phone.

God...one hundred and eight missed calls. He's frantic. The urge to call him and comfort him is overwhelming. What the hell is wrong with me? I know what he did to me and yet, when someone says something bad about him, I immediately defend him, and I still want to comfort him when he's hurting.

I'm pretty sure that makes me a masochist.

I need to talk to him. That's the only answer I have right now. I need to know what he's thinking and feeling, I don't feel right not knowing, the anxiousness nearly choking me.

My phone buzzes in my hand with an incoming call and I stare at Ryan's picture for a minute before answering.

"Hi."

"Baby," he breathes into the phone. "Please come home."

"I don't think that is a good idea, Ryan."

"Sweetheart, I swear I didn't mean to hurt you. I love you so much. Please forgive me and give me a second chance. I'll make it up to you."

Chewing on my bottom lip, I look up at the ceiling as if angels with descend from heaven and offer me divine wisdom.

"I need some time, Ryan."

"Time for what, Emma?"

"I just need time to think."

A heavy sigh comes across the phone and my eyes burn with unshed tears.

"How much time?"

"I don't know."

"Okay, baby," he agrees after a minute.

"Thank you."

"Don't stay gone too long, baby. I miss you so much. This house is so depressing without you." A tear falls down my cheek and I know I need to hang up the phone.

"Bye, Ryan."

"I love you, Em," he responds and I hang up the phone without responding. Then the tears are streaming down my face.

Will I ever be able to get over this?

Chapter Twenty-Four
Then…

Arriving at work, Moe's eyes grow wide in shock as he looks at my jaw. It's been a couple days, but the evidence is still there.

Turning to Trey, he grits his teeth. "What the hell happened to her?"

"Don't know exactly," Trey responds. "She won't tell us." Moe turns back to me, his eyes softening as he approaches.

"Sweet girl, you best be tellin' me what happened."

I bite my lip and look down. "It was just an accident, Moe."

His hands clench at his sides. "Darlin', I could put my fingers exactly where his were. It wasn't an accident."

Suddenly feeling defensive of Ryan again, I straighten my spine and look Moe in the eye. "It was an accident and I am fine," I say, my voice hard and unwavering.

"I'm callin' your daddy."

"Sure, you know what, why don't we just take out an ad in the fuckin' paper so then everyone can know?" I snarl and Moe raises an eyebrow at me.

"Keep the spunk, girl. You're going to need it," he says before walking into the office and shutting the door behind him.

What the hell does that mean?

*　　　*　　　*　　　*

A commotion by the front door drags my attention away from the bar and I gasp when I see Ryan arguing with Trey. Ryan looks up, his eyes meeting mine, and I feel like I'm in a trance. I start moving toward him, unable to stop myself, and a small smile plays on his lips. Trey glances over his shoulder and sees me coming.

"Get in the back, Em." I ignore him until he wraps an arm around my waist. "Em, please, I don't want you to get hurt."

Turning to look at him, I give him a reassuring smile. "I'll be okay, Trey. We're just going to talk."

Trey shakes his head adamantly. "No, I don't like this."

"This is between me and my girl."

I shoot Ryan a look of annoyance. He is so not helping this situation.

"Yeah, I can see what conversations between you two look like on her face!" Trey snaps and Ryan takes a step in our direction.

"Enough!" I yell. "Ryan, outside...now!"

Spinning back to face Trey, I reach for his hand and give it a squeeze. "I'll be okay." He grumbles but lets me go. When I get outside, Ryan is leaning up against the side of the building.

"Ryan, why are you here? I told you I need time."

"I know you did baby but I just miss you so damn much. I was sitting at home and it was so hard. The house is so quiet and it feels so empty now." A desperate look crosses his face. "Listen, I was thinking today and I'm not sure that time apart is the best thing for us. We need to spend time together so you can see that things will be different."

I have to admit that what he says makes sense but I still have a small bit of hesitation inside me. He must see this because he steps forward and cradles my face in his large hand.

"Baby, I need you. I'm going crazy without you. You mean everything to me."

I don't trust a single word that is coming out of his mouth. I can't afford to. "I can't do this anymore."

A look of pure panic flashes across his face and he tries to pull me into him but I back away.

"Baby, please. I need you. I can't live without you."

I shake my head. "I'm sorry, Ryan but I'm done."

His eyes travel frantically all over my face and I swear, I can hear him thinking.

"Will you come talk to me after you get off work? I feel like we can't talk here and I want to try to fix this."

I think about his request. As I look up at him, I realize there is nothing he can say that will fix this. I am well and truly done, but I do need a few things from the house. Finally, I nod.

"Okay, Ryan. I'll come talk to you." I have no intention of giving into him but at the very least, I can get some essential things that I'll need until my brothers can get everything else. He smiles at me and kisses the top of my head. It takes every ounce of strength I have to not flinch.

"Thank you, baby. I'll see you tonight."

*   *   *   *

I pull up in front of the house — my house for the last nine months and I feel a little sad. When we moved in here, I had so much hope for us, for where our relationship was going. It's sad to see it end this way. But, I know this is right. I have to get away from him.

I take a deep breath and slide out of my car before making my way up to the front door. I'm not sure what to do. It doesn't really feel like my house anymore, despite the fact that all my stuff is in there. After a moment of debate, I raise my hand and knock.

The door opens almost immediately and Ryan shoots me a puzzled look. "Hey. Why didn't you just come in?"

I shrug. "I don't know. It just felt weird."

His eyes cloud with sadness and I second-guess my decision to come over here tonight.

"Well, come on in." I follow him inside and he sits down on the couch. I stand there, awkwardly, and stare at him. After a moment, he sighs. "Do you want something to drink?"

I nod. I can feel the nerves building as I play what I'm going to say to him in my head. He stands, making his way into the kitchen. I look around the living room and tears spring to my eyes. It hurts so much that this is all ending. I thought I had found my happily ever after.

Ryan comes back into the room and freezes when he sees me. He sets the drink on the end table and walks over to me. "You came here to end it, didn't you?"

My breath stutters and I nod. His hands fist and his jaw clenches. Instinctively, I take a step back. He reaches out, lightning fast, and grabs ahold of my arm. The tips of his fingers dig into my bicep and a squeak of pain slips through my parted lips.

"No. You're not leaving me. I gave you a chance to come to your senses and now I have to remind you who you belong to."

Panic skyrockets inside me as I imagine what he might do. "Ryan, please. Let me go."
He yanks on my arm, hard. I fall into him and he holds me there, our faces almost touching.

"Never." His voice is so low and so terrifying that a shiver races down my spine. I have no idea what he's capable of and that scares me more than anything else.

"Please stop."

"You are mine, Emma. You have been since the moment I met you and you will be until the day you die."

Without another word, he turns and drags me down the hallway, to the bedroom. I try to plant my feet but he keeps pulling on me, locking us in a tug of war. I fight him with everything I have, afraid to give up and find out what awaits at the other end of this hall. He gives another good yank and I feel my shoulder dislocate. I scream out in pain and my knees give out. I collapse to the floor but Ryan keeps pulling me along. Pain radiates out from my shoulder into my chest and all the way down my fingers. It hurts so badly, I don't know how I haven't passed out yet.

Ryan reaches our room and drags me inside. I glance up and through the haze of my agony, I see rope sticking out of the back pocket of his jeans, and I scream. I scream as loud as I possibly can, hoping that someone will hear me. Ryan pulls on my arm until I'm standing and slams my body up against the wall.

"Shut up!" he snarls in my face as his palm connects with my cheek.

The hit stuns me for a moment as my head whips to the side and the room falls silent. A moment later, I'm screaming again. My throat hurts but I don't stop. I use every ounce of energy I have to call for help. Ryan looks murderous but I don't care.

"I said shut up, you little cunt!"

This time when he hits me, it's with a closed fist. All the air whooshes out of me and I know my cheek is starting to swell already. Ryan grabs me and tosses me onto the bed, causing me to hiss in pain when my injured shoulder makes contact. He climbs on top of me, straddling my hips, and pulls the rope from his back pocket.

I scream some more as I try to buck him off, but it's no use. He leans down and clamps his hand over my neck, squeezing until it's difficult to breathe.

"Shut. Up."

This time, his threat works, but I still struggle to get free. He grabs my bad hand and is able to quickly tie the first rope around it. He pushes me up the bed until he can tie the other end around the wrought iron headboard. When he's done, he pulls my body back down the bed, stretching my arm out, and I howl in pain.

When he tries to grab my other arm, I fight him. I claw at his arms, not letting him grab me. After a moment, he gets frustrated and slams his fist into my belly. The wind is knocked out of me and as I try to suck in a breath, he quickly ties the rope around my other hand, extra tight, and secures it to the bed. He looks at his handiwork and smiles. It's disgusting. He pulls off my pants and panties, running his finger along my slit, and I suck in a breath. With another deep inhale, I do my best to shut down, to steel myself against what he's about to do to me.

He quickly shoves his jeans down his legs and his boxers follow a second later. When he's undressed, he tries to spread my legs so he can settle between them. I use all my strength to press my thighs together and try to twist away from him. He finally gets them apart and settles his hand over my core.

"This is mine." He pulls his hand away and lines himself up at my entrance. I squeeze my eyes shut because I know this is going to hurt. I can't stand to watch him do this to me. I know if I watch him, his face as it looks now will be burned into my memory. He spits on me and the first sob escapes me.

When he forces himself inside, I squeeze my eyes shut tighter and try to think of anything else to get me through this. He moves and every pull and push of his cock is like I'm being stabbed. Tears leak from my eyes and trail down the sides of my face as he begins the chant that I'm his.

A part of me dies inside, as though all the light and love is being wrung out of my body with every thrust of his hips. He's taking something from me, something so precious and I'll never get it back. I will never be the same.

His rough hand grabs my breast, squeezing hard, and another sob slips out. He groans and bile rises in my throat. I'm going to throw up. He starts moving faster and a part of me is glad because I know it's almost over though it hurts so much more. Finally, after another agonizing minute, he tenses above me. My breath falters as I realize it's over.

He pulls out of me and quickly unties my hands. He moves the injured one so that it's resting over the top of my belly and he kisses my forehead. "You're mine, baby," he whispers and flops onto the bed next to me. I remain still, afraid to move, or even breathe.

After a couple minutes, he starts snoring and I release the breath that I had been holding. Everything comes out of me as I try to sob as quietly as possible. I sit up from the bed and look around the room. With silent cries racking my body, I tiptoe around the room, collecting as many clothes as possible and I shove them in the first bag I find in the closet. I pull some shorts on my legs as fast as I can with one arm.

Every time Ryan shifts or makes a little noise in his sleep, I freeze, petrified that he will wake up and find me trying to escape. But he doesn't. I finish packing my bag and silently make my way through the house.

Grabbing my purse and keys, which fell to the floor when Ryan grabbed me, I slowly turn the handle on the front door, my breath stuck in my chest.

Once it's open, I make my way outside and creep through my front yard to my car. Each step feels like my last as I imagine Ryan waking up and coming after me in a rage. Thankfully, I make it to my car and lock the doors without incident. Only then am I able to breathe.

I start the car and just drive. I have no idea where I'm going. My brain is too busy shutting down so I don't have to relive what just happened. After a while, I look up and realize that I'm pulling up to Tucker's house. I climb out of the car and stumble up the walk. I pound on the door as loud as I can and I don't stop until the door flings open to reveal Tucker standing there with a scowl on his face. When he sees me, his scowl instantly changes to a look of concern just before I collapse into his arms.

Chapter Twenty-Five
Now

It's just after eight o'clock in the morning when the four of us walk into the police station. I'm surprised that I'm not feeling that nervous, shocked by the strength flowing through me. This is what I need to do.

A young officer looks up from the front desk when we walk through the door. "Can I help you?"

"Yes, I need to speak to a detective." Nix gives my hand a squeeze and even I want to smile at the authority in my voice. I'm not taking any shit today.

"About what?"

"I need to file a report against my ex-fiancé."

The officer looks between Nix and me, focusing on our joined hands, but I remain firm. After a moment, he nods.

"Okay. Follow me." He turns to lead us further into the station.

"Excuse me, one more thing." The officer turns back to me. "Can you tell me which detective I'll be talking to today?"

He shakes his head. "I'm not sure. Does it matter?"

"Yes. It can't be Detective Wheeler."

His eyebrows shoot up in surprise and he has an interested look on his face. "Why?"

"He's my ex-fiancé."

He watches me for a moment before nodding his head. "Okay. I'll make sure it's not him."

"Thank you."

He nods again and begins leading us through the station to the interrogation rooms. The whole way, I feel nervous, wondering if Ryan can see me or if someone already told him that I'm here. I swear I sense his eyes burning holes into me but I don't see him anywhere. I do however get a look of surprise from Detective Nelson. My suspicions are raised.

We finally reach the small room with a metal table in the middle, surrounded by four metal chairs.

"Can I get you guys anything to drink?" the officer asks.

I shake my head. "No. Thank you."

He leaves us alone, shutting the door behind him. My brothers stand in the back of the room, leaning against the wall with their arms crossed over their chests, looking every bit the bodyguards they've been playing for the past few months. Nix pulls a chair out for me and I smile up at him as I sit. He slides into the chair next to me and grabs my chair, pulling me closer to him.

"You doing okay, sweetheart?"

"Yeah, I'm all right."

"You are so strong, baby. You can do this."

I lean into him and he wraps an arm around my shoulders, giving me a little squeeze. "I love you," I whisper and he kisses my forehead in response. We're interrupted by a knock at the door followed by Detective Nelson and someone else I don't recognize entering the room.

"Miss Harrington, what can we do for you today?" Nelson smirks down at me and I find myself clenching my fist and wishing I could punch him in the face. In that instant, my suspicions are confirmed and I know that I can't trust him.

I turn and take in the other man who entered the room. He's older, probably in his mid-thirties, with black hair and brown eyes. I arch a brow and he leans forward, extending his hand.

"I'm Detective Rodriguez, it's nice to meet you."

"Nice to meet you, too. This is my boyfriend, Phoenix West." I gesture to Nix beside me. "And my brothers, Tucker Harrington and Trey Davis."

"Like I said, what can we do for you?"

I square my shoulders and look directly at Detective Nelson when I say, "I need to file a report against my ex-fiancé, Ryan Wheeler."

Detective Rodriguez nods and sits down in the chair opposite me, pulling a notepad out of his suit pocket. I keep my eyes focused on Nelson as he stares back at me, contempt clear on his face. Finally, he sits in the other chair and clears his throat.

"Why don't you tell us what happened?"

From behind me, Tucker growls at the sarcastic tone he's using, and Nix's knee bounces like crazy under the table. I lay my hand over it and his gaze flicks over to me for just a moment before focusing on the slimy detective again.

"One question first, is Ryan watching this through that mirror there?" I point to the two-way mirror behind the detectives and Nelson laughs.

"That's just a mirror."

I glare at him. "Let's get one thing straight here, I'm not stupid so stop treating me like I am." Fire is flowing through my veins as I take them on. I don't know where it came from but I love it. Nix places his hand on my leg, just above my knee, and squeezes. I glance over at him and he nods, with a small smile playing on his lips.

"Get Wheeler out of here," Detective Rodriguez calls over his shoulder and I roll my eyes. Of course he was here.

"Any more games?" I direct my question at Detective Rodriguez. He may seem more sincere than Nelson but I'm still not sure that I can trust anyone here.

"No, Ma'am." I study him for a moment before nodding. "Please tell us what happened."

"I started dating Ryan Wheeler a little over two years ago. We moved in together after dating for a few months and shortly after that, he began getting violent with me. He would grab me or hold me down, squeezing hard enough to leave bruises behind. Things were getting worse and when I caught him cheating on me, I tried to leave. He grabbed me, tossed me into our spare bedroom, and locked me inside. He left me there for twenty-four hours with no food and no water."

"Isn't that like, kidnapping?" Tucker snaps from behind me.

Detective Nelson smashes his lips into a thin line. "Technically, yes."

I resist the urge to snort in disbelief. Technically. No, it was kidnapping.

"Go on, please," Detective Rodriguez says, shooting a look in Nelson's direction.

I take a deep breath. "He also raped me several times. The last time is when I was finally able to get away from him. I went and saw my doctor the next morning. I have her report here." I rummage around in my bag and pull out the folder of all our evidence before sliding the report to them across the table. I see Nix's raised brow out of the corner of my eye. I didn't tell him about the report. I didn't tell anyone. I never wanted anyone to know any of this.

"How long ago did this happen?" Detective Nelson's voice drags me out of my thought and I look up at him.

"Over a year ago."

"Why are you just coming forward now?"

"Because he's been stalking me and making threats."

"Why didn't you come in sooner? Like when this originally happened."

"Actually, I did make a report. Right, Detective Nelson? What ever happened to that?" That has Detective Rodriguez's attention instantly and he whips his head in Nelson's direction.

"I'm sorry. I have no idea what you're talking about." I knew it. He probably never even filed that report. God, how stupid can I be? I should have never trusted anyone here.

"Ma'am, do you have any evidence?" Detective Rodriguez asks and I direct my gaze back to him. I slide the rest of the folder across the table and pull the jewelry out of my bag.

"All right, we're going to need to go over every detail of the attack described in this doctor's report," Nelson says. The sick satisfaction in his voice only serves to piss me off more. If he thinks this will break me, he is sorely mistaken. I take a deep breath and Nix rubs my back in support.

"We had broken up but he asked me to come over so we could talk. As soon as he realized that I wasn't going to take him back, he grabbed my arm and dragged me down the hallway, toward the bedroom."

"Is this what caused the bruises on your arm and the dislocated shoulder?" Rodriguez asks as he reads the report from my doctor.

"Yes."

He nods. "Please go on."

"When he got me to the bedroom, he slammed me into the wall. I started screaming, hoping that someone would hear me. He slapped me once and punched me to shut me up. Then, he threw me on the bed and tied my hands to the headboard."

Nelson and Rodriguez whisper to each other, pointing to things on the paper for a moment.

"And then what?" Nelson asks.

"And then he raped me."

Tucker makes a choked sound behind me and Trey coughs, gruffly. I close my eyes, feeling bad that they have to hear all this. Nix has his hands balled into fists in his lap and his knee is shaking. At least he's not screaming like he did after I told him this story last night.

"What happened afterward?"

"Afterward, he untied me and fell asleep. I was able to get out of the house and I went to my brother's house."

"And when did you go to the doctor?" Nelson asks.

"The next morning."

"Can you confirm this?" Detective Rodriguez asks Tucker.

"She did leave the house for about two hours that morning but I didn't know where she was going." Detective Rodriguez nods and Detective Nelson scowls at the doctor's report in his hand.

"We'll go get Detective Wheeler's statement and be back. Please wait here." They stand and leave the room with my folder full of evidence, shutting the door behind them.

"I'm so proud of you, baby." Nix wraps his arms around me.

"Thanks," I whisper, collapsing into him, suddenly feeling exhausted from reliving everything with the detectives.

"I love you, Emma."

"I love you too, Nix."

*   *   *   *

"Emma, why didn't you ever tell us about everything?" Tucker asks as we sit in the room, waiting for the detectives to come back.

"I…it's…I guess I didn't want you guys to think of me like that."

"Baby girl," Trey whispers, shaking his head and looking at the floor.

"Why didn't you tell me about the doctor's report?" Nix asks.

"Because I could barely get through it. I wasn't going to let you guys read it." All three of them pale as they imagine what could possibly be written on that report. "Exactly."

"Fuck," Tucker growls.

The door opens and Nelson enters the room again. He sits across from us with a stern look on his face.

"Well, we've talked to Detective Wheeler. He said that you have a history of mental health issues, is that true?"

"No."

"He said you see a Dr. Ingrid Fields?"

"Yes, but only for a couple sessions after I was raped."

How would he possibly know that? I guess I really shouldn't be surprised since he's been stalking me but it's still hard to hear that he knows every move I make.

"Right. He also said that he never even saw you the night you claimed he raped you. He read the report and he's very concerned about who did this to you. We all are. We just need you to tell us the truth. Do you know who did this to you?"

"You're joking, right?" I ask, my emotions somewhere between disbelief and some kind of sick humor.

"No ma'am." Nix growls from beside me and I put my hand on his knee.

"Are you going to file this report?"

"We can't until you tell us who really did this to you," Detective Nelson says and the gleam in his eye tells me all I need to know. Besides, I know that what he just said is a total lie. He could file the report, he just chooses not to.

"I would like to speak to your boss," I snap, fed up with *Detective Nelson* and his smug attitude.

"I'm sorry. He's not available right now."

"Fine." I stand to leave and Nix follows suit.

"Ma'am, you can't leave."

"*Actually*, I can. I haven't done anything wrong and you aren't arresting me so I'm free to leave at any time." I grab my things and the folder off the table and shove everything into my bag before walking out of the room with the guys on my heels. I stop short when I see Ryan standing there watching me through the window.

"The level of unprofessionalism here is astounding."

Ryan smiles and takes a step toward me. My brothers rush in front of me, making an impenetrable wall while Nix stays with me. "I knew you were still in there, baby. I love your feisty spirit."

"Fuck off," I snap and Nix chuckles softly behind me.

"I love you," Ryan says. "I won't give up."

"Careful, Ryan. You wouldn't want these people to know what a monster you truly are."

His eyes widen and his face turns red as he stares me down. I realize I just poked the bear. He is going to snap and I'm worried about what he will do when it happens.

*   *   *   *

"I'd like to talk to a reporter," I say to the receptionist in the newspaper's office.

"About?" After the day I've had, her bored tone annoys the hell out of me.

"I have a story I think they'll be interested in."

"Why don't you tell me what it is and I'll pass it along?"

I shake my head. "No, I need to talk to a reporter."

"I'm a reporter. What can I help you with?" A tall woman with golden blonde hair and gray eyes says, smiling back at me.

"I have a story I think you'd like to hear."

She studies me curiously. "Sure, come with me."

She leads Nix and me behind the closed doors of an office. Little cubicles form rows all through the large room with larger private offices along the walls. We follow her to the back corner where she has an office tucked away. She sits behind the desk and motions for us to sit in the chairs across from her.

"I'm Carly Mills, by the way."

"Emma Harrington and this is my boyfriend, Phoenix West."

"It's nice to meet you both. So, what's this about?" she asks, crossing her arms over her chest.

"It's about the police department covering up domestic abuse and rape."

Her eyes light up. "Well you've certainly got my attention. Mind if I record this?"

"Not at all."

She pulls a recorder out of her desk drawer and sets it up on the desk. "Okay. Go ahead."

"You've got to be shitting me," she exclaims when I finish telling her my story, shaking her head.

"I wish I was. I have all this proof." I start digging in my bag for the folder. I hold it out to her after I find it and she opens it and scans through the papers.

"Ho-ly shit. And they just dismissed all of this?"

"Yes."

"So, why did you come to me?"

"Well, as you can see, he's stalking me and threatening me. I'm concerned about what he is going to do, and the police won't take me seriously. When I asked to speak to their boss, I was told that he was unavailable. If, God forbid, something happens to me, I want the world to know what is really going on. If I get hurt, I want Ryan and the police department held accountable for their actions."

She nods in understanding and something like pride sparks in her eyes. "All right, I'll do what I can. Can I make copies of all this?" she asks, pointing to the folder.

"Oh, those are copies. You can keep them."

"Why did you bring the police copies?"

"Because I guessed that something like this would happen." She nods again in understanding.

"Don't you worry, Emma. I'll take care of this," she assures me and I smile.

"Thanks, Carly."

Chapter Twenty-Six

"Hey, Em! Come out here!" Nix calls from the living room. I finish running the brush through my hair and walk out of the bedroom to join him.

"What's up, babe?"

He holds up the morning paper and smiles. "It's in here."

I'm suddenly nervous. I've done a pretty good job of shoving all this to the back of my mind for the last few days but I can't avoid it anymore. "Have you read it yet?"

"Yeah, babe. It's good." He holds the paper out to me and I take a deep breath before opening it to the article.

I quickly read through it. The last few words send a chill running through me, citing that an investigation should be done regarding my attempts to file charges sooner rather than later.

Before it's too late.

"It's kind of short." I look up at Nix, trying to shake off my unease.

"It is." Nix nods. "But I think it gets the job done."

I set the paper down. "Yeah, it does."

He extends his hand to me, and I take it. He pulls me into his embrace. "You okay, baby?"

"Yeah. That last line just got to me."

He squeezes me tighter, his heartbeat pounding beneath my hand. "I'll protect you, baby. He's never going to hurt you again."

"Nix, you know that isn't true. You can't be everywhere. There is a possibility that he'll get to me." He doesn't say anything, only squeezes me even tighter and I sigh. "Baby, I love you but if this is too much, you can leave. I'll understand."

He tenses and leans back a little. "I'm not leaving, Emma."

"Nix, it's okay, I get it. You didn't sign up for all of this."

"Stop!" he yells and I flinch. "Stop pushing me away. I'm not going anywhere, ever."

I can feel myself shutting down. It's instinct after everything Ryan did to me. "Okay," I whisper, emotionless.

Nix growls. "Goddamn it!" He slams his fist into the wall and marches out of the room and into the bedroom. I hold my hand over my chest and sink into the dining room chair as tears start running down my face.

This isn't fair. I know Nix would never hurt me but as soon as he raised his voice, I couldn't help my reaction. I just don't know if I can do this to him anymore. He has every right to be frustrated here. It's me who can't handle it. He's been so amazing to me through all this, so understanding. I'm just so messed up and he deserves better. He deserves someone who can give him everything.

"Baby," Nix whispers from behind me, and then he's kneeling in front of me. "Baby, I'm so sorry. I handled that all wrong."

I'm momentarily shocked that he's not blaming me. But, he's not Ryan so of course he's not blaming me. "It's okay." I wipe the tears away from my face.

"No, it is absolutely not okay. I let my emotions get the best of me and I made a mistake."

I smile, clearing away the last of my tears. "Do you know how I know that you're nothing like Ryan?"

"No."

"Ryan would have come out here and blamed me. He would have blamed all the stress at his job. He would have said that I just wouldn't let him love me. And then, he would have said 'forgive me.' He never said sorry. Not once. That's how I know you are nothing like him, and that's why it *is* okay. But Nix, if this is too much for you, if the stress is more than you can handle, I will understand. You don't have to stick around."

"No, you listen to me, I'm not going anywhere. I would rather be stressed and have you in my life than be carefree and without you."

"Okay."

He places his hand against my cheek. "I love you, Emma."

"I know and I love you, too."

*   *   *   *

"Saw your article yesterday, baby girl," Trey says.

"Yeah, you're a total badass, sis," Tucker adds from his seat on the other side of the bar.

I let out a laugh and shake my head. "First of all, it wasn't *my* article, and second, I'm just doing what I have to."

314

"Like I said, total badass."

I laugh again. Glancing up, I see two members of the Bayou Devils, Storm, and Chance, walking in. "Hey, boys, can I get you anything?"

"Beer," Chance says and Storm nods in agreement. They sit on barstools next to Tucker and I slide them their beers.

"What's up?"

"Just on babysitting duty," Storm growls and I shoot him a look.

"Hey, Storm, did you get your name from your usually sunny disposition?"

Chance laughs. A grin is tickling Storm's lips but he holds it back.

"Naw, it's his eyes," Chance says and I give him a confused look.

"Huh?"

"One of the old ladies said it looked like he always had a storm brewin' in his eyes and it just kinda stuck."

I understand what she was talking about. His gray eyes look just like storm clouds.

"And how did you get your name?"

He grins. "Just my name, darlin'."

"No nickname?"

"Nope."

"Now, wait, what's an old lady?"

"It's a term of respect for a member's woman. It's like wife status in the biker world," Storm explains.

"Ah, okay. Makes sense."

"YOU BITCH!" someone roars from the front door.

Ryan stands there seething, fists clenched and face bright red from rage.

"That's our cue," Storm growls and hops off the barstool, Chance on his heels. Ryan gets halfway across the room before the guys reach him and start dragging him out.

"I'M COMING FOR YOU, EMMA! YOU WILL ALWAYS BE MINE!" he screams right before Storm and Chance take him outside. As soon as he's out of sight, I release a breath and brace my hands on the bar.

"Whoa there, baby girl. Come on, come sit down," Trey says, wrapping his arms around me and guiding me to a barstool.

"Think he saw the article?" I joke, my voice shaky. Both boys laugh but the tension is still there. My hands are trembling, and I flatten them against my thighs to try to get control of myself.

"You okay, Emmy?" Tucker asks and I offer him the best smile I can. "That's not very convincing." His response earns a shrug from me. I can't find it in me to care right now.

"I think you should take the rest of the night off, Em."

I'm about to protest when Moe chimes in, "I agree."

"Moe, I need to work or I'm never going to be able to pay my bills."

"You need money?" He pulls a large wad of cash out of his pocket and begins thumbing through the bills.

"Ugh, stop! Fine, I'll go home."

"Not by yourself, I'll call Nix," Tucker commands and I groan.

"He's gotta work too, guys. I can go home by myself."

"Are you fuckin' insane? Right after he just showed up here and said he was coming for you?" Tucker barks.

"He's got a point," Trey says. I glower at my brothers but they do have a point.

"Fine. Tucker, you take me. Storm and Chance can stay with me."

He nods. "Let's go."

*　　　*　　　*　　　*

I scream when I walk into the apartment and find Nix sitting there, reading. I was so lost in my head that I didn't even notice his truck outside or the fact that the door was unlocked.

"Oh, you're home." I sigh, pressing my hand against my chest, trying to calm my racing heart.

He grins and quirks an eyebrow at me before saying, "Home, huh?"

"Uh, yeah." I scowl as I try to figure out exactly what he's up to. Maybe if I wasn't so frazzled by Ryan's little visit to the bar twenty minutes ago I would be able to catch on quicker.

"Have you decided something and not told me?" His grin grows as my scowl becomes more severe. I honestly have no idea what he's trying to get at here.

"Huh?"

"You know, like us moving in together."

Oh.

OH! God, that was the furthest thing from my mind tonight. All I can seem to think about are the threats Ryan spewed at me. "Um, no, I haven't."

"I think you have."

"What?"

"Well, you said, 'you're home,' so whether you realize it or not, I think you've come to a decision."

"I think you're reading too much into it." Even though I know that I'm taking my stress out on him, I can't seem to stop. The fear and anger are just bubbling out of me. He frowns and watches me closely for a moment.

"Hey, what's wrong? I was just teasing."

I lean my forehead against the wall and sigh. "I know. I'm sorry."

He's behind me now. So close the heat from his body seeps through my clothes and I want nothing more than to have him hold me. Gripping my shoulders, he kisses the back of my head.

"What's wrong?"

"Ryan came by the bar tonight. He saw the article."

His muscles tense up slightly before he releases a breath, relaxing again.

"What did he say, baby?" He loops his arms around my waist and I lean into him. Tears build in my eyes. But it's not from the fear or anger I was feeling just a few seconds ago. It's from the intense relief of being in Nix's arms.

"Well, first he called me a bitch then he said that I was his and he was coming for me."

"What happened to him?" His body is rigid again, anger rolling off him in waves.

"Chance and Storm took care of him."

"Good," he growls. "I can't believe he was stupid enough to say all that to you with so many damn witnesses. Especially after the article."

"I think he's losing control, Nix. It makes me even more afraid."

He squeezes me tighter and plants a kiss on my neck.

"I know, sweetheart."

Words that Ryan practically drilled into me run through my mind. That he couldn't live without me, that he needed me. Is all of this my fault?

"I didn't do this, did I?"

He spins me around in his arms. "Do what, baby?"

"Did my leaving make him like this? Is this all my fault?"

"No!" he barks. "Absolutely not. You listen to me, he screwed up his life. This is all on him."

"He always said that he needed me. That he would be lost without me. What if this is all my fault?" Now that the thought has entered my mind, I can't seem to let it go. Could I have prevented all of this? Nix's arms tighten around me and I look up to see him glaring at me.

"Emma, I want you to listen to me very carefully. None of this is your fault. Not a single thing."

"But—"

"Not a single fuckin' thing."

I chew on my bottom lip as I watch him. It's hard to convince myself that I'm not responsible in some way. Remembering everything that Ryan did to me helps a little though. Nix is right. Ryan did this to himself. He made these choices.

"Okay," I finally reply and he releases a breath.

Leaning down, he kisses my forehead and pulls me into him. "Come take a shower with me?" he asks after holding me for a minute.

"Yeah, that sounds good."

He winks and scoops me up with a playful grin on his face. I can't take my eyes off him. I love everything about this man, from his sexy smirk to his unending patience with me, and everything in between.

I try to remember a time that I was this happy with Ryan and I can't think of a single instance. Sure, there are times when I was happy, but not *this* happy. Sometimes, it feels like I've known Nix forever even though we only met a few months ago. I have to wonder if I'm crazy for thinking of a forever with someone I've known for such a short time. But this really isn't something that can be controlled. When it happens, it happens. Love has no time limits or requirements.

"I love you," I whisper as we enter the bathroom.

His eyes are swimming with so much love that I can *feel* it. One look from him and I can feel his love, my body soaking it up like a sponge. It's another thing that lets me know that this thing is real. It would be so easy to lie, for him to say the words that I want to hear, but you can't fake the love pouring out of his eyes right now. You can't fake the total devotion on his face, or the way he holds me like he never wants to let me go. It's so different from the way Ryan used to look at me.

Though I didn't realize it at the time, when he looked at me, he was putting up a front, pretending to love me. I wish I could have seen it then.

"I love you, too, Emma." He cradles my face in his hand, thumb stroking over my cheek, and my eyes flutter closed. His lips pressing against mine has my brain shutting off completely, and the world around us fades away. He pulls me even closer, molding my body to his. I moan when his erection presses into my belly and he takes advantage of my parted lips, slipping his tongue in between.

His tongue strokes against mine as he fists my hair, his other hand grabbing my ass and rubbing me against him.

I pull away, panting, and sigh. "Nix."

He groans and rubs against me again. "It's been way too long since I've been inside you."

Smiling, I shake my head. "It was this morning."

"Uh-huh. Too long." He slowly moves down to capture my lips again. I rise on my tiptoes to meet him halfway. As soon as we connect, he grunts and grabs each of my legs, right under my ass, and lifts me into the air. My arms loop around his neck and my legs encircle his waist as he presses me up against the wall. As his lips move down from my mouth to my neck, he grinds his hips into me. The inferno inside my body burns hotter than ever before and I throw my head back, threading my fingers through his hair as he rains kisses down my neck.

"Strip." He pulls his lips away from my skin and sets me back down. I watch him, my eyes glued to his magnificent body as he gets undressed faster than I've ever seen. His chest is heaving, a physical reminder of how much I effect him right here in front of me. It turns me on. A rush of wetness pools between my thighs.

The fire in his eyes has goose bumps popping up over my flesh. He slides his hands under the material of my tank top and pulls it over my head. I quickly unbutton my jeans and he helps shove them down my legs, along with my panties. His eyes stay locked with mine as he reaches behind me and unhooks my bra, sliding it down my arms and tossing it to the floor.

He surprises me by dropping to his knees. I cock my head to the side and shoot him a look. He just smirks up at me before pressing his face into the apex of my thighs. My breath stutters and I lean my shoulders back into the wall. He grabs one leg and hooks it over his shoulder.

"Nix," I moan.

He kisses me softly just before his tongue circles my clit. I cry out, automatically grinding down on his face. His grip on my hip tightens as he slides one finger inside me, his tongue still working the sensitive bundle of nerves. My fingers slide into his hair and I pull him into me. He groans and removes his hand, replacing his finger with his tongue. He moves it in and out of me, several times, before returning to my clit. I can't take anymore.

"Nix. I need you."

A second later, I am in his arms with my back pressed against the wall. Jesus, he's fast. He smashes his lips onto mine and I moan, desire racing through every inch of my body. I can taste myself on his lips and it only adds to my fire. It's erotic. God, when did I become this wanton woman?

"God, baby," he groans against my mouth, rubbing his solid length against me. "I'm hard as a rock. You drive me so fuckin' crazy." He nips at my bottom lip before kissing down my neck again, and my body trembles with anticipation. His teeth sink into my neck, causing me to cry out and arch my body into his.

"I need you, Nix." I'm so amped up I'm going to explode. I'm desperate. I need his hands on me, need to feel him moving inside me.

"Jesus, I love hearing you say that." He makes his way back up to my lips as he lines himself up with my entrance. He plunges into me and my inner muscles immediately clench around him. He groans and buries his head in my neck as he begins moving inside me. Warm breath rushes over my flesh as he pants and grunts with each thrust into me.

I lean forward and kiss his neck and shoulders. He powers into me, never losing his stride, and my climax builds. My fingers dig into his shoulders and he groans loudly. He picks up the pace, slamming into me a little harder and faster each time, until reaching a punishing rhythm that makes it impossible for any thoughts to form in my head.

All I can do is feel. I'm completely high on him and this incredible feeling we create when we're together like this. He pulls back and kisses me quickly, saying, "Open your eyes."

I fight my body's desire to keep my eyes closed, blindly soaking up every divine moment of pleasure he can give me. As soon as our eyes connect, another wave of pleasure rushes through me and my eyelids feel heavy. I do my best to keep my gaze on him as he thrusts into me. The look in his blue eyes would knock me clean off my feet if he wasn't holding me. So much love, so much happiness stares back at me it's overwhelming. But not in a bad way. It adds to my impending orgasm.

I squeeze around him again and his eyelids flutter before he focuses on me.

"I'm not gonna last much longer, baby," he says through gritted teeth. I grab his face in my hands and pull him to me, sealing my lips over his. I kiss him, trying to put every ounce of love that I have for him into it, and he groans in response. He reaches between us and swirls his thumb over my clit. The climax takes me by surprise, crashing over me. I rip my lips away from his and throw my head back, moaning.

He buries his face in my neck again and grips the back of my head as he pounds into me faster, chasing his own release now. The hand on my ass squeezes tighter as he jerks inside me. A moment later, he groans loudly before going still, just clutching me to him.

After a couple seconds, I place kisses on every inch of his skin that I can reach in this position, and he smiles against my skin.

"Holy shit, Em." He releases a breath and sets me back on my feet. "You're gonna kill me."

I giggle and shake my head. "You're the one who had to have me right that second."

"It's cause of that ass." He smacks my butt, the slapping sound bouncing around the bathroom. I jump and squeal as I cover the spot he just hit with my hand.

"Brute."

"I'll show you brute," he growls, lunging at me.

I squeal again and duck to the side but he hooks his arm around my waist and pulls me back to him. He scoops me back up in his arms and carries me to the shower, flipping it on. When it's ready, he sets me under the warm water and spends the next thirty minutes gently washing my body and caressing me, showing me that he's anything but a brute.

Chapter Twenty-Seven

No one has seen or heard from Ryan since he showed up at the bar three weeks ago. He has literally dropped off the radar. All the guys are increasingly anxious as they wait for his next move. I know that it's naïve but there is a small part of me that hopes he'll just decide that this isn't worth the trouble. That *I'm* not worth the trouble. I'll admit that a part of me wondered if Storm and Chance took care of him — permanently — but they have assured me that he was very much alive when they left him.

"Babe, we're gonna be late," Nix calls from the living room.

Sighing, I check my make-up again before making my way out to him. I'm beginning to feel suffocated by all these alpha males around here. They won't let me go anywhere without an escort…or two. I get it, I really do, but it doesn't change the fact that I would love just a little space every once in a while.

"Nix, you know I can go to the doctor on my own, right?"

"Not with that asshole on the loose."

I sigh again, giving up because I know I won't win this.

"Fine, but you have to stay in the waiting room."

"But what if he—"

"No! Absolutely not. If he shows up, there will be plenty of people around and I can scream for help."

"All right." A deep frown mars his face, letting me know that he is really not happy about this. He grabs my hand and laces his fingers through mine as we make our way out to the car. I don't miss the fact that he is scanning every inch of our surroundings. He opens my door for me and shuffles around to his side after I climb in, still looking around him.

Good lord, this has got to stop.

I love him but he's driving me insane.

He climbs into the car and starts driving. "So, why are you going to the doctor?"

"To get my birth control shot."

"Oh, okay." He holds my hand as he drives to my doctor's office and I lean back in the seat and relax.

Ten minutes later, we pull up in front of the office and Nix tells me to wait in the car while he comes around to get me. Rolling my eyes, I throw the door open and step out, earning a scowl from him.

"I told you to wait."

"Nix, I need you to relax. You're going to make yourself and me crazy."

"I'm just worried."

"I know, and I love you for being so worried about me, but seriously, you need to calm down, or I won't let you stay at the apartment tonight."

He gapes at me. "Are you serious?"

"Very."

Sighing, he shakes his head. "Fine. I'll try to relax."

"Thank you," I say, kissing his cheek.

"I love you, Emma."

"I know, baby."

*   *   *   *

My doctor walks into the room and sits down on the rolling chair by the desk. She offers me a warm smile and I get the sense that something is off here. Dr. Greene is an older woman, probably in her fifties, with gray hair styled in a pixie cut, and a slim figure. More than once, I've pictured her as a weed-smoking hippie in the sixties.

"So, Emma, how are you feeling, dear?" she asks, still giving me that warm smile. Dr. Greene is always nice but she is usually a straight shooter. The fact that she is even in here to talk to me is weird. Most of the time, the nurse just gives me my birth control shot.

"I'm fine. What's going on?"

"Well, you're pregnant," she states in her usual no-nonsense tone. I choke on air and gape at her.

I'm pregnant? How? I'm religious about my shot. I'm never late and I never miss.

"I…uh…what?" I can't wrap my mind around what she said. God, how will Nix react? Will this freak him out?

"I know this is probably a shock, Emma, but no birth control is one-hundred percent effective."

"Holy shit," I whisper, my mind spinning but somehow blank at the same time. The timing couldn't be more awful. Ryan is still out there and he could get me.

"It's going to be all right, dear. We'll do an ultrasound to see how far along you are and go from there."

"No!" I yell and she jumps. "Sorry. It's just…my boyfriend is in the waiting room and he should be here for this. And I need some time to tell him."

"Oh. Of course. What's his name? I'll have one of my nurses go get him."

"Phoenix."

"Okay. Be right back."

She leaves the room and I drop my head as my mind begins to race again. God, how am I supposed to tell him that we're going to have a baby? The last word gets stuck in my head and all I can picture is a sweet little baby. I'm going to have a baby. A stupid grin slowly spreads across my face as I lay my hand over my belly. A wave of love and warmth flows through me as I think about the child growing inside me at this very moment.

"Hey, little one, it's your mama," I whisper and run my hand across my belly. Tears build in my eyes and I laugh as they spill down my cheeks. I hear voices through the door and my tears quickly vanish as I start to worry about telling Nix. We've only been together for a few months and this was obviously not planned. Will he be mad? Happy? Jesus, we haven't even talked about kids or marriage. I have no idea what he is going to think.

Just then, the door opens and Nix walks in. As soon as he sees my face, he charges over to me and holds my face in his hands. "Baby, what's wrong?"

"I'll give you two some time." The nurse leaves, closing the door behind her.

"Em, what's going on?"

"I'm okay." I don't want him thinking that there is something wrong with me. Sure, at first, I was shocked but I'm quickly coming around to the idea, and I want him to be excited about this.

"What's going on? I can tell you were crying." I look up into his eyes, and a picture of a little boy with matching ones fills my mind. "Em, please tell me. My imagination is running crazy over here."

"I'm pregnant," I say, and he jerks in shock. Biting down on my lip, I watch him nervously, waiting for his reaction to the news.

"What?" he asks, like he didn't hear me the first time.

"We're going to have a baby." He looks a little bewildered and I can't say that I blame him. It was a shock to me, too. Frankly, I'm surprised that I'm handling it so well right now.

"We are?"

"Uh-huh." A smile slowly spreads across his face and I breathe a sigh of relief. "You're not upset?"

"Hell no, I'm not mad!" he exclaims, shaking his head. "Why the hell would I be mad? This wasn't exactly my plan but I could never be upset." He lays his hand on my belly and grins. My heart expands at the simple but powerful gesture.

"But we never talked about anything like this and now it's happening."

"Sweetheart, I never talked about it because I didn't want to push you and scare you off but I want it all with you. I want you to be my wife and I want us to make lots of beautiful little green-eyed babies, and I want to grow old with your hand in mine. You're it for me, Em. You're my lobster."

"Nix," I sigh, tears welling up in my eyes again.

"I love you, Emma. So much."

"I love you, too."

He leans down and seals his mouth over mine, showing me everything he just said with his lips. A throat clears behind him and we break apart. He turns and grins at my doctor, who blushes.

"We all ready in here?"

Nix looks back at me in confusion. "Ready for what?"

"They're going to do an ultrasound and look at the baby."

"Fuck yeah, we're ready," he exclaims and then adds, "Shit, sorry, Doc."

Dr. Greene and I both laugh as she shakes her head.

"That's quite all right. I wish all my expectant fathers were this excited." I watch Nix while she is speaking and when he hears the word *father* his chest puffs out and he grins. I can't fight the smile taking over my face at the look of pride in his eyes. How did I ever think that he would be anything but happy about this?

"Go ahead and lie back. Pull your shirt up and we'll try to get a good look at your little one," Dr. Greene instructs me. I do as she says, lying back on the exam table and pulling my shirt up to my chest. "You stand right there, young man, and hold her hand."

Nix listens immediately and moves to stand by my head, grabbing my hand in his.

"Okay, this may be a little cold," Dr. Greene says just before squirting gel on my belly.

It is cold and I jump slightly when it hits my skin. Nix smiles down at me and I shake my head at him. She presses the wand to my belly and begins moving it around. Both Nix and I direct our attention to the screen as we wait to see our baby.

"Do you see that right there?" Dr. Greene points to a little blob on the screen.

"Yes," I say while Nix nods his head.

"That is your baby."

"He looks just like a peanut."

"He?" I ask. "What makes you so convinced that it's a boy?"

He shrugs his shoulders, a smile plastered on his face. "I just know." Something that sounds like a galloping horse fills the room and I look back at the monitor.

"That is your baby's heartbeat," Dr. Greene says, and I stare at the screen in wonder. Tears spring to my eyes as I listen to the quick heartbeat of our little peanut.

"Oh dear," Dr. Greene murmurs, and Nix's gaze shoots over to her.

"What? Is something wrong?" He panics, squeezing my hand for comfort.

"No. Nothing is wrong. Do you see this here?" She points to another little blob on the screen. No way. "This is your other baby."

"Two?"

She smiles at me and nods. "Yes. Twins."

"Oh my God." Lying back on the table, I look up at the ceiling and try to wrap my brain around having two babies.

"Do twins run in your family?"

"No," I reply at the exact same time that Nix says, "Yes." My head whips in his direction.

"Who?"

"Baby, my dad and Moe are twins," he says, holding back a laugh.

"No, they're not." I picture both men. Sure, they look alike but I just thought they were, ya know, brothers.

"Yeah, they are, sweetheart." He laughs and I shake my head at him. I can't believe I never noticed before. To be fair though, I've never seen the two of them right next to each other.

"Let's see," Dr. Greene interrupts. "I estimate that you are about five weeks along so that makes your due date January tenth."

"Is there anything we need to do? Anything she needs?" Nix asks, seeming really nervous all of the sudden, and I have to bite back a giggle.

"I'll give you some information to take home and there are all sorts of books you can buy if you want."

"Okay. Thanks, Doc."

After she leaves the room, I wipe the gel off of my belly. When I sit up on the exam table, he pulls me into his arms, clutching me to him.

"I'm insanely happy right now." He leans away and the huge grin on his face makes the tears well up again.

"I can tell."

"Come on, let's go get that information and get you home."

He sets me on the ground and I gather up my things. Loud giggling takes over my body as I think about telling my dad and brothers about this.

"What's so funny, gorgeous?" Nix asks, wrapping his arms around me from behind.

"You have to tell my brothers," I answer, still laughing, and his body jerks behind me.

"Shit!"

Chapter Twenty-Eight

I sigh as I sink back into my pillows, completely exhausted from the day. Telling my family about the babies went as expected. Tucker and Trey got all pissy with Nix, like this is his fault or something. Well, I guess it's half his fault but I wouldn't change it for the world. Once my shock wore off, I was ecstatic. Daddy reacted about the same as my brothers — asking Nix when he planned to marry me — but Mama made him back off. She was also thrilled, once she got over the surprise.

I think Moe had the best reaction of all. He just smiled, the same smile Nix gives me that makes me melt, and thanked me for bringing his family back together. Blaze, however, is a different story. Of all the people we told, he was the most excited. I thought he was going to do a happy dance. I have to admit, I would love to see that big, bad biker acting like a little kid.

"Hey, Em, can I talk to you about something?" Nix asks, directing my attention to him.

"Sure, babe. What's up?"

He nervously licks his lips three times before finally speaking. "I really want you to move in with me." When I just stare at him, he continues. "I want to spend the rest of my life with you, but I know you may not be ready for that yet so we can go at your pace. Just let me be there for my babies, though. My house has more room than the apartment and we can set up a little nursery for them."

I've been thinking about his request to move in together ever since he asked me that night and I had pretty much decided to say yes. Plus, everything he just said makes sense. His house does have more room, and there is a yard for the babies to play in when they are older. Two days ago, I probably would have freaked out about the thought of marriage and babies, but not anymore.

I know this is different than Ryan. Even as I said yes to Ryan's proposal, I had lingering doubts, and if Ryan ever brought up having kids, I tried to change the subject. Now, though, I find myself wanting to sit here and talk baby names all night long. Somehow, deep down in my gut, I know this is right.

"Baby, please say something."

I giggle in response. "Yeah, I'll move in with you."

"Really?"

"Really."

"We'll take things as slow as you want. Hell, I'll keep paying for your apartment if you want so you have a place to go."

"You don't need to do that, Nix."

"Baby, I'll do whatever I have to do to keep you comfortable. I don't want to rush you and mess this up."

"Phoenix, I want to move in with you. Not because of the babies, but just because I want to live with *you*. Besides, I'm not sure you could do anything at this point to mess this up. I'm head over heels in love with you."

"How did I get so lucky?" I shake my head. "Yes, Emma. You know, I wasn't looking for anything.

I was pretty happy with my life and then you walked into my tattoo parlor and my whole world changed. I couldn't imagine going through a day without seeing you. I thought about you all the time and even though I knew it would be hard, I wanted to be with you. I've had to be careful sometimes but it's all worth it."

"Don't treat me with kid gloves, Nix. I want to be your partner, not someone that you have to take care of. I'm strong enough to handle whatever you can dish out."

"I won't treat you with kid gloves then. Promise." He draws an "x" over his heart. "I know you're strong enough, Em. I just didn't want to do something that would remind you of him."

"You could never remind me of him, baby. Never."

*   *   *   *

The sun shines down on me, warming my skin as I sit in the rocking chair on the porch, watching him and my brothers carry my things into Nix's house.

Or *our* house now, I guess.

It took about a week to get all my things loaded up in boxes. Of course, Nix wouldn't let me lift a finger. He made me sit down and order him around. And the crazy thing? He actually seemed to enjoy it. I don't know where this man came from but I thank God every day for him.

"You could help us out, lazy," Tucker teases.

"Nope. I was ordered to sit right here and relax." I shoot him a smug grin and lay my hand over my still flat belly.

"That's right," Nix agrees, coming out of the house after dropping off a box. I beam at him, and he winks at me as he leans down and kisses my forehead. "You feelin' okay, baby?"

"Yeah, I'm good. Don't worry about me."

Two days after finding out about our little bundles of joy, the nausea set in and I've been puking my guts out ever since. Nix was practically frantic at first, wanting to rush me to the doctor to make sure the babies were okay. I made him call Mama, who assured him that it was perfectly normal, especially with two little ones on board.

"Oh my God! What is that smell?" I exclaim when the scent of something delicious drifts past my sensitive nose. All three of the guys turn to me and sniff at the air.

"Smells like barbecue," Trey says and my stomach growls, loudly.

Nix laughs and crouches down in front of me. "You hungry, baby?"

"Mmhmm." I nod my head and he laughs again.

"Would you like me to go get you some food?"

"Yes, please!"

"I'm on it. You want barbecue?"

"Oh my God, yes! And pickles!" He chuckles again and my brothers join in.

"Anything else, princess?" Tucker asks, still laughing.

"Not right now but if I think of anything, I'll be sure to make you go get it," I growl, narrowing my eyes at him.

"Shit, she's scary when she's pregnant," Trey says and Tucker bobs his head in agreement.

"I love you, baby. I'll be right back," Nix interrupts, grabbing his keys from his pocket.

"Thanks, baby. I love you, too."

As soon as his truck is out of sight, Trey and Tucker sit down on either side of me. "How you doin', baby girl?" Trey asks.

"I'm really good, Trey."

"Yeah. You seem good."

"We just want to make sure you're one-hundred percent sure about this guy before you go moving in with him and stuff," Tucker adds.

I turn to him and cock my head to the side. "I know it probably seems soon but it's different with Nix."

"You're different with him," Trey observes.

"Good different or bad different?"

"Definitely good different. You seem almost like your old self," Tucker answers.

"I don't think I'll ever be totally back to that girl again and I am getting better everyday. I haven't had a bad dream about Ryan in a long time and I'm feeling stronger."

"That's good, sis," they both say.

"You guys like Nix, right?"

"Oh, hell yeah, he's like way, way better than that other asshole," Tucker exclaims and I laugh.

"Yeah, he is."

"We definitely approve, Emmy," Trey adds.

"Thank you. You guys are always there for me."

Tucker growls. "I wish we could do more. We should have done something to stop him while it was happening. If I had known everything, Emma...I swear, I would have—"

"Hey, it's okay," I say, laying my hand on his shoulder. "That was part of his control. He made me feel isolated from you guys. I couldn't even trust myself."

"Will you ever tell us everything he did to you?" Trey asks.

I shake my head. "No, you guys don't need to hear all that."

They both nod in what I assume is understanding. "Yeah, okay."

"Whelp, we better get back to work if we ever want to get out of here," Tucker declares, jumping up off the porch, and Trey follows him, smirking at me. We both know that Tucker has never been good with the emotional stuff.

*   *   *   *

"Hey, Chance, how are you?" I call out as he walks through the front door for babysitting duty.

Nix had a client scheduled for a late appointment today so he called Blaze to have someone come hang out with me. A small voice inside my head that tells me this is all ridiculous. We haven't heard from Ryan in over a month. Sometimes, though, I wonder if that voice in my head is actually Ryan. It seems convenient that it's always telling me I'm being dramatic.

"Hey there, little mama. I'm good. How are ya' feelin'?"

I smile at his new nickname for me.

"I take it you heard about our news?"

"Oh yeah. Blaze is so damn excited that he can't shut up about it."

My grin grows. "I'm glad everyone is so excited. It really could have gone either way."

He shakes his head at me. "Naw, not with a cute little thing like you. They were bound to love you."

"But Nix and I haven't really known each other for that long."

He just shrugs his shoulders. "What does that matter in the grand scheme of things? Listen, I've known Nix a long time and I've never seen him like this. We all knew you were special the moment we saw ya'll together."

I blush, growing a little uncomfortable with the conversation. I've been getting better but I'm still not as confident as I was before Ryan.

"Do you want somethin' to eat?" I ask, changing the subject.

"Uh...I was instructed to not let you do anything. I heard there was frozen pizza I could make. Does that sound good?"

I sigh. I wonder if it was Nix or Blaze that told him to not let me do anything. Honestly, it could be either one.

"Yeah, that sounds good."

He smiles a carefree smile and I sit on one of the barstools while he turns on the oven and gets the pizza out of the freezer.

"Hey, Chance, can I ask you something?" His gaze flicks up from the pizza box in his hand and he nods. "Why do you guys do this?"

His brow furrows and he sets the box down on the counter before walking closer to me. He crosses his arms over his chest. "What do you mean?"

"Why do you guys help women like me?"

Darkness clouds his green eyes almost immediately.

"We all have our reasons," he answers with a shrug.

"Will you tell me yours?"

He watches me for a moment and I can see the indecision wearing on him. Finally, he sighs.

"I guess, in the realm of abuse, mine is a fairly common story. I watched my mom get the shit kicked out of her by different boyfriends for the majority of my life. Each time she met a man, she would be so hopeful that 'this time will be different,' but it never was. She just attracted assholes. When I was thirteen, she met this guy and he really was different. He was so good to her and good to me, too, but she didn't believe it. Couldn't believe it, I guess, and she left him. After that, she never tried to date again. She just drank herself to death."

I gasp and my hand flies up to my mouth. "Oh my God, Chance. I'm so sorry."

He smiles but I can see the sadness lurking there. "Thanks."

"How many other guys in the club have personal experience with abuse?"

"Enough. But those are their stories to tell, not mine."

I open my mouth to thank him but a loud knock on the front door interrupts me. I jump and press my hand over my heart. Chance glances toward the front of the house before turning back to me and pulling a gun out of his waistband.

"Stay back here, darlin'," he commands and my head bobs up and down.

I've never seen Chance be anything but funny and playful. Right now, he looks like a trained killer as he creeps closer to the front door, gun raised.

"Holy shit," I whisper to myself. Of course, I knew that I was in danger but it really sunk in in this moment. Dread washes over me, and the hairs on the back of my neck stand straight up. I can't shake the feeling that something really bad is about to happen. The screen door behind me creaks as someone opens it and in that moment, I know.

He's here. He finally got to me.

"Hey baby," says the voice that haunts me day and night, making my body go rigid from fear. I suck in a breath and turn around, coming face-to-face with the man I once loved, the man who claimed to love me and the monster who beat and raped me.

"Ryan." My mind begins to race. Different scenarios keep flitting through my head as I try to figure out how I can get out of here, get away from him. My eyes flick to the front door and I pray that Chance will walk through it at any second to save me. Straining my ears, I try to hear where he is.

"He's a little tied up," Ryan says and a sinister laugh spills out of him at his own joke. Nausea turns my stomach as I realize that I have no way out of here. God, I was so stupid. Why did I think that he would just give up? How many times did he tell me that he wouldn't? And I just didn't listen.

Maybe I could run…

"What do you want, Ryan?"

He smiles and my unease increases. His face is devoid of any emotion. He looks like pure evil.

"I want you, Emma." He inches closer and I take a step back, trying to put even a tiny amount of space between us. "It's always been you, baby. I told you, I need you. I'm lost without you." He takes another step forward and I mirror his move. I need to fight.

"You can't have me anymore."

His face clouds over with anger. He lunges at me and I see my opportunity. I kick my foot out, catching him in the shin. I hear him fall to the hardwood floor as I turn and sprint for the front door. As I run, I pull my phone out of my pocket and quickly dial Nix's number.

"Hey, sweetheart, I'm only gonna be a little bit longer," he answers and I can hear the smile in his voice. Tears well up in my eyes at the thought of never seeing it again. I know I'm not in the clear yet. This could still end very badly.

"Nix! He's here!" I scream into the phone. I'm tackled into the grass from behind and the phone flies out of my hand, falling a couple feet in front of me. I can hear Nix screaming on the other end but I can't make out the words.

I love you, baby, I think, just before my world goes black.

Chapter Twenty-Nine
Nix…

"FUCK!" I roar and slam the phone down on the table. "I gotta go, we'll do this later," I bark at the guy whose tattoo I've been working on for the past three hours.

"Seriously?" he growls, balling up his fist.

"Do I look like I'm joking, asshole? I gotta go!" He stands up and throws his shirt over his head as he follows me out of the shop.

Shit.

I've gotta get to her.

Rushing to my truck, I pull out my phone and dial my dad's number. He answers on the third ring. "Hey, boy, what's up?"

"He's got her!" I curse. "Who was out there with her?"

"Chance. Let me call him. I'll meet you at the house."

"Yeah, okay." I'm driving like a maniac, going twenty over the speed limit and weaving in and out of traffic. I can't believe I let this happen. I told her, promised her, that I would protect her and our babies.

Fuck. The babies.

I'm not a religious man but I send up prayer after prayer that I'll find my woman and my kids safe. My phone rings. I scoop it up from the cup holder to find that Tucker's calling me.

"Shit." I forgot to call Tucker. "Tucker, you gotta get to the house," I rush out as soon as I answer the phone.

"What? Why?"

"He got her."

"What the fuck? How?!"

"I don't know anything yet. Just meet me there."

He hangs up without saying a word and I press down harder on the accelerator.

"Please let her be okay," I whisper, over and over again.

When I pull up to the house, the scene before me makes my stomach roll. Blaze is untying Chance from one of the columns on my front porch, and there's blood everywhere — not a lot, just little droplets all over the porch that tell me someone's hurt. The rocking chair has been kicked over and the top part of the screen on the door has been ripped off.

God, she fought him.

Of course she fought him. I've always known she was strong. She's gotta be terrified right now, though.

Shit, what is he doing to her?

"Son," Dad barks and I look up at him. He snaps his finger in front of my face and I blink. "Focus, kid. We'll get her back, okay?"

"How, Dad?"

"Holy shit," I hear whispered behind me and turn to find Tucker and Trey standing there.

"What happened?" Tucker growls.

I start to respond but my dad interrupts me.

"Chance said that someone knocked on the front door. When he answered it, they hit him over the head and tied him up over there. He woke up right before she came sprinting out of the house. He said she fought like hell."

"Of course she did," Trey says. "She knows what he'll do to her."

Hearing those words, I lose it. Balling up my fist, I smash it into the side of my house, repeatedly as a growl tears through my lips.

"Phoenix, look at me!" Dad barks and I do. "Chance saw the license plate. You know Streak is a genius with all that tech shit. We'll find her," he assures, but it doesn't calm the violent storm raging inside me.

"I can't believe I'm even asking this but should we call the cops?" Tucker asks and I laugh.

"Leave those useless fuckers out of this. They are the reason she is in this situation." Everyone nods in agreement.

"All right, let's get to the clubhouse," Dad orders and my body kicks into action.

We'll get her back. I'll do whatever it takes. I just need her to hang on.

*   *   *   *

"Fuckin' find her, Streak!"

"I'm tryin', dude! The camera is out at this intersection. Somewhere between these two cameras, I lose the van. I'm sorry." Streak prospected in at about the same time I was supposed to and he's a good guy.

Also, the luckiest son of a bitch you'll ever meet, hence his name. Someone said his life was like one giant lucky streak.

"Well, try harder," I snap, running my fingers through my hair and pacing across the worn carpet of the clubhouse.

"Nix! Take a breath," Dad orders and I growl.

"I won't be able to until I can see that she's safe."

"Sit down!" he barks, his voice leaving no room for argument. "You're going to give yourself an aneurism."

I ignore him and continue pacing as I think about what he could be doing to her right now. I glance down at my watch and curse.

He's had her for two hours already.

"We'll find her, Nix. You gotta relax, man," Kodiak says and I send a glare his way.

Fuck all of them. They have no idea how this feels, the agony of knowing she's in danger. Involuntarily, my mind drifts back to the story she told me not so long ago about the night he raped her. Jesus, is he doing that to her right now? My head feels like it's going to explode and I know I need to distract myself.

"Chance, tell me again. What happened?"

Chance glances up and offers an apologetic smile.

"Sure. Uh, so I woke up tied to the column and she sprinted out of the house a second later, talking to you on the phone. Ryan came running out right after her and he tackled her on the grass. I think she passed out for a couple seconds, enough time for Ryan to stand up. She kicked him in the junk and ran back for the house. He caught her again just as she was opening the screen door. She grabbed onto that door like her life depended on it." His face pales as he realizes what he said.

"Keep going." He nods.

"So, she was hangin' onto the door and he was yankin' on her, trying to get her to let go. That's how the screen ripped. She was hanging on so tight that it just tore right off the frame. He finally got her to let go and she threw her elbow back, hitting him in the nose, and he started bleeding all over the place."

"So the blood was all his?"

"Yeah, I think so."

"'Kay, what else?"

"He had her around the waist and he threw her in the back of a white van. I watched the license plate until they pulled away so I would remember it."

I nod again and run my hands through my hair. God, she fought so hard. "How long between when they left and I showed up?"

"Ten minutes, tops."

God, I can't believe we lost her in such a short amount of time.

"What the fuck are you doing here?" I hear Tucker snarl from near the doorway. I turn to see Detective Rodriguez standing there.

In an instant, I'm standing toe-to-toe with him. "Where is she?" I ask, my voice so menacing that he flinches.

"I don't know for sure but you need to know that Detective Nelson has been helping him this whole time. I was suspicious after you guys came in to file the report but I couldn't prove anything."

"So, what? You just let it go and forgot about it. Forgot about my sister?" Trey shouts, shocking the hell out of me. Trey is a pretty levelheaded dude. I've only seen him get worked up one other time.

"No, I didn't forget. I've been trying to find evidence, I swear, but they were careful."

"Wait a minute, why is the other guy helping Ryan?" Dad asks and I'm curious to know the answer.

"Their dads were partners. They've been best friends their whole lives," Rodriguez says.

"Why are you here?" I ask, growing impatient with all this useless information.

"I've been running surveillance on Wheeler. I approached my captain after we spoke last time but he brushed my concerns under the rug so I had to do all this quietly. As soon as I showed the video of Wheeler kidnapping your girlfriend to him, he couldn't ignore it anymore. We're here to help."

"He's here?"

"Yeah, him and about ten other officers are outside."

Holy shit.

*　　　*　　　*　　　*

"What a fuckin idiot!" Streak exclaims as he works over the computer.

I jump up and rush over to him, rubbing my eyes. It's been six hours since Emma went missing and we've been working tirelessly to find her but every lead turns out to be a dead end.

"What?" I ask. "What is it?"

"What a stupid motherfucker!"

"Streak, I like you, I really do, but if you don't tell me in the next two seconds, I'm gonna kick the shit out of you."

"All right, calm down. This idiot turned his phone on. I've been watching it but I figured no one would be that stupid but he is. Being a cop, you would think he'd know someone could get his location from his phone."

"Do it! Now!" His fingers start flying over the keys. "Tucker! Trey!" I yell and both of them come running.

"Did he find her?" Trey asks.

"Ryan left his phone on. He's getting a location on her now."

"Got her! They are driving down I-10 but I lost the signal. Hold on, I'm gonna try to get it back."

"Nix, Wheeler's phone just turned back on at a gas station just outside Prairieville."

"Got it. Text me with updates!" I holler back as I sprint outside.

"We're right behind you," Rodriguez says.

"Let's go," Dad calls out and brothers start spilling out of the clubhouse. The rumble of motorcycles fills the air and I jump in my truck, peeling out of the parking lot.

Hang on, Em. Just a little bit longer.

Chapter Thirty
Emma
Six hours earlier...

"Good morning, sleeping beauty," *his* voice says, the sound so vile that I shiver.

A small part of me is frantically praying that this is just a dream but I know it's not. The pain in my shoulders from my hands being restrained behind my back tells me all I need to know. It's not a dream. He's here and I'm living the nightmare now.

My mind drifts to Nix, even a vision of him in my memory giving me the strength to fight against the monster I was going to marry. Nix and the babies are all I can think about. I need to get back to him and I need my little ones to be safe.

"Come on, Em. Open up those gorgeous green eyes of yours." His tone has gone all sugary sweet and it makes me want to vomit. He's fucking delusional, talking to me like we're anything more than victim and abuser. I hate him but I won't let him win. I won't let him take my strength away from me again.

Slowly, I peel open my eyes and glare at him with all the loathing I feel for him.

"Ah, there she is. I knew you hadn't lost that feisty spirit, baby." He runs his fingers across my cheek and I jerk away.

"Fuck you," I spit. Glancing around the dark room, I take everything in. He's got me tied to a chair in the middle of the room and I'm dismayed to find that there isn't anything else in here. How the hell am I going to get out?

"Baby, why do you treat me like this? All I've ever done is love you and you treat me like shit on your shoe."

I laugh. I can't help it. What he said is so ridiculous that all I can do is laugh. "Are you serious right now?"

His face morphs into one of anger and his jaw ticks. My laughter dies immediately. I know that look. My body knows that look. It tenses in preparation for whatever pain he's about to inflict. His hand closes around my throat and he squeezes. My eyes widen with a mixture of shock and fear.

"Listen here, you little bitch, you will show me some respect," he growls, increasing the pressure of his hand. It's becoming difficult to breathe and tears sting my eyes. I nod my head, praying that once I do he'll release me. For once, my prayers are answered as the pressure of his grip disappears, and I suck in air, tears running down my face.

He crouches down until he's face-to-face with me and his expression softens. "Why are you doing this, Emma? We could be happy again, baby."

"We were never happy."

His hand snaps out and smacks my cheek, pain radiating through my entire face. I don't cry out. I don't even flinch. I just hold his stare, refusing to back down.

"Stop doing this. We were happy. We're together again. I finally got you back so we can be just as happy as we used to be."

"It was all a lie, Ryan."

Shooting back up to a standing position, he roars in frustration. He runs his hands over his short hair and grits his teeth as he paces. After a couple seconds, he stops in front of me, pulls his foot back, and kicks me in the shin. I cry out in pain and he rears back and kicks me again.

"Why do you have to be such a fuckin' bitch?!" he yells, kicking me again. This time, when his foot connects with my leg, the bone snaps and I scream at the incredible pain. Tears pour down my face as I sob and Ryan seems to reach some kind of clarity.

Just as he opens his mouth to say something, someone cuts in. "Ryan, I need to talk to you." I look over to the door and gape when I see Detective Nelson standing there.

What the fuck?!

"What, Evan?" Ryan growls.

"Just get your fuckin' ass over here."

It all clicks into place. They have been working together the entire time. That's why he wouldn't take my statement and that's how Ryan was able to get to me. Evan is the one who tied Chance up.

"I'll give you a little time to think about everything," Ryan says and leaves the room with Evan. I'm so disgusted with this whole thing that I can't even bring myself to call him Detective Nelson anymore. What kind of sick, demented person does something like this?

My mind drifts back to when they took me and I shiver. It all happened so fast but I can remember every moment with excruciating detail. From waking up face first in the grass after Ryan tackled me to kicking him in the balls and sprinting back for the house. The splinters from hanging onto the screen door with all my might still sting my fingers. My entire body aches after everything I've been through tonight and I want nothing more than to crawl into Nix's arms and go to sleep.

God, Nix. Thinking of never seeing him again fills me with a pain that I've never known. It leaves me breathless and my heart physically hurts. I have to find a way back to him.

*   *   *   *

Ryan strolls back into the room with a smile on his face. I have no idea how long I've been here but it's long enough that my eye is almost swollen shut from the blow he delivered earlier. I watch him warily, as best as I can with only one eye. He stops in front of me, sitting down in a chair he brought with him.

"So, I had an idea, baby," he says, his voice light and cheery. This man seriously fucks with my mind.

"What?" My voice is hoarse from being stuck in here with no water for God knows how long. I'm absolutely exhausted and I don't know how much longer I can stay conscious.

"We're going to remember the good times."

I hold back my scoff.

"There were no good times, Ryan."

"Your family and that asshole have gotten to you. They've tainted your memories of us. That's why I am going to help you remember."

"Fine." I don't have the energy to fight him. I need to save it for when I get my opportunity to get out of here.

"Good." He scoots his chair closer to me and gently runs his thumb over my swollen cheek. It takes every ounce of self-restraint to not jerk my face away from his touch. It feels so wrong. That is Nix's thing and I love it. Feeling Ryan do it is so messed up that I want to scream. "Do you remember when I asked you to be my girlfriend?"

"Yes, I remember." The screen plays perfectly in my mind. Ryan walking out of my bathroom wearing only his jeans, sitting down on my bed and telling me that he didn't want to see anyone else. That he wanted everyone to know that I was his girlfriend.

"See, baby? It was so good. We were so good together."

His words have the opposite effect and I remember one more of the bad times. He showed up at the market and stormed over to my booth. Screaming about how I was always neglecting him for my art and that I didn't bring in enough money to make it worth my time. I remember the intense disappointment that I felt, thinking that I wasn't good enough.

"Do you remember?" he asks, bringing me back to the present.

"Yes, I remember, Ryan." I don't tell him what I was just thinking of but I remember clearly. It would be so easy to fall into old patterns with him.

"What about the first time we made love? Do you remember that?"

"Yes." When I look back on this so-called good memory, all I see is bad. I see the manipulation that I couldn't realize back then because I was so blinded by his charm. The way he controlled my emotions, the way he *made* me fall for him.

It's all tainted.

Even if he didn't know what he was doing and he got some help, changed his behavior, it could never work between us again. I'll always remember what he did to me. I'd always be wondering if he was telling the truth or just trying to control me.

Plus, he's not Nix.

I have to fight a smile as I think about Nix. I never thought I would date again and then there he was, charging into my life, and he healed me, *he* loved me. I can confidently say now that Ryan never loved me because I know what real love is. I know what it feels like to be adored and cherished by someone.

"See? It was so good."

"Do you know what I see in that memory, Ryan?" I ask, and he scrunches up his brow.

"What?"

"I see you using sex to manipulate me and make me think you were a good guy. I see lies. All of it was a lie."

"Emma, no. You let people get into your head and tear us apart. I begged you not to do this."

"You don't understand how much you hurt me, Ryan," I say, still trying to keep the peace but unable to lie to him. I can't pretend that the things he did never happened or they weren't that big of a deal.

I just can't.

"I didn't mean it, babe."

"I don't know what to believe."

"You believe me, baby. I love you," he says and leans into me. I pull away, not wanting his lips anywhere on me. "Fuckin' seriously?" he growls.

"I don't want that."

"Yes, you do, Emma. I know you and I know your body. You want this."

"Stay away from me," I growl, my every defense raised as I remember all the times Ryan forced me into having sex.

"You don't really want that, baby." He laughs and unties me from the chair.

"Yes, I do!" He pulls me down to the ground and lies down next to me.

He laughs again and pulls me closer until our bodies are touching. Panic takes over and I begin to shake. I can't do this again. I can't let him rape me. I struggle against him but he holds me tightly.

"Get off me!"

"Come on, sweetheart."

Hearing him call me that makes me cringe. It sounds so fake and it's not his. It belongs to Nix. I belong to Nix. He growls and fists his hand into my hair, gripping it tightly and yanking. A squeak of pain escapes me and he manipulates my head toward him and kisses me.

I fight against him as best as I can with a broken leg and my arms tied behind my back but it doesn't do much except make him angrier. "Why are you such a bitch to me?"

"Get away from me!" I half beg, half demand, tears welling up in my eyes.

"Bitch!" he curses and releases me. "Everything I do is for you and it's just never enough. You're never happy."

He's fuckin' delusional. What part of all this is for me?

"How is raping me, for me?" I snarl, unable to get control of my emotions.

"Are you kidding me? I would never rape you! I was just trying to remind you how good we were! You know what, I'm out of here. I'll give you some time to think."

He stomps over to the door. I hear it slam and lock. My mind is spinning and I think I'm slowly losing my sanity. This is just more of his games. He knows that he raped me, there is no way that he can claim he tied me up for fun.

Well, actually he could claim that but it's not true.

This situation grows more hopeless the more I sit here. How am I going to get away? I don't think I'll be able to run on this leg.

Sighing, I look down at my belly. "Any bright ideas you could share with Mommy, peanuts? We gotta get out of here."

I stare down at my belly with renewed resolve. I have to keep my little ones safe so if I have to run a mile on this leg, I will.

As long as my babies are okay.

*   *   *   *

"Wake up!" Someone snaps from above me. I pry my eyes open and come face-to-face with Detective Nelson.

"Evan," I growl.

"It's Detective Nelson to you, bitch."

"You don't deserve that title." His foot rears back and then connects with my stomach. I gasp and fold myself over, trying to shield the babies from any further attack.

"Evan! What the fuck!" Ryan barks.

"She disrespected me!"

Birds of a feather, flock together, I think to myself and hold back the giggle. God, my emotions are all over the place. Maybe I'm in shock.

Or maybe I'm just crazy.

"Go down to the van!" Ryan demands and Evan grumbles before doing as he says. Ryan leans down in front of me and palms my face. My mind locks onto the word *van*. Oh God, are they taking me somewhere?

"Baby, I'm so sorry. I can't believe he hurt you."

My eyes widen.

Oh, the irony.

I have to mash my lips together to keep from scoffing. This is also the first time he's ever said, 'I'm sorry.'

"It's fine," I say, trying to keep it safe.

361

"Come on, we gotta go."

"Go? Where are we going?" Panic consumes me.

"It's a surprise. Come on," he says and drags me up. As soon as I put any weight on my leg, I scream in pain and collapse again. Ryan kneels down and inspects my injury.

"Mmm, babe, I think it's broken."

"No shit, Sherlock," I growl and gasp when I realize that I actually said it out loud. "I'm sorry. I didn't mean that."

He glares at me for a moment before nodding his head. "I'll let it go this time because you are probably in a great deal of pain."

Sighing, he produces a cloth and grabs the back of my head, holding it in place while he moves the cloth over my nose and mouth.

No!

I try to struggle but it's too late. I see Ryan's lips moving but I can't hear what he's saying and then my whole world goes black again.

Chapter Thirty-One

I wake up, lying on my side with my hands still secured behind my back and my head pounding. I take inventory of my body and wince at the result. My leg is throbbing and my face swollen. My belly aches where Evan kicked me and the cable ties are digging into the skin of my wrists, blood trickling down my fingers.

Please, God, let my babies be okay, I pray, looking up at the ceiling.

Wait, where am I?

I look around and realize that I'm alone in the back of the van again. Oh God, where are they taking me? How will anyone ever find me? We hit a bump and I bounce off the floor before slamming back down.

I hiss in pain on impact. The van comes to a stop and I strain my ears, trying to hear anything around us. Muffled voices carry through the metal of the van and then one of the doors opens and closes. I sit there, waiting for someone to open the back doors but they never come.

Where the hell are we?

"I should get her some water," Ryan says right outside the van.

"Yeah, all right but hurry up. We don't want to be here long." I glare in the general direction of Evan's voice.

After about ten minutes, Ryan comes back. "'Kay, go get whatever you need."

"Be right back."

A door opens and closes again. I wish I knew where the hell I was or where they plan on taking me. If they get me out of the state, I don't know how anyone will ever find me.

Ten more minutes pass and Evan returns to the van and gets in.

"I better go give her some water," Ryan says.

"What the fuck, dude?" Evan growls. "We need to go."

"Yeah, I got it, Ev!" The door slams. A moment later, I'm squinting at the bright morning light streaming in.

"Come here, baby. I've got some water for you."

I scoot toward the light and my leg throbs the entire way there. I try not to whimper or show any sign of the pain I'm in but I don't do a very good job. Once I get close enough, Ryan holds the bottle up to my lips and gives me small sips. The cool water coats my mouth and I almost moan in relief.

"Why are you doing this to me, Ryan?" I ask once he pulls the bottle away, my voice scratchy.

"What are you talking about, Emma?"

"Why am I tied up in the back of van while you're giving me small sips of water? Can't you see that this isn't the way to love someone?"

His eyes soften and he runs his hand over my cheek. "It's necessary for right now, baby, but I promise I'll make it up to you."

"Where are we going?"

"I found us a little cabin. You're going to love it," he answers, his eyes bright and dread fills me.

God, no one will ever find me if he gets me out in the wilderness.

"I don't want to go to a cabin."

He narrows his eyes at me. "Is this because of him?"

"No, I'm just not an outdoorsy person."

"Don't lie to me! This is about that guy! How long is it going to take for you to realize that you are mine?"

"I'm not yours," I growl.

He leans in close and grabs my face. I wince but he keeps holding me tighter. "If I can't have you then no one can."

Jesus, what is he going to do? Kill me? I want to say that he wouldn't but I really can't be sure. I have no idea what Ryan is truly capable of. If his delusional idea that he loves me keeps me alive then I guess I have to roll with it.

"Okay, Ryan. I'm yours."

"There's my girl." He beams, leaning in, and kisses me. I fight my body's every instinct to retch and instead kiss him back. Pulling away, he wipes his thumb across my cheek and smiles.

"Scoot back so I can close the doors, babe."

I allow my body to follow his directions. I'm so exhausted and I just want Nix. I don't have much fight left in me.

He closes the door and goes back to the driver's side. The van starts up and he curses.

"What?" Evan asks.

"We need gas."

This time Evan curses. "Man, we can't hang around here long. Do you want to get caught?"

"We'll be fine. It'll take five minutes."

"We've already been here for close to a half an hour!"

"Chill out, Ev!"

My mind spins as Ryan sounds completely aware of what he is doing. He knows this is wrong, he just doesn't care. I feel better knowing that I'm not the one losing my mind here. The van begins moving, only to stop a short time later, and someone jumps out after it shuts off.

"Man, hurry the fuck up! I'm not going to jail for that cunt!"

"Shut up! Don't call her that!" Ryan calls back.

"Yeah, yeah, sorry. She's your girl, I know."

It grows silent as Ryan puts gas in the van.

"Jesus! How long is this going to take?" Evan barks.

"Dude, it's got like a thirty-gallon gas tank. It's gonna take a minute."

Suddenly, the rumble of motorcycles fill the air and I hold my breath, praying with every ounce of strength I have that it's Nix's dad. Police sirens join the roar of the bikes and in that moment, I know I'm saved.

He found me.

I don't know how but I know without a doubt that Nix found me. Now, all I need is for my babies to be okay.

"Shit!" Ryan yells.

"Motherfucker!" Evan adds. "I told you, Ryan! Damn it! How did they find us?"

"I don't know!"

"You stupid idiot! Did you turn your phone on?"

"Shit, sorry, dude. Come on, let's get out of here."

"What's the point, asshole? They'll just follow us. We're screwed!"

"NO! I'm not going to lose her!"

My relief dies when I hear those words. In an instant, I realize that this could get much worse.

Do they have guns?

Of course they do, they're cops.

"Get out of the van!" Tucker barks and I almost sob at the sound of his voice.

"Where's Emma?" Trey demands and the low rumble of the motorcycles dies down as everyone turns off their bikes.

"You had better start talking, asshole," Nix says and this time a cry rips out of me.

"Nix!" I scream, hoping that he can hear me through the walls of the van.

"She's mine. I'll die before I let anyone else have her," Ryan says and Nix laughs.

"Sounds good to me."

"Nix!" I yell again. When he doesn't respond, I scoot over to the side of the van.

"Where is she?" Nix yells. Using my good leg, I slam my foot against the side of the van. "Emma?!" I kick again.

"Hold on, baby. I'm comin'. Tucker, keep an eye on this douchebag."

"Got him."

Light floods the back of the van as the doors fly open and I see Nix standing there.

Finally able to fully relax, I release a breath and sob. "Nix!"

"Shhh, baby. I'm here. Can you scoot toward me?"

"N-no, my leg is broken."

"Okay, Em. I'm comin' in to get you. Which leg is it?"

"Right."

He nods and crawls into the back of the van with me.

"Hey, baby," he coos when he reaches me and cradles my face in his hand.

"Nix," I breathe. "I love you."

"Oh, Emma, I love you, too, baby."

"I thought I was never going to see you again," I say and fresh tears spill down my cheeks.

"I would have spent the rest of my life searching for you. I never would have given up."

My sobs grow louder and I bury my head in his chest. He strokes my hair and rocks me back and forth.

After a moment, he wipes the tears from my cheeks. "Ready to get out of here, baby?"

"Yeah, let's go." Nix scoops me up in his arms, careful not to jostle my leg too much, and carries me out of the van. We emerge, the morning sunlight overly bright, and both of my brothers rush up.

"Nix, she's bleeding," Tucker says, pointing to my legs. Nix's face loses all color as he shakes his head.

"No."

"Hey, we need an ambulance over here!" Trey yells and I look up at Nix, his panic-stricken face the last thing I see before I pass out.

*   *   *   *

My mouth is really dry and my entire body aches as I slowly crack open my eyes and look around. There's a whiteboard on the wall in front of me with my name and a doctor's name on it. Nix is on my left, fast asleep in the chair next to the bed. His lashes fan out against his cheeks and his eyes twitch as he dreams. He has his arms crossed over his large chest and his head is bent at an awkward angle.

I groan and his eyes shoot open. "Hey, baby," I whisper, barely loud enough to be heard.

"Hey, honey." His voice is still heavy with sleep. He moves the chair closer to my bed before grabbing my hand and bringing it to his lips. "Do you need anything?"

"Water, please."

He jumps up and grabs a cup off of the tray by the bed. "Here you go, baby." He places the straw next to my lips and I wrap my lips around it and take a drink. After I'm done, I sigh and relax back on the bed.

"What happened?"

"Well, the police arrested Ryan and Detective Nelson—"

"Evan," I interrupt.

"Right, Evan. Then, you passed out on me and we rushed you here, to the hospital. They took you into surgery and set your leg."

"What about the babies? Are the babies okay?" I ask, suddenly remembering the kick Evan dealt to my stomach earlier.

"Both babies are perfectly fine, sweetheart."

"Are you sure?" I still feel panicked, like they could've missed something on the ultrasound.

"Emma, I promise. They are both good."

"Okay," I sigh. "How long have I been out?"

"Only a couple hours. Babe, I gotta ask…did he…rape you?" he asks, an agonized look on his face.

"No, Nix. He didn't."

"Oh, thank God." He lays his head down on the bed and I run my fingers through his hair. He hums in appreciation and then looks up at me.

"I thought I was never going to see you again."

His lips curve up in a sweet smile and he runs his knuckles over my cheek. I soak it up, loving how perfectly right it feel when he does it.

"I think you seriously underestimate my love for you, Emma Harrington. I would have looked for you until my dying breath."

"Phoenix West, you are too smooth for my own good."

He grins and shakes his head. "Naw, baby. Just for you, it's always you." He stands and leans over me, pressing a soft kiss to my lips, and contentment washes over me.

"I love you," I whisper against his lips.

"I love you, too, Em." He kisses me again.

Someone clears their throat by the door and Nix pulls away as I glance in that direction. An older man in a police uniform stands in the doorway.

"Can we help you?" Nix asks, sounding annoyed, and I can't say that I blame him. After everything we've been through with the police, I don't trust a single one of them.

"Yes, I'm Captain Cole. I wanted to offer my apologies regarding the...situation yesterday." He sounds very insincere and I question his motives immediately. Nix starts to speak but I put my hand on his arm to stop him.

"Thank you for stopping by, Captain."

He nods his head and tells us to have a good day before leaving.

"That guy was full of shit," Nix says, his tone laced with venom.

"Yeah, I know but what are we gonna do about it?"

He sighs and runs his hands through his hair. "I don't know but we should do something."

Chapter Thirty-Two

"How's our girl?" Tucker asks as he and Trey come barging into my hospital room.

"I'm good, guys. No need to worry about me." It's the truth, I really am feeling better and have been up for a couple hours now. And Ryan is locked up behind bars so life is pretty good right now.

"I won't stop worrying until that fucker is dead," Tucker growls.

"Yeah, okay, Macho Man."

Nix and Trey bust up laughing but Tucker just glares at me.

"This isn't funny. Have you thought about what you're going to do?" "What do you mean?"

"Well, I was talkin' with Dad and we both think you should consider filing a case against the city."

His comment takes me off guard and I just stare at him for a moment. I had never really thought about doing anything like that and I can't say that I'm terribly fond of the idea. It's just not who I am.

"I don't know, Tuck."

"Just think about it, okay? You may not be the first victim of their carelessness but you could be the last." That strikes a chord in me as I think about other women going through the same kind of abuse.

I know that I got lucky. It's a weird thing to think given Ryan did some terrible things to me but it's true. I had my brothers, Nix came into my life, and I got away from Ryan. Some women are stuck and they need an ally.

"Okay, I'll think about it."

"Thanks, baby girl."

"Sure."

"So, are you going to go to the bail hearing?" Trey asks.

"Yes. When is it?"

"Monday."

I scrunch up my face and look at him. It's Saturday, why are they making him wait until Monday? I thought bail hearings happened pretty quickly.

"Why Monday?"

"They don't do it on the weekends," Trey answers.

"So, Ryan is stuck in jail until Monday?" I ask and Trey nods. I immediately start giggling. "Oh, that's great."

"You seem totally unfazed by everything that has happened to you, Emmy," Tucker comments and I shrug.

I don't know what I'm supposed to be feeling here but all I am is relieved. Ryan is in jail, my babies are okay, I'm okay — what more could I ask for?

"I feel pretty good." Tucker scowls at me and I roll my eyes. "What, Tucker? Spit it out."

"I'm just worried that you're going to crack up in a couple days, or a week, or a month, ya know?"

I roll my eyes again. "Ya'll don't give me enough credit."

"I know you're strong, baby," Nix says and I smile lovingly at him.

"Oh, sure! Throw us under the bus, why don't ya?" Trey complains and I laugh again. It feels good. With Ryan in jail, it's as if a weight has been lifted off my chest, and I can finally breathe again.

*   *   *   *

"Want me to carry you up the stairs, baby?" Nix asks.

I look down at my pink cast and pout. "Yes."

He smiles and scoops me up in his arms. "It's all right, sweetheart. I'll carry you everywhere, if you want."

"No!" I complain, burying my head in his chest. "I want to walk. Stupid cast…and stupid Ryan!"

His lips brush against my forehead and he kisses me, softly. "It will heal, baby. Just like you did." My body relaxes in his arms. We enter the bedroom and he sets me on the bed.

"Can I get you anything, baby?"

"No, just come lay with me," I answer, patting the bed.

"You got it, boss." He climbs into bed and I shimmy down off the pillows and roll into him. He tucks his arm underneath me and pulls me closer.

"You know what the worst part was?"

"What?"

"Thinking about never seeing you again or the babies getting hurt. I didn't care what he did to me as long as I got home to you and our babies were okay."

It's so weird. I spent so much time being scared of this, being unsure, but when Ryan took me all I could think about was spending the rest of my life with Nix. I'm not scared anymore. I know that this is what I want.

"I love you so much, Emma."

"Marry me," I blurt out and he jerks away.

"What?"

"You heard me."

He looks down at me for a moment before smirking and shaking his head.

"You are seriously stealing my thunder here, babe." He tries to sound irritated but I can see the smile growing on his full lips.

Giggling, I say, "I know but will you marry me anyway?"

He sighs and reaches into the pocket of his jeans, pulling out a black velvet jewelry box. My mouth forms a perfect *O* as I watch him open the box. Inside is a princess-cut diamond ring, with smaller diamonds surrounding the center stone and lining the band. The light catches the gems and they sparkle back at me as tears well up in my eyes.

"You already had a ring?"

"Yeah. I bought it the day after we found out about the twins. I told you, baby, I want it all with you."

"Oh, Nix."

"Will you let me do this right?"

I nod, eagerly. He climbs out of the bed and struts around to my side before dropping to his knee. Even though I knew it was coming, the sight still has me tearing up.

"Baby, from the day I met you, I knew couldn't live without you. I don't want to spend a single minute of my life without you as mine. I told you, I want it all. The wedding, babies, rocking chairs, and the rest of our lives. Will you marry me?"

"Yes."

He smiles a brilliant smile and pulls the ring out of the box before sliding it onto my finger. My heart swells with happiness as I think about this man being my husband.

Husband.

The word sends butterflies dancing through my stomach and has me giggling. It's just too much joy to hold in my body. I am insanely, completely, out-of-my-mind happy. I didn't think it was possible, but his smile grows and his eyes shine with pure love.

"I can't wait to make you my wife, baby."

I just can't take it. My face hurts from all the smiling and just when I think I've reached my quota of happiness, he says something else to make me even happier.

I'm going to explode or something, right?

"I love you so much, Phoenix."

"I love you more, Emma."

I wrinkle up my nose and shake my head. He laughs and jumps on top of me, kissing me senseless.

*   *   *   *

"I'm freakin' out, Nix!" He wraps an arm around my shoulders and pulls me closer as we wait for them to bring Ryan in for his bail hearing. I fidget again and Nix lays his hand over my belly.

"Everything is going to be okay, honey. Just relax." His voice chases some of the stress away.

"How do you do that?"

He grins. "I hear lobsters have very special abilities." He winks and I mash my lips together, fighting a smile. He kisses my cheek and I can't stop it, a smile stretches my lips and I gaze at him adoringly.

There is a commotion over by the door and Ryan enters the room, glaring at Nix. His eyes move down to our hands on my belly and they widen in shock before I see rage burning there. When I glance down, I realize that he saw my ring.

Oh God.

This is not going to be good.

"I can feel you tensing up, baby," Nix whispers in my ear. "Just relax. I've got you." His words work their magic again and I lean into him for support. He kisses my forehead.

The judge enters and gets right down to business, asking Ryan what his plea is.

"Not guilty," he calls out, and I want to jump up and call him a liar.

"What is the prosecution's recommendation in this case?" the judge asks.

The prosecutor, a woman in her early thirties, clears her throat. "The people recommend no bail in this case, Your Honor."

"That's ridiculous!" Ryan's lawyer snaps. "Mr. Wheeler is a detective with the Port Allen Police Department—"

"A position he used to abuse and kidnap his ex-fiancé!" the prosecutor cuts in, and I feel like I'm watching a tennis match as they go back and forth.

"Allegedly!" his lawyer states. I've never hated a word so much in my life. It's not alleged, I lived it. "And Mr. Wheeler has extensive ties to the community. He is the exact opposite of a flight risk."

"Seeing as how Mr. Wheeler was fleeing to California with his victim tied up in the back of a van when he was caught, we consider him the definition of a flight risk."

"What is your request for bail, Mr. Richardson?" the judge asks Ryan's lawyer.

"We request that he be released on his own recognizance."

"That's preposterous, Your Honor!" the prosecutor exclaims. "Mr. Wheeler is very dangerous. Miss Harrington, her two unborn children, and her fiancé are in grave danger if he is allowed release."

Ryan turns to me with narrowed eyes as soon as he hears that I'm pregnant.

Well, I guess all my secrets are coming out today.

"Your Honor, Miss Harrington has a history of mental health issues and has falsely accused my client of assault, rape, and kidnapping."

"Oh, please—"

"That's quite enough," the judge says, cutting the prosecutor off. "I'm ready to make my ruling. Bail is set at five hundred thousand dollars."

I tense up and Nix squeezes me to him. I can't breathe, it's like there is a hundred pound weight pushing down on my chest.

Just when I thought I was free.

"I will, however, grant Miss Harrington and Mr. West an order of protection. You are not allowed to come within one hundred yards of either of them, young man. Do you understand?"

"Yes, sir."

I can hear the sick satisfaction in his voice. How do these people not see it? Is he really that good at fooling everyone?

"Bailiff, please escort Mr. Wheeler back to his cell," the judge orders and a man in a police uniform guides Ryan out of the courtroom. My breath stutters. Tears threaten as I remain frozen in my seat and the rest of the people in the courtroom file out.

"Hey, baby, look at me," Nix commands, softly.

I turn to him slowly and he lets out a pained moan at the expression on my face. "Emmy, I hate seeing you like this."

"I can't believe they let him out. What are we going to do?"

Nix flexes his jaw and I know he's barely holding it together. I need to be there for him just as much as he's there for me.

"I'm sorry," I whisper.

He blinks and his eyes widen in shock. "What on earth are you sorry for?" His brow furrows and he cradles my face in his hand.

"I only think about me. I'm over here freaking out and this is hard on you, too."

He shakes his head with a small smirk gracing his lips. "Babe, I think it's safe to say that this is a whole lot harder on you."

"Maybe it is but that's not the point. I care about how you feel, too."

"I know you do," he assures me, stroking my cheek with his thumb. "I'm just so worried about you. As far as what we're gonna do, I'm not leaving your side until this is resolved. We'll get my dad's help again."

I sigh in frustration. "I hate asking your dad for help again. I'm sure he's got his own life to live."

"Baby," he scolds, "my dad loves you and he's so excited about being a granddad. We're his family and he wants to do this for us."

"Okay, Nix," I agree, giving in. I honestly don't have a better option so I'll suck it up if I have to. It's not just about me anymore. I have to think about our little ones.

"Come on, babe. Let's get you out of here."

I let Nix lead me out of the courthouse, readying myself for what comes next.

Chapter Thirty-Three

"So, what's the plan here?" Tucker asks as we all gather in our living room. I haven't been able to relax since that judge granted him bail this afternoon. He's probably already out. Lurking in the shadows, just waiting for the perfect opportunity to get to me.

"I don't think there is anything we can do." Nix lets out a growl from behind me and wraps his arms around my waist. I snuggle closer to him before turning back to my brother, and continuing. "He's not doing anything wrong by being out on bail right now. We just have to wait."

This time, all three boys growl and I roll my eyes.

"I don't like it," Trey says.

"Me either," Tucker grunts.

"I don't like it either but she's right. Unless he breaks the protection order, there is nothing we can do," Nix adds.

My brothers grumble a little but they don't disagree this time. There is a knock at the door and every head in the room whips in its direction.

"Come in," Nix calls and then turns to us. "It's my dad."

Blaze, Chance, Storm, and Streak strut into the room, nodding hello to all of us. They find chairs and settle in before Blaze gets things rolling.

"So, anyone have a plan?"

I shake my head. "Not really."

"All right. Well, I'm gonna have two guys on her at all times."

Chance grumbles something and I frown at him. I know he feels guilty about me getting taken. He showed up at the hospital to tell me how incredibly sorry he was. Not that I ever blamed him.

"Chance, it wasn't your fault."

"Yes, it was."

"No," Blaze barks, "it was mine. I made the call to only send one guy over." He turns to me and offers an apologetic smile. "I failed you, darlin' and I'm sorry. It won't happen again. I promise you that."

"No—"

Blaze holds his hand up to stop me. "Now, along with the two guys, I'll put a guy on that asshole so we can keep tabs on him." Everyone in the room nods and even I have to admit that the thought of knowing where he is at all times eases some of my stress. Blaze turns and speaks directly to me. "We'll keep you safe until this thing is taken care of."

"When is this going to be taken care of? When is it going to be over, for good?" Everyone in the room looks down, not wanting to answer my question, and in their silence, I find my answer.

This will only end when one of us is dead.

*   *   *   *

"Emma," *his* voice wakes me from a deep sleep, and instantly, my body goes on alert at the danger it knows is there.

No!

No, he can't have me. I won't let him take me again.

His hand wraps around my upper arm and he squeezes, his fingers digging into my skin. "How many times do I have to tell you that you are mine, bitch?" he snarls. "You'll never get away. You'll never be free."

"No!" I respond, surprised by how strong my voice sounds. I will fight back this time. I'm stronger than the last time he turned me into a victim.

He laughs, the sound sending chills all the way to my toes. "You don't get to say no, Emma. You have no control here."

That one sentence haunts me more than anything else.

You have no control.

"I won't go with you!"

Fight, Emma, I think to myself. Don't *let* him take the control from you.

"Open your eyes," he commands and my body obeys, my lids blinking open. I focus on his empty hazel eyes in front of me.

"Leave me alone," I plead.

He slaps me across the face with one hand while the other digs into my arm harder. Blood streaks down the inside of my arm.

"Never."

"Let. me. go," I demand, stronger this time.

He laughs manically and shakes his head. "I'll never leave you alone. We will be together always. Until death do us part…"

"NO!" I scream and shoot up off the bed.

"Emma! Jesus, baby, what's wrong?"

I look around the room and realize the only other person here is Nix.

It was a dream.

I release a breath and tears drip down my cheeks.

"Shhh, it's okay, honey. You're okay," Nix coos, pulling me into his arms and rocking back and forth.

I gasp for breath as I sob and clutch Nix's arm for dear life.

"Calm down, Em. You're okay."

Streak, Chance, and Tucker bust into the room, the door banging against the wall, and causing me to jump and scream again. Nix's arms tighten around me.

"Everything okay?" Chance asks.

"Yeah, she just had a bad dream," Nix answers.

Streak scans the room while Tucker keeps his eyes locked on me.

"All right, we'll leave you to it," Chance says. Streak and Chance leave the room but Tucker stays behind, watching me.

"It's all right, Tuck. I've got her," Nix assures him and after a moment, he nods.

"Love you, Emmy."

All I can do is nod in return. He seems to understand and leaves the room.

"Come here, baby," Nix lowers us back down on the bed. I rest my head on his shoulder and curl into him, needing to get as close as humanly possible.

"It was just a dream, Em. It's not real. You are okay," he says, stroking my hair and kissing my forehead.

"I'm sorry."

"You have nothing to be sorry for."

"He's coming for me," I whisper as I stare at a spot on the wall. I feel as empty as Ryan's eyes looked in my dream.

"I know, baby."

I shudder. A foreboding feeling rushes through me. It's almost as if my dream is a message, a warning. What it is saying, however, terrifies me more than anything else.

It won't be long now.

*   *   *   *

It's been a week since I woke up screaming in the middle of the night and each passing day puts me more on edge. I'm stuck, waiting here for death. I just don't know if it will be his or mine. Blaze's guy, Fuzz, lost Ryan the day after my dream and no one has been able to find him again. They've been scouring the area but nothing has turned up. Fuzz, aptly named because he used to be a cop, assured me that he would find him again. They left the biggest guys, Kodiak, Moose, and Smith here to guard me.

Nix hasn't left my side either. I can barely go pee by myself.

My brothers also decided to stay here with us and they brought my girls with them. So, I've been able to de-stress but only slightly. Addy and Daisy have been helping me plan the wedding. We decided to have a small, intimate ceremony in the backyard by the water next month. I really wanted to get married before I got too big to fit into a dress.

Sighing, I grab a couple beers from the fridge and pass them out among the guys. Storm smiles when I hand one to him. "Thanks, darlin'."

"No problem." When I turn to walk away, he reaches out and grabs my wrist. My brow shoots up as I look back at him. He nods his head to the chair across from him. I slowly sink down and meet his eyes.

"How are you doin' with all this?"

"Oh, I'm fine." I wave my hand through the air to brush off his concern, but he's not buying it. He raises an expectant brow and stares me down. "Seriously, I'm okay," I add.

He shakes his head. "I know that's not true."

"How could you possibly know that?"

He's right, damn it, but I don't want him or anyone else to know it. I really thought I had been doing a good job of hiding it.

"Have you ever heard about the work we do?" I nod my head, assuming that he's referring to them sheltering abused women. "We do that because enough of us in this club have dealt with abuse in our lives. So, I know from experience that you are not okay right now." His words and the seriousness in his tone make me pause. Chance's story comes to mind and I wonder if Storm has a similar tale.

"Have you dealt with it personally?"

He takes a swig of his beer. "Yeah." I open my mouth to ask him what happened but he shakes his head at me. "I don't talk about it."

After a moment, I stand. "Okay." Just as I'm walking away, he gently grabs my wrist again.

"You're family now, Emma. We'll do whatever it takes to protect you."

Whatever it takes. Those words eat at me, both from Ryan and Storm. Both sides are willing to win by any means necessary, and I'll be at the center of an all out war. Is there any way to get out of this in one piece?

I force a smile to my face and nod. "Thank you." Then I slowly make my way into the living room and Nix looks up when I enter.

"Come here, baby." He pats his leg and I go to him, sitting down and curling up in his lap. He presses his full lips to my forehead and I sigh. "You okay?"

"I guess so," I reply with a shrug and he squeezes me to him. He doesn't have to ask what's wrong, he already knows.

"It will be over soon, sweetheart. I promise." I pull back to look at him.

"How can you possibly know that, Nix?" Love and reassurance shine in his eyes and he brushes his thumb over my cheek. Closing my eyes, I soak up his touch. One single tear slips down my face. Nix kisses it away.

"It will be okay, Em. We will end this."

"Thank you," I whisper, my voice so soft that only he can hear me. I lean down and press my lips to his.

This kiss isn't full of heat or need like they so often are between us. Instead, it's full of the love and reassurance I need in this moment, and I love him even more for that. He always knows just what I need. When I pull back, I smile at him, feeling a little lighter.

Several loud pops ring out through the air and I jump in Nix's lap. He stiffens just as Blaze, Storm, Kodiak, Moose, Smith and my brothers go running to the back of the house with guns drawn. Nix jumps out of his chair, clutching me to his chest and marching with determination to his goal — the front door. Deja vu washes over me.

"Wait!"

Nix jerks to a stop and stares down at me. "What, baby?"

"Something isn't right." Why can't I shake this feeling? The shots are coming from the back of the house so logically, we should go out the front but I can't help but feel like that would be the wrong decision. Then, it hits me.

"Emma!" Nix snaps, his body trembling from the rush of adrenaline.

Fear overwhelms me. Ryan is here. This is it. This is the moment I've been waiting for and dreading for the past week.

"Go to the kitchen." As soon as the words are out of my mouth, his eyes widen and he gapes at me.

"Have you lost your mind?!"

"Please, baby. Trust me."

His gaze flicks back and forth between the front door and the kitchen. Uncertainty vibrates through him but finally, he sighs and marches into the kitchen.

The moment we enter the space, someone yells, "It's a fuckin' recording!"

Nix gazes down at me, his eyes full of astonishment.

"How did you know, baby?"

"Do you remember when Ryan took me?" He nods. "He had Evan at the front of the house to draw Chance out while he snuck in the back. He was counting on you wanting to get me as far away from the gunshots as possible."

I look up at him and he gazes back at me but his eyes are blank. My brow furrows in confusion as he slumps to the floor and I come face-to-face with Ryan.

I gasp and my hand flies up to cover my mouth. Ryan throws a piece of wood off to the side as he takes a step toward me. He inches closer and I quickly take two steps back, trying to keep distance between us. He smiles at me and it scares me more than anything else. It's maniacal, inhuman almost. How did I ever fall in love with this man?

He rushes me and I don't move quickly enough to escape him. His arm hooks around my waist as he moves to stand behind me and yanks me into his body. I fight against him with every ounce of power I can muster up, but it's no good. He pins my arms at my sides and secures them there with one arm. I've never felt so defenseless in my entire life. The tip of his nose trails a path along my neck and he buries his face in my hair, inhaling deeply. My skin crawls.

"God, I missed you, baby." His free hand strokes over my arm and I have to bite down on my lip to keep from sobbing. I can't help but remember that last time he touched me. "Did you miss me, Emma?"

I should probably lie right now. I should tell him that I've missed him so much and that I could barely get out of bed without him but I refuse to lie. I refuse to encourage him.

"No."

His arm tightens around me. "You're mine and you always will be. Did you forget that?"

I shake my head. "No, I'm not."

He chuckles. The sound is so out of place in this desperate, dark moment that it grates on my nerves.

"Yes, you are," he growls, right in my ear. His breath washes over my skin and I want to claw it off. "You and me are going to get out of here, baby. We can be happy again, you'll see. We just need to get rid of these things." He jabs a finger into my belly and I suck in a breath. Oh God, no. Not my babies. His arm tightens further and I hold back the squeak of pain that so desperately wants to escape. "I'm so fuckin' mad at you, Emma. How could you do this to me?" His finger digs into my belly and this time, I whimper. "How could you give him what belongs to me?"

"I'm not yours and I gave myself to him because he never demanded a single thing from me."

A growl sounds from deep in his chest as he grabs my face and twists my head so I'm looking back at him.

"You. Belong. To. Me." I shake my head in his grasp and he grits his teeth. "So Goddamn stubborn." He releases me and my face aches where he was grabbing me. I know the feeling well. I'll have his signature fingerprint bruises there tomorrow morning.

I don't know why I'm taunting him. If I was listening to logic, I would go along with his delusion, but I just can't do it. I don't love Ryan anymore and I never loved him the way I love Nix.

"Let me go, Ryan."

"Never. How many times do I have to tell you that you are mine?"

"I'm not yours and I never will be again."

Suddenly, he's gone but I don't even get to breathe a sigh of relief before he's standing in front of me and wrapping his large hand around my neck. He squeezes and my eyes widen and start to water as I struggle to take a breath.

"Shut up!" he seethes. "After we leave here, I don't ever want to hear you talk about him again. You belong to me. End. Of. Discussion." When I remain silent, he loosens his grip slightly.

Nix groans and my breath catches in my throat.

Ryan quickly moves behind me again and pins my arms to my sides. Nix's eyes flutter open and he looks around the room in confusion. His blue gaze finally lands on me and his eyes widen as he staggers to his feet. When I can tell that he is okay, tears of relief drop down my cheeks. He stares at me and I can see the torment that this is causing him.

"How nice of you to join us," Ryan sneers and Nix looks to him for only a moment but when he focuses back on me, I can see the rage lighting up his eyes.

"Let her go," Nix demands and Ryan laughs.

Nix takes two quick steps forward but freezes at the same moment that something presses against my belly. When I glance down, I see a pistol, pointed right at my babies. In a panic, my eyes fly back to Nix, who looks equally horrified.

"That's right. We wouldn't want to do anything to hurt the little bastards, would we?"

Nix's entire body tenses and fury builds in his eyes. He looks capable of murder.

"You hurt my girl or my kids and I can promise you that it will be the last thing you ever do." He never once takes his eyes off mine as he delivers the threat. We stare at each other, silently saying so much. Ryan's grip gets harder around me and I wince from the pain. Only then does Nix look to Ryan and his intent is clear. He is going to kill him.

Ryan shakes his head as the gun digs into my skin. "She's not yours." He squeezes me and tears start falling down my cheeks. I've never been so scared in my whole life. I don't know how to get all the people I love out of this mess.

"Take a look, asshole. That's my ring, those are my kids, and I'm the one that she can't take her eyes off of."

"Shut up!" Ryan roars and his body is shaking with anger. What is Nix doing? How is making Ryan mad going to fix anything?

"Face it, Ryan. As long as I'm alive, you'll be second place in her book. A consolation prize."

Jesus, what the hell is he doing? His plan becomes clear just as Ryan pulls the gun away from my belly and points it straight at the love of my life. A sob racks my body as I shake my head at Nix. He just gives me that easy smile that I adore, his eyes shining with so much love and devotion that I know he's prepared to die for me, for us. It makes me cry even harder and Ryan is getting angrier by the second, his body shaking in rage.

"Shut up!" Ryan yells, shaking me. He cocks the gun and the fear works its way up my throat, clawing at me, choking me.

No! I can't lose him.

Come on, Emma! Think! Think of something.

"Even if you kill him, I'll never be yours again. If he dies tonight, he will be immortalized in my mind as the love of my life and I'll blame you for as long as I live. *I will hate you.*"

A look of absolute horror creeps over Nix's face as Ryan lets out a shriek of frustration and points the gun to my head.

I blink away my tears and lock eyes with the man in front of me. I need to see him. A part of me wants to tell him to look away but I can't waste one second of what's left of my life on anything but him. It's selfish, I know, but I need it. I hope he knows how much I love him. I hope I've done enough to let him know that he is everything I ever wanted and that I'm so incredibly lucky to have gotten the time I had with him.

Ryan buries his head in my hair again and Nix's gaze flicks to him for just a moment. I can practically see the all-out war going on in his head. He wants to rush over to me, to go after Ryan, but he also realizes that it could get me killed just as easily. I know what he's feeling very well, the fear of not knowing what to do leaving you paralyzed.

"Why do you make me do this to you, Emma? If you had just done what you were told, we could have been happy again, but you chose him. You've left me no choice." He presses the cold metal into my skin and I can feel his hand shaking. I take a deep, ragged breath. This is it. This is the end.

I want so many things in this moment, to walk down the aisle and marry Nix. I want to watch our babies be born and see how they grow. I want to grow old with him, sit in rocking chairs on our front porch and watch our grandkids play in the yard. The terrified part of me that can't even move right now wants to close my eyes and just wait for death, but I can't take my eyes off of this wonderful man. He's shaking his head, frantically. Intense pain clouds his eyes as he looks at me and I know he's trying to think of some way to get me out of this.

"I love you," I whisper.

"Emma, no," he chokes out and takes a step toward me just as a shot rings out.

Chapter Thirty-Four

"It's perfect!" Mama sings as she stares at my reflection in the mirror.

Twisting to the side, I catch sight of the back and sigh. She's right, the dress is absolutely perfect. I knew it was the one the second I laid eyes on it. It's a V-neck sheath dress with beaded lace applique and a stunning low back that dips all the way to the small of my back.

It's hard to believe that only three weeks ago, I was standing downstairs in my kitchen with a gun to my head — sure that I was going to die. When I heard that shot, I squeezed my eyes shut and waited. Waited for the pain or the light or something. But, none of that happened. I had a brief moment of panic where I thought Ryan had shot Nix, but I opened my eyes and found him staring back at me. It's then that I realized that Ryan was no longer standing behind me.

Storm had snuck in through the back door without a single one of us noticing and he was able to get a clean shot. He kept his promise and he saved my life and the lives of my babies. I owe him everything.

"Are we ready to go?" Daddy asks from the doorway.

I turn and nod at him, beaming. "Yeah, I'm ready."

"We'll see you down there," Addy says, kissing my cheek before she and Daisy hustle downstairs to walk down the aisle.

"You're absolutely stunning, sweetheart," Mama says and kisses my other cheek.

"Thank you, Mama."

"I love you, baby girl."

"I love you, too."

She nods and files out of the room, leaving me alone with Daddy.

"Shall we?" He holds his arm out to me and I link my arm with his. We start off down the stairs. "I'm so proud of you, Emma. You are far stronger than I ever gave you credit for."

"Thank you, Daddy."

We walk into the kitchen and I peek out the window, gasping when I see how beautifully Daisy and Addy put everything together. The sun is just beginning to set over the line of trees behind the house, orange, red, and purple streaking across the sky. Lanterns and strings of pearls hang from the canopy created by the oak trees, casting soft, warm light around the yard. A white aisle runner is laying on the ground between rows of white wooden folding chairs that lead to an arch overflowing with pink and white roses and calla lilies.

"Can't Help Falling in Love" by Ingrid Michaelson drifts through the backyard. Daddy and I stand at the door waiting for our turn. Addy and Trey go first, walking down the aisle before taking their places. Daisy and Tucker quickly follow, and I take a deep breath. When they reach their spots, Daddy gives my arm a squeeze and we begin walking. Butterflies dance in my stomach as everyone's eyes turn to me, but there is only one person I see.

My handsome man is standing under the arch of flowers, decked out in a black tuxedo that looks incredible on him. I thought he was sexy in jeans and a t-shirt but he's downright sinful right now. He lifts his head, a smile stretching across my face as I lock eyes with Nix. His blue eyes shimmer with so much happiness and love that I feel it all the way to my toes. It's like I'm floating down the aisle as a complete sense of euphoria fills me.

We finally reach him and he holds his hand out to me with a look that practically has me melting into a puddle of goo.

"Who gives this woman to this man?" the preacher asks.

"Her mother and I do," Daddy answers, placing my hand in Nix's upturned palm.

His fingers curl around mine and he guides me up under the arch with him. I hand my bouquet to Addy and when we reach the preacher, we turn toward each other and hold hands. The preacher begins talking and I lose myself in Nix's eyes.

Sometimes, I can't figure out how I ended up here. It feels like just yesterday that I was living that nightmare with Ryan. Then one morning, I woke up and everything had changed. For a year, I muddled through my life, faking it, and then I met Nix and he lit a spark within me. He brought me back to life. I left Ryan and somehow found this incredible man who never pushed me and who showed me what it meant to be truly loved by another person.

I'm lucky, I know this, but it's not just the fact that I got away. That alone, made me lucky. So many don't get away, they pay the ultimate price for falling in love with the wrong person. Yet, I got more than that. Not only did I get away but my nightmare is officially over. Ryan will never come for me again. He will never hurt me and he will never hurt my babies. And I get this amazing guy for the rest of my life.

I am infinitely blessed.

"Emma and Nix wanted to prepare their own vows and they will exchange them now," the preacher says, snapping me out of my daze.
Nix grins down at me and I briefly wonder if you could bottle the power of his smile and use it as an antidepressant.

It's sure doing a number on me right now.

"Emma, I've always considered myself to be just a regular guy and I was happy in my life until the day I met you. You showed me how much better things could be by just being around you, and I knew in an instant that I would do whatever it took to make you mine. I was living a monochrome life and it was nice, comfortable. But the moment you stepped into my shop, vibrant color exploded into my world and I could never be without it, without you. You are, without a doubt, the strongest, most incredible person I've ever known. Your beauty, inside and out, lights up entire rooms. There aren't strong enough words to describe what you do to me. You render me speechless, your love knocks the wind out of me. I promise to you that I will work every day to be the man and husband that you deserve. I can't promise that it will always be perfect because we are both pretty realistic people and know that's not true, but I can promise you that no one will ever love you more than I do. I'm so incredibly lucky that you said yes to me. I love you."

His vows take my breath away and I have tears rolling down my face as I absorb his sweet words. He smiles at me and it's like sunshine for my soul.

"Emma," the preacher prompts and I clear my throat to begin.

"Nix, for a long time I was pretty pissed off at life. I didn't understand why I had to go through the things I had suffered through. It didn't seem fair. Then, I got to thinking the other night and I wondered what would have happened if I never met Ryan. It didn't take me long to realize that I probably would have never met you. So, in spite of the pain and suffering, I'm glad for it now because it led me to you. And I would do it a hundred more times if you were waiting for me at the end. I'll never be able to thank you enough for all that you have done for me but I can promise you that I will never run from you. You are my partner and we will weather whatever storm comes our way, together. I love you with every piece of me and I'm so lucky that I get to call you mine and the father of my children. I love you."

Nix coughs, covering up a stray tear or two, and chuckles ring out around us. He quickly recovers as the preacher hands Nix my wedding band.

"Repeat after me," he instructs. "With this ring, I thee wed."

Nix slides the band up my left ring finger until it meets my engagement ring. "With this ring, I thee wed."

"Emma, repeat after me," the preacher says again, handing Nix's ring to me. "With this ring, I thee wed."

"With this ring, I thee wed," I repeat, sliding the ring onto Nix's finger. Nix grabs my hand as soon as I'm finished and squeezes, exhilaration shining in his blue eyes.

"By the power vested in me by God and the state of Louisiana, I now pronounce you husband and wife," the preacher says. "You may now kiss your bride."

Grinning, Nix cups my face in his hand and pulls me to him, planting his lips on mine. The thought strikes me that I'm kissing my husband now and I smile against Nix's mouth. He changes course, leaning down next to my ear. "I love you, Mrs. West."

When he pulls back, I return his grin and say, "I love you, too, Nix."

"It is my honor to introduce Mr. and Mrs. Phoenix West," the preacher calls and everyone begins cheering as we turn to them, big stupid grins plastered on our faces.

*   *   *   *

I watch as the last guest pulls out of the driveway, gravel crunching under the tires of their car and smile. Today felt like a dream. I've heard that things always go wrong but it was literally perfect. I couldn't be happier.

The fact that I was living a nightmare not that long ago makes it all the more surreal. I didn't know if I would ever get to this point. It scared me to hope for this. But now, I've got this incredible man as my husband and two little babies growing in my belly.

It's more than I could have ever hoped for.

"You happy, baby?" Nix comes up behind me, and loops his arms around me, laying his hands over my belly. I position my hands over his and lean back into him, his warmth and smell surrounding me, wrapping me up in him.

"Deliriously," I answer and his lips stretch into a smile against my neck.

"I love you, Mrs. West."

My heart flutters at my new name and I squeeze his hand. "I love you, too, Mr. West."

"Ready to go inside?" he asks, backing away and turning me around.

"Dance with me some more?"

He smiles and pulls the remote for the sound system out of his pocket. "Anything you want, dear."

"You're catching on quick."

A startled laugh slips out of his mouth and he shakes his head at me.

"You're gonna keep me on my toes," he says, almost to himself, and chuckles again.

"Definitely." He grins at me while pointing the remote over to the stereo and a second later "Make it to Me" by Sam Smith rings through the air. He slips the remote back into his pocket and saunters over to me.

"Well, someone seems quite pleased with himself."

He nods. "I am a very happy man today, wife."

"Glad to hear it, husband." His arm encircles my waist and he links his other hand with mine, holding it over his heart while we sway back and forth to the music.

After a moment, he leans back slightly to look at me. "Did you mean what you said in your vows? That you would go through all that shit again for me?"

"Nix, I meant every single word that I said to you today."

He gazes over my shoulder, lost in thought for a moment before shaking his head. "I'm kind of speechless."

I smile and cuddle back into him as we dance around our backyard. The chairs have been cleared away but the lanterns and pearls are still hanging from the trees and reflecting off the water. I know that this moment right here will be branded into my memory for the rest of my life. At night, I'll no longer have nightmares about Ryan's torment. It will be moments like right now that fill my dreams.

"Did you see your brother and Daisy today?" I giggle as I think about them.

"Oh yeah, I saw."

Tucker never left Daisy's side once tonight. They danced and laughed all evening. I've never seen my brother look at anyone the way he does my best friend.

"I'd put money on him proposing soon."

My eyes meet his. "Why? How do you know?"

"He's just got that look, baby."

"What look?"

He smiles and runs his thumb back and forth across my cheek. "The look a man has when he's thinking about forever; the same look I saw in the mirror not too long ago."

"Nix," I sigh, at a loss for anything else to say. I snuggle back into him. "You know, you claim you're not a romantic guy but you say such perfect things."

"I just tell the truth, baby. If it's the perfect thing then it's because of you. You're the other half of me."

"See! That right there! Perfect."

He laughs. "Only for you, Emma."

"No, I'm pretty sure any other girl would melt if you said that to them."

He shakes his head at me, exasperated. "Maybe, but you are the only woman I've ever said them to, and the only woman I ever will say them to so this conversation is a little pointless."

The song changes again, this time playing "Mirrors" by Justin Timberlake, and I glance up at Nix. "Did you plan that one?"

He laughs. "No, definitely not."

"You're so smooth."

"Only—"

"Yeah, yeah. Only for me, I know," I interrupt, and he chuckles again.

"I love you, Emma."

"Forever?"

"Forever, baby."

Epilogue
Six years later…

My phone starts ringing and I grin when Nix's picture pops up on the screen. "Hey, honey."

"Hey, baby. How's it going?"

I open my mouth to tell him but end up giggling when I hear screaming in the background.

"Maybe I should be the one asking you that."

"Naw, they're all right."

I shake my head and smile as a new customer checks out my booth.

"Is my house going to look like a war zone when I get back?"

"Mmm," he hums. "Can't say."

I hold back another laugh. We both know that cleaning is not his forte, so I'll be stuck picking up whatever mess my wild children have managed to make.

"Yeah, yeah. Okay."

"So, how's it going?"

My eyes sweep over my booth and I grin again.

"Pretty good. Sold a couple pieces."

I started coming back to the Market about three months after the twins, Grady and Corbin, were born. It was the final piece of me that was still missing after everything with Ryan. Nix says he fell even more in love with me after I started painting again. That I had a vibrancy about me that was sometimes lacking before.

"That's great, baby," he says, just as something crashes in the background. I sigh.

"Nix, maybe we should just hire a sitter when I do the Market. It's not like we can't afford it." After Ryan's second attack on me, I decided to file the lawsuit that my brother suggested. It wasn't really for me. I just wanted other women to have a chance. A week after the wedding, the city offered a settlement of ten million dollars. When I first heard the number, I choked on air. I had never even thought of having that kind of money. I accepted on the condition that the city would find a way to deal with this kind of thing better and they did. They created a special unit that deals with domestic abuse and sex crimes.

"No, I don't want to do that. You know I like spending time with the kids." Nix and I may have all this money but we don't let it affect us. We still live in the same house and we both still work — just not as much now. "Harper, NO!"

I have to bite down on my lip hard to keep myself from laughing. Harper came along two years after her brothers and she is a handful, to say the least. Nix likes to tell me all the time that she's just like me and I won't admit it, but he's right. She is the spitting image of me with her dark brown curls and smoky green eyes while the twins look just like their daddy.

"Are you sure? For your sanity?"

He chuckles. "Yeah, I'm sure."

A young woman approaches my booth and I offer her a warm smile.

"Hey, I gotta go. Someone just walked up."

"All right, babe. I love you. Oh! Don't forget the ice for the barbecue tonight."

"I won't. I love you, too."

I hang up and greet the woman with a wide smile on my face, so happy to be feeling like myself again.

*   *   *   *

"Nix!" I call out from the back bedroom as I'm getting ready for the barbecue.

"Just a sec, babe."

"Mama!" a little voice squeals from the doorway.

I twirl around just in time to see my crazy three-year-old daughter sprinting right for me. She jumps into the air and I catch her, spinning around with her in my arms. Her sweet little giggle fills the room and she squeals again. A smile spreads across my face as I stop spinning and kiss the top of her head.

"Hey, baby girl, what are you doin?"

She pouts. "I pick dress. See?" She points down to the bright yellow sundress on her little body. I wince when I see the orange shoes she paired with it.

"Yeah, I do see, honey. Can Daddy maybe help you find a different color to wear?"

She blinks up at me, her eyes an exact match to mine and cocks her head to the side. "I wike this color!" she exclaims, pointing to the bright orange shoes on her feet.

Nix chuckles as he walks into the room, catching the tail end of our conversation.

"Hey, princess," he coos and my daughter's face lights up.

"Daddy!" she squeals loudly and squirms in my arms. I shake my head and hand her off to Nix.

"Can you go to your room? Daddy will be there in a second to help you."

"'Kay, Daddy," she says and jumps out of his arms, landing on her feet like a cat.

I shake my head in exasperation. "That child—"

"Is just like her mama," Nix cuts me off, chuckling.

"Remind me to apologize to my parents."

He roars with laughter. "Oh, they'll love that."

"Where are Grady and Corbin?" I turn back to the mirror to check my outfit again.

"On the couch watching cartoons."

Well, thank God for that.

"Baby," Nix growls, wrapping his arms around my waist and biting my neck. "Are you sure we have to have people over today? How about we just send the kids with my dad and spend the day in bed?" He kisses the side of my neck and runs his hand over my body.

"Nix," I groan and spin around, unable to fight it. I lock my lips with his and throw my arms around his neck. He echoes my moans as his tongue slips between my lips and strokes the inside of my mouth. He palms my ass and squeezes, pulling me into him, his hard cock pressing into my lower belly.

I reach between us and rub against him and he groans again. "We can be quick."

"Okay," I pant, totally caught up in his spell.

"Daddy!" Harper yells, just as he's reaching for the button on my jeans. He lays his forehead on my shoulder and growls, drawing a giggle out of me.

"Hold on, princess," he calls before pulling back and looking at me. After a second, he smiles and shakes his head. "I love those kids, I really do but—"

"Later," I tell him and his eyes light up.

"Promise?"

I nod. He repeats the move and kisses me quickly before pulling away. He adjusts himself as he backs away from me and I giggle again.

*   *   *   *

I sit down in the padded lawn chair and tip my head back, closing my eyes and soaking up the warm rays of the afternoon sun. Someone sits down in the chair beside me and I open my eyes, a grin spreading across my face when I see Daisy.

"Hey, hon."

"Hey." She flashes me a tired smile and I give her a sympathetic look.

"How are you feeling?"

Her smile morphs into one of complete bliss and she looks down at her sleeping newborn daughter, June, in her arms.

"I'm good." When she meets my eye again, I can tell that she means it. She may be tired but I know she wouldn't have it any other way.

"Good. Where's that annoying brother of mine?"

"Trying to keep Jacob from jumping in the swamp." She nods her head toward the water, where Tucker is scooping their three-year-old into his arms as he makes a flying jump for the murky water. We both giggle when Jacob starts screaming and Tucker looks pleadingly back at the house.

"Here, hold your niece." Daisy hands June off to me and marches off to the swamp. I'm not sure if it's Tucker or Jacob who are in trouble. Tucker and Daisy got married about two years after we did and little Jacob came along not long after that. Nix was right. My brother had the look.

I look down at the sleeping baby in my arms and gently stroke her little face with the tip of my finger. She's so perfect. She looks just like Daisy except for her dark hair. My heart flutters.

"We should have another one," Nix whispers in my ear, surprising me.

I jump and poor little June startles, her arms flailing out in front of her. I stroke her cheek again and shush her, ignoring my husband's comment. He chuckles and he's still close enough that his warm breath rushes over my skin. My eyes drift closed at the delicious feeling and I shiver.

"Jesus, get a room, you two," Addy hollers and my eyes pop open.

I nod toward the house with my brow quirked. "Uh…this is my house, lady." She beams and plops down in Daisy's abandoned seat beside me. "Where's your husband?"

"I'm right here, baby girl," Trey says, shuffling out of the house with a beer in his hand. He leans down and kisses my cheek. I smile up at him. Trey and Addy officially got together after our wedding and were married three years ago. When I asked her about it, she told me that everyone had been so worried about me that they weren't really focusing on figuring out what was going on in their own love lives. I felt guilty until I realized that it all worked out in the end so I shouldn't feel that way.

"Good to see you," I say and Trey smiles at me.

"Okay, ya'll. Food's ready," Mama calls and we all stand and make our way over to the table.

I smile at all the faces around me. My parents, my brothers and my best friends. Even Blaze, Moe, Storm, and Chance are here. After the attack, Storm and Chance became really close to our family and we all hang out a lot. It's like Storm said that day — they're family now. I hand June off to Daisy and sit down beside my husband. He wraps his arm around my shoulders and pulls me close.

"Love you, baby," he whispers just before he presses his lips to my forehead.

My eyes close and I lean into him. It doesn't happen often but every once in a while, I have to stop and wonder how I managed to survive Ryan and all his torment. I know that I'm so lucky to even be alive but I have so much more. This amazing man next to me is always there for me, he's on my side, and we are truly a team. And I have three beautiful, smart babies that make my world go round.

"Love you more."

He shakes his head against mine and I smile. I open my eyes just as Mama brings the last of the food out of the kitchen. She sets it down and finally sits herself, motioning for everyone to dig in. Everyone starts reaching forward to grab food when Trey starts clinking his beer bottle with his knife.

"Hold up, ya'll. We have an announcement before we eat." My gaze flicks from my brother to Addy, who is glowing. A smile slowly curls my lips and she glances my way. When she sees me, she knows that I already know. I can't believe I didn't see it earlier. "We're having a baby!"

The table explodes with cheers, clapping and laughter. I jump up and rush over to them. I wrap Addy up in a hug first.

"I'm so excited for you," I whisper in her ear. Addy and Trey have been struggling to have a baby for a little over a year now. She's spent many nights at my house, crying her eyes out because nothing was happening, so I know how happy she is right now.

"Thank you." Her eyes shimmer with unshed tears. "I wouldn't have stayed sane if it wasn't for you."

Before I can say anything, Mama pulls her into her arms and I smile at the tears running down her face. It doesn't matter how many grandbabies she has, she always cries like it's the first one when someone gets pregnant. I look around our large table and all I can do is smile. Some of the people here may not be blood but they are our family and there is so much love surrounding us.

*   *   *   *

"Come on, baby," he urges. "Let's have another one." His lips press against the skin of my neck and I arch into him. He works his way back up to my lips and his tongue slips inside my mouth. I moan as he expertly works me up.

"Nix." Even after six years, he still gets me as eager and desperate for him as I was that first time. I don't think that will ever change.

"Say yes."

"Nix, I can't think when you're doing this to me!"

He kisses back down to my neck and nips at my ear. I moan again.

"Stop thinking, sweetheart. I love you and you love me. Let's have another baby."

I'd be lying if I said that I hadn't been thinking about it. Ever since June was born, I've been preoccupied with the idea and hearing him say he wants more babies tips me over the edge.

"Okay."

"Okay?"

I nod and smile up at him as he hovers above me. He groans and seals his lips over mine. My hands immediately slide into his hair and I moan, loving the feel of him.

Just him.

I love everything about this man. That easy grin that makes my heart thump in my chest, the smoldering look he gives me every time he sees me, and the way he loves me with his whole heart, no reservations and no conditions. After all the pain and heartache I endured, I finally got my happily ever after.

Acknowledgments

First, I want to thank my best friend, Niki. You are always down to read whatever story my crazy head comes up with and you've always got my back. You encouraged me and reassured me that I could do this. You cheer me up when I'm having a crappy day and I love you.

To my editor, Lea Burns. Thank you so much for helping me make this book what it is today. I learned so much working with you!

To my Beta readers, you guys rock! Thank you for your honest feedback. Your love of Nix and Emma and their story was overwhelming and I love that you love them as much as I do.

To everyone that read Nix and Emma's story, thank you. It's because of you that I'm able to make my dream a reality and I appreciate each and every one of you more than you'll ever know. I hope you loved these characters as much as I do.

Check out my Facebook page
for news on new projects!
https://www.facebook.com/pages/Au
thor-A-M-Myers/1489055591368098

Made in the USA
San Bernardino, CA
30 October 2015